AFRICAN WRITERS SERIES

204

The Smoke That Thunders

Michael Marodde

The Smoke That Thunders

DOMINIC MULAISHO

LONDON

HEINEMANN

IBADAN · NAIROBI · LUSAKA

Heinemann Educational Books Ltd
48 Charles Street, London W1X 8AH
P.M.B. 5205 Ibadan · P.O. Box 45314 Nairobi
P.O. Box 3966 Lusaka
EDINBURGH MELBOURNE TORONTO AUCKLAND SINGAPORE
HONG KONG KUALA LUMPUR NEW DELHI KINGSTON

ISBN 0 435 90204 0 (paper)
ISBN 0 435 90647 x (cased)

British Library Cataloguing in Publication Data

Mulaisho, Dominic
    The smoke that thunders. — (African writers series).
    I. Title II. Series
    823'.9'1F   PR9405.9.M

    ISBN 0−435−90204−0

Phototypeset in 10pt Baskerville by George Over Ltd., London and Rugby
Printed in Great Britain by Cox & Wyman Ltd., London, Reading and Fakenham

To Father and Mother

Introduction

The island of Kandaha lies like a giant banana in the Zambezi River, the muddy waters of which flow and eddy around it, fluctuating with the seasons. Politically distinct, Kandaha is unique in other ways — the world's largest island in the main course of a river, and geologically a veritable fossil of the oldest rocks faulted up and preserved in the younger sediments filling the great rift valley of the Zambezi. The long low island, seldom rising more than a few hundred feet above the river level, is gently rolling and presents in the dry season, a brown, dry, parched appearance fringed by a bushy green at the water edge. Beneath this stark surface lie immense mineral riches in a fortuitous duplication of those same geological conditions that make the Witwatersrand the world's greatest gold mining centre, and here in Kandaha the steeply dipping reefs have been followed down to great depths. An hour's drive away, at the far end of the banana island, the colourful capital city of Musasa contrasts with the desolate mainland on either side of the river, while only a short way downstream the river plunges into the great *Musi-O-Tunya*, the Smoke That Thunders.

I

The heavy door closed on them. The metal was cold against his skin. Katenga sat meekly, stripped to the waist. It was his third job in six months. He needed the job — he needed the money — so did the rest. There were thirty of them, all lined up on the metal bench, impaled between two rails and each of them in his own cage. They waited. The heat began to come on, a damp moistening heat. At first it felt as though someone had spat warm saliva at them. Then they began to perspire. Soon, drops of sweat formed on their foreheads. The drops grew larger and heavier until, no longer able to hang on to the faces, they coursed down their chins into pouring sweat.

The excited jabber had died down. A further wave of hot air hit their faces. It was cloudy, steaming dampness in there, on and on until the temperature rose higher and yet higher. They were new recruits. They were sweating it out. They called it the 'acclimatization chamber'. In reality, it was a sweatbox, the sweatbox of the Bristol Gold Syndicate. Its purpose? To sweat them out so when they went underground, down to 3,608 metres below, they would not dry up. A good respectable phrase for it ... to immunize the workers from heat prostration. ...

Katenga had not travelled far to come to that chamber, just forty miles from Musasa, the capital town of Kandaha.

Most of the other fellows in there had travelled many hundreds of miles. As he watched their glistening skins, now a soggy mess, Katenga felt a hatred for them, hate because they had succumbed to the white man's enforced labour policy. He had come there of his own free will. They hadn't. At least he could quit any time. They could not. Not until they had worked two years unless, of course, they wanted to be clapped in jail.

The silence in the chamber deepened. The chamber was getting hotter and hotter. He had never known such merciless damp heat before. Hands were going up to their faces, cupping off the perspiration. Katenga looked at the fellow next to him. The fat fellow, a big daddy, who had been prattling most when they entered the chamber, thought that perhaps it was a big joke. But he kept silent.

Big daddy showed signs of wilting. One would never think he was the noisy type. His face began to show much strain. The whites of his eyes were beginning to roll up. But there would be another three hours in the sweatbox. Katenga settled down to the steamy heat. If big daddy could keep up that fight for three hours, he would break the world record. Big daddy looked at the heavy door, closed, barred and sealed. There was no hope that way. A further hiss of steamy heat mounted. Big daddy raised his arms in desperation.

'I'm dying!'

Katenga looked at him. He would have asked, 'What?' but his dry, parched lips couldn't reply. That was what life was about. To feel what you have to say and not really say it. He and Katenga were in the sweatbox, the doors locked, the keys outside and help- less. What the hell was the point in bothering, or even listening to your life wishing to live on when it was impossible?

It's fellows like this, Katenga thought, the scared ones, who mess things up on the mine. They were usually villagers, giving in to the white man, and that's why conditions didn't improve. They had nothing on their backs except their skins. When they found jobs, they found their heaven and the white man, their god. Villagers, thought Katenga, should be banned from coming to the mines to work.

He too was beginning to feel dry. But big daddy entered a new phase. His tongue moved as though it had taken over from his lungs. A steamy haze of heat swept the chamber again. Several voices gasped, but some sat still, quiet, knowing that they would have a job as soon as the sweatbox door opened. Big daddy was still restless. Two hours gone and there would be another two. And another four days of this.

I'm probably too harsh, thought Katenga. He began to wonder what persuaded the big daddy to stay when the recruiting team came to his village. Maybe he was looking for a job to end his wife-nagging, 'You see what my friend is wearing.' Maybe his children needed school money. But if he only knew that there was no future for a black man in Kandaha! Sweat and more sweat. For a moment Katenga had forgotten where he was. Scooping the sweat off his face, he decided that there was no point in worrying about the rest.

Strangely enough, the big one seemed to be coping better with the heat. Perhaps there was a flicker of hope for a job.

Ten minutes left. There was a stir low down the row. Men were jumping up but a fellow down the line slumped over the railing. There was little that any of the others could do for him outside of climbing out of their firmly secured cages. Someone would have to. The short small fellow appeared lifeless. No one stirred for fear that he might lose his job. Finally, Katenga shouted:

'Help your friend, you sons of dogs!'

Still, no one moved. Big daddy, fully awake now, looked on bemused. Katenga climbed out of his cage, rushed over, tripped and fell. He pulled himself back up and managed to reach the man in distress.

'Water!' demanded Katenga.

A final whiff of steamed up heat swept through the chamber. Katenga rushed to the door, knocked forcefully with his fists. The heavy steel door remained silent.

'A person is dead!' Katenga shouted.

The doors opened. The four hours was up. A tall fat uniformed black man appeared.

'Get out, all of you.' He unlocked the cages. 'Are there any rats to pick up?' he asked.

'One man has died!' protested Katenga.

'Then get him out!' replied the uniformed fellow.

Five men picked him up.

'Put him into the jeep. He must be rushed to the hospital,' Katenga stated.

'There's no room for corpses there,' replied the uniformed man examining the fellow. As he felt the pulse, he laughed aloud: 'The little rat, he's not dead. Take him to the Mine Hospital.' He turned to Katenga. 'You, talkative one. We don't like your type. Get out of here.'

The sun was shining brightly. Coming out from the sweatbox, Katenga could only feel relief. However, after a few minutes of recuperation, he realized that he still had no job.

As Katenga walked from the industrial giant. the Bristol Gold Mines, he was frustrated. By the time he had reached the main shopping area, he was angry. He was thinking what chances did an African have, in his own country, where he was born? He saw African babies playing, what opportunities would these babies have in the land of their fathers?

By the time Katenga reached the bus stop for Musasa, he was

3

frustrated, mad and thirsty. While waiting for the bus, he went into a nearby tavern to have a beer with his few remaining pence. While he savoured his cold beer, white-coated white men were sitting at their desks in the mine offices and laboratories. Lepton, the underground manager, was explaining the shaft system from a model in the office to visitors from overseas. These were important American visitors. The two men were Eximbank men. Plans for the installation of increased ore-crushing facilities had been under way for some time. If everything went well, this loan would finance the American portion of the equipment required. OECG (Overseas Export Credit Guarantee) had indicated interest. But Her Majesty's Government had been dragging its feet. Kandaha, like Angola, could be an area of big power conflict. You don't fight from outside and that's why the blacks' clamour for independence must continue to be ignored. If Britain went out with great flourish and magnanimity, the commies would come in.

The two men had spent a whole day yesterday with John Turnbull down town in Musasa. Number two Colonial Avenue was after Government House, the most important house in the whole of Kandaha. It was called Bristol House after the name of the Bristol Gold Syndicate. Set back in a luxury of evergreen lawns and shrubs cupped by, curiously enough, the Fountain of Peace, it was a real marvel of modern architecture. The house rose six stories. Its sandy walls and the verandah space encircling every floor gave it an atmosphere of wide girth and sprawling comfort. In the basement was an art gallery. 'Europeans Only.' From the basement right up to the top floor ran a beautiful mosaic of bright splashy colour.

Lepton sat listening optimistically to the burly American.

'We've discussed the financing with Mr Turnbull. We reckon we could help you. We still have to talk around the rate of interest. We're most impressed by all we've seen. We've now got the OK for investment in this part of the world. Secretary of State is deadly keen that we do something here.'

Lepton had previously showed them around the plant and now explained the main problem of the mine.

'It's pressure and excessive water. It's wetter than Konkola out in Zambia, and that was, until recently, the wettest mine in the world. Now we've taken over the world record. But we are coping. Recently, we've had to put in an entirely new pumping station at 2,600 metres. Pressure is, of course, a serious problem. But it's understandable with all deep mining.'

Responding favourably, the American said:

'I see. It's a pretty good set-up you've got. We've seen gold mines in South Africa and the Soviet Union. This one is as good as the best of them.'

Lepton interrupted:

'Of course, there are many other things we could do if we had the money and, of course, if Bristol House would agree. But everything you take up there, they look at it as though it was a Trojan Horse. You know what I mean?'

The burly one knew what Lepton meant. His first impressions of Turnbull were of an abrupt overbearing executive who knew it all.

'We need better housing for our black workers, for example. But up there it's regarded a luxury. One of these days things will blow up into our faces. Naturally, when the chairman, Lord Ventrical, out there hears of it, it will be down our necks that Bristol House will be breathing fire.'

'Yes, yes.'

'We haven't had a general manager here for the last twelve months since Jose Smithley moved to head office in London. Bristol House thinks it's unnecessary. So I manage my side of the business and the metallurgical manager runs his outfit. We all go to agree or differ in Bristol House, forty miles away. I know he's been trying to get a slimes treatment plant going for some time. It seems such a shame we can't export the real gold bars out of here. Our slimes have to go all the way to South Africa for smelting and refining.'

'There's now a slimes treatment plant on the Copperbelt in Zambia. You could surely use that now, couldn't you?'

Lepton looked at the two. Americans were always naïve, weren't they?

'Politics,' he said.

'Politics?' asked the burly one. 'It makes perfect economic sense to me.'

'We're not on talking terms with Zambia because this country is a colony. Zambia and the blacks here want the white man out. It's been deceptively quiet out here, but believe you me this little island will outdo Angola when it explodes.'

The two looked at each other. Turnbull had briefed them that politically everything was nice and happy.

'What about your other neighbours?'

'Rhodesia?'

'Yeah, they're in a hell of a mess, aren't they?'

5

'They are a great deal better than us. At least they've cast their vote for civilization and Old Smithy's sticking to his guns. Here, we don't know if we're coming or going.' Lepton leaned towards the two men. He whispered, 'The trouble here is the Governor. Weak. He won't tell the blacks where they get off. But so far, PALP — that's the black agitators — haven't made any headway here on the mine.'

'You call it what?'

'PALP — don't ask me what it means. But there's talk of big changes within PALP coming. They only need to get a demagogue to lead them and we are in real trouble.'

The two men thought briefly. They were not political men but politics were obviously relevant to their appraisal. Ten million United States dollars needed some security beyond just the assets of the Company, huge though these were. They would be seeing Thomson, the Secretary for Native Affairs, the following day anyway. And maybe even the Governor. The burly one looked at the chart on the wall:

BRISTOL GOLD SYNDICATE

Tonnes milled per year	1·5 million
Average ore grade	12 g/t
Reserves	10·5 million

'It's a good mine all right,' he said.

'Happy?' asked Lepton.

The one who had said, 'It's a good mine allright' said:

'I see no reason why not. Just as long as we can clear up those points about the rate of interest. We gotta know where we stand on that.'

Lepton looked up, surprised:

'Oh, I thought John Turnbull had discussed that.'

The man replied:

'To be perfectly frank with you, he talked, we just listened.'

Lepton asked:

'Okay, what precisely is Eximbank's position?'

'Well, first of all, on paper the deal looks most attractive. But, we're all men of the world, we know that what's on paper is not always what is on the bottom line. Still, money has been alloted for this project. So put your mind at ease. What we would like to see is this venture done with Eurodollars.'

'I see no reason why not. Dollars on deposit in Europe are just as good as dollars anywhere,' said Lepton.

'But there are a few things we want from you.'

'Oh, what are they?'

'Now there you go, looking at us like we're a couple of hoss thieves.'

The man smiled.

'I think what Jack is trying to say is, the Secretary of State is rather keen that the Americans play an important role in terms of investments, in this part of the world. If we invest hard dollars here, in two or three years we wouldn't like to see little slant-eyed men, wearing dark suits with cameras around their necks, snooping around here. That would make us most unhappy.' It was the second man called Harold.

'That would not be desirable to me or my colleagues,' said Lepton.

'So you can't use Zambia, eh?'

'No. Politics,' said Lepton again.

'Politics, hell! It's a question of dollars and cents,' said Jack.

'Yeah,' said Jack after a moment. 'Looks like Old Smithy's got caught crapping without any toilet paper.'

Harold said:

'Yeah, they are in one hell of a mess. A good businessman knows when to cut his losses. It's only a matter of time. They have to give up. Rhodesia, that's the only way Vorster can hold on to his slice of cake, by throwing Smithy to the wolves. It gives him another twenty years to rape the country.'

'Well, I told you at least, they've made up their minds there,' said Lepton.

'Old Smithy is a fool,' said Jack. 'He ain't no poker player. He's playing from a weak position. He's gonna wind up with two pairs of aces, while the niggers walk away with a Royal straight flush.'

They thought a moment. Harold looked at Jack, then he said:

'Jack, is there anything you would like to add?'

'Well, we're talking about a lot of capital, ten million dollars to be exact. Let me be perfectly frank with you, Mr Lepton. As I see it in a nutshell, you might have a revolution here or you might not have one. Our position is to make money for Eximbank. Now, if we don't make money our stockholders are upset, the chairman of the board is upset, our President is upset. The whole USA is upset. Now that's a whole lot of people to be getting upset. Our organization, for want of a better word, is run like a family.

We stay away from anything that smacks of controversy. We vote straight Republican. Now, that might seem a bit old-fashioned but that's our policy.'

Harold added:

'If I might interject here, what Jack is trying to say is, we were led to believe that you had no race problem here. We were told that by John Turnbull. Like I says, if that's not correct then we need some more security. I would not like to get in bed with Bristol and a year from now, a bunch of rag-tail natives takes over the country.'

'I don't know what to say.' It was Lepton.

'Don't say anything. Why don't you run it up the flag pole, what we have said to you. Tell your people, if anybody salutes it, we will talk again,' said Jack.

'We won't be flying back to Dallas until the middle of the week,' added Harold.

The two Americans stood up.

'We can show ourselves out,' said Jack. Then he added shaking Lepton's hand warmly, 'Great mine you got here. We all can make a lot of money.'

The two Americans left. Lepton slumped back in his chair. He had a headache. 'Bloody American, "run it up the flag pole if anybody salutes it". What kind of English is that?' he rasped.

At Elwyn Shaft the morning shift was just coming out. A fellow called Nkolola — who had gone underground to report back on a personnel problem that had arisen there — led the exit from the lift. Most of his time was spent on surface and it was, therefore, quite a tiring experience to climb up and down these endless ladders underground. An armed guard marched the group to the change room. The whites went their way but the guard remained with the blacks. Nkolola, leading the group, was called in.

'Strip!'

When he hesitated after removing the overall, the white inspector barked:

'Down to your skin!'

He did as he was told. They searched his hair, ears, eyes, mouth, armpits, bottom and right down to the toes!

'You can go,' said the inspector. 'All these blacks need to wash,' he said to the armed black fellow.

When the search was completed, the group left under guard until they were well out of the mining area.

Things were going on well both on surface and underground. Nkolola stepped out from the Bristol Gold Syndicate mine and in the distance he could see the miners' houses, people going to the market, children playing. As Katenga awaited the arrival of his bus at the station located north of the mine, he too saw the microcosm of the Bristol Gold Syndicate. Mine shops, euphemistically termed 'supermarkets', were within walking distance of the white residential area. Houses here did BGS real proud. Gardens maintained by mine labourers were beautifully laid out and each different from the other in design. The African compound, a sprawling treeless expanse of land with ten thousand, two-bedroom red brick houses all in enormous unending rows. Not a blade of green grass was in sight at this time of year. At the end of the compound were recreational facilities — a bare football pitch and a welfare hall which at any one time could not take more than fifty children without complaining. For the recruits from the villages, this was their heaven. A blaring public-address system hooked on to every house. Then there was the public radio system. There was no way of turning it off if you didn't want to listen to whatever Radio Kandaha out in Musasa was broadcasting. This was the life that people came to see in the towns.

Katenga's bus arrived and he boarded it. Nearby, a European woman known by everyone as Mrs Eckland wound up her shopping for the afternoon, her last stop at the butcher's.

'That will be £2.1s.6d.'

Mrs Eckland dipped her fingers into the money purse. She peeled off the £2 from a wad of notes. She put them into the man's hands and smiled wistfully.

'No discount for cash as usual?'

The man shook his head.

'No.'

She rummaged into the purse again and gently slipped the 1s. 6d. on to the counter.

'It's a very nice cut. Thank you!' She picked up her parcel.

Outside someone shouted:

'Get off the pavement, nigger!'

Mrs Eckland hesitated and then turned to the butcher:

'They are getting rather rude, these Africans. Aren't they?'

'Very,' replied the man.

'I've been here ten years now,' she confided. 'Never seen a black walk on the pavement. And now here it is! I remember the first year John and I came here. In Musasa two Africans were hanged for jostling a white woman on the pavement. That put paid to that.'

'I wish they'd strap someone up by the balls — I mean feet.'

'Yes,' said Mrs Eckland thoughtfully.

'It's this politics business. Kaffirs like Santasa being made to feel they can rule this country. As far as I'm concerned, Mrs Eckland, 'twill be over my dead body. Norris is right. We whites must take over this Kandaha from the Colonial Government.'

'Yes, I do remember Sir Ray. Such a delightful man. And d'you know last time he came here he took my little hand in his two large hands and shook me warmly. He says, "Mrs Eckland, we're in this thing together. We've got to preserve civilization in this part of the country!" '

The butcher said:

'Ja, man. Christ! We'll fight same like we pushed out the Muntus (blacks) in the south and have kicked out the British in Rhodesia.' Simon Malherbe growled his vocal chords, leant sideways and spat through a hatch behind him on to the blacks' side of the butchery.

Simon Malherbe, once a road-mender in the Chipata District of Zambia, was a stubby, hairy chested white man. He had darkish skin. His arms were large and also hairy. His hands were hard and corny. He had a rather flat nose for a white man. Some of his enemies called him a genetic throwback. Malherbe had come from South Africa — or the Republic as he used to call it — more than twenty years ago. Strutting there in the butchery — open neck, shorts, hairy and muscular arms and legs and a pugnacious mouth always ready to hurl an insult at a Muntu (African) — he was a natural for frightening off the Africans.

Outside, the man who had shouted to the African to get off the pavement was getting into his car. Mrs Eckland made for the door and gently closed it behind her.

Simon Malherbe, the butcher, leaned over the counter. Business was slack. Keeping a whole butchery open for just five or ten white families was not exactly a lucrative business. Now and again people dropped in from Musasa and they made hefty orders.

A black voice shouted through the hatch:

'Dogs' meat finished, Bwana?'

Malherbe uttered quietly:

'Christ, man! These blacks can send one round the bend.'

Nevertheless, he liked the sound of brisk business behind the wall. Money was money and it didn't matter who touched it.

Every evening he would pack up all the day's takings and stash them under his pillow until banking the following day. He didn't have any dreams about dirty money from Kaffirs. And if there were any dreams, they were dreams about his lily white, fresh-complexioned Joan Chessman, the highly educated girl who had crossed his path and who was now firmly his mistress.

Simon Malherbe had come from South Africa some twenty-five years ago to work on the roads of Zambia, then of Kandaha. He'd risen to the position of road foreman but no further. Then he'd left Government service and came to the Bristol Gold Syndicate and opened up as a butcher.

He had a grudge against the English, but with Joan he had a love-hate relationstip. He cared for her, yet he treated her the way he wanted to treat the English. He wanted the English to respect him and that meant he had to accumulate money and maintain a high financial status. He wanted to show the English that he was better than them.

Malherbe looked through the window. Two whites ambled along the pavement outside. For a moment, they hesitated. Hoping that they were customers, he straightened himself up and put on his best smile. The pair returned his smile with a wave of their hands and went past. He felt a little annoyed but he quickly turned his eyes to Kruger the dog who wagged his tail lazily. He too was feeling the boredom of doing nothing.

Suddenly, Malherbe's eyes darted to the large window. A black woman shuffled clumsily towards the door. He looked at her and felt strange. Didn't Mrs Eckland just say that two blacks had been strung up for walking on the pavement ten years ago? The black woman hesitated at the door. Then her eyes settled on the carcasses of meat hanging up behind Malherbe. She pushed the door open, her money held ready in an old dirty piece of cloth. Malherbe stood transfixed behind the counter. Such a thing had never happened in all his years at the estate. Halfway towards the counter the woman stopped. She took another step forward. It was her first day in the estate. She had come from a village in the north of the country, following her husband who'd been pressganged two years ago. She said:

'Meat.'

'Shit!' said Malherbe. *'Wena inzwa* (Do you understand)?'

Her only knowledge of the white man was the District Commissioner who went round the villages exhuming people, levying taxes, and of course, making sure they built wide roads — even though they didn't need them.

'Get out! *Forsek!*' bellowed Malherbe behind the counter. '*Ena aikona butchery ka lo Kaffir* (This is not a Kaffir butchery).'

The village woman looked puzzled.

'Kruger! *Bamba ena!* (Kruger, catch her!)'

Kruger leaped up from his half slumber, his long agile body slithered towards the woman like a snake. He growled at her and showed his fangs. The woman panicked.

'Mama!' she cried.

'*Aikona thawa!* (Don't move!)' barked the master, outdoing his dog.

But it was too late. Kruger leaped at her as she tried to run, bit into her thigh, ripped off her loosely wrapped loin cloth. Blood! The master ran to Kruger ordering him to stop. The wounded woman, attempting to escape, was attacked again. The butcher stroked Kruger to calm him down. Kruger, responding to him, got down on his fours and scratched his ear. Malherbe cut him a generous chunk of sirloin steak and Kruger, very content with his reward, ambled off.

The butcher went back to the woman lying on the floor and pushed her out on the pavement with his foot. He turned to walk back into the shop, then suddenly paused, and returned to the bleeding, crying woman, pushed her with his foot until she was in the street clear of the pavement. Satisfied, he calmly ambled back into the entrance exclaiming:

'Jesus, what nerve these Kaffirs have!'

Katenga was around the corner. He got off the bus.

The women, the boys (servants), the crowd, then the miners. They come. The woman, she is trying to get out of the gutter into which she has rolled. Blood gushes off her thigh. She falls. They look on speechless. Then she cries:

'Mama I die!'

Malherbe looks through the window, opens it slightly and shoots a heavy phlegmy spittle towards her.

'Kaffirs!'

Had he said it? Was it he? Someone cried:

'Butcher!'

The crowd seethed forward without understanding. Then it understood. From nowhere stones, sticks rained on the butchery. Malherbe stood his ground. The door lock gave way. The mass seethed in. Malherbe dashed to the telephone in the office.

'Blacks gone berserk man.'

Someone cut the phone. Malherbe looked at him. Fiery eyes of a white master. They commanded respect. The man flinched and let his hands drop.

'You'll pay for this, Christ man!' rumbled Malherbe.

A police siren sounded. Huge trucks ploughed into the crowd. The mobile unit police squad jumped out, their guns drawn at the ready. Malherbe said:

'Just look outside.'

The people looked. Their intestines froze. Would it be 1935 over again when many miners were gunned down by colonial guns for daring to go on strike? The crowd outside stood hushed. The whimpering voice of the woman could be heard clearly. Someone in the crowd cried in a clear strong, unbroken voice:

'Stand your ground!'

A lean anthracite black man strode to the front. He raised the bleeding woman up. His face was blacker than ever with anger. No miner's helmet. Just a simple short-sleeved white shirt. . . .

The armed police are advancing. Their boots crunch into the cobblestones of the road. They halt. An African policeman hails:

'Disperse or we fire!'

'My people will not disperse until . . .'

The man points at the woman.

'Disperse or we fire!'

'My people! Hear me! Don't!'

There's a movement in the crowd. Stones fly at the police. The people caught up in the butchery run out. Belching smoke. The butchery's been set ablaze. That is victory. The crowd seethes forward. The man who said, 'My people' marches forward at its head. Forward to the police. Forward into the mouths of their guns. Stones, bricks, everything, anything flies.

The police leader, droplets of perspiration form on his forehead. He feels faint. He cries:

'Charge!'

The mobile unit moves in, brandishing batons and teargassing the crowd. There is confusion here. Cries of pain as the batons home in into skulls. The crowd surges backwards. The man in the simple white shirt cries:

'Don't!'

He joins hands with someone. The crowd is joining hands. It's

13

moving forward again in the hailstorm of stones, batons, etc.

'Charge again!' cries the policeman.

More teargas. High-pressure water hoses. But the linked up crowd of several hundred marches on. Some are collapsing as the baton cracks down into them. One big man — about forty — has broken off the chain. He's running away. A child of ten has intercepted him. The child is wielding a knobkerry.

'Don't run away!' it cries.

The crowd moves forward. The flames are lapping up the butchery.

'Charge!'

'You can kill us all,' cries the man in the white shirt. A baton crashes into his stomach. He falls but he staggers up. He starts a song. 'Let us march together with one heart!'

Police re-enforcements arrive. These carry the real guns. An FLN crashes into the air. Its echo rumbles throughout the whole compound. A deathly silence falls on the crowd. A white officer comes forward as a detachment of the police battles with the blaze gutting up the butchery.

'You!' he says to the black in shirt sleeves, 'what's your name?'

The black one looks at him unflinchingly.

'Listen all of you to Mr Turnbull,' says the white officer.

Mr Turnbull had dashed down to the mine in the hope of putting in a further word for his company with the two Americans who had seemed doubtful about recommending investment. But he had missed them. Mr Turnbull comes forward.

The young black man walks up to Mr Turnbull. His eyes, piercing with anguish, yet proud and firm, look into Turnbull.

'Tell your company, tell your police, tell your Governor that these people will not go back to work until their demands for equal working conditions and privileges have been met!' The paramilitary stood unflinchingly, awaiting orders. The man glanced in their direction, unmoved. Turnbull stared at him. He was speechless.

'Arrest this man!' he said.

The police stood still. They could not take orders from a civilian even though he was a white.

'Who is this fellow?' asked Turnbull. The man took a step forward. Looking right into Turnbull's face he said:

'I am Aliko Kawala of PALP. I left here five years ago, Mr Turnbull, because of this kind of stupidity. Now I am a Party Worker and I am prepared to make it hot for you here.'

Kawala, tall and wiry, his back straight like a rod and his skin a shiny black, looked at Turnbull in the face. He had a slightly protruding forehead which gave his small sharp eyes the impression of being sunken. His face was oval and handsome. He was cleanly shaven and dressed in a simple but clean white shirt. His hair was combed back. Turnbull blinked. Kawala's narrow red eyes were like hot metal burning into him.

Shifting his tall frame uneasily, Turnbull said:

'I'll sack the whole lot of you if you don't get back to work.'

Away in her three-bedroom house, Mrs Eckland dried her meat over a low fire. In another day or so, it would be excellent biltong. Jeke, the house servant, always looked forward to this day. He would receive a generous portion of it for his children. Sometimes he joked about the Ecklands giving him so much meat because they had no teeth to chew it up themselves. But that was of course not serious. They looked after him well. They also employed his wife.

And Mrs Eckland, wasn't she a busybody? Always going to the welfare hall to teach black women sewing! Perhaps it was something to do with her past. Jeke puzzled. Mrs Eckland's voice came through. The fire was too high and it was burning up the meat.

The Ecklands had spent many years in Indonesia before coming out to Kandaha. Having no children of their own, they had adopted a little native girl. Such a beautiful, copper-skinned little girl. They adored her. Her father had died a leper a few years before and her mother had died in a drowning accident. The white neighbours had not liked the idea very much. But for Mrs Eckland, this was her little world. Then the white children began to play with her and every time they would pick her up, Mrs Eckland would sit worrying and fretting until she returned. But one day she and her playmate didn't return. Their little bodies were found washed down the beach. They had got on to a raft, the usual children's pranks. The tide had swept them out. They had panicked. But it was the way these two little bodies lay on the beach. Hands locked firmly, the little white and copper faces shot with fright. Might they have been trying to save each other?

So as Jeke told her the news of the rioting, Mrs Eckland closed her eyes. In that moment the two little girls ran full tilt into the sea. She could see the waves building up into huge mountains. The children were now small specks confronting the waves. Then there was a roar and a gasp.

She opened her eyes.

'Did anyone drown in the water?' she asked.

She checked herself. A hose-pipe was not a sea. Turning to Jeke she said:

'Here take all the meat for yourself.'

Jeke looked at her with surprise.

'You have a daughter?'

'Yes, ma'am. Donna.'

Jeke looked at her. He wanted to ask. Ask why she was so different from the other white donnas. Mrs Eckland turned away. Mr Eckland would soon be back from work. She would need to fix him some tea.

2

House number 113 was the only house in the compound which boasted a tattered flag which hung limply upon a burdened and unwilling bamboo flagstaff. That was the flag of the 'might' PALP. It had an axe for an emblem, and although the privileged residents of Samaka had at first scoffed at the idea of 'a stupid little cloth pretending to be the Union Jack', there were now many who were becoming courageous enough to salute it in place of the Union Jack.

But, whatever else Hut number 113 might not be, today it was the centre of the universe. Elections for a President of the party were taking place there or rather in the nearby welfare hall. A new candidate had emerged from nowhere to test the strength of the incumbent – Santasa. Kelvin Santasa had managed to hold the lid of resentment against his leadership firmly for these last five years. The younger men had complained that he was ineffective and that was why the Colonial Government, through its Governor Sir Elwyn Baker, continued to oppress the people and allowed Norris to thrive. Something had to give. The clouds were full of the promise of thunder. All that was needed was a spark. Santasa was not that spark. Naturally, Santasa was resentful of the challenge. But the motto of the party was 'Let the people speak'. And so he had to go through with it, this frivolous and unnecessary election.

Santasa arrived early at the conference. He walked around and mixed with the 'delegates' with an air of confidence. He was a forceful orator and he preached violence even though none had really been organized by the party.

When the elections began, it appeared that Aliko Kawala would not turn up, someone in the audience stood up and proposed that the conference confirm Santasa as the only candidate. Suddenly there was a stir in the crowd. A tall young man with a striking bearing and a face which looked as though its eyes were looking at each one of the three hundred or so delegates and visitors, strode into the hall. He wore khaki shorts, white canvas shoes and a neatly patched white short-sleeved shirt. Kawala had arrived. He made his way to an empty seat near the front. He had no sooner sat down when someone in the crowd — Chimuko, it was — stood up and proposed Aliko Kawala for President of PALP, the People's Army of Liberation Party.

At 5 p.m. outside Hut number 113, Samaka Compound, this same Chimuko stood up and moved into the empty seat on his left. He crouched a little. A dusty mild wind swept through the crowd squatting on the floor under the big leafy, mvungula tree. Another gust started — a stronger one rose on the wake of the first one, blowing papers all over. It caused a disturbance, such that Patrick Chimuko, the youthful publicity secretary to PALP, the young man with a voice that always sounded as if he had just emerged from a drinking session, shouted people back to order. As the chatter of the voices settled down, he announced:

'The newly elected National President, Aliko Kawala is about to address the nation!'

The three hundred delegates rose to sing the African national anthem.

As the hymn, 'God Bless Africa' ('Nkosi Sikelela Africa') neared the end, Kawala took in the large crowd before him with one sweep of the eye. He, by now, knew, with varying degrees of intimacy, most of the people there. There were a few, perhaps even as many as fifteen, who were not militants. There had been some debate about the wisdom of inviting these people who were all part of the white man's colonial establishment. The four or five African secondary-school teachers who behaved like emperors when a 'not-educated' visited them in their 'African graduate houses'. There was the African medical doctor, who had learned more than medicine from the European. Then his eyes rested on Kakonkawadia. Of all the intellectuals there, he knew that Kakonkawadia held first place, for no one else there worked as a real civil servant of the Colonial Government. There were also some visitors who had come in just because they were curious.

As if suddenly distracted, Kawala cast his eyes at the setting sun, for it was now beginning to get dark. That sun was not being snuffed out by dark racing clouds, nor did it appear to be in any hurry to give way to night. Instead, like a triumphant fighter stalking away from his victim, its shaft of bright rays were piercing the horizon upwards in a halo. Those rays appeared to be scorning the approaching night and to be saying, like the triumphant fighter, 'We shall return tomorrow'. He raised his hand to shield his eyes from the brightness of the gorgeously beautiful setting sun as its bright red yolk slithered slowly down below the horizon.

He breathed in deeply as though he wanted to suck in all the fresh air and for a while he held it there in his lungs. His black glazed face took in the large crowd that had gathered outside the party office to welcome him to the Presidency. They would be looking for a pointer to the new direction in every word that he would say. He was not a public speaker. To a certain extent his election was an accident based only on his stand at the Bristol Gold Syndicate's southern estate and the very speedy manner in which he had re-organized the party in the southern province. These were strokes of luck which could not keep repeating themselves over the following years of his tenure of office. What should he tell them? He hardly knew Musasa and its ways of the big city. When the dust had settled down, would the people of this city accept him, basically a villager, to lead them? Lead them to what? Could he take on Elwyn Baker, the Governor? Could he take on Norris, the leader of the whites? Could he take on Turnbull the financier of the white party and the most powerful single man because he presided over the Bristol Gold Syndicate, the most important single company in Kandaha? Could he take on Santasa? Wouldn't that be more difficult and delicate than anything else?

He took another look at the crowd and suddenly, setting aside the written speech, he felt strengthened.

'Today I say to you we have come from bondage, are still in bondage, but we go forth to freedom. I would like to believe that my election signals a new phase, a phase in which no sacrifices shall be evaded, no trouble spared, to achieve freedom. I will spare myself no effort to do by you what I know to be my duty. You, fellow countrymen, assure me in turn: are you willing to fill the colonial jails in the cause of freedom? Are you willing to starve? Are you willing, above all, to die for freedom? And when freedom shall have been won, are you willing to lay your arms down and give way to the young generation so that the freedom that you have won shall be consolidated?'

There was sustained applause. Kawala raised his right hand.

'I, Aliko Kawala, affirm before you that I am ready. Together with you we will talk to the Colonial Government only so long as there is a chance of victory for peace through negotiation. But when that chance is no more, know all of you that we shall fight for our birthright. If there are any jackals among you who fear to fight, let them leave us now because beyond this, they will be traitors. We have talked too long about the injustice of this colonial régime. The time for action is now . . . !'

If he had looked sideways at that time, he would have met the doubtful eyes of Santasa. For what was Kawala saying? Was he not saying that previous leadership had failed? What did a naïve newcomer like Kawala really know about politics at the presidential level? Was this not an insult to Santasa? For how much longer could Santasa go on putting up with such insults? Not even a word of acknowledgement of the work that he, Santasa, had put into the party!

'I speak to you as I do because I know that the foundations from which the attack against slavery will be launched have been well and truly laid,' said Kawala. 'For the success of our new efforts, I will depend on all of you. But most of all on those from whom I and my new team takes over. They have done a good job and I thank them.'

Santasa let out a scarcely audible sigh of relief.

'But no job is good until it is completed. So to my predecessors I extend the hand of co-operation so that even as they started the fight they may be counted with us as we complete it. . . . And now for our targets. Independence must come within twelve months. We will give the colonial reptiles two months within which to meet our demands for a one-man-one-vote independence constitution. We will not talk to Norris. We will spend our time organizing our people. After two months, and if nothing concrete comes up, violence, I say violence, will take over. Keep your vigilance. Weapons will come.. I do not say that you may need them — you *will* need them. Long live free Kandaha! Long live free

Africa!'

It was a fetid September night. The wind was refusing to blow. Just still heat, but, fortunately, dry and not steamy. The darkness was deep. Stars show off best against this dark sky. As usual, there was noise and drumming all over the compound. Through this, Kawala walked home. He was jittery and on edge. It was not like he was a nobody way out in the southern province. He was National President. The responsibility. Could he make it work? Fortunately, he'd now managed, just managed, to put together his Central Committee — a kind of Cabinet in waiting. Most of those fellows — Chimuko, Shakala, Kakondkawadia (a surprise), Mama PALP — were keen. Older hands like Santasa would come around and he was earnest. But where to go from there? That's what was worrying Kawala that night as he walked to his home. The night was dark. Cicadas were chirruping in the trees. A lonely owl hooted off the roof top of a house. That was a bad omen.

'You!'

He turned. Something hammered into his face. Stars swam in his mind. He fell back. A hand reached for his throat. It was a heavy clamp. He gasped for breath. The squeeze tightened. He struggled. A deep black voice said:

'You, we don't want any Kaffir nonsense in this compound.' Raising him by the one hand and throwing him back against a tree the voice again said:

'We don't want you! Final warning!' Kawala thought he had broken his back against the tree. Two men were running away. He felt faint and then ...

He awoke about an hour later. He felt his face. It was a bloody mess. Where was he? He stood up. He staggered to a communal water tap nearby and washed off the blood. Fortunately his face wasn't very bad. It might all swell up over the night. He prayed it would not because he didn't want his wife Ana to know. It would worry her so much.

'Tata' ('Daddy'), greeted Kawala. It was his seven-year-old daughter, Jena. 'Tata, next time you must come early, you understand?' Jena had a rounded up cherubic face and the kind of real black finish that was very beautiful. A bit like her mother. Unlike the boys who were always going away to play, she stayed at home with Mummy or at Grannie's to eat. She had a puckish, mischievous twinkle about her. She was his dearest, and she knew it too.

'Next time you come late, I'll lock you out like Mummy did last year.'

In fact, 'last year' was only last week. Mrs Kawala had had a visit from the police late one night. They had wanted to know where Kawala was. Then, when she had said she didn't know, even though she knew he was at the party headquarters, they had scoffed at her saying:

'Watch it woman. No Kaffir stays out so long without another woman!'

She had dismissed it — but then doubt crept in and when he returned she refused to open the door. Kawala walked back to the party office a mile away. He felt sorry for his wife and understood. But it was only the beginning. With time, she'd understand. . . .

'You've been behaving, Jena?' he asked, smacking his lips and looking into her face. The little girl jumped into his hands, laughing.

'Tata,' she said, putting on her most pleading voice, 'Charlie beat me.'

'Why?'

'I don't know. I did nofing.'

'He's asleep?'

'Yes.'

'We'll see him tomorrow then. Now go off to sleep darling.'

'But, you'll beat him? I go tell him now?'

'Sssh!' said Kawala. 'Goodnight now!'

The little girl hesitated. 'Tata you like me?'

'Yes, darling.'

' 'Cause I not naughty like Charlie and the others?'

'They'll also stop being naughty.'

'Goodnight Tata.'

She again jumped into his arms and within minutes fell fast asleep. Kawala carried her to the reed mat spread out on the floor. There was a tattered blanket. He pulled it over her body. His wife who had been preparing his supper in an adjoining small black sooty room came over. Her eyes were watering from the smoke of the wood fire. She was feeling tired. She had been standing on her feet all day at the market. But she managed a smile.

'How was the day?' she asked.

'I was elected President tonight. I'm worried. 'Twill be a long haul. But now, how are you Ana-Jena?' he asked, looking into her eyes.

She tiptoed into the only other room where the children were sleeping. Six of them laid out in peaceful sleep. Even the little girl who'd been waiting for daddy was now asleep. She looked at the cargo laid out before her. Healthy competing snores. If she could only make a little more money at the market! A little meat — offals certainly — once or so a week could do wonders. He was in the house and there they were. What else could a woman wish? Kawala stood up. He too tiptoed to the room. He stood close to her until their sides touched. He put his arm round her waist. For a moment the two were lost in the admiration of these children of theirs. He squeezed her waist. She smiled into his face. What else could a man wish?

'I must get your supper.'

They walked back stealthily. She to the kitchen and he back to the little room which was at once, the foyer, parlour and bedroom for them.

'You are tired,' she said.

'Not any more than you.'

He closed his eyes. What was their future? If there was one, what use was it if they arrived at it maimed and distorted in their minds? He'd read an article once about the psychology of mercenaries. How pathetic! All to a man, they were the produce of unstable homes. Could a home be stable without the father spending time with his children? He closed his eyes yet more tightly. It was no longer his children alone that he was seeing. There was the myriad of children, black, coloured, in chains from the day of birth, condemned to colonial domination because they were not white. That was the alternative.

She set the food down on the rickety wooden table in the corner of the room.

'It's very difficult at the market.'

'Yes,' said Kawala.

'They're chucking out all known PALP supporters.'

'I've heard so.'

'And naturally they came to me and harassed me to get out. They say the white men are complaining that PALP is stopping people from buying meat.'

'Ana-Jena' ('Mother of Jena'). Although Jena was not the first born, he liked to address her as such. 'I'm sorry. How shall we live without you selling at the market? If they can't allow you, we shall live somehow or other. But let them watch it! Soon we shall flush out the colonial lackeys from that market. It will be us who will demand PALP cards for anyone selling there. The party is getting organized and tomorrow we are leading a rally into town, we'll . . .'

He stopped. His wife sat meekly on the floor mat. She liked listening to him. She was not sure that she could go the whole way with him, but she understood. People made faces at her at the market. But she could not change herself, could she? She was his wife. With that title would go many humiliations. She had to put up with them. Come tomorrow, she would be at the market again. She stood up, her tall slender frame belying the long years of child-bearing. Anywhere in the crazy world of good looks, she might even have made a model. The saucy twinkle of her eyes which she shared with Jena. Was it not that which had attracted Kawala to her first? She stood up. She always rose from the floor like a creeper straightening up. So gracefully she did it. She said:

'Your water for your bath. I've forgotten to put it on the fire.'

She turned her back to him.

Kawala said:

'You're tired. I can do with a cold bath.' She turned on him and her face exploded into a criss cross of laughter. She was remembering their first days of marriage. He was then Nathaniel. She'd never heard of the name Nathaniel until she met him. There was something bewitching about the sound of that name. Maybe it was just in her head, but it was there all right.

Kawala had come from the next village to visit his cousin, her brother. Then he saw her. From there she could still not remember what happened. Just a delirious sunshine joy. And then the tribal wedding. So simple and yet so symbolic. Then the church wedding. When Father Lafayette heard his protégé had contracted a marriage 'of the outside,' wasn't he angry with him! So the Christian wedding, the 'proper' wedding, as Lafayette had called it, had followed. It had all been so strange to her. The white flowing gown. The priest in white vestments. All so strange. But Nathaniel had been by her side. That was all that had mattered.

Again she laughed. But this time it was a loud hearty laugh.

'You didn't use to approve of cold water.'

'That was when you were young.'

'Why, am I not still your girl?'

They laughed. Kawala's face had a way of surrendering itself into sheer laughter. He held her by the two hands and his eyes twinkled gleefully into her large dreamy eyes. She looked into his again and said:

'You used to be a difficult one to please. The water was never the right temperature. Always either too hot or too cold. And I used to get so angry with you.'

'I know,' he said laughing into her face. 'But now I don't. Without you, what would I be? Come, let me warm up your water.'

She could have been flying on wings. He heard her chatter away:

'One of these strange crosses women have to bear. It's either a man who hates water on his body like a mother-in-law or someone who thinks he's so dirty that he must always wallow in hot water.'

'You don't like water very much, do you, my dear,' he joked.

'If we both kept so scrubbed clean, there would be no human smell. You would not even find out where I'm lying in the dark, would you?'

They laughed. Kawala said:

'Well, I'm finished with your food. It was very good, just what I needed. I really like dried vegetable relish. Now, how about some water, girl, to wash down the food?'

As they lay on the reed mat in their room, they went on talking and joking. Little talk about the small things that really mattered — the children, their old folk and the little things that they had done together for so long. But as Kawala drifted off to sleep, the last thing that nagged in his mind was, 'Where to go from here?'

Aliko Kawala was not the first born of a family of twelve. He was the third but the first two had gone 'into the ground' when they were less than a year. He was born Nathaniel Harris Aliko Kawala, two Christian names which he subsequently dropped, and Aliko, which meant 'God is there' because his mother had believed that his life had been made possible because of the intercession of the spirits. Perhaps it was this realization that he might not have been which made Kawala a lonesome and withdrawn character, over sensitive perhaps, but certainly very compassionate. His father had been a headman of the village, and that had meant that the missionaries, in this case, the Jesuits—Catholics, who had the nearest missionary station nearby would be interested in him. Hence the two Christian names.

In his father's village and at the village school, Kawala grew into a useful fellow who was always at the elbow to help his many brothers and sisters and his classmates. He knew that as the surviving eldest of a family of ten children, only he could help them if his father was away. His father did go away one day and the following day someone came across his body in the forest. But the tragedy did not end there. One morning, a year later, an early riser heard moans and sobs coming from a thicket. He went into the thicket to investigate. He found a woman badly burnt. Tongues of flame were still greedily lapping up the stunted grass around her. The woman just had time to say, 'I die,' when her body convulsed in agony and she passed out.

That was how Kawala's mother had died. It was a mysterious death and no one really ever found out how she had been transported to that bush that night. Some said that she had taken her own life. And others said that some witches had changed themselves into flying hyenas at night and that such ones had whisked Kawala's mother to that place of death.

Although Kawala and his brothers and sisters had lost their parents early in their lives, they grew up a happy and close family under their grandmother and, when she died, under a childless uncle.

Kawala had gone through Form II and had then obtained a job as an 'African trainee' with the Bristol Gold Syndicate. He had been sent to the UK for administrative training, and had come back and worked in the personnel department, one of the few Africans so honoured, when a riot took place some five years ago. After the strike, he became a full-time member of the People's Army of Liberation Party (PALP). He was given some form of political education and sent to organize the southern province. He rose quickly. He had come to the mine to look up old friends. In fact he had been just about to return to Musasa when the whole business of Turnbull and police happened. There had been rumours that the party was not happy with Santasa's leadership. Indeed, some had said that at the forthcoming meeting of the party, Santasa could lose his job. He had lost it and now Kawala was President.

3

Katenga woke up in jail. It hurt him to move. Yesterday he had got a new job with the National Milling Company. On the way home he had stopped at the PALP meeting where Kawala was elected President. Katenga was one of the curiosity seekers.

He had never really been interested in politics and he had only slipped in because the crowd, with all its noise and boisterous behaviour had interested him. But as he left that evening to make his usual round of pubs in Musasa, he could not forget the deep look of the man who had just become President of PALP. He did not waste much time to talk about the new man.

'Where does Kawala come from?' He took a deep draw on his bottle of beer. Then he thought a moment. 'I don't like it much. He's too much a villager. The other man sitting with him in Sanga Bar said:

'He could pull it off. Old Santasa hasn't been exactly effective, has he? Always wasting our time on this or that rally and it comes to nothing. Maybe what we need is an ascetic chap like that fellow, lean and hungry. He could go on for years without food, that chap.'

'And I understand he worked for a while at BGS,' continued Katenga.

'Yes indeed he did, but Turnbull made sure he didn't come back. Ugh, I think politics is not my kettle of fish,' responded his drinking companion who suddenly became distracted by someone.

Just five or six paces away from where he and Katenga sat was a woman colourfully dressed. She wore a short blouse, fitted and cut low in the front as well as the back. Her chitenge (cloth) wrapped around like a skirt was so tight that she seemed to have difficulty walking. Her eyes were heavily made up with black and her complexion appeared orange. The orangey colour was restricted to her face. Everywhere else, she was a rich brown which indicated that she was one of a number of women who used skin bleach.

Unable to continue their political discussion, he nudged Katenga to share his view of the woman standing close to them. Katenga's companion looked and he and Katenga smiled approvingly.

'She's good, isn't she?'

'Sort of,' responded the companion.

'Well, don't sit here saying, "sort of". She's looking for a beer and maybe fun, eh? Why not call her over?' Katenga suggested.

The woman came readily.

'You're new here?' asked Katenga.

She nodded affirmatively.

'So you're not married?'

She giggled foolishly and said:

'I am, but it doesn't matter.' She was obviously high but she was not finished. 'You buy me a beer?'

Katenga considered her briefly. He was feeling a little hazy. Maybe it was the drink catching up with him. That was strange because his normal consumption was twelve pints and he had only had three. From Sanga, he would be moving to the Red Lion Bar in town and then to Africa Bar to complete his twelve. So why the haziness? he thought.

'You,' said the woman, nudging him in the stomach, grinning in his face.

He closed his eyes for a moment. No, he wasn't drunk. Was it something Kawala had said that disturbed him, or was it simply his expression from the meeting? Didn't Kawala say that time had run out? For what? How could time run out when there was beer around? Wasn't life pleasant having beer, women and smoke? He reached in his pocket for a cigarette.

'Want a fag, Mama?' he asked her.

'You joking with me, brother. No African woman smokes, at least the good ones,' she replied.

'I know,' Katenga responded quickly. 'Do you want a fag?' he asked again.

A little irritated she asked for a beer. He ordered her a beer, looked into her large brown eyes and said:

'You owe me a dance, Mama.'

Katenga went to the juke box and slotted in the sixpence for his favourite, *From a Jack to a King*. With a cigarette in his mouth, he swept her in his arms.

'You take me home tonight?' she asked.

'Don't know.' He was uncertain. It was going to be a long evening as usual and he didn't want to commit himself so early.

'There's good music at Africa Bar,' she said trying to persuade him. 'There's also roast meat there. Didn't I see you there yesterday?'

Becoming impatient, he snapped, 'If you talk too much, I'll leave you.' She gave in to him.

'OK, OK, brother, I stop, but will you take me with you?'

Katenga looked at the ceiling. It was a pleasant mellow yellowish colour. The drink tables spread all around the dance floor looked very good indeed. It was really a different world. Fancy how the most drab night club looked so bright and plush at night after a few beers. *From a Jack to a King* was drawing to a close. Katenga pointed to his companion to get some more beers. The woman squeezed him tight. As he looked at her, her lips approached his.

'Not in public', he said restraining her.

'Ah! So you fear to love me in public? You have a girl here?'

He pushed her away. They returned to the table, Katenga muttering:

'Next time, only half a beer.'

Going to the Red Lion that night in a thumped automobile, Katenga said to his friend:

'You know in two months' time there will be fighting here?'

'Who says?'

'Kawala did and mad men like him can mean what they say.'

'Don't spoil the evening then. If there's only two months to go then we better live it up.'

They both laughed. The owner of the car said:

'Do you know this man, Kawala? They say when he was in the southern province, he told the whites where they got off.'

'How?'

'Well, they say it was like this. But I don't know if it's true or not.' The man changed into the lower gear slowly to negotiate an incline. 'They say that a white bwana shot himself. Woman trouble. Four hundred miles away from here. No mortuary. So the DC ordered clear out of all meat from the deep freeze in the African butchery.'

'And what did Kawala do?' asked Katenga.

'Well, but I don't know if it's really true. But they say he stopped it and threatened to dump the body in the whites-only butchery.'

'How could they do that?'

'My friend,' said the driver. 'Whites don't think a black is a man. That's why I think Kawala has a point. And between ourselves — you don't mind my saying it, do you? — that's why I think we are fools not to listen to him.' The man lifted his foot off the accelerator so that the car just coasted along. 'Take me here. Why do you think I'm driving you all the way to this sordid Red Lion of yours? I've got enough education to equal at least Norris'. What's he? A railway spanner boy turned into a big bwana and leader of the whites. Large house, large everything. The richest company — BGS keeps him in the money. Why? Have you asked yourself, why? Because Norris stands for no good jobs for the black, no opportunity, no nothing. And BGS likes it that way. Then they can continue to take money out of this country to feed their kith and kin in England.'

He dropped them at the Red Lion. For most of the evening, Katenga sat hunched up in the corner. A white man came in. He was one of those stray whites that made news by fraternizing with drunken black women. Katenga looked up at him. He knew the man. Often Katenga noticed that this white man came in near closing time to pick up women.

'Mary,' the white man commanded. 'Let's go!'

The street girl named Mary, stood up, disappointed in Katenga, approached the white man. Katenga, surprised that the white man was addressing the woman he was with the whole evening, shot up from his corner of the bar.

'You won't go?' he asked. Mary looked at him contemptuously, saying:

'I don't go with Kaffirs.' Mary, staring at the white man, said, 'Baas here is my boyfriend.'

'Do you mind?' said the white man interposing himself between Katenga and his catch. He was a tall, threateningly large man, the sort you would not have associated with scavenger operations in black bars. Katenga pushed the man aside and yelled to the woman:

'Who's a Kaffir?' Then without waiting for an answer, he told her. 'You are only an African woman. I'll beat you up, you prostitute!'

He slapped her hard on the face. The woman screamed. The white man grabbed Katenga by the jacket and lifted him up saying:

'You Kaffir!'

Katenga slipped through his hold and landed a heavy blow on the white man's throat. He staggered but made a dive for Katenga. Someone rushed to get hold of Katenga.

'Stop it! You'll get in trouble. This is a white man.'

The white man recovered his balance. Katenga struggled to break the hold of the black hands. Katenga was helpless now.

'Beat this cheeky bastard up!' the white man ordered Katenga's captors.

Katenga felt a stinging blow on his head. Then another and another until the whole bar participated. Two black policemen walked in, their handcuffs ready. The barman shouted on seeing them:

'We don't want any Kawala thugs here.'

Yes, he had been pulped up by the police before being chucked into the cell in which he was now the occupant on an exclusive basis. He would have laughed at the thought of having a room all to himself. But his head ached. His lips were swollen. Maybe that's why they call us 'thick lips'. Then he heard a shuffling of feet. Someone was fumbling with the door lock. Not again! He missed several beats. The door opened roughly. He jumped up, his shoe ready in the right hand. The constable stopped in the doorway, a slightly comical smile on his face.

'Glad I worked you over well. You can use some more. But here, first.'

He dropped him a cigarette. Katenga's insides went cold. The constable looked at him again, at the large gash above the eye, the swollen bulbous face, the congealed blood and decided he would defer the treatment. He peeped into the shit bucket in the corner.

'You don't pass up your routine, eh?'

He laughed loud and left.

Waking up in jail the following morning, a little disorientated at first, he recalled the previous night. An African constable accompanied by a familiar white man approached Katenga's cell.

'This is a bugger. If nothing is done to him, I'll report the matter right up to O'Flaherty himself. You know that unlike Jefferson, your Commissioner of Police, O'Flaherty is a guy who stands no nonsense from these Kaffirs.'

This was Katenga's first taste of a police cooler. And the police finished off the work which the white man had started on him the previous night.

Later another policeman came with a woman to Katenga's cell. She was Katenga's woman. Katenga, a bit relieved when seeing her, called her name, 'Delia'.

'Is this not the pig you are after?' the police asked her.

'Katenga what are you doing here? I've been looking for you the whole night.'

Katenga suddenly became irritable.

'And who told you to look for me?'

'Am I not your wife? Haven't I beared you a child?'

The woman pinched the child who was strapped on her back. It began to cry.

'Don't talk rubbish woman. Get away from here. I never married you. You're just a street woman, a child collector, like that woman I saw yesterday.'

'So, you've been sleeping with other women?'

She broke loose from the policeman and began to claw his face. Katenga tried to fend her off but it was no use. The policeman just laughed.

Released in Delia's custody, they continued their hot discussion.

'What's this I hear about you?' asked the woman as soon as they were out of the police station.

'What?'

'Your friend, the one who picked you up from Sanga said you are a Kawala fan.'

'When did you meet him?'

'He came straight to me after dumping you at Red Lion. He said you were pissed.'

'So he is your boyfriend?'

'You are jealous?' He looked at her. He could see that she had calmed down. So he smiled and said:

'Not really. Now I remember him. Yes, I thought I'd seen him somewhere before.'

'He's my uncle. He's a driver for BGS and he's often around in the evening ferrying people up and down. A funny fellow that. Comes all the way, forty miles from BGS to run a night taxi service.'

Katenga thought for a moment.

'Are you really a Kawala thug as they say? He's a mad man that man,' Delia asserted.

'Why?'

'Why does he leave his wife alone to suffer like that? Always at the market selling this and that caterpillar worm, dried relish, firewood. Name it and she's got a bit of it. And what a mean wife she is too!'

'You mean he's not been staying with his wife in the southern province?'

'Ha! What man stays with his wife if he can get away from her these days! Why do you think he entered politics? To get away from her. That's why he left his job at BGS and sent her down here.'

'You know, Delia,' said Katenga as they approached her hut where he was a frequent visitor. 'That man, Kawala. I think he's our future.'

'Why doesn't he become the future of his children first?'

'But I think you are wrong.'

'Me? Every women here knows it. And what's more she herself has now found it out.' Delia lowered her voice, 'These days she comes very late from the market. Very late at night. What does she do there when the market is closed?' She opened the door.

A woman next door said to her husband:

'Some women are not ashamed. Going all over Musasa to look for a man who is not your husband!'

'Come in.'

'No,' said Katenga to her invitation. 'I must get myself some sleep. I can't go to work today.'

'I will make you some tea.'

'All right. If you don't claw me again I'll lie down in your bed a while.'

He smiled. She said:

'Hasn't your girl friend told you you look like an owl with all those swellings?'

He said:

'You haven't.'

She looked into his eyes, lionish eyes that always burnt her. Always shifting, never looking her fully in the face. Eyes of an adulterer! And suddenly anger welled up in her chest. Her throat was choking. The hairy-chested brute! Getting. Getting. Taking. Always taking and never giving. Her body froze as she looked at his unkept visage. She wanted to vomit, vomit in disgust at herself. And then ... all out of the blue, Katenga swept her off into his powerful arms. Smothering and biting into her mouth until it hurt, he growled,

'I will eat you!'

She melted into his arms. He threw her back.

Katenga hadn't had much sleep in the cooler. Fatigue overwhelmed him and soon he sunk into a deep sleep after he entered his hut made of timber boards and two concrete slabs for a bed. Completely oblivious of the hours passing, he slept through his job at National Milling. The following morning he no longer had a job, but this was no surprise. Most of his jobs had ended similarly. Finding a new job was going to be difficult — work was scarce. He thought about Kawala again rather than where he could find employment.

The following night, there was an inspection of all the huts in Musasa. He didn't have any job card because he no longer had a job. The National Milling inspection found him in bed with a woman — not Delia. The girl jumped up and ran into the other room — the small kitchen. One of the guards flashing a torch into his face said:

'Job card and marriage certificate.'

'What's all this about?'

'Show me your job card and the paper that says you can sleep with that woman, Kaffir.'

'I don't have them here,' replied Katenga. 'I lost them.'

'You've got no job, Kaffir. Let's go. Jump on to the truck. You'll be in good company there.'

Katenga tried to run but the other man slid a truncheon between his legs and he tripped and fell. Holding him there the man said:

'Pick it up, next time you try it, I'll bash your brains.'

The first guard looked round the room.

'Do you walk naked, Kaffir? Where's your clothes? Oh, rags, eh? And that slut goes for you?' With a wink to the other guard he said, 'I'll join you in a minute. Take him to the truck.'

He went into the kitchen where the girl had run into. Within a few seconds screams were heard from the girl in the kitchen. Katenga tried to jump off the truck. The others — some fifty — laughed.

'You think we were found in church?' said one of them.

Jail wasn't as bad as Katenga expected. Although he couldn't have beer, there was plenty of politics, Kawala always being the main issue. The prisoners boasted that Kawala would set them free. The warder chuckled at that and said:

'You must be joking. He'll be next in here.'

'You are a stinking fool. Your father has a stench. Your mother's father was slave. You are a dog only,' said Katenga to the warder.

With that outburst, Katenga, instead of one week got three. But during his extended stay, he and the warder became buddies. After all, he'd committed no real crime. And to Katenga's surprise, the warder himself was a supporter of PALP. So the chats became more friendly.

'The superintendent is on the war path. Two prisoners escaped last night,' said Msonda.

'Good. I hope they'll come back and burn the place down. Any news of Kawala? Is it true he was really beaten up? Did they find out who did it?'

'Compound thugs.'

'Like you.' Katenga grinned. Then he added, 'No, of course not. You are official.' Then seriously, 'But why?'

'Kawala is the only fellow who can set us free. Do you think I like torturing my fellow blacks? But I've got five kids. Money is money. But it's not a good life this. My father used to tell me, "Msonda, laugh with as many people as you can." I don't get that here. Instead I have to beat you up or I lose my job.'

Just then there were loud footsteps outside. It was the white superintendent. No black warder wore shoes.

'I'll hit the wall and you'll cry,' whispered the warder to Katenga. Katenga could have laughed. Instead he let out a yell and the superintendent outside said:

'That's it Msonda. Fix the loafer.'

'He's tamed now, sir,' said Msonda.

'Well, if he's tamed, what's the use of wasting good space keeping him here?'

But Msonda knew better than to take his commander's words literally. So after a few days he went up to his office.

'It's the prisoner Katenga, sir.'

'What about him, warder?'

'Well sir, we have broken him.'

'You think so?'

'Yes sir.'

'He's tamed?'

'Well sir, this morning he begged me not to hit him again. There were tears in his eyes.'

'Tears!' exclaimed the superintendent. 'We don't measure repentance by tears here.'

Then he smiled. He liked Msonda. There was that something about the man which always made him feel by merely listening to his reports about prisoners breaking down that he was doing a good job and could go on ordering flogging.

'Do you think he will return?'

'No sir.' The warder shook his head vehemently.

'Right. Release him. We need the space.'

Msonda clicked his feet to attention and saluted. Then the superintendent said:

'These two prisoners that escaped last night.'

'Yes sir,' replied Msonda.

'It was your shift, wasn't it?'

'An accident, sir.'

'Accident! It's three times now in one year.' The superintendent stood up.

'It won't happen again, sir.'

'Yes, I know it won't happen, warder. He can go.'

The warder again clicked his feet together and saluted. This time he hoped the bwana would not speak again.

'Good man,' said the superintendent as he watched Msonda go. 'I could use more like that.'

That evening Katenga was released. Msonda, waving a secretive goodbye, said:

'See you don't come back. You'll never get out of here.'

A few days later as Kawala walked out of a shoe store, Katenga ran to him and said:

'I don't think you know me. But you have done something good for us. My name is Katenga.'

Kawala offered his hand to Katenga. The eyes of the two men met: one pair narrow and sunken, but piercing, the other bulgy and criss-crossed with reddened veins. Kawala's face was smooth and clean shaven: the other's was rough and wore a fuzzy goatee which fluttered ominously in the small breeze.

'I have lots of time. I'm unemployed. Can I join the party?'

'We don't allow loafers.'

'No, I mean, I'm tired of my life. Drink, women, from one job to another. I'm tired of living for myself. I know I can get a job any time, but . . .'

Kawala looked into his face. He felt a mysterious togetherness with the man standing before him. What was it? Katenga did not batter his eyes. He too was looking into Kawala's face steadily.

'Show you can keep a job first. Then I'll know you can stick the rough life of party workers.'

Katenga tore off his hand from Kawala's. Grunting with disgust he said:

'I'll make it my own way,' and walked away.

They're all the same, these politicians of Africa, Katenga was thinking. They come in with a bang and die with a whimper. Santasa must have been the same when he entered politics. Where did it get him? To decency. To understanding everything so completely, such as why we the blacks had to suffer, that he had no strength left for action. And now here comes this Kawala. He dares ask me for my credentials. The credentials of subservience to the white man. Who has ever kept a white man's job unless they accepted to be slave to the white man? Villager only! That's what Kawala is. Spending all your life working on a farm is as good as living in the village. Does he know that here in town we suffer? That to sleep on the floor where the white man sleeps on a mattress is worse than sleeping on a reed mat? How long has he been even at the Bristol Gold Syndicate? One year. Where was he before that. A villager. Teaching Christianity in a village. Katenga's bulldog chin jutted out. His boots crunched up the loose road surface as his protruding red-shot eyes gaped into nothing. In his heart he was still saying, 'I'll make it my own way. Whites are swines only. They killed my father and that's why I came here to town. If the axe that one is given to cut wood for the mother-in-law is blunt, throw it away. I must have a certificate from the white man to join the party. ... *Dear Mr Kawala, I confirm that Katenga has been a good Kaffir. ... Obedient to the white man and all that. I recommend him to you unreservedly. ... He'd do the job of killing the white man just as obediently. ... Yours, John Smith (white man).'*

'Shuck!' exclaimed Katenga loudly.

The sun shone mercilessly hot as Katenga walked to nowhere. In his mind he could see the verdant grass of what he thought was Kawala's spawn disintegrate into red heat and crumble into the black ash of dried grass just burnt.

'I'll make it my own way!' he repeated to himself.

4

Katenga was sitting with some friends in a tavern. He had many friends in taverns, in any tavern that he went.

'Did you hear what Kawala said about independence?' asked Katenga.

'What can he do?' asked one companion. 'You can't get rid of bosses like Norris, the Governor and all of them just like that.'

'Watch, he'll soon be in Central Prison,' volunteered another.

'Eh, Norris! That man!' stated the first. He could have been about forty-five.

'Yah,' replied the second. 'With large tattooed arms ... bloodshot eyes. On the railway we called him Mbatatisi (potatoes) because he always used to roast local potatoes on the engine when he drove the train from Kapiri to here. His wife died ... years ago. Has a son. Funny thing about the boy, teaches in an African school. Has African friends. Bwana Norris — a crude Polish man — changed his nationality to English — now, he's *Sir* Ray Norris. Bwana Norris!'

They all took a drink. The first companion, Katenga had forgotten their names, resumed:

'Norris wants to be another Smith.'

'Ah! He wants to be the next Governor. To be Governor Sir Ray Norris, the ex-Polish defender of British European civilization. He wants to be Governor. And Kawala wants to be Governor or

President, my friend,' replied the second. 'But who can side with an African, a villager? Eh! Europeans are Europeans. They even make this beer that we are drinking.'

Katenga broke in:

'Kawala is not fighting for himself! He's fighting for you, you drunk! That's the trouble with you Africans. You always want to be slaves.'

'We are not slaves!' interrupted companion number two. 'But we will be slaves if Kawala takes this country. My boss, a very good white man says this, and I believe it! He says he is sorry for us that we allow such a demagogue.'

In the Kandaharian Legislative Council (the law-making body in a British colony) that afternoon, Sir Ray Norris, the leader of the Unofficials stood up to make an important statement. The Kandaha Legislative Council was composed of ten civil servants who were designated the Officials. The Officials together with the Governor constituted the Executive Council which was the policy-making body in minor matters, while the Colonial Government decided directly through the Governor in major issues. One of the Officials, Mr Thomson, represented African interests in the Legislative Council. Thus, if the black community in Kandaha — ninety-eight per cent of the population — was aggrieved, it had, through a maze of institutions, to get its views up to the Secretary for Native Affairs, Mr Thomson. The Unofficials numbered ten also. They were the representatives of the white men. Mr Thomson, a thick-set little man, had crossed swords with the Unofficials before — especially Norris. So that afternoon as he walked into the little debating chamber — very much a microscopic miniature of St Stephen's chapel he felt supremely confident.

The private members' motion would be defeated as usual. Although the Unofficials equalled the Officials, they never maintained a consistent voting pattern. It didn't matter whom you represented, if you were a trader, you had to have your import licence and also the foreign-exchange allocation. And that did not come from the Unofficials' side. You barked with them, but, naturally, you worshipped with the Officials. Thomson looked around the chamber wistfully. Norris sat across the floor. His face was fixed and the jaws set. His bushy brows fell over his eyes ominously in sharp contrast to the thinned-out skull and forehead. The large hairy arms, dark with sunburn, twitched nervously at each movement of his pencil. He was in a sullen mood. He meant to win and take all. Thomson looked at him, a trace of anxiety crossing his face. He looked at the order paper in his hands. It read:

'Honourable Sir Ray Norris to move:

That in the view of the House, the Colonial Administration has continued to commit grave errors of administration in its handling of the African peoples.

That

WHEREAS the Colonial Government has continued to behave as though the white people and their representatives in this country did not exist;

WHEREAS it has been established beyond any reasonable doubt that the Colonial Officials are contemplating a deal with the blacks for the purpose of ensuring the demise of the representatives of the white people of this country;

WHEREAS the representatives of the white people have on several occasions made it categorically clear that they have not, are not and will not consider blacks of this country fit persons with whom to share power either in the forseeable or distant future;

WHEREAS the white and freely elected representatives of the white electorate are able and capable of taking over the reigns of Government from the colonial civil servants whose homes are still in the United Kingdom, and who, unlike the representatives of the white electorate who go home every day, go home for six months every three years;

WHEREAS the white citizens of this country are more Kandaharian than even the blacks and are for that reason better equipped to protect these natives because they know in what place the natives belong;

WHEREAS the Colonial Government for reasons of personal aggrandizement among its officials here in Kandaha has continued to accept to be misled in regard to the time and noble intentions of the white people towards their primitive charges;

And WHEREAS further in the Republics of Rhodesia and South Africa the white race has clearly demonstrated its strategic import-ance as a bastion against the onslaught of communism;

And WHEREAS further black ruled régimes to the north, east and west of this country have evinced unbridled rapacity, racialism and sheer incompetence in the governance of people and a complete betrayal of civilized government.

The House now

RESOLVES

1   That black political activity and its demagogues should be banned forthwith.
2   That representatives of the Crown in the form of nominated civil servants sitting in this Legislative Council and the Executive Council should be withdrawn immediately, and
3   That both in the interests of establishing civilized and responsible government and in the interests of securing the country's investment potential, Kandaha should become independent forthwith under the existing franchise which will ensure that government does not pass into the hands of irresponsible and uncivilized people.
4   That considering the intemperate and immodest utterances of African heads of state, Kandaha is in a state of siege and responsibility for the control of its armed forces should move forthwith from the Governor and the Colonial Government to the representatives of the civilized people.'

Thomson snatched off his glasses. Again he looked across at the padded green bench where Norris sat. For a moment, he closed his eyes to think of the day when five years ago he himself had personally recommended a Queen's Birthday honour for Norris. What had Norris been before that? A mere uncouth, rabble-rousing, white racist orator. Only the Afrikaans people, those on the farms and those on the railway where he came from had taken him seriously then. But with the MBE then the OBE and two years ago the CBE, Norris had become accepted even in the most pure English circles.

'I'm damned if I'll stomach this,' said Thomson. 'Personal aggrandizement indeed!'

The Speaker, a tall, furtive but sharp-eyed man appeared in the doorway.

'Honourable Members of the House, the Speaker!'

He walked in swiftly, hardly enough time to allow his tall frame to unwind and bow again to the other side. When he ascended to his chair, he too swept the Members with a ferocious and somewhat charging look. His eyes rested briefly on Norris and moved on. He too was a colonial civil servant, white, of course, nominated by the Governor.

'Let us pray.'

His voice boomed across the floor of the small chamber. His eyes, in an effort to locate his God, possibly trapped up there in the ceiling, lighted harshly on the capacity-full press gallery. He enjoyed clever repartee with the wayward and somewhat recalcitrant Members on the floor. He knew the Press simply loved his sharp thrusts. Had they packed the gallery to hear Norris or to enjoy the superb phrase of the Speaker? He tugged at his robes then started again:

'Let us pray. Almighty God, Who in Thine infinite wisdom and providential goodness hast appointed the offices of Rulers and Parliaments for the welfare of society and the just government of men, we beseech Thee to behold with Thine abundant favour, us, Thy servants, whom Thou Hast been pleased to call to the performance of such important trusts in this land. . . .'

After preliminaries which appeared far too long, the Speaker then called upon 'The Honourable and Learned Member'. He shook his head and said:

'Sorry.'

But that was his way of telling the press that Sir Ray Norris was simply not just not learned but was an uneducated railway spanner boy graduated into a 'Sir'.

'I mean, The Honourable Member for Musasa West.'

Norris stood up. He wiped his massive forehead. He'd been perspiring in spite of the air conditioning. He looked up and, in spite of the high walls, he thought he could hear the wind outside blowing through the fronded palm trees and whispering softly over the verdant lawns that surrounded the House. The House was of colonial architecture. Heavy and dominating grey walls. High roof. Mazes of corridors and offices. Thomson, the leader of the House sprang to his feet. It was after all, not Norris' business to move motions.

'Mr Speaker, sir, I beg to move that the House do now debate the Members' motion before it.'

The Speaker rose.

'The motion is that the House do now debate the Members' motion before it.' He paused then looked up. 'Any debate? Any objection?' He straightened himself up. 'The motion is that the House do now debate the Members' motion before it. Will as many as are of the opinion say, "Aye!" '

'Aye!'

The Unofficials were at their vociferous best.

'Will as many as are not of the opinion say, "Nay!" The "Ayes" have it. It is resolved in the affirmative. The Honourable Member for Musasa West.'

Norris stood up again. He smoothed out the creases of his crumpled coat. As a widower he did not care much about clothes. They were there to perform just one function — 'to stop people running away from me' as he used to say. He looked squarely into the Speaker's eyes — Norris was a hard worker in everything that he touched.

'Mr Speaker, sir. I rise with a profound sense of gratitude to have been permitted, so early after my return from the United Kingdom, the Mother of Parliaments, to address this distinguished Council, nay Parliament. This oasis of civilization in a continent wracked and torn asunder by the savagery, rapacities, nay chicanery of the so-called black parliaments and their sabre-rattling, tinpot dictators called "Presidents".' He swept his eyes over the benches in front of him and then turned back to look up at the press and visitors' galleries. 'It is indeed a good feeling to come from the Houses of Parliament at Westminster and to behold here in this chamber nothing but Honourable Members, yourself, Mr Speaker, and men and women in the galleries testifying to the presence in our midst of a long and arduous history of culture and civilization. For I do not perceive any black man in this House. Am I now to understand that this will not be so for very much longer, that black locusts will soon descend upon this chamber, shrieking and swooping and gouging out the very eyes of Aryan civilization lest with seeing it it should re-incarnate itself?'

Sir Ray Norris paused. Then he opened out his arms until they embraced the whole House. Shaking his massive chiselled head, he said:

'Mr Speaker, I refuse to open my mind's eye to this prospect. For if there are Honourable Members here in this House bent on treachery against their own race, I would like to warn them that the white race all over the world is ready to defend its civilization. I . . .'

'On a point of order, Mr Speaker.' It was Thomson. The Speaker rose.

'Point of order.'

Norris sat down.

'Is it in order for the Honourable Member to intimidate the House?'

'I'm not intimidating the House,' cut in Norris arrogantly.

'The Honourable Member is in order and he may continue.'

'Thank you Mr Speaker for your protection.' Thomson threw his papers into the air in exasperation.

'Mr Speaker, sir, I was saying before I was rudely interrupted, that . . .'

'Mr Speaker, sir, is it still in order for the Honourable Member to refer to an honourable and learned colleague of this House as "rudely" interrupting him?'

It was Thomson again.

'Point of order.'

Norris sat down — or rather crouched, ready to resume.

'The Honourable Member for Musasa West is out of order. He must withdraw the adjective.'

'It was an adverb, Mr Speaker,' said one of Norris' men.

'Adverb, adjective, full stop or whatever it was, I must insist.'

George Norris Junior, sitting in the visitors' gallery, smiled. As a teacher, he liked a fine use of words.

'Mr Speaker, sir, I withdraw the word unreservedly and apologize to my honourable and learned colleague. If I may now continue. Mr Speaker, sir, . . .'

'Mr Speaker, sir.' It was the Secretary for Transport. He'd risen from shovel work on the roads right through to becoming Secretary for Transport. 'Secretary' was the equivalent of Minister in independent Africa. 'A point of order.'

Norris again sat down. But this time not before he had grunted: 'Rubbish!'

'Is it in order for the Honourable Member to refer to the Officials as conducting government business for the purpose of self-aggrandizement?'

'The Honourable Member for Musasa West has not said any such thing to the best of my knowledge. But I dare say that as compared to the Honourable Secretary of Transport, my knowledge is indeed very little.

There was laughter because Members and the press and visitors knew that the Speaker was a silk while the Honourable Secretary for Transport was a windbag who could never have occupied any post in the administrative service for which ability to read and understand a book page was a prerequisite.

'But it's here, sir,' he said in a sing song and pointing to the order paper. The Speaker stood up. He looked at the galleries and down to the Members and when he was sure of attention, he said:

'Yes, the Honourable Secretary for Transport is right. It may be there. But it hasn't been said as yet.'

When Norris resumed, it was a vigorous, angry and fighting speech.

'The Colonial Government in London has no right to sacrifice us. Do they want us to tell them that we are no longer part of Britain? Do they want us to utter and commit rebellion? Do they know that our dear colleague, Ian Smith, was pushed too far to the wall? If they still don't know, I tell them that we are ready. I tell them that for us, the white people of this country, no cause is sweeter than the defence of our own rights; that no omission or sin is more heinous than unquestioning submission to the plot to elevate the black nigger into a human being enjoying an equal status with us. . . . If Britain is serious about its nigger-saving mission, then let not her citizens act as though the black man stinks. For that is what they are doing now there in Britain. They are hounding out the black West Indian, the black African, the brown Indian. And yet these people who put up this fight against coloured immigrants are in my opinion the brave sons and daughters of Britain. Britain should have cause to thank them. But alas, they are fighting a losing battle. We here are not fighting a losing battle: we have not even started to fight. Try us and you will see.' He looked towards the Officials briefly and continued.

'To condemn South Africa for practising apartheid is like condemning the human hands for being a separate organ from the legs. We, the white people, are different from the blacks. If we are different, it follows we live differently. Have the Honourable Official Members across the floor ever tried living with their cookboys? There is a difference between black and white: but there is no difference between blacks, no difference between a black professor and a black cookboy. That is the problem. That is the crisis. That, Mr Speaker, is the tragedy, a tragedy of over-reaching human proportions, a tragedy which if not contained can hound civilization, the white race, out of this world.

'Don't you know, Mr Speaker, sir, that the hallmark of black is savagery, that the onrushing lava of black savagery is cascading towards our very doors and that we have but little time to stop it?'

George Norris Junior stood up. Something that the father had said appeared to have upset him much.

Sir Ray spoke on. When he finished there was tumultuous

applause. Of course, Thomson would move in to butcher the motion. But that is not to say that Sir Ray Norris had not made a moving and at times thoroughly convincing speech. What was more, he had not isolated the Officials for unwholesome mention. In fact, he had risen above factionalism to make the dramatic appeal to all white people. 'I may hate what he says,' said Thomson to himself, 'but I defend his right to say it.'

That evening, Norris' visage loomed large in all the news bulletins. It was as though a hitherto unknown colussus had overshot the cloudy skies into the brightness of the shining sun.

'Well son, what did you think of it?'

George sat back in the well-padded chair at Norris' farm house. It was called 'Mtendere Haven' which means 'Peace Haven'. Mtendere Haven was a rambling 5000 acre estate just twelve miles west from the Musasa Post Office. The land rose towards the centre of the estate where the house was perched. All around it a lush of green coffee trees fell away. At the northern edge of it, a stream bubbled through thick foliage. Norris had made twelve ponds off it, all stocked with fat river bream. He had sunk all his railwayman's savings into this farm, not borrowing even an *Ngwee*, cent or penny from anybody. That was how Norris worked, independent at every stage of the game. He often teased his followers about the need to die independent, 'independent from niggers, independent from death itself'. He was proud of his home. This was home, home where he returned to after all the glamour, excitement and sometimes utter wretchedness of the political day.

George, the old man's only son thought over his father's question. Norris Senior walked over to the bar, poured himself a stiff brandy — the previous drink had been a neat gin 'to lay the foundation' — and gulped it down. George said:

'Dad, you're drinking too much.'

'It's the pressure my boy. Being Leader of the Opposition isn't easy. Not when the Colonial Government wants to stiffen itself up by setting the blacks against us. They've been excellent as nannies and houseboys. I don't see what else they need. Anyway, George, what did you think of my performance? ... God, I love this place.' He sniffed the cool evening breeze that was coming in through the open windows.

'This is how God meant the white man to live. Independent. Independent from niggers. Independent from death itself. Home is the sailor, home from the sea. It's been a long voyage. Well son,' he said, stopping to look at George, 'what did you think of my speech?'

'Not much, Dad. In fact, I left before it finished.'

'You what!'

'Yes, Dad.'

'Why?' Norris Senior stomped into the thick carpet furiously. He poured himself another brandy.

'Dad, you remember how you brought me up. Not having a mother so early in life was quite tough. You had your work to do. You bought me toys, train toys, airplane toys, ships and what not. These were my companions. But you did more. You encouraged the cookboy's sons to play with me. First they thought I was a curiosity, but soon we began to get on very well together. Then they offered me their food, *nsima*. At first you would not have me eat with them. But eventually you relaxed the rules and these boys used to come in, even sit on your chair, and eat with me.'

George looked up to his father. The father said:

'Yes I remember.'

'Now, Dad, these two boys never went to school. Michael is now working for you driving the tractor and John died — of malnutrition you said once.'

'Yes.'

George stood up, a lemonade in his right hand.

'But I was lucky. You knew what was good for me and you made sure I had an education. Overseas University and all that. But do you know that the best friends I have ever had were these two boys?'

'Then?' Sir Ray's anger was returning.

'And now my own Dad says, tells the world, blacks are no good. My own Dad says this old cook who still cooks for him, the man who washed the dirt off my nappies, is only a savage. My Dad, whom I loved most because he was such a kind man to all of us, who made me feel I was not alone because these black piccaninies were part of the family, says they are savages. Dad . . .'

'Blacks are OK for cooks, but can't you see the point George? Can these piccaninnies rule you, rule this country?' Sir Ray's voice rose. He was again perspiring profusely. 'My God!' he exclaimed. 'My own son! Is that why you went to teach in a nigger school, to look for your piccaninny Johns and Michaels?'

'No, Dad. Tell me that when you taught me to share what I had with these little brats, you were telling me what you didn't believe in. Tell me you've lied to me all my life. Why *you*? Why you of all people? You who clothed your servant and all his two boys and five girls when you were only a railway man earning very little?'

'They were not a threat then.'

'And now they are?'

'Yes!'

'How?'

'Because they want to meddle in government. I'll not have it I tell you! You know what's happening in other black states, don't you?'

'No, I don't. That's the most racist thing I've heard you say!'

'But it's the truth. Look around you.'

'What about Ghana, Nigeria, Zambia, Zaïre, Kenya, Tanzania and all those countries?'

'What about Zambia? They seem to do all right without the white man's help.' It was not meant to be a sneer but his upper lip curled up somewhat.

Then he continued, 'Take Zambia for instance. Twelve years ago it was no more than a train stop. Fourteen years after Kaunda and UNIP kicked out the British, it is one of the most up-to-date countries in Africa and a real pain in the neck for Britain. They have a university, an educational system, medical set-up, that will rival anything that we have here.

'You took me to Zambia on my thirteenth birthday, remember? Our plane landed in a cow pasture. What a laugh we had about it!' George laughed. 'Well, you should see it now. An air terminal that will rival anything anywhere, and for that matter even your South Africa. Dad, it's the thirteenth hour, everything around you is burning. Your luck is running out.'

Norris poured himself another drink:

'You've never been this vocal before.'

'Dad, like you I love this country. I don't want to lose it. Don't want to see another country where whites fucked up their chance because they were too selfish and everything went up in smoke.'

'You know there's oppression of the white man. There's mass killings of their own people. There's no democracy.'

'Dad, where is there democracy in the white world today?'

'You are a commie!'

'No I'm not. But if you want me to tell you, I've lost confidence in the so-called civilization which you seem so keen to safeguard. How long did you stay as a Pole before you were kicked upstairs to Sir, Dad? Don't you remember the many youngsters who superceded you merely because you were a Pole and they were English? Isn't that why you became a naturalized British citizen, just so you could become accepted in their society? And you call that civilization? You call Hitler's liquidation of the Jews civilization? Where is the democracy where you can get to the top without money, without this lovely estate, without hurting and treading on the poor and helpless?'

'George, I won't have this starry-eyed idealism in my son.'

George moved closer to his father. He was a clear foot taller than the old man.

'I'm grown up,' he said.

The clock on the mantlepiece chimed seven o'clock. Norris poured himself another brandy and said:

'Go get changed. We're expecting some visitors.' Then when George had disappeared into his temporary bedroom, Norris Senior called after him, 'Black tie. There is a set on your bed.'

George came back.

'At home?'

'Yes', replied the Senior. 'They're important people, my boy. No shabby Kaffir talk anymore.' Then he added, 'You are growing up on me. You've never talked back at me like that!'

'You're my father and I love you.' George looked away, a trifle ashamed of himself but also angry.

'Then why are you trying to break my heart?'

'The trouble is, Dad, you see yourself as a white man. I see myself as a man.'

'You are deserting me to join the mob.'

'Dad, it's you who are deserting me.'

Shortly after that, headlights appeared from low down the estate. They wound their way up the meandering, tree-lined avenue to the house. Norris Senior downed another brandy. He coughed a little and said:

'That must be the Turnbulls,' and went out to welcome his distinguished visitors.

Mrs Turnbull, a tall and beautiful blonde was dressed in a turquoise flowing gown, tipped at the ears by diamond-studded earrings. Turnbull had married her only a year ago having lost his wife the year before. He was his usual cheery and bright self. A tall handsome figure, greying somewhat, but a most warming and charming man. Next came the Thomsons. Thomson, short, chubby and somewhat portly, as usual complaining about a touch of gout. Quick to add — not good living but sitting cramped up in Parliament. Mrs Thomson — or Lady Thomson, if you went simply by her behaviour — was a tall lady. Fairly close to double Mr Thomson's height. There's always something about short men marrying tall women. In her mid-fifties. Heavy make up. Slight bags under the eyes. Voice a little imperious and just a trifle hoarse. Bushy grey in the eyebrows and a bit crow-like in her looks. The nose long and slightly squatting over the upper lip — evidence of weakening props. In her youthful days she must have been a terrific catch for Mr Thomson — politics, philosophy and economics at Oxford, Diploma in Public Administration at Cambridge and LL.B. at London.

'Ah, this then is George,' said Turnbull rising up when George made his debut.

George greeted them all.

'You're a nice lad,' said Mrs Thomson admiringly. 'Just make sure you follow your father's footsteps. He's going to be a great man.'

'There. There she goes,' teased Thomson. 'Darling, I thought we'd agreed not to talk politics this evening.' He laughed.

'Politics! It's not politics. Ray is right about these Kaffirs and I'm glad he told all of you stuffed-up civil servants off. That's why I'll never allow my girls to come here. It's too dangerous with Kaffirs around. You are here for a visit?'

'I work in this country,' George replied.

'Where? I've never seen you before.'

'Er, my son teaches in the Secondary School,' Ray Norris cut in.

'Ah, that's right. The Musasa European Secondary School is very good,' offered Mrs Thomson. 'Just make sure it remains so. And my boy, there's only one way of keeping things good. Just make sure no blacks get anywhere near there.'

Mrs Thomson's poison was gin. She liked it always large or double. Turnbull's was Bloody Mary to start with and whisky on the rocks thereafter. Mr Thomson drank anything. As the second, most important man to the Governor he had to drink whatever was offered lest he should embarrass his hosts. Mrs Turnbull looked as though she was just going — not come back — from honeymoon. Always looking up to Turnbull with thirsty glittering eyes as though he might run away.

'You think it will be all right for me to have a drink honey?'

'Oh, yes, darling.'

'Ah!' she sighed delicately. 'Let me see.' The servant waited. 'What a lovely room this is Sir Ray. That painting. What an abstract!' She stood up to examine it closely. 'Ah! It's a Picasso. Is it an original?' she asked excitedly. 'I always pester John to get me a Picasso.'

John Turnbull felt hot under the collar. The small childish ways of his angel sometimes got him hot under the collar. Sir Ray could not answer the question. In fact he had not even known whether it was a Picasso or not. What more an original? It was just one of those things people put up to fill up a wall and to 'arrive'. Then she sat down and her eyes caught a skin hanging on the wall.

'Isn't that gorgeous John? These people here do the skins so well. Is that a lion or a leopard?'

'Lion, my dear.'

'Done by Africans?'

'Yes,' replied George.

'They're clever people these blacks, aren't they John?'

There was a moment of silence. Thomson looked at Ray Norris. Mrs Thomson said:

'Yes, as far as spearing animals is concerned. I hate cruelty. I've been trying for years now as president of the Royal Society to stop this business.' Whenever Mrs Thomson talked of the Royal Society for the Prevention of Cruelty to Animals, she always referred to it simply as the Royal Society. 'I suppose I can now have my drink. It's such a lovely room, Sir Ray. Let me see. A Campari and soda?'

The waiter bowed and said:

'Yes madam.'

The clock on the mantlepiece chimed eight o'clock. Sir Ray switched on the radio for the BBC news. With luck, they might even mention what he had said in Parliament. After all London was very interested in events here. Indeed they did. The BBC talked about how he had warned of severe white rebellion outclassing Ian Smith's revolt and about how the Government had narrowly escaped a censure vote.

'Well, Ray,' said Thomson, 'you are making news.' Then he joked, 'I hope you'll have jobs for all of us.'

For the first time Ray Norris relaxed his huge frame and laughed.

'How do you think the Governor will take this?'

Thomson thought for a moment. Then he said:

'Don't really know.'

'A bit inscrutable is our little friend, isn't he?' Turnbull was putting out a feeler.

'Don't know,' said Thomson again. 'Why don't we have a drink? Cheers to Ray!'

They raised their glasses to Ray Norris, and sang 'For he's a Jolly Good Fellow'. After the singing Ray Norris said:

'The trouble with the little Governor is that he sits there like a little God and thinks the whole world is under his feet. If you, Harry, were Governor, it would be different. And I'm not saying that just because you are here.'

'Tell him,' said Mrs Thomson. 'I keep telling Harry here that little Elwyn's too much under the boot of Lady Elwyn Baker. The two of them are a total disaster. And Harry, my dear, you'd better look out.'

'There she goes again,' said Harry Thomson laughing. 'Darling, no politics tonight. Just drink and food. But I'll tell you what. Ray keep on the pressure. That's the only language the British Government will understand. I'm sure they would be anxious to avoid another UDI. Now they know it can happen if, as you said, the whites are pushed too far to the wall.'

The waiters brought in the hors-d'oeuvres. Absolutely delicious snails in hot buttered sauce. There was some silence as the guests made headway with them. Not for long though as Mrs Thomson was asking imperiously after two minutes:

'Are there any more where these little creatures came from Ray?'

Then followed the main dish — a Tournedo Rossini, the meat, a beast slaughtered on the farm and sent over to a butchery in town for professional parcelling up.

At ten that night Ray switched on the radio again. News time. BBC — Norris was no longer headline news.

'In Jango,' the announcer started, 'more than five hundred people were today killed in inter-party clashes.'

Norris shot up, looked at his son and then at Thomson and said:

'You see. That's what will happen here if blacks take over.'

The son, no longer able to keep quiet said:

'That's what happens when we hold on to power so long and we don't train the blacks for it. Jango is not a condemnation of Africa: it is Europe, we, who are being judged there.'

Turnbull looked at the young man with surprise. Mrs Thomson curled her upper lip up in an aristocratic sneer. Norris Senior felt embarrassed.

'Yes,' said George. 'You watch what will happen in your paradise land of Rhodesia. Smith cannot hold out forever. One of these days he'll go. And who do you think will take over? Blacks. What will happen? There will be inter-party, inter-tribal clashes. There will be genocide against the white man. Why? Because the white man there is selfish, he's never bothered to share power. That's what will happen here.' He stood up. 'We are living in a fool's paradise, deceiving ourselves that all this luxury here can continue when millions of people are poor, starving. Was it the blacks who chopped off the blue-blooded necks of the aristocrats in the French Revolution? No, it was the masses of oppressed, hungry and starving poor whites.'

'George, sit down!' cried the father. But George ignored him.

'I read what Kawala says. He talks of love for fellow men, white or black. Kawala says any people who are oppressed are slaves and they should fight off oppression. He says any people who oppress are also slaves because they are enslaved by selfishness. He believes in a basic goodness of man. What do we the civilized race believe in?' The glass of cognac in George's hand trembled. He looked at the seated guests and then he sat down saying, 'I'm sorry.'

Mrs Thomson said:

'Young man, you should be ashamed of yourself preaching communism in Sir Ray's house and to important people like these.'

'Communism!'

Norris Senior held George down by the hand as he tried to stand up again. But the young man continued:

'What is communism? Can any of you here tell me what it is?' There was no answer. 'I am black. I go to school, even to University in the UK. I come back here. I can't get a job like you would because I'm black. I've to live in noisy crowded compounds because I'm black. In the office I can't use the same toilet as you because I'm black. My children cannot go to the same schools as yours. When I'm sick, I cannot have the same good doctors, the same hotel luxury time of hospitals as you can. I fight for this and you tell me I'm a communist. Don't you think I'd prefer communism?' George stood up and saying, 'Excuse me,' he left for his bedroom.

They retired to the drawing room for coffees, cognacs and cigars. Rich cuban cigars in spite of ideology. The ladies went through to powder their noses and returned quickly. Mrs Turnbull sat close to John Turnbull. Whoever told her he might run off with someone like Mrs Thomson? At least that was the amusing thought that crossed Thomson's mind.

'Now boys, no more politics here and that's final,' said Helen Thomson, laughing.

'What do you expect when you get too old war horses like Sir Ray and Mr Thomson in the same corner? Politics and niggers!' There was general laughter. Ray looked pleased. Then he looked at his son who had just returned to the room. He wasn't laughing.

'Sir Ray is right, though,' cautioned Turnbull. 'I'll not allow my girls to come here so long as Kawala is running loose. Damn Kaffirs and niggers.'

George's coffee cup dropped to the ground. The coffee soaked the lily-white Wilton carpet in an ever-enlarging circle. There was silence. Everyone looked at him. He looked at Sir Ray. His lips were about to move, but he picked up the cup and merely said:

'I'm sorry.'

As if to ease the tension, Turnbull said to George:

'Funny we've never met before. Did you say you teach at the Secondary School?'

Helen Thomson said:

'I'm on the Board of Governors. Everything that 'Lady' Thomson was involved with was always in capital letters.

'I'm not . . .,' said George.

'My son is not the most sociable man in the world. He's not like his father,' said Norris. Then looking at Thomson he added with a smile, 'fighting lost causes'.

'You say the most awful things Sir Ray,' said Mrs Thomson, smiling. 'Still the Musasa European Secondary School is the best school in Africa. Just keep the niggers out.'

Mrs Turnbull said to John Turnbull:

'Dear. This obsession of yours, I must say it's begining to bother me. They can't be as bad these people.' She corrected herself and said, 'Niggers.' Then she sighed. Ever so delicately. 'Dear do you think it will be all right if I have a Tia Maria?'

'You know what that drink does to you, darling,' he replied.

She knew it wasn't a rebuke. She turned to Norris and said: 'Sir Ray you simply must do something about this horrid man I'm married to.'

'John is what this country needs, ma'am,' replied Ray. 'A ten-cent cigar, as the Yankees say.'

They had a good laugh over it, over their coffees, Tio Pepes, Irish whisky and varying degrees of inebriation.

'What a lovely room,' said Helen Turnbull looking around. 'That is an original, isn't it Sir Ray?'

Sir Ray stood to look at the picture closely, closely like someone who has so many valuable works that he has to look closely to recognize the one.

'Oh yes,' he said 'it's from Pablo's Blue Period. Rather like it. Picked it up in Bond Street, London.'

'It's super,' said Helen. 'And that's a Makishi mask. I know something about that. I must say, some of these Africans are clever and even good looking, well in a savage kind of way.'

Mrs Thomson eyed her with a slight sneer. Helen turned to George.

'Don't you think so George?'

George's nerves had calmed down. But now, looking at Mrs Thomson's sneering face and listening to Mrs Turnbull's childish prattle he could not contain himself any further.

'Mrs Turnbull,' he said, 'when the white men were painting their ladies' bodies with blue paint, living in caves, worshipping idols, these so-called savages had already invented medicine and were teaching it to the white man at the universities in Alexandria, and the lot. They had astronomers, mathematicians, poets, architects, philosophers and surgeons.'

George had stood up. There was a hushed silence. Sir Ray stood up and said, somewhat embarrassed:

'Calm down my boy.'

George held up his hand:

'I haven't done, Dad.' His heart pulsated. 'Please let me finish, Lady Thomson.' He said 'Lady' with a cynicism. 'When Hannibal made his famous trek across the Alps, himself by the way an African from Carthage, just in case you didn't know it, and the son of a famous African General called Hammilcar of Carthage, just who do you think met Hannibal on the Alpine Way? A Roman general? No. He was met there and defeated by Scipio Africanus, another black man who, at the age of twenty-six, commanded the garrison of Rome. Mrs Turnbull . . .'

Norris, beside himself with anger said:

'George, these people are our guests. . . .'

'I haven't finished!' exclaimed George. 'Mrs Turnbull you are a woman of some taste. The most refined Latin scholar and ecclesiastical historian who lived from 160 to 220 A.D.'

Mrs Thomson cried:

'Really, Sir Ray!'

Turnbull's face flushed with anger. Mrs Turnbull was entranced.

George continued:

'Mrs Turnbull, his name was Tertullian. An African.'

George looked at them. At that moment he felt a supreme contempt for them. For the culture for which they stood. For the civilization, the hypocrisy and the sheer smugness. He was not talking to grown-ups. Yes, even his father. He was talking to children. Worse children than the little brats he taught at the Kamolo African Secondary School. He would prise their heads open, flush out all the prejudices and indoctrination and teach them the facts. Unconsciously his hand went up to the wall as if in search of a blackboard. He lowered it.

'St Augustin of Hippo, one of the most famous theologians of the Christian Church, the Church which you people profess, was an African. The Zimbabwe Ruins in Rhodesia were not built by Phoenicians. They were built by Africans. And now, they are among the wonders of the world. Did the European accept this? No. He said they couldn't have been built by Africans. Now that all the facts pointed to the black man he has now come back with a new theory. Yes, they were built by Africans, blacks, because the walls are crooked. That is what he says now!'

He felt his throat dry. He felt a strong temptation to gulp down a brandy or anything strong. No he wasn't going to. Instead he swallowed hard and said, 'Tshaka Zulu, one of the greatest military strategists of all time. Yes they teach him at Sandhurst. They teach him at West Point. He too was black. Are we not living in a fool's paradise? Won't it come tumbling down around us?' He stopped. He hesitated. He wanted to get away from these people. Away from Mtendere (Peace) Haven. To simply run and run. But he sat down. Norris' face was red anger itself.

'Well, I must say!' said Mrs Thomson. Then she said, 'And what does our famous little professor of history teaching in a black school say about the niggers, the blacks whom I now understand we have called savages?' She summoned all her venom to say it. And she looked hard in Norris' direction. 'I thought your father would have taught you blacks are evil!' She hugged her shawl to her shoulders and faced away.

George moved. Norris stood up and cried:

'Sit down!'

But it was too late. George had stood up, but this time he was not feeling any anger. Just concentrated disdain for Mrs Thomson.

'Mrs Thomson, don't put me on.'

'Young man, this time I'll take you on. I read in a book that the world is in danger of being wiped out by niggers. Here we hang them if they go to bed with a white girl. But there are other countries where they don't, never mind your list of "famous" blacks. Zambia, Tanzania, Malawi, Botswana. Even America. Have you been to Washington lately? Or shall I say "ever"? All the streets are chock-a-block with seething masses of blacks. Ten years ago it wasn't so. Do you know why? I will answer you in a moment.' Mrs Thomson reached for her drink — it had come full circle back to a large whisky. She took a long draw and then said, 'Because black men have been copulating with white girls. Just remember young man that only white on white can remain white. Black on white or white on black will be black. One of these days a Kaffir will curl his ugly finger around the trigger of the most powerful nation in the world. A nigger President of the United States. And we'll all be finished.'

She paused to recharge her prophecy. Unexpectedly George said: 'And all this because he's a black President?'

Mrs Thomson replied emphatically:

'Yes.'

'Why aren't we finished in the African countries? I mean, why haven't we been liquidated in the independent countries?' asked George.

'Because their native presidents know they haven't got the power.' Mrs Thomson's voice was hoarse and husky — from the oratory and whisky. 'In America he would have the power. The hot larva of black savagery is cascading down into the white valley. It will consume us in flames before we know where we are. But unlike you young man, we haven't given up hope. We can fight it — and we shall. Black is savagery.'

George smiled at her. Her passion was too laughable for words had it not been pathetic. Thinking about it all made him think of something else that wasn't just a 'something else' for him. He kept quiet for a while. Mrs Thomson waited to challenge him. But he was not really with them. Then anger began to burn into his heart. He did not mind them. Not even his father. But it pained him that these people in the room with him now would despise what his mind and heart were now pouring over.

'Mrs Thomson, I hope you know the African proverb — the beauty of the fig and yet inside it there are only ants.'

'I'm not a Kaffir philosopher,' cut in Mrs Thomson.

'As if I didn't know!' George's anger had returned. 'But can I hope you know why you and I and all of us are white — and therefore sitting here, downing drinks that killed the Roman Empire?' He moved his chair to her. 'The only reason why you are white Mrs Thomson is because the *melanocyte* cells in your skin are smaller and more sluggish than those in a black skin!'

'There he goes again, your child, Sir Ray.'

'By the way, the colouring substance called *melanin* is made exclusively by these cells which are interspaced among the basal cells of the epidermis.'

Mrs Thomson said:

'Really, Sir Ray, we must go.'

Mrs Turnbull said:

'How fascinating!'

'Genetic albinism or acquired vitiligo are the result of the synthesis of melanin being blocked even though the melanocyte cells are present. So if you are black this is because your melanocytes are larger and more hard working. If you are white that's because they are smaller and less hard working. If you are an albino that's because the formation of melanin is blocked. That's the only reason why people are white or black.' George paused. He had talked too much for one night.

They laughed. For the first time Turnbull who had remained quiet stood up. He said:

'You haven't explained anything young man. Supposing I put it to you that the black's savagery lies in the very fact that his melanocytes or whatever you call them, are so much larger and work like mad. Have you got a formula Magi, for toning them down and shrinking them so we can all be one happy white civilized race?'

'How fascinating!' exclaimed Helen Turnbull again.

'Well, I must say,' said Mrs Thomson.

'Prattle,' said Thomson.

'Shut up,' his wife said.

They laughed.

'George and Mrs Eckland would make a fine pair,' said Mrs Thomson.

'Which Mrs Eckland, dear?' asked Thomson.

'Why, I thought you would have known the little dried up woman at BGS! Everyone here knows her. Always at the Kaffir welfare hall. Teaching black women this and that. Between ourselves, she's a gypsy. That's why she's always on the move. Do-gooder. Among cobras. One of these days she'll get it right between her eyes.'

'What?'

'Well, what business of hers is it to work among the black women? She says she's English. She's not. Nor is her husband. They're Dutch.' Then she turned to George, 'Why don't you tell her to go back to Indonesia, Java, wherever the goddam Dutch Empire was?' There was an embarrassed silence.

5

Joan Chessman didn't like the combined Monday morning current affairs class. It took in all the kids from grade three to seven. They also had a similar lesson for the grown-ups, grades eight to eleven later on in the morning. But as the lesson menu was the same, the teacher who took the lesson with the juniors also took it with the seniors. This particular Monday morning she was feeling awful. She'd been to a carousel with her regular number, Mr Simon Malherbe, for most of the night. The party had started most innocently — simply as a *braai* for one of the ever-so-many good white friends who were emigrating. There had been cheese, wine, punch and, oh! what a hell of a lot to drink.

Mrs Jackson had been the hostess. Parties at that house were always in the name of Mrs Jackson because Mr Jackson was always so meek. They said she carried him in her petticoat and all that. She was certainly a lovely chuckling lady, middle-aged but desperately trying to be a young nineteen. So she liked inviting the young girls and their boyfriends. Of course, she preferred the young husbands to come without their young wives. The party had been fantastic. As usual, there had been swimming — some of it naked — in the early hours of the morning. She had not forgotten to put on her usual act. At around 3 a.m. and as the eggs were being broken for breakfast she had served wine stark naked. Anyway, it had been a good party and Joan made sure Simon never left her eyes. With Mrs Jackson around you just didn't know.

Ever since the burning of the butchery at the Bristol Gold Syndicate, Malherbe had migrated to Musasa to live full-time with Joan Chessman. He treated her rough, but she stuck all the more. Joan wasn't exactly pretty but she was wholesome and very fresh-complexioned. She'd come to Musasa four years back having read history at London University. A very religious High Anglican background — in fact her grandfather had been a priest of the church. She had led a cloistered and protected life. It sometimes surprised Joan when she thought back and then looked at her life with Malherbe. But here she was now. She knew life with Malherbe was like life with a pig. Illiterate, crude mannered, impetuous and selfish. That's why even if he had asked her, she wouldn't have married him. But he *didn't* ask her. That perhaps was what made her dislike him so much on occasions. Now and again she'd told him about this or that girl who had asked her boyfriend to marry her. Some of these girls had even made quite a scene. But every time Malherbe's reply had been, 'Christ man, why buy a fuckin' cow if you can milk it?'

The Musasa European Junior and Senior School was, of course, the best school in the country. After all, sons of famous big people went there and it had to be good. Teachers there were in a special social class of their own. It was like teaching at Eton or Harrow. The assembly hall where now Joan stood was quite something — carpeted wall to wall in rich velvet — covered comfortable seats, air-conditioned, mobile stage and all that. On the wall hung a large portrait of the Queen. On the opposite wall was a small portrait of the Governor of the colony, Sir Elwyn Baker. Some kid had pelted it with a rotten egg only that morning. So when Joan said to the vast sea of little white faces, 'Quiet,' and a squeaking voice further down the hall piped, 'Nigger!' she knew she had run into rough weather.

'Well children, can you tell me what happened last week?'

A little fellow in grade four jumped up.

'Sir Ray told the niggers where to fuck off.' The little ladies and gentlemen burst into a titter. The speaker said, 'I heard it from Daddy. Daddy sits in Parliament.'

Joan would have said to the boy, 'Your bloody father!' but she put on an encouraging smile.

'Johnny, you know you shouldn't use words like that! I'm sure Daddy has told you it's rude, hasn't he? Well, well, let's see now what you know about current affairs. Where was Sir Ray Norris talking?' Hands went up.

'Me!' Someone clicked his fingers.

'Yes, Andrew,' said Joan.

'In Parliament, Miss Chessman.'

'Very good, Andrew. Now, what's Parliament, children?'

'Parliament is where no niggers are allowed and where Sir Ray makes good speeches.' It was John again.

'Any other answers?'

'Yes, me, me, I told you where Sir Ray spoke. Parliament is where . . .'

The other children laughed because Andrew had a funny, high-pitched voice.

'Sir Norris only don't like bad Africans.'

'Doesn't,' corrected Joan. 'Who are bad Africans, John?'

'Kawala!' several little voices shrieked up. 'Daddy don't allow us to mention that name,' piped one. 'He says that African no good. He's spoiling our servants. They say he's a bastard.'

'Mark!' cried Miss Chessman.

'I'm sorry Miss Chessman.'

'Now children,' said Joan after the noise had subsided. In her heart she was feeling very sorry for these children. Such strange ideas about Africans that were not true. She was thinking of the Headmaster, Colonel Wiltshire. How the more liberal members of staff had complained about the anti black indoctrination the children were getting in their homes. They had said that he should warn the parents firmly. But always it had been, 'Don't know that it would be right.'

At that point Colonel Wiltshire walked into the hall. All the children stood up and cried, 'Good morning sir!' He did not so much as reply but merely signalled to them to sit down. He drew Joan Chessman aside and said:

'The police have found a bomb in my office and we're clearing out all the children from school.' He twirled his moustache. His fingers trembled somewhat. His face was an ashen colour.

'For how long?'

'I'd say the whole day, but the children mustn't know. Tell them it's a holiday.'

One child, straining to overhear the whispers in the corner picked up the word 'holiday'. He cried to the others, 'It's a holiday!' The kids scuttled out even before Miss Chessman could confirm it.

Malherbe was seething with anger as he went to pick up Joan. He was mumbling to himself, 'Kawala, that fucking bastard! I'll kill the savage son-of-a-bitch! Should have killed him when I had the chance!'

The 'chance' had been a few months or so ago. It had been on a Sunday when Malherbe had wanted to ride down to Gunsbury.

'Gunsbury's too far. Much too far,' Joan had protested. 'I've got classes tomorrow.' But Simon had a sunny smile — just like a cloud burst. But for Joan it was sunshine.

Malherbe had jumped into his decrepit Ferrari and revved up the engine. He zoomed off, stopped suddenly, then zoomed backwards to Joan, stopping again suddenly.

'Come on, man! Get in!'

She did.

The car had leaped to ninety, then to a hundred miles an hour. They'd passed Kaori and after an hour of hair-raising and hell-rousing driving, the elegant skyscrapers of Gunsbury, the other world of Kandaha, gleamed on the horizon. He had let out a sigh of relief and lifted his foot off the accelerator slightly. He'd looked at Joan, fast asleep. For a moment he thought she was beautiful — her full lips and rounded, pink-nippled bosom accenting his thoughts, and he wondered why this pretty English doll didn't stop jazzing around him.

He was just about to run his rough, horny fingers over the tip of her breast when suddenly a huge truck, speeding like a rogue elephant running amok, lurched upon him from around a hairpin bend. The truck driver slammed on the brakes. He'd overshot the bend. Malherbe had veered violently to the left. The truck had swerved, flattened a tree, and then with a horrendous screech and roar, rolled over and over and burst into flames. It was as if it had happened in a movie, yet it was happening in front of his unbelieving eyes.

Malherbe had jumped out of the car and run towards the inferno. A man lay sprawled out near the burning wreck. He held him by the feet and dragged him clear of the fire. The man was dead. He'd been thrown out on to a boulder as the truck overturned. He looked around frantically. No soul to be seen. Then he heard a low but shrieking wail behind him. He ran towards the direction of the wail, thinking someone might still be alive. It was a child, thrown off the huge truck. It lay on its back, its head within inches of his rear right-hand wheel. It was bleeding profusely, one arm had been severed at the elbow. What to do? Wait for the police? And let the child die? He snatched Joan's cardigan. Bound up the bleeding arm. Joan jumped up, shouting, 'Oh God!' as she took in what had happened. She jumped out of the car. They threw the little groaning child into the back seat. Joan's sweater was a mass of blood as the severed arm sprayed the whole car. The child was screaming a prelude to death.

The Ferrari lurched forward. He had not stopped for any red lights, his mind recorded. The sleekness of the city, with its gleaming white-driven cars and black-driven lorries, burst upon him. Motorists honked, swerved and swore at him as he rushed by. At the bottom of Cecil Avenue, he turned sharp left. Then careering through the red lights, narrowly missing a police car, he drove on. He turned into a private road. Within seconds he was outside the Gunsbury General Hospital, hooting continuously to attract attention. Would there be a doctor on duty? He looked in the back of the car. Joan was sobbing quietly as the little thing writhed with pain. She was holding it in her lap. Her dress was by now a mess of blood.

A black maid ran to the car, looked in and her jaw dropped.

'Get help for Christ's sake,' Malherbe shouted.

The maid ran back into the hospital and returned dragging a middle-aged white woman who turned out to be the Matron.

'Come see Matron,' the black maid said.

The Matron looked into the car and then slowly walked round to Simon. Shaking her head she said:

'Sorry sir. You'll have to go to the African Hospital. We don't take natives here.'

'Christ!' said Malherbe. 'It's a black child!' realizing for the first time that the child was black. The picaninny lifted its pained eyes towards him as he turned back to look at it. He turned away.

'But this is an emergency, Sister. The child will die,' Joan said.

'That's the regulation, madam,' snapped back the Matron.

'An' where's the Kaffir hospital?' asked Malherbe.

'Some four miles from here in this direction,' she replied. 'There are plenty of African Police who can show you the way.'

Simon turned the ignition key, pressed the accelerator and sped on, searching for an African hospital — or better still, a Kaffir hospital.

Perched on a stool at the Grand Hotel Bar that evening, Simon could still not understand how it had all happened. Joan had been so shaken that they had to stay the night. As he sat there drinking, one gin after another, she was fast asleep in a friend's home in Westlea. He had had to report to the police after taking the child to the African Hospital. The police had said it would not be necessary for him to return to the scene of the accident. The dead African had already been taken to the mortuary where he had been certified — yes that was the officer's word — 'dead and drunk'. Simon Malherbe slung one gin after another and every time he remembered the screaming infant lifting the bleeding stub that was his arm at him and yelling, '*Mai, Mai*,' his nervous hand shot out for the counter calling for another gin and tonic.

The Grand Hotel is always crowded with all types of whites, except the very high ranking Government and business executives. But on Sunday evenings, the bar is usually deserted, with a few of the hardy perennials the only occupants. However, tonight was different. The clientele was still all white, but the bar was not empty. Instead it was bustling with people, with people, as they would have said, except for the bar assistant's assistant.

Simon looked at his watch nervously. He did not know Gunsbury and he would have to make ready to collect Joan. Someone in the corner was starting a song. It was 'Happy Birthday to You'. The whole group in that corner stood up and joined the chorus with the vigour of a people who are happy. Then there followed laughter and when the same man started the next song the bar was frothing and trembling with the reed of discordant voices. Someone threw a beer at Nothing, as the bar assistant's assistant was called. Nothing grinned at the merriment and at the beer which through habit he had learnt to catch adeptly in mid-air and without losing a single fluid ounce. Nothing enjoyed his work immensely and what was better than seeing satisfied customers? Mr Nothing, a little man in an immaculate black tie and shining coat lapels, nestled the beer in his hands and then dexterously turned it upon his upturned mouth so that the whole spectacle looked like a deft piece of Chinese juggling. Simon Malherbe looked at the African. He jumped off his stool, swept his glass off the counter and sent it hurtling towards the African. The glass whizzed towards the upturned bottle. Nothing tried to duck but it was too late. A loud crash as the pieces splintered upon his face.

'I die Mother,' he cried, falling backwards.

'You baboon,' growled Simon Malherbe leaping over the counter and crashing another glass into the man's head. 'Who told you to drink in a white bar?'

For a split second the crowd was dumbfounded. Then someone laughed aloud.

'That's the way chum!' cried Mr Smith.

The man whose name was Mr Smith had not come to the Grand Hotel to attend the grand birthday party. He had simply been found there, like the way you find a piece of furniture in a room. He had left the game park where he was the warden, two days before having got a lift into Gunsbury. He had liked it and determined to stay put in the bar of the Grand until either his money or his own self gave out. In the event his money had held out, as he had experienced unprecedented hospitality from the other patrons, perhaps out of sheer respect for his endurance. That was why Mr Smith, whose self showed no danger of deterioration, continued in this third day to superintend the mirth of the bar. And that was why Mrs Smith, so many miles away in the game park, and who knew well the habits of the great keeper of animals, did not worry.

Nothing staggered, his white shirt now scarlet with blood.

'Get out, you baboon!' roared Malherbe again, crashing a blow into his stomach. He screamed, doubled up with pain and slumped down, hitting his face upon the concrete slab. 'We don't drink with niggers in Musasa,' shouted Malherbe to the stunned crowd.

Then a tall fellow shot up and leaping over the counter grabbed Simon by the collar and grated:

'An' who d'you think you are? This is our barman and not an ordinary native.'

'It doesn't happen in Musasa,' shouted back Malherbe. 'Let me go!'

'Musasa?' said the man shaking Malherbe by the collar. 'That's where all the trouble comes from, there in Musasa. You treat the blacks like animals and that's why Kawala and his lot are causing you problems!' The man spoke in a heavy accent. 'Here, my friend,' he said swallowing hard, eyes wide open with fury, 'here my friend, we rule the native but we treat him like a native and not like an animal.'

'You're right Johannes,' shouted Mr Smith. 'That's the way chum.'

The whole bar stood up and several voices shouted:

'Chuck him out, chuck him out.'

Malherbe felt a violent pull at his shoulders. He hurtled into the air. Then there was another upward push against his chest and before he knew what had happened, he had been hurled out of the bar, his head crashing against the glass door.

'Kawala and the damn lot of you can hang,' he growled. He passed out.

He jumped up at midnight. He was having a very uncomfortable dream. People battering his head and someone saying, 'All white here will be butchered tomorrow. You are only the first one.'

'This is our land,' he screamed as he jumped out of sleep. His hand flew to his throbbing head. The hand pulled off a ream of cloth. He looked at it. It was covered with blood. A shudder. Was he really being murdered? 'Kill all blacks,' he shouted. Joan turned in her sleep. 'Kill all blacks,' he shouted again, this time shaking

Joan vigorously.

'Are you all right dear?' asked Joan, getting up. Then he remembered how he had acquired that bandage in his hands and asked:

'Did I tell you?'

'Yes, if it's that,' replied Joan sarcastically. After all, she'd been waiting for him for the whole night. 'Very good news.'

'Bloody shit of good news,' swore Malherbe, touching his head again. 'Drinking with blacks. Shit!' He coughed and spat into his handkerchief. The phlegm was bloody. He thought for a moment, then said, 'You. You'll have to phone Musasa. I should be fit for work tomorrow.'

'I rang a friend last night and told her we wouldn't be back for work today,' replied Joan. 'What about the child, don't you think we should go and check what's happened to it?'

Malherbe kept quiet for a moment. Then:

'It's not ours, you know,' he said.

Joan's face flushed red. He was at it again, making insinuations about her not bearing him a child. How could one dare have a child with that coarse, ill-tempered and selfish brute?

'And whose fault is it?' she exploded. Malherbe looked at her through swollen eyes, as if to say 'that is not what I had intended to mean'. In that simple sentence, 'it's not ours, you know,' his thoughts had gone back in time to five years ago when he had been in the rural areas in charge of roadwork there. He had fallen in love with an African girl and, well, not married her but they had stayed together like husband and wife. Officially she had been his servant and certainly in public there was no question of her being anything else. He did not reply. Joan, her anger subsided, asked:

'Shan't we see it?'

He nodded. After breakfast, they went out to the Gunsbury African Hospital.

There was a large crowd of Africans at the main gate of the hospital. Joan held Malherbe's arm tightly.

'Maybe we shouldn't go in,' she whispered.

She was afraid. Malherbe did not reply. When they entered the corridor of the children's ward they found a cluster of Africans arguing heatedly with a white nursing sister.

'This is the uncle,' one short man was saying. 'He must go in and see the child.'

'I don't care what uncle he is. The visiting hour is over and that's it,' said the exasperated sister. 'Now, clear off all of you. This is not a beer hall. It's a hospital. . . .'

'But the child in there is his nephew,' said a short man with a heavy but cleanly shaven face. 'We must go in or there will be trouble. If we were Europeans, you would have let us in even at midnight.' The short man's eyes flashed at the woman. 'We've travelled the whole night from Musasa to come and see this child. This man here has lost his brother in the accident in which this child was hurt. His brother is in the mortuary. There!' said the man pointing at the little red brick house.

'I'm sorry, I can't allow you to come in and I don't care if you've lost nephews, brothers or what have you!'

She was closing the double door on them. The one with the heavy face pushed her off the doors and clenching his fists, he roared:

'You'll let us in, white woman!'

Just then Malherbe and Joan walked up to the door.

'There's a piccaninny we brought in last night sister. He had a severed arm and my wife here would like to see how it's getting on.'

The sister sighed with relief. At least there was a white man around.

'Come in,' she said, brushing by an African. 'Here he is,' she said at last when they had reached the bed. 'He'll be all right,' she said to both of them. 'But it will take some time.'

Joan bent over the child, her hair almost covering its face.

'Aren't you a beauty,' she whispered, laughing into the little fellow's closed eyes.

'He's still asleep you see. We had to take him to the theatre last night for an emergency operation.'

'Happy?' asked Malherbe, looking at Joan. 'A beautiful child. I'm so glad he'll be all right sister.'

They walked away stealthily. The sight of the child reminded her of the Christmas crib and somehow it made her heart feel warm.

'Thanks awfully sister,' said Joan as they came out. 'Maybe next time we are here we could visit again? What are the visiting hours?'

'Oh, I wouldn't worry about visiting hours. Just pop in any time you're around. After all, Musasa is quite far and you can't be expected to arrive on the dot.'

As they turned to go a man took a long step towards them. Malherbe looked at him with faint disgust. The man was tall and coal black. His hair combed back and he had a slightly protruding forehead. His cheeks were long and sunken and the red, fiery-looking eyes were narrow slits, brooding under black eyelashes. In contrast with the short man standing by his side, he was clean shaven and cleanly scrubbed. He wore a short-sleeved white shirt.

The man stretched out his hand towards Malherbe and whispered:

'How is the child? I am it's father,' and then he added, looking down into Malherbe's eyes, 'in the African sense, that is. I understand it was you who saved my child yesterday. I want to thank you for this act of kindness.'

Joan looked into the man's eyes. Although they were sunken she could see that he had been weeping. Then, as if in answer to her question the man said:

'My brother is the one who died in that accident.'

'Let's get out of here. Drunken blacks driving. That's what happens. Jesus!'

'Young man,' called Kawala after Malherbe, for it was he, 'do not insult the dead.'

The small crowd around Kawala stood dumbfounded looking at the disappearing backs of the two white people. Someone said:

'This is a bad omen. Perhaps another bad thing is about to happen.' Just at that moment the nursing sister who had closed the door on them, opened it roughly and said:

'You can come back at 1.00 p.m.'

Dr Lal Naik, F.R.C.P., looked at the disappearing black figures from his window in his surgery. He knew what it was all about — Africans being turned away even when a dying man was groping for a hand that he knew to whisper his last meaningless jabber. He had protested to the medical superintendent about it. That had been a luckless day for Naik. Dr Craw M.B., B.Sc., had simply rasped back, 'You're only an Indian doctor. Mind your own business!'

Naik thought for a while. There was something about the tall man in a white short-sleeved shirt which he couldn't quite make out. As they passed his window Naik peeped out and said:

'Is anything the matter?'

Of course he knew what was the matter and he got it right straight out from Chimuko.

'Matter!' As if he isn't part of it. These Indians!'

But Kawala had stood still to look at Naik.

'It's very kind of you.' Then uncertainly he asked, 'Doctor?'

Naik nodded:

'Dr Naik.'

'Maybe, maybe you can keep an eye on the little child? Operated on last night. An accident.'

Naik nodded, but he kept his eyes on Kawala. In his mind he was thinking, 'Something strange about the fellow.' Naik, consulting paediatrician, knew about the child.

That was how Malherbe had met Kawala. And that was how, perhaps, he'd missed his chance to 'kill' him.

6

Kawala got off at the Samaka bus stop near the party office. He found the young publicity secretary, Patrick Chimuko, waiting for him. Santasa too, now Vice-President, was also waiting. They'd been told that morning that if the central committee wished to operate, all its members had to have native passes. Kaffir passes. It was as simple as that and the man had hoped they would understand because that was what Decompol (Deputy Commissioner of Police) O'Flaherty, had said.

'And if we refuse?' asked the young publicity secretary.

'You'll be classed as dogs I suppose.' Kawala smiled. 'If we're fighting for human liberty, I suppose we could do with someone certifying that we are not dogs.'

'But we can't accept this,' protested the young man. 'We must burn them up.'

'Why don't we wait until we have them to burn?'

Santasa nodded agreement. The three would go up to the office of the Commissioner of Police, get the passes and then . . .

John Jefferson was a real seven-footer. Ruddy complexioned, somewhat flabby around the belly, but a very upright figure. He'd seen service in the old colonial Northern Rhodesia, now Zambia, and it was from there that he had come to Kandaha when Zambia became independent. Before that he had served in the West Indies, Hong Kong and Nyasaland (now Malawi). He had a kindly and fairly handsome face, the front teeth distinctly tanned with a fungal mouldy black from smoking. Whenever he smiled, you had the impression he was feeling sorry for his teeth. But he did smile quite a bit, perhaps a bit too often for a Britisher. But then he was a

Scotsman, born fifty-eight years back in a village in the Hebrides. That sort could be weather-beatenly rough. But it could also be warm. He had personally given instructions for the trio to report to him. A bit unusual. But Jefferson had been to colonies before and he knew that in Africa 'demagogues' always became Presidents.

He looked at the three briefly and then said:

'My deputy will see you.'

'But we've been told to see you. We haven't asked for this interview.' It was Chimuko. 'We can't be pushed around from boer to boer like this as if this is not our country.'

Jefferson regarded Chimuko kindly. Except for the fact that the youngster was coloured, he could have been his son. Patrick Chimuko, born twenty-five years ago, was the great-grandson of a famous English pioneer, Throggmorton. He'd come down to Rhodesia at the turn of the last century, worked his way up north through the hostile African tribal chiefs. He had met up with Rudd and helped him to secure the so-called Rudd Concession which, by the mere mark of an 'X' on a parchment of Lewanika's (the king of the Lozi) secured for the British South Africa Company (BSA) the total ownership of all mineral rights over an area covering the whole of present day Zambia and Kandaha. Throggmorton had moved on and then settled in the eastern part of Kandaha where, in the words of a notable Afrikaans historian, he 'determined and married seven black *mafazi* (women) and produced a howling pack of fifty-one coloured children.' Patrick St John Throggmorton was a product of a grandson of the old man. Unlike the rest of his progeny, John St John Throggmorton, his father, had diluted the white colour further by marrying back in to the black colour. The father had died within weeks of the boy being born. But John St John Throggmorton had died a social leper and so it was that the young child's uncles and cousins never visited the native woman, his wife, in the village. But more by way of cleansing and retrieving the family's honour, the whole generation migrated to Rhodesia and South Africa, where up to now they live racially unadulterated as assistant white men.

The young man was brought up and lived as an African — by his loving mother. He struggled through school, doing odd bits and pieces to earn his fees. He passed his School Certificate. Could have gone to University, but his headmaster had blacklisted him. There had been a hysterical debate with the motion that Anthony Eden, the former British Foreign Minister, was right in invading the Suez Canal. The young man had argued eloquently that he was definitely wrong. The vote had gone against the motion. The white head-master had demanded a re-vote saying, 'You will all vote that Sir Anthony Eden was right.' It didn't work. Except for the fact that it was a month to the Cambridge School Certificate exams, the boy would have been dismissed. That was five years ago. Patrick St John Throggmorton had gone into life, then entered politics and had also changed his name to Patrick Chimuko. He was bright but mercurial. Always impatient but honest. He had a sunny, sanguine face which always charmed even his worst enemies. And being of a lighter colour in a pack of black-coloured fellow fighters, God knows, he needed his charm. A tall strippling of a lad, he was the publicity secretary of the party. Invective was his weapon and he knew just how to use it.

Jefferson looked at the young man again.

'You are a trouble-shooter,' he said.

'That's our business,' Chimuko replied. 'If we are going to be called trouble-shooters for obeying your summons, we might as well go. We aren't seeing anybody else.' Then he turned to Kawala who stood gravely. 'Comrade National President, we've got the people on our side, why should we bother about these whites? Does Norris require to be registered before he can speak all that bumf of his?'

'It's not registration. This is not South Africa. All we require is for you to give us your full biography. Everyone in politics has to give us his full and documental history. That's the law.' Jefferson pulled his large frame up. He was not really feeling angry about the young man. Maybe that was because he knew where the hornet's nest would come. 'You will have to see my deputy. He's set up for this kind of thing.'

Kawala for the first time looked into Jefferson's eyes. Jefferson also looked into his. He (Jefferson) felt uncomfortable. He'd never seen Kawala so close. They were hot burning eyes, eyes that held yours there. He'd never seen these eyes before. He hesitated. Then he said:

'Right?'

Kawala turned to go. To O'Flaherty's office. To the office of the Deputy Commissioner of Police of the colony of Kandaha.

O'Flaherty was a lank, hungry-looking individual, sunken cheeks, tousled hair greying heavily around the temples, a sharp nose and a mouth that was always on the verge of some provocation or other. His khaki uniform, the belt of rank and badges hung on him limply. He had a habit of constantly tugging up his stockings even though they were tightly fastened to his calves by rubber bands. His eyes were a murky steeliness, anxious to avoid something. But his facial features were so distinct that any attempt at anonymity through the vagueness of his gaze was unsuccessful.

'Keep standing my boys,' he said, as the trio made to sit down. 'If you think I'm going to add to the load of trouble that I already have by allowing you to go on addressing meetings and whipping up fanaticism, you are very mistaken.' He strutted up and down the little office peacock fashion. 'Let me tell you a thing or two. When we, Her Majesty's Government, have finished with this country, we'll hand it over to the whites, to Norris and his crowd and not to you. Norris is the leader of the Unofficials in the Legislative Council. He is initially the leader of the Opposition. So when we go, it will be he taking over. Government, my friends must remain in responsible hands — and that means white hands. Right?'

O'Flaherty was in fact Irish. But there was nothing for being a patriotic Englishman than being an Irish policeman in the colonies. Through sheer doggedness and a ruthless streak, he had risen to the number two position in one of the last remaining colonies of Her Majesty's empire. His wife, an elderly nervous ruin, saw to it that he succeeded and whether it was that whenever he spoke to Africans he remembered the way his wife berated him, there was no doubt that his bark could have been an authentic copy.

'No Africans, no blacks, will be allowed any political activity.'

'Even though PALP is a registered party?'

'Registered!' exclaimed O'Flaherty, staring into Chimuko's face. 'You are a bloody coloured mulatto, anyway. What the hell are you doing with these niggers? Which of your old men committed adultery with who?'

Kawala's hand rose in the air. He let it drop down. He said:

'You're too dirty for me to touch,' and walked out.

A few hours later, Katenga had walked into the party office. 'Come in, comrade. Can we help you?', said Chimuko.

Katenga said to Chimuko:

'My name is Katenga. Look at this. That's all I've come to show you.'

His voice was gravelly. Maybe he'd been drinking the previous night. But maybe not. Chimuko regarded him briefly. He had been told something about Katenga. He looked at him again. He decided he didn't like his bloodshot protruding eyes.

'What's the letter about? We are very busy up here, comrade.'

'It's about people. My people. Why don't you read it? Why don't you even open it to find out how people are suffering while you sit here talking politics?'

Chimuko's head jerked up.

'Who tells you we're doing nothing?'

'What have you done?'

'Don't you see we're attacking racialism?'

'What's that?' Katenga stood up. 'You should not waste time attacking racialism. That is to admit that when we rule ourselves we shall have no racialism. Are you going to give these white jackals the same treatment as ourselves when you take over? What's the use of independence then? Do you think the people in the village will benefit from your breaking racial barriers here, from your being able to sit drinking beer with unwashed whites merely because they are white? Read this letter,' he cried, thrusting it before Chimuko's nose.

'Who are you, anyway? You don't even belong to the party. What are you here for?'

Katenga struggled to contain his temper. But he exploded:

'I'm a black man. Is your party not fighting for blacks? Or is it fighting for coloureds?' That cut Chimuko to the quick.

Katenga thumped hard on the table in front of him. His fuzzy beard descended ominously over Chimuko's face.

'Listen, young man,' he lowered his voice. 'I've come here to tell you what I can do for the party. But I'm prepared to go it alone if you still don't want me. I'm unemployed. But don't think I'm coming here for a job. I can do without a job. But the only way to talk with these whites is to frighten them? Is that what you are doing here? Katenga looked round. There were piles of brochures and other printed material. 'Paper is not guns. We must fight the whites with guns,' he said. 'But read this letter. I'll come back in a week's time. I've to go to the village now. Maybe I should tell them you people don't care. Isn't that so? Maybe I should tell them the party does not want any outsiders.'

'Wait,' said Chimuko. 'We know your individual "own way" position, and your bomb threat at the school, and other things. I will read your letter.' He ripped the envelope off the letter and read.

Loved one Katenga

If you are well, my grandson, we are also well here. But here we are in many troubles. There are strange things happening here, things which could only happen to dogs in the past. Yesterday we were all rounded up by the white man's messengers. All my young able-bodied men have been taken away. They leave today for Chibalo (forced labour). They tell me that some will go to Johannesburg to work in the white man's mines there. Others will come there to work for the white ones.

But it is not this I object to. It is the way these young men were beaten up and led off like sheep to the police jeeps that were waiting. One, Nsokolo, you remember your old friend Nsokolo, his child died the day before. Yesterday, as we were preparing to carry the coffin away for burial these messengers came. He was one of those they took. Snatching a father from his son's coffin! These messengers, I don't understand them. They are people like us and yet what they do! Does the white man's money really brutalize people like that?

So all the able-bodied men are gone. This village of Nampande is now like a deserted village. And this coming only a few weeks after the white man's policemen arrested twenty people. This Boko District is no longer a country of peace; this Nampande Village is a place of fire. They do not tell us why they do these evil things to us. But, my grandchild, we hear that the white one wants to kill our worship. I do not know if you still practise our faith of the Holy Ones. I hear that there in town it is laughed at to worship The Holy of Holies. But if you still do or you do not, remember that we are being persecuted here. The white one thinks we hate him even as it was not the white angel who was saved at the gates of Jericho but a black one.

Last week they came — I mean the white one's police. They burnt our Assembly (Church). But even as the Holy of Holies said He would rebuild the synagogue in three days, we rebuilt it in these many days. We know that the evil one will continue to torment us. Only the other day my brother, your grandfather, went to the Boma at Boko. As the big white bwana the District Commissioner passed near where he was squatting on the floor, waiting to license his gun, this big bwana says to the messengers, 'Arrest this black one.' My brother protested. He told him because he had not stood up when he the bwana passed by. Is it good manners in our tribe to stand up when a big one passes? Is it not good manners to sit down on the floor and even disappear into the very earth that you sit on? We have not seen our own since then and now we understand he is in jail. Every morning they wake him up to carry away the buckets of faeces for the other prisoners. An old man like that! (Are his years not more than all your fingers and toes and mine and those of your grandmother and your small grandmother put together . . . ?'

'Come,' said Chimuko when he had finished.

Katenga found himself standing before Kawala in the adjoining room. For a moment their eyes met. Quickly Chimuko ran through the story of Katenga and thrusting the letter before Kawala he said:

'This. We've protested, asked to see Thomson. Nothing happens. In the meantime, they continue to do this to our people.'

When he had read, Kawala again raised his eyes to Katenga, Katenga did not drop his. Kawala remembered his first encounter with the man. . . . 'I'll do it my own way. . . .' He moved a little. Then he said:

'Comrade, do you still want to join the party?'

Katenga, his gaze now raised into the roof said:

'Yes, if that is the only way to stop that.' He pointed at the letter lying on Kawala's desk. 'Will the party protect people like this grandfather of mine or is the party concerned only with breaking down racialism so I can drink off the same pub as a white? Drink off the same cup may be with my . . .' He stopped. He blew his nose loudly onto the floor. Maybe to make his point.

Kawala took a close look at Katenga. He (Kawala) had grown up in a house where you could not take everyone and everything for granted.

'Comrade Katenga, you interest me. Have you lost an axe?'

'An axe? No.'

'But you're looking for one, aren't you?'

'Why?'

'I'll tell you. You're interested in joining us only because your people have been hurt by these colonialists. Aren't we the axe which you wish to wield for the sake of your blood relatives?'

'No.'

'Yes.' Kawala stood up, his tall frame over-towering Katenga. 'Here in the party there is neither relative nor enemy. There is neither black nor white. There is only a band of people determined that Kandaha shall be free.' He looked deep into Katenga's face then he continued, 'Your relative of today may be tomorrow's enemy of Kandaha. If that happens will . . .' He could not bring himself to say the word. But Katenga said:

'Yes, I will kill anyone who is an enemy of Kandaha. All whites are enemies also.'

There was a momentary silence. Then looking into the roof Kawala said:

'I sincerely hope it will never come to that. I have thought and prayed long after my own god for Kandaha to be delivered whole from this bondage. A man who denies you your freedom, does he not deny you your right to a full life? Does he not murder you? Do they not say 'an eye for an eye, and a tooth for a tooth?' He recollected himself. Katenga stood eyeing him deeply. Kawala said, 'I don't know who has sent you here. Maybe it is fate. The party has been working quietly. The hour has come. Later, you will take the oath of allegience. From then on you will be a militant.' Then a smile broke through Kawala's firmly pursed lips. 'And maybe you'll do it your own way.'

Katenga left Kawala thinking. Something about Katenga made him feel that a kind of watershed had come. What it was he could not fathom. But the situation in the country was moving to a crisis. Could the crisis be averted? Could it be averted when it was now open talk that Norris had threatened white rebellion and whites were being armed? Where did the answer lie? Did it lie in the Governor showing his teeth and telling Norris, 'Get lost!' Did it lie in leaving Norris and his fanatics to steamroll the blacks into submission? Did it lie in the party? He closed his eyes. In his mind's eye he could see frothy rivers of human blood cascading to nowhere. Voices of pain shrieked in his ears. Was such a price necessary for liberation? Could it not be done any other way? Did blood have to be shed to get that which by birthright already belonged to one? At half-past two that afternoon Kawala stood up from his rickety chair in the party head office to go home. As he walked through the streets he could feel an uneasy calm around him. People on the streets looked at him. Some were pointing him out to their friends and whispering things.

After leaving Kawala, Katenga had lingered a little at Sanga Bar. 'A Coke.'

'What? No money today, eh?'

The barman had laughed. In fact Katenga had had enough money for at least two beers — from Delia, the usual source. He had kept quiet. His mind was still on Kawala.

'We don't see you much these days?'

'No.'

'Do you know what happened last night? You remember that girl you danced with some time ago? Well, she was here again last night. Seemed to be looking for you. But she had a tall white man. I think the same fellow you went to prison over. Remember?'

Katenga gulped up his Coke, paid for it and left.

'Why?' the bar man called. Another Kawala, eh? No good for

Over
about K
how int
why did
he had

7

Sir Ray
to talk
He dia
'Priv
'Sir
'His
turbed.
'Tell
Priv
an A.I
'Rig
'H.E
you lik
'I'll
to carr
take m
The
'Thi
school
childre
now th
duty t
questi
murde
was ge
'Th
'You
'Th

business that one. No wonder he wears such a long face.'

Katenga walked over to Delia's house.

'Have you remembered your child today or is the money finished?'

'Delia, I want to talk to you.'

She was cleaning up her pots outside at the community water tap. She had a loin cloth strapped over her waist, a longish dress and she wore a duku on her head. Her feet were bare. But that did not stop her looking pretty, with her high cheek bones and a face that looked always fresh and optimistic.

'To me! What's come over you? The only thing you do to me is beat me up, curse me. Talk to me! I've no money, if that's what you want.'

The other women listened.

'Look, I can't talk with all these women around.'

'You've beaten me publicly before with all men looking on.' She shielded her eyes with her hand to look at him in the afternoon sun. Something appeared to have come over him. She said, 'Right, I'll be coming right away.'

When she sat down in the house he said:

'I've had a letter from home.'

'They want you to disown the child? You can tell them you disowned it already. Don't you tell them that you never see the child?'

'No, its not like that Delia. The white Government is harassing them.'

'White Government. As if there can be a black one! We are all being harassed. Not even by your white Government. By hunger. By you. What do you do about it?'

'I want to do something now.'

'Something? O ho ho!' she loooked into Katenga's face. She stopped laughing.

'Delia, the other day I went to town.'

'As if you do anything else except loitering around.'

'A white youngster rode into me and I fell on the road. Do you see this bruise?' He showed her his freshly scarred arm.

'Drunk as usual. Look what do you want to say?'

'Do you know he called the police there and then and do you know what they said? That I had struck his bicycle and they fined me.'

'Who paid?'

'Someone lent me the money.'

'And you've come to get the money so you can pay him?'

'No. But they are doing worse things to people in the villages.'

'Your Excellency, don't tell me I didn't warn you. There's going to be chaos in this country. If that happens I'll have no alternative but to order the Europeans to defend themselves. We're just not going to put up with threats to our safety.'

'Are you threatening violence?'

'No, I'm threatening that we will exercise our right to self-protection.'

'Outside the law?' asked the Governor. His chin jutted out.

'The law provides for self-protection,' replied Norris.

'Outside the law?' repeated Baker.

'By your standards, yes.' Norris puffed at his cigarette.

The party offices buzzed to the clanking sound of the duplicator. There was Murphy. For him Norris was the man who would save Kandaha from chaos. The Africans had to be grateful that there was a man like Norris to protect them from the rapacities of their self-styled leaders. Then there was Hannah, silently clipping away the sheets of paper that spewed out of Murphy's maternity labours. Hannah was a kind of part-time secretary for Norris. Norris used to refer to him and Murphy as the 'Norris staffers.' The broadsheet would be going to all white houses in the town that night. There would be a meeting in the Hindu Hall the following night to decide on the formation of the People's Home Guard. The Home Guard would protect all white families in the city. Malherbe, still smarting from the wounds of the burning down of his butchery at the BGS waited in his van outside to deliver the broadsheets. He had moved to Musasa after the incident.

Dear Voter, read the broadsheet. You must have heard the news of a savage attack this morning. Your school was nearly razed to the ground and your dear children massacred. . . . I know that the Colonial Government will do nothing to bring the perpetrators of this heinous crime to justice. I fear that they will see in this fresh eruption of violence an excuse for hastening the diabolical plot to hand the country over to the Africans . . .

We have no objection to Africans ruling this country provided they are civilized. We have the right to insist on this condition because, unlike the European colonial civil servants who go home on leave for six months every three years, we go home at the end of each day.

This Kandaha is our home and we are going to bring up our children here and our children's children will also live here. We are not here just for three years or just for twenty years. We are here for eternity. So we must be involved in the vital decisions that affect our lives. The most important of these decisions is who should rule this country? The answer is clear. We don't say that Europeans should rule. Nor do we say that Africans should not. We simply say that civilized people should rule this country. The Africans are not civilized. They are primitive; they would have to come down from the trees to receive independence. Take a look at their so-called leaders. They are demagogues. They have no respects for the rights of man. Theirs would be a reign of terror, oppression, torture and revenge.

The brochure then went back to the incident at Kamata in the Southern Province.

In case some of you do not know the origin of all this savagery, I will tell you. A native who did not know that there was a PALP-wide ceremony in that province, a ceremony at which 'colonial oppression' was meant to be buried, committed the unforgivable sin of going to work at the Boma that morning. PALP youths set on him. They called him names and accused him of being a member of another native party. The poor man — an innocent, law-abiding messenger — stood his ground. He said he had work to do. They booed him. The poor native brushed them aside and went straight to his post. The PALP ruffians set a rabid dog which they kept in chains on him. The dog roared and growled and sank its putrid, disease-ridden teeth into his skinny flesh and then they beat him up. When the District Commissioner found this out, he was furious and ordered the mob to disperse. The mob did not disperse but instead charged at him, shouting insults and throwing faeces at him. That was when District Commissioner Brighton—Jones ordered the police in to intervene. They were overpowered. The natives went mad, looting and burning everything in sight — including your own European school. They speared a white official. They shed your blood . . .'

Sir Elwyn Baker could hear the grinding noise of something like a duplicator in the background.

'Tell him to get stuffed,' said Hannah, cupping his mouth to Norris.

'Yes, we are forming Home Guards, Your Excellency, if you must know,' said Norris into the telephone. 'The police are no longer capable of guarding us. The African ranks are infiltrated. Investment is being scared away. Turnbull has been to me on several occasions, expressing his anxiety. I've written you memo after memo and all I get is an acknowledgement card. Signed by your officials. Nothing more. No action.'

The Governor put the receiver down. Lady Baker had been waiting. They had to go to the annual dinner of the Bristol Gold Syndicate. Mr Turnbull, tall and benign as usual, would be there to receive them and his wife would, as usual, be talking bridge and cakes. Sir Ray would also be there, always choosing a seat directly opposite his and crouching over the table like a fighter resting against the ropes. He reached for the copy of the dinner speech in his pocket. Would he need to change the text after what Norris had said on the telephone? He decided against the idea. He would go ahead as though nothing had happened. The Bristol Gold Syndicate would be praised for its show of confidence in the country. It would be praised for its enlightened programme of Africanization. It would be praised for its continuing expansion because although Mr Turnbull might well be a man with three tongues — not that he was not already double tongued — he had assured him personally that plans for expanding his company's activities were going full-steam ahead.

Elwyn Baker smoothed his once blonde hair and adjusted the black bow tie on his neck. He had always been a perfectionist about clothes and maybe that is why he rarely looked his age unless he was very very tired indeed. Tonight he was feeling tired. His wife said:

'You look tired, darling. Couldn't you have asked Thomson to do it on your behalf? I hope that leg of yours does not trouble you again. Why, you have a slight limp!'

Sir Elwyn had had a touch of phlebitis some years back before that malady acquired the more pronounceable name of 'Nixon's Disease'.

'I'm sure Mr Thomson would love it,' he said airily. 'But that wouldn't please our friend Turnbull. I'm sure his speech will have all the barbs for the reigning Governor.'

Lady Baker thought for a while. She didn't like Mrs Thomson, or Lady Thomson as people called her. But then, the feeling was mutual. And yet they both had to pretend in public they were so close. After all, were the two not the most important ladies in the country?

'Let's move,' said Baker. 'It's nearly eight.'

They came out on to the porch. The chauffeur drew up slowly with the gleaming black Rolls Royce bearing the Union Jack and simply the gold embossed crown instead of a number plate. The black chauffeur saluted them as he let them in. The police out-riders in front of the car started to rev their Honda motorcycles and in a moment the splendid procession weaved into the mean-dering darkness of the Government House road to the Louise Hotel. The idea of a meandering road had been Lady Baker's. So had the idea of the luxuriant shrubs that lined its sides.

The Louise Hotel was some five miles away. Not quite in the city centre but close enough to it. It was like walking into the Trinidad Hilton. The reception, banquet hall and facilities all on the top floor. To get to the rooms you took the lift underground. It was six floors deep. Naturally, no blacks were allowed here except as servants. The banquet hall into which Elwyn Baker now walked was a vast hall with a dome-shaped ceiling and massive gold-lacquered chandeliers hanging off it. The carpet was a deep bloody crimson and the tables were covered with white Irish linen which threw up to good effect the multi-coloured bouquets of flowers over the tables.

The dinner promised to be a success. Mr Turnbull's sanguine smile, a little condescending perhaps, but bright like the leaves of his coffee trees against the shining sun, was most warming. There must have been at least two hundred guests there. A bomb dropped there would have wiped out the political, civil-service and business leadership of the whole colony of Kandaha.

As the dinner continued into the coffee, Mr Turnbull stood up. He adjusted his bow tie and looked up into the faces of the glittering guests before him. He started off, after the preliminaries, with a few pale jokes about rugby and religion. Then he repeated some jokes which he claimed he had heard from no less a person than His Excellency himself. But then His Excellency was not smiling. His hands were resting on the table and the tip of his thumb was just touching the base of his cognac glass. He was not much of a drinker.

Then Turnbull charged into his speech.

'Private business has a critical role to play in this country. But it will not come here unless the political climate is right and investors know where they stand.' He coughed a little. From the way he was sticking to the text, it was obvious that Lord Ventrical, the London-based chairman of the group had personally approved its contents. 'The political climate of Kandaha is, ladies and gentle-men, to say the least, uncertain. Political thuggery is on the increase and it would appear to those of us whose business it is to seek out valuable investment opportunities that tension is mounting between the Europeans and the Africans as never before. This country needs and will continue to need both people, the one to supply the resourcefulness so essential to any development, and the other to execute the routine functions which are also so necessary to industry. If is the sincere hope of my corporation that Her Majesty's Government will indicate its position on the whole question of the future of this country in clear and categorical terms, that in so doing it will take fully into account the gross limitations for good government so much evident in the black members of our society, and that it will realize the tremendous fund of good will towards these protected persons which exists in this country amongst the white population.'

There was acclamation.

'Let me speak plainly and say that so long as the threat of a possible concession to black pressure exists in this country, there will be very little investment, if any at all. We need our black brothers. They need us more.'

He continued. The guests listened. He turned to politics. He called Kawala a desperate hungry man. Africans, he said, were most dangerous when they had nothing to eat. That brought him back to investment. It was a brilliant speech, delivered consumately with the kind of ease only possible of a man who knows that fifty per cent of the country's tax revenue derives from his company. As the speech progressed, the Governor looked visibly shaken. His face was ashen and his fingers no longer rested peacefully on the long head table, but tapped the table cloth impatiently. When Turnbull concluded his address and called on the guest of honour, His Excellency Sir Elwyn Baker, there was a thunderous applause. Sir Elwyn Baker stood up. He looked briefly at the expectant and silent guests. It was clear that the majority of those guests agreed with everything Turnbull had said. Lady Baker looked at him. His face was still pale and the papers in his hands trembled a little. Turnbull waited, a vague smile on his face. When seated, the standing Governor was only about six inches taller than himself. The Governor spoke in a slow measured tone. He and his wife were delighted with the guests. The Bristol Gold Syndicate had contributed a great deal to the welfare of Kandaha and Her Majesty's Government appreciated that contribution enormously. Foreign investment had an important role to play in Kandaha and he personally welcomed the confidence that the company had shown in the country.

'Talking about confidence,' he said, after a brief silence, 'I must here make categorically clear Her Majesty's position. Her Majesty's Government refuses to be intimidated, ladies and gentlemen.'

Everybody sat up. The Governor abandoned his prepared speech. He was angry with Turnbull for his highly popular but completely unacceptable remarks. He was angry with the guests for showing so much approval.

'Her Majesty's Government will not be blackmailed into pandering to the whims of anyone, whether rich or poor, black or white. I want you all to understand this from the outset. . . .'

He spoke on for a further ten minutes. It was a fighting speech. Her Majesty's authority would be upheld. The rule of law would not give way to that of the jungle, no matter the colour of the perpetrators.

As he concluded his fifteen-minute speech and was saying again, 'Neither this Government, nor Her Majesty's Government will be intimidated,' a waiter brought a note on a burnished tray to Mr Thomson, the Secretary for Native Affairs. Being the second-most important man in the country, Thomson was somewhere on the left-hand side. He too had not been very amused by Turnbull's speech even though as he unfolded the note, he was thinking that the Governor's reply had been somewhat heavy-handed.

It was a police radio message. As he read it his forehead moistened.

Immediate. From OC (Officer Commanding) to COMPOL (Commissioner of Police) *Repeated* SNA (Secretary for Native Affairs) Following for H.E. Yelling mob at village in Boko District NP attacked lonely white farmer and wife at 18 GMT tonight. Police reinforcements rushed to farm five miles ex Boko Boma at 19 GMT. Mob wielding pangas, axes, spears, hoes and guns charged at police as others looted place. Police fired warning shots in air, but mob charged yelling PALP slogans − One Man, One Vote, Down with imperialism, etc. Riot quelled after one hour. Three women and two children killed. Casualties could be up to seven. Whereabouts of white farmer and wife not known, but bedroom soaked in blood.

Thomson had stopped listening to the Governor. He folded the note, pushed back his chair and stood up. He walked round Turnbull's back and set the note before the Governor who was just sitting down to a perfunctory acclamation. The Governor furrowed his brow as he read it. His forehead was feeling damp. Turnbull whispered aloud to him in his benign way:

'That was a fantastic speech, Your Excellency.'

Baker abruptly pushed back his chair and said to his wife, who was on the immediate left of Turnbull:

'Darling, we most go.'

Turnbull tried to say something but the Governor had stood up. Then he announced:

'His Excellency, the Governor, will now leave, ladies and gentlemen.'

Baker was already half-way down the large dining hall, when Jennings stopped him and said:

'Your Excellency, the National Anthem is playing.'

'Long live our noble Queen . . .,' Baker heard the throaty guests accompanying the stereophonic record player, 'God save the Queen.' Then, 'Send her victorious, happy and glorious,' and suddenly the guests seemed to explode, 'Long to reign over us, God save our Queen.' Before now Baker had not realized how long the National Anthem could take.

After the Governor had left, the guests settled down to the cognacs, Rémy Martins, Irish coffee and the lot. At that point it was time for the specially arranged cabaret. Chairs and tables were re-arranged. The hotel manager came especially to whisper something into Turnbull's ear. It was something about there not being a white artist because of the short notice. Management had, however, improvized and the improvization, as far as Turnbull was concerned, seemed to mean precious little that was not offensive.

'You know we hold a substantial interest in this hotel.'

'Yes,' replied the manager. 'But it was a choice between something or nothing.'

Turnbull thought for a moment. He himself had in fact enjoyed the black singer who would be appearing. But he wondered how others would take it.

'OK, then!'

Half an hour later the black singer came on to the stage. Naomi had a rich, full, cooing voice. She was slim of build. She had a confident air. You had to look at her closely to realize she was beautiful. Under the lights of the stage her finely textured dark skin came up very well. She heaved the sharp breasts below the soft lingerie gown which she wore. Her earrings sparkled. She looked blankly into the audience. There was a sadness about her face so that when she smiled and her white teeth showed it was as if she was reproaching the audience. She shook her head and said:

'Ladies and gentlemen, it's nice to have all of you good people here tonight.' She brought the microphone closer to her mouth and cooed, 'It's really great.' Such a rich whispering voice that the audience looked up. 'I'm going to sing you an African song because you are all good people. It's a Zulu song and it's called "*Iyo Patapata*". It's African,' she said with a graceful movement of her body, 'but I'm sure you good people will enjoy it.'

She stiffened up, her face suddenly serious. In a high pitched voice, she started '*Iyoo patapata, iyoo!*' The band took it up. Her face broke into a smile of joy. She was not really rejoicing at the people seated there. She was rejoicing at herself, at her ability to sing the song of her own people. Her eyes shone through the make-up and her full beauty came out. The audience sat entranced as she crooned, riggled and contorted through the music. She was fabulous, so good that an outraged elderly female admirer walked on to the stage and said, 'Get out!'

The editorial in the Kandaha Times stated:

There will be no proper government in this country until only the people who live here have the only and final say in the affairs of the country. Whatever may be the Governor's ideas about what constitutes the people of this country, we are quite clear that 'the people' does not include the criminals who are terrorizing the country. We are determined that government will pass from the effete colonial order into the hands of civilized and effective men and not into those of PALP or any other African party. To use his own phrase, the Governor needs to be told that we will not be intimidated.

The white population of Kandaha has always given the Government full backing. This backing has been irrespective of the individual who was Governor — or shall we say in the present circumstances — in spite of the individual who is Governor? We have done this believing that the Governor is the Queen's representative and therefore above politics. Last night, we witnessed a strange spectacle. Her Majesty's representative, has apparently decided to enter politics, batting of course and, as usual, with the Kawalas of this world.

Among the many unwholesome things the Queen's representative said was the arrogant statement that the Europeans of this country must leave everything to him. Does the Governor realize that unlike the Africans, we are a mature people fully capable of taking care of ourselves? The Europeans of this country are fed up with a Government that has become so ineffectual that it cannot govern.

That Thursday afternoon was Turnbull's day off. That meant golf with Nel Prattley of Barclays, Jim Fender of Standard and now and again with Norris himself. But on that day Britain had devalued and all dealings had been suspended. So Nel and Jim could not make it and there was just Norris and himself. The Chainata Golf Club was one of those most exclusive clubs. With a membership fee of £300 sterling what else did you expect? Fairways deep and green like greens themselves. Sparkling water hazards chlorinated lest the Club's precious members should catch bilharzia. And the lay of the land, what a gorgeousness of sheer undulations so that when you stood at the club house it seemed as though long sweeps of sheer green carpet fell off you, twisting and turning in the brilliant sunshine. And yet the club house itself was nothing more than a plain, and in parts, collapsing edifice. They said that it was an exact replica of another club house in Scotland and so any drastic renovations were out. Even the chairs on which you sat, the bar stools and the beer mugs, each of them had a legend of vintage.

Norris said after a little wait:

'Well John, looks as though you'll have to be content with old political bones today.'

Turnbull was not exactly happy. His after-dinner remarks at the annual dinner of the BGS had drawn a long letter of anger from Government House. In a letter copied to his Chairman in London, Lord Ventrical, the Secretary for Native Affairs had warned him to keep clear of politics. He knew Lord Ventrical to be very sensitive to these matters and he wondered just what good his being seen publicly with Norris could ever do now.

'I'll tee off first if I may,' Norris rumbled his chest, stretched his arms and body with good feeling. 'There we go,' he said, recovering from the breathlessness of putting the tee into the ground and resting the ball on its top.

With Jim and Nel, Turnbull would have said, 'Remember lad you've only got two,' but his relationship with Norris did not go that far down. Norris felt his No. 1 wood delicately, moved it up and down to the ball and then said to Turnbull:

'My stance all right?'

'Sure,' he replied.

'There's something about me, you know. They say I hit them long. Do you know why?' Norris chuckled and his massive eyebrows descended upon his face as if to say to the mouth, 'You're not supposed to laugh.' 'I just says to myself, "Now Ray, that ball's a nigger's head. You smack it hard and you've bashed off Kawala's head." So here I go.'

He coughed a little, raised his club and then brought it low onto the ball and swiped it. The little white ball rose higher and higher, then it began its descent, hit the ground, rolled further and stopped short of the green. For a par four that was something and Turnbull applauded.

When Turnbull had teed off and they fell in step, Norris said:

'John, we've got problems.'

'Telling me,' said John Turnbull.

Ray Norris turned round and saw the caddy.

'Run for the ball piccaninny!' Then he turned to John and said, 'You've always to watch these caddies. They'll try and get close to you so they can hear what you're saying. But as I said, we've got problems. I don't mind telling you I'm desperate.'

Turnbull nodded. He reached for a four iron. His first shot hadn't been so good. He addressed the ball. Turnbull never took practice swings. He raised his club. It came down slowly and gracefully, but he shanked it.

'Lousy golf,' he muttered.

Norris said as they walked on:

'My followers are in a bloody mood. That bomb business with old Wiltshire and the little Governor's stupid remarks at your dinner have upset them no end. The whites feel they've no protection and rightly too. So we had a meeting of the party executive last night and we're forming home guards.' Norris stopped walking as they came up to Turnbull's ball. 'We are going to need guns. KF (Kandaha Front) hasn't got the money. You and ourselves are in the same boat. Without BGS this country is finished. We are also finished. But without us you are also finished.'

Turnbull looked at Norris. For a moment he forgot his ball.

'You mean . . .'

'Just that. That's how old Smithy has survived, isn't it? Patriotic companies like yours must chip in. We've got to find the guns for the boys because Baker won't protect them. You heard that for yourself, didn't you?'

Turnbull shook his head:

'Look Ray, we couldn't help you. Our stake in this country is much too high and Ventrical just wouldn't hear of it.'

'Are you sure Ventrical wants BGS to collapse?'

'No, on the contrary.'

'Well, just wait. When all these boys begin scuttling off because there's no security here then you will collapse.' They moved further down towards the green as Turnbull took his shot. 'We need the money and it's not an awful lot. We could get the guns on discount from across the border in Rhodesia.'

'What if the Government knows we're financing this thing?'

'Do they have to? They don't need to, I'm telling you. This whole deal could be done overseas and no one here be the wiser. You could pay into a numbered account in Switzerland. In fact that's what the dealer wants.'

'Ventrical couldn't accept that apart from everything else. He'd have to be sure that money could be allowed from here. You know that things are becoming sticky up here.'

Turnbull, lying four steadied for his fifth shot. He hit it. The ball flew off furiously and smashed into his caddy's ankle. The caddy screamed, holding up his smashed ankle in his hands. Turnbull ambled over to the howling little monster, looked at the ankle briefly and said:

'OK?'

He hit the ball again and this time it landed on the green. Norris, lying one — a fantastic achievement — chipped lightly on to the green. As Norris, furthest from the hole, made ready to putt, Turnbull, relaxed by the success of his last hit, smiled lightly. Norris' putting posture was really something to behold: the rotund stomach further forward and the back really out with the legs in a knock-kneed fashion. If it had been Nel or Jim he would have said, 'Steady lad, just remember that hole's a virgin and you are about to ravish her. So, don't miss.' But it was Norris and there wasn't very much in common between them — age-wise at least.

After the nine holes they strolled back to the club house. The caddy who'd been hit and the other one followed them to their cars. Norris said:

'We don't have change, boys. We'll go into the club now and you can wait for us outside until we get some change.'

They stayed in the club for two hours, talking intensely in a corner all by themselves. The two men seemed very happy together.

'I'll tell the boys it's a deal,' said Norris shaking Turnbull's hand warmly.

'Only along the lines we've agreed.'

Norris raised his thumb up. The two boys were still waiting outside. Norris threw two shillings at his caddy. Turnbull gave his four and they were off.

8

Kawala coughed a little. In the deep stillness of the dark night that cough seemed to pierce into the bushes around. A lonely hyena laughed out loud in the distance. A monkey chattered from the opposite end. But these were not the voices and sounds which the men gathered in that bush dreaded. So Kawala lit a candle and held it in his left hand. For if there were danger that monkey chatter and the laughter of the hyena would be repeated three times. Once meant all was clear. These were the instructions the men keeping sentry had and they were more than a quarter of a mile away.

At this meeting were: Chimuko, Kakonkawadia (whom everyone now called comrade Kako) and Mama PALP. Mama PALP was a large woman with a very captivating face. She was also a spell-binding orator. She'd challenged the black women of Kandaha once 'never open your thighs to the cowardly men until they have promised they will wipe out the white man! We will only bear free children!' She was chairman of the Women's Brigade.

There was Shakala, the treasurer in a party with no money. He was tall and lanky, always restless and fumbling with something or other. He had steely eyes. He was a man of few words. He did not trust educated Africans.

Standing before this group, stood Katenga and eight other new recruits. Kawala was speaking:

'Comrades, you have of your own accord taken this oath of allegiance to our organization and the cause for which it is fighting. From now on, my brothers and sisters, you will give selflessly of all that you have, including your blood, your very life in the struggle for the liberation of our people.' Kawala paused. 'But there are some things that you will not give away, for to do so would be to become the vilest and most unforgivable traitor. You will not divulge any secrets of the People's Army of Liberation, which embodies on the highest level the aspirations of our people and you will never give up your faith in our people and our ultimate victory. You will be disciplined at all times. You will study so that you will be able to fully understand why PALP embodies on the highest level the aspirations of our people. You will study to learn the tactics of our enemies, and who our friends are.'

After the ceremony, they sat down around the candle in discussion. Kawala said:

'Comrades, now you are real comrades. On this occasion let me remind you all what our mission in life is. It is to liberate this country from the yoke of imperialism and colonialism. We are fighters for our people and "our people" means all peace-loving people, black, white, yellow or any colour. Our enemy is colonialism. It is also racists like Norris. These we must single out and attack until they are dead.'

Katenga stubbed his foot into the ground at the word 'dead'. Kawala continued:

'I do not have any quarrel with Norris. I have a quarrel with the sedition against humanity which he represents. If tomorrow, nay tonight, Norris were to say, "I am wrong, the majority must rule, all men are equal", I would be the first one to embrace him.'

Katenga looked sharply in Kawala's direction. Shakala coughed.

'But Norris does not say this. On the contrary, he is arming his racist whites. Is it not the sweat and blood of *our* people toiling away at the gold mine?' Kawala paused. He tried to speak but an impossible stammer seized his lips. His heart burned within him. Then the words tumbled out in a staccato.

'Arming the whites. Have we become animals to be stalked day and night? The bomb. That's the excuse they are using. Is this the first time a bomb has been left in an office in the world? The Colonial Government killed our people at Nampande Village only recently.'

There was a murmuring through the little crowd. Santasa said: 'It is true.'

Katenga exclaimed:

'Exactly!' He stamped the ground. His eyes went wild and the lips trembled as he exclaimed again, 'Exactly!'

The following morning, despite having had a sleepless night,

Kawala, Katenga and Santasa, the Vice-President of PALP set off for Boko District in the northern province. Boko was five hundred miles away from Gunsbury. Nampande Village, where the massacre took place, was only a few miles from the Boko Boma.

It was a bright cheery morning when they finally arrived. The sun shone brightly. The sky was a sheet of blue virginity unblemished even by a single cloud. Morning birds chirrupped liquidly. They had arrived at Nampande Village. They stood before a forest of tall leafy bloom. The village headman said:

'It's in there, under those tall trees. That is where they are.'

He led the way. They followed. A little crowd gathered behind them. Kawala lowered his frame to avoid scraping his head against the overhanging creepers. He was feeling stiff. For a while they trudged silently. Then they came to a clearing. The headman said:

'It's there, those five new graves.'

The silent crowd stood back. Kawala followed by Santasa and Katenga walked on to the mounds of new earth. Santasa and Katenga halted. Kawala walked on. Now he was close to the graves. He bowed his head. He lowered himself to the ground. Over and over he kissed the earth of the grave before him. Santasa wiped a tear from his eyes. Katenga stood, his head bowed. The women wept.

The village headman stepped into the arena. A thin little man with short, hardy body and a bald head. He wore a black cloth which hung loosely from his shoulders. He coughed a little. He was trying to suppress a tear. He coughed again and spat at the side. Then he said:

'Today we are thankful to God and to our spirits that you, our leaders, have come all the way from Musasa, a place where in the days of our fathers it took more than three moons to walk to. You have come up all this way to see how we, your people, have suffered at the hands of the white one. There is not much that I can say. Everything that could be said was said already when I buried these, my children and grandchildren.' The little old man paused. He turned to the graves and pointing them out one by one, he said, 'You, our chiefs who have come from Musasa, do not know who lives under each of these mounds. That one there is Chalo, my son because his mother and I were born from the same womb even though our fathers were different. My father married my mother first and bore me. Then, hunger, the hunger that was called *cigumula* descended on this land. People died like flies. He too died. That is how my mother later on was married by another man, the one who bore the sister of mine who produced Chalo who is in that new grave. My sister herself is buried there,' he said, pointing to an uncleared patch. 'She died in childbirth many years ago.' Then the man turned to the next grave and on to the remaining two. When he reached the fifth, a tiny grave, he said, 'This is my grandchild. She, too, was killed by the gun of the white one. Yes. Yes, let me say it now. By the gun of the white one. Why? What could a baby have done to be given a bullet instead of the soft teat of its mother?'

He turned to look at Kawala.

'There are many people who will tell you that the white man's black policeman shot at us because we were plundering the white one's goods, that we attacked the white farmer. We have lived with the white ones at that farm these many years, lived with them as a slave lives with his master. When the Bwana has been short of labour he has come to our village and I, with my own mouth, have convinced the young that it is good to work for money with which to buy the white man's goods. But when the village has run out of water and we have tried to get it from the only well that never dries up at his farm, we have been chased away like dogs. These things have happened for these many years, I will say ever since the Bwana's father died for he was a good, kindly man.'

He cleared his throat, looked at the sun creeping up into the sky, and then resumed.

'On the evening when these sad things happened, we of the village were on our way to the funeral of village headman Twatha. He had died suddenly, witchcraft without a doubt. It was too dark for us to take the path that skirts round the Bwana's farm because the Bwana's farm is a large one. It is as large as this whole country. There was a short-cut through the farm. So we took it thinking that if we could explain that our journey was a journey of sorrow, the white one would take pity on us and allow us to pass through his farm. After all these was nothing growing there, this being the dry season. It was not as if we wanted to steal his wealth.

When we were right into the farm and only a few yards from his house, a strong light like the white light of a ghost, flashed into our eyes. We panicked. The women screamed. The children cried. Then suddenly we heard a loud explosion like that from a muzzle loader. Chalo touched his chest, 'I die!' he cried and fell to the ground. Then we scattered in all directions, even into the mouths of the guns that were shooting us. We were sheep.'

He looked into the crowd.

'They say that we carried axes, pangas and knobkerries. Yes, that is what we heard on the radio. They say that we attacked the white ones. How could I, with all my manliness, have allowed men to attack a woman — a white one at that. No. We carried an axe, yes. We carried a spear, yes. We carried a panga, yes. We carried these three weapons between all of us. It was dark. The sun had set. What man is it who walks in the dark without a weapon to fend off the lion with?

It was the Bwana and his people who attacked us. It was the police from there at the Boma of Boko who came to finish the job of blood which he started. We were beaten up as if we were not people in sorrow. When the work of the white man had been done there were five of ours dead. These are the graves. I myself hit the gun off the white donna as she levelled it at my head. She was hurt. I hurt her, but I did not kill her. She still lives on even though they said on the wireless that she was missing.'

He stepped back into the arena. His voice charged, he said:

'The God of heaven, the God of the city of Jericho will come down in ten years' time,' he clapped his hands together, 'to judge the world, to condemn and burn the sinners to ashes. We in this village do not worship the God of Christianity, the God of the white one, the God of war. The God of Jericho is our God. Jericho is our city of hope, the city to which we shall go when the world will come to an end. The God of Jericho protected us from all harm, including the harm of the bullet of the gun. Our ancestors were immune to bullets. They were immune to any harm. They could fall down from tall trees, high mountains, and never dash even their toe. Now we who are their descendants have lost that immunity. We are like cows and goats and even the white man's knife can kill us now. Is it because we have lost our way to Jericho in this valley of sin that we now suffer so much that even a white woman's gun can kill us?'

He stepped back and, obviously reciting, cried:

'Repent. O you sons and daughters and heirs to the paradise of Jericho. Lose not this city to sin, the city which your God has given you from times and days without number. You parted with the religion of Christianity because that religion was the religion of the worship of idols. That religion taught you to worship white statues and the white man. You deacons present in this crowd, lift up your eyes to the Lord and pray that the God of Jericho will once again protect you, smash the religion of statues and the makers of these statues. A religion that rules by the sword, by a government of the earth, by hate, will be crushed by the heel of the God of Jericho even as he crushed the head of the black mamba in Chapter 3,

Verses 5—10, of our own bible.'

Headman Nampande turned to Kawala. In his village he was the archdeacon of the Church of the Holy Ones. The Church of the Holy Ones was a breakaway from the local Catholic Church. Its leader, Nicodemus Simalonda, the Holy One, had at one time been a seminarian at the international seminary which Kandaha still shared with Zambia. One night and six months from his ordination to the priesthood, Nkonde Simalonda then called Nicodemus Simalonda, had dreamed of a colossal heavenly battle between Lucifer and Michael the Archangel. Each of their armies was racing from the city of Jericho. Swords flashed through the ethereal atmosphere steeped in brilliant sunshine. The archangel's sword large and long, smote into Lucifer's head. The head exploded into a wild and roaring fire but Lucifer went on fighting as his army raced towards Jericho in the trail of his smouldering head. Then, as the two armies reached the gates of Jericho besplattered in blood, Nicodemus Simalonda saw himself standing in the doorway, his hands now turned into glittering wings and his whole body an angelic form glowing with celestial crystal beauty. He raised his wings towards the embattled armies led by Michael and Lucifer each of whom had his long nail deeply planted into the other's throat.

'Neither of you is fit to enter the heavenly city of Jericho,' he heard himself say. 'You have been weighed and found wanting. The God for whom you fight, Michael, and the God whom you fight, Lucifer, is the God of war, the God that has brought the plague of war and slavery to the peoples of the earth. Cast your eyes down', he heard himself cry, 'many miles below you and see how the messengers of your religions bear the sword of war against the heirs of Jericho, the innocent black children of God who neither know how to fight nor to kill.'

Michael and Lucifer listened in amazement.

'Amen, amen, I say to you. From now on these very lowly sons of the God of Jericho shall be the real heirs of their father's city. The spear, swords and guns of your messengers shall neither pierce them nor wound them. They shall fall from the cliffs of heaven, from the trees and mountains of the earth but shall never be harmed. Like the innocent birds of the air, they shall flee from their enemies on wings even as I, the Archangel of Jericho, have wings.'

Then Nicodemus Simalonda saw his white apparel turn into a glowing black robe, glistening in the bright reflection of the sun shining down into the earth. He spread out his gleaming wings. The celestial heavens roared thunder and the sun streaked across the empty atmosphere like a lightning bolt hurled by a giant. Then the skies broke into angelic music and trumpeting and a host of black angels descended upon Nicodemus and lifted him further into the sky, carrying away with them the floating gates of the city of Jericho. . . .

Nicodemus woke up in a sweat. But a figure, robed and luminous, appeared to him and said:

'I am the Lord and Son of man whom they call Jesus. But you shall call me the Holy One, the Lord of Jericho. You have seen me. Now go about my Father's work.'

The figure vanished.

For the next four days Nicodemus lay prostrate, unable to speak. On the fifth day, he got up and told Father Rector that he was abandoning his vocation. He vanished into the wilderness for forty days. There he prayed and thought much and when he came back it was with a new religion, the Church of the Holy Ones.

Headman Nampande said to Kawala:

'In this village and many others we follow the law of our founder Simalonda, the Episcopal Archdeacon of the Holy Ones. We do not raise arms against men because we do not believe in the earthly kingdom. But we shall rise and overthrow those who frustrate our worship of the Holy One. Already the messengers of the religion of iniquity, those religions whose leaders the Episcopal Archdeacon of the Holy Ones stopped from entering the gates of Jericho, have been here and told us to close down our churches and worship the very God from whom our founder turned away. They have accused us of supporting PALP, your party. We know no earthly kingdom. Therefore, the struggles for power here on earth do not concern us. We know only of the black man's destiny to enter the city of Jericho after death even as our founder entered it when his soul left his body. Your man Katenga here, even though he may fight like you for power here on earth, knows that as a member of our worship his home is in Jericho. But this,' said Nampande, staring into the graves, 'this is too much. This was not meant to punish us for PALP: out children have paid in blood the sin of belonging to the church of the Holy Ones. We are being punished for living together in a community where there are neither relatives nor foreigners. We are being punished for refusing to accept the authority of the white man because it is the authority of people who worship statues and the authority and power of this passing world. We are being punished because we will not pay taxes, we will not allow our own to go to hospitals and be cut up like goats as if each of our bodies was not the house of the Episcopal Archdeacon of the Holy Ones. For us, there is only love, love of fellow men even as we love ourselves. For this, too, we are being hunted down like animals as if the message of total love is not the foundation of goodness. There was a time once when the unbelieving weapons of death could not kill us. But that time it seems has now passed. Today we are like cows and goats and even the unbelievers' knife can kill us. Is it because we have lost our way to Jericho in this valley of sin that we can now suffer so much that even the gun of the infidel woman, even the white woman, that killed our people, can kill us? Dimintolo must come. Let him come down from his kingdom in Tanzania to hear how we, his flock, have corrupted ourselves even as the City of Jerusalem fell into the pit of iniquity.'

That afternoon, Kawala held a meeting of all the provincial officials of the party. The meeting started off well. There was going to be a big meeting — in fact a seminar — in Musasa followed by a rally. He hoped that all the regions and constituencies were ready with their delegates. Then before he could continue, the provincial secretary asked:

'What shall we do about all these killings comrade, National President. Our buttocks are worn down smooth from passive sitting. The people here are ready, especially in this village. They have sworn that if the farmer returns to the farm they will kill him and all his cats and dogs. When they do and they are taken to court and condemned to death, shall we just sit and watch their execution?'

Kawala looked in Santasa's direction. He had not yet changed his face of sorrow for a face of business.

'Comrade, National President,' said Santasa feeling somewhat uncomfortable, 'whatever you think will be right.'

Then Katenga spoke.

'These people here must advise us. We sit there in Musasa five hundred miles away from the scene of the killing. We must go by what the colonial radio says. We don't know the people, comrade National President.'

'What do you mean?' challenged Kawala. 'If I don't know my people, do you know them better?'

'Comrade National President,' said the provincial secretary, 'comrade Katenga is right. If the forthcoming meeting produces no action, these people will act on their own. What we hear on the radio is no good and I hope you can assure us that the colonial press wants to divide us. Today the central committee says this.

Tomorrow someone else is saying something completely different. We don't want peace, because after all these killings this would be the peace of cowards.'

Just then a choir led by a blind guitarist came forward. The man smiled vacantly at the dignitaries seated under a tree and then said:

'You respected dignitaries, we are very happy to see you in our country. This is a country of guns and death, so do not tally around too much. He that has leprosy must be left on his own lest he should infect the healthy ones. Here we are blind. Chalo was a blind man. That is why instead of running away from the gun of the white man he grinned into it. But we have come here to entertain you. No more of this.'

He set down his guitar and did a slight caper. Waving his hand at the seated dignitaries he began to recite a verse of praise. As he did so, he darted from one corner to the other, haranging them in the local vernacular with all the fury and mockery of his oratory.

'Welcome, welcome to this country of fire,
You great Kawala, the eater of fire, the scourge of the white men.
You great lion, you the owner of all the rivers, mountains,
The owner of the whole land, the land they want to steal.
Welcome, welcome, you the spirit that vanishes in thin air,
The keeper, guardian, protector and defender of your people.
Welcome to you the eagle of many talons,
The talons that will claw the colonialist animal
Until its festering belly will be torn up in cavities
For the flies from his faeces to fill, fatten and breed maggots.
Welcome to you great one who knows that many tongues never
    built a home,
You have told us to prepare ourselves for war and we know you
    mean war,
We know you don't mean the war of peace,
We know you mean the war of fury.
The war which trounces the enemy, cuts off his head,
The war that eats his eyes and urinates the urine of anger into his
    skull.'

The man broke off. Looking vacantly he exclaimed:

'Where is that guitar, the guitar of the white one?' When it was put in his hands, he set it down and then crushed it with his foot saying, 'Take away this useless thing of the white one. Bring me our own native drums.'

In a moment the drums stirred into action. First the uncertain beat of the deep-voiced drum with a bulging belly. Then its sound quickened. The other drums followed. The blind man started a song, his face lighting up with joy. He cocked his ear to listen as the drums took him up. He shook his head. Someone was out of tune. Then he started the song again. As the melody of the different drums joined in, he smiled with joy. Then jumping sky-high he put it back to them. The drums replied with bouncing tropical hilarity. The man laughed, laughed into the drummers' faces, into those of the dignitaries before him. Then he started to dance. It was the *Kalela* dance, the most famous tribal dance in the northern province of Kandaha.

The blind man, Fwebashya, was a well-known dancer in the area. He was popular with everyone, especially the girls. He was tall and muscular, his teeth white and sparkling, and when he laughed, it was as though he had been promised eyesight. Kawala listened. What were eyes for in a land where one was not free? As if reading his thoughts, the blind man laughed in his direction. He was bliss itself and Kawala envied the simple, uncomplicated happiness of one who did not know. Then the man sang:

'When that day comes, we shall all have eyesight,
The eyesight that comes from our minds being free,
Even if the free body, eyes and hands may be crippled.
Kawala you told us the day would come,
The day when we would be ourselves, eat honey and drink milk,
The honey and milk of deliverance from the yoke.
Save us, save us. Tell us are there slaves where they come from?'

The drummers took up the plea and as the small ones chatted away excitedly, the big ones vibrated as if punctuating the chatter with, 'No, no!'

'Oh, tell us the truth,' resumed Fwebashya. 'Is there really
  independence?
How could they have forgotten it if it is true,
Their own feeling of their own independence these white people?
When you drink the beer and it is good,
Couldn't you be proud to give to another because he would like it?
Or are they not people these white ones?'

Once again the little drums took up the challenge and the big ones roared their, 'No, no.' There was something pathetic about a blind man crying for freedom from the colonial yoke. Was it not a reproach to the sighted ones?

When the dancer and his troupe bowed out, the people cheered them. Someone put a shilling into the blind man's hands. The blind man would have started dancing again except that he was shepherded off by the others.

So the meeting resumed.

9

Upon returning from Boko, there was a meeting. After Kawala's report, Chimuko stood up.

'Comrade National President, we are in a war situation. War cannot be waged with peace. We must all go to the bush. The liberation fight in South Africa is hotting up. Here we only sit, talk and wait, waiting in case these colonial enslavers here in the shape of Thomson, Baker and others are different from Vorster and his gangsters. They are not. Our friends are fighting against the white here. What are we waiting for?'

Katenga exclaimed excitedly:

'I agree.'

Shakala put a spear in Kawala's hand. Kawala closed his eyes as he held the spear before him. He could see the watershed before him. The hands of destiny were quickly closing in upon the arch devil of oppression.

'The whites. All the whites!' exclaimed Katenga.

Ignoring him, Kawala said:

'As I close my eyes I see a sea of human faces crying out from the depths of the inferno. Their voices are rising to our ears. They are calling us to save them from the fire of slavery. These cries of anguish, the cries from the throats of our own people asking to be redeemed from slavery must not be betrayed. Nor should the cries of many other millions on this globe. For even among the mocking voices of those who oppress us there are others who call us to liberate them from their own evil of racialism and oppression. There are the abysmally poor among the abysmally rich. These, too, call to us to be saved from the exploitation of the rich. Fellow travellers, we are launching tonight on a long perilous journey. But this journey must not stop with the destruction of colonialism. This and others are only instruments of exploitation of man by man. Having won that battle we must brace ourselves for the major onslaught. For we cannot be truly free when all Africa is not so. We cannot be truly free when man the world over continues to be exploited. The canvas we set ourselves here is a wide one. Let us recognize our fight for independence as the small, first, uncertain step that it is towards the larger goal. If we do that, then we shall see that it is an objective within our means. It is a goal that must be reached, achieved and . . .', he swung his spear into the air, 'acceded to quickly.'

'Where do we begin?' asked Katenga. Shakala looked at Katenga and nodded as if to say, 'That's right. Where?'

'With the workers,' replied Kawala. 'Plenty's happening there. And maybe we're letting them down.'

Kawala lingered behind. His mind was not at ease. He loved his people. Would they all live through the violence that had to come, or would they be the people who would suffer while the colonialists lived on to become more ruthless than ever before? He badly wanted to talk to someone. Who could he talk to? Then he remembered Fr Lafayette. He had not seen him for a long time now. He hesitated. Had Lafayette ever spoken out for the people's rights? Would Lafayette open his door to him at such a late hour? 'You must talk to him. These are moral matters of great importance,' a voice within was saying to him. 'He's the only man who can understand you as a simple, worried human being. Don't forget he brought you up, even though he may be white.'

Lafayette had been ordained priest thirty-five years ago at Monte Christi, the famous monastery, rising out of the waters of the sea at Marseilles. Five years later he had been posted to North Africa. Then an SOS came from a Monsignor in the northern province of Zambia. There was a crying need for a man who could heal both the wounds of the soul and those of the body. Such a man would have to be a practical type. There were lepers to be tended. Ritual murders to be stopped. Adultery, paganism, idolatry. The black man needed salvation. Christ was calling for sacrifice. Conversions in black Africa could be richer because the African did not have a stubborn religious and cultural past. Young Lafayette had read that appeal over and over. Then he had read the works of Father Damien, the famous Belgian healer of the lepers of Hawaii. That was it, and a year later he found himself among the white fathers of the northern province of Zambia (then Northern Rhodesia). It was from there that he came to Kandaha — twenty years ago. All these twenty years except for the last five had been spent in the rural missions. He had built schools and clinics wherever he went. Some called him the Fire of God because of his ardent preaching. Others had called him a slave driver because he worked so hard and drove his workers like a slave driver. At one mission where he had stayed seven years he had come in contact with young Nathaniel Kawala. Such a keen little pupil he had been. He did not know why, but Lafayette had always taken a personal interest in the young fellow and followed his career. It was he who had blessed their marriage. Even after Kawala left the Bristol Gold Syndicate and vanished into the country, Lafayette had always followed his career with interest. But since his return to Musasa, Kawala had not been in contact. He'd never called at the little church on the edge of Samaka Compound.

'To Samaka Church,' said Kawala to the man picking him up in a little old Morris Minor half a mile away from where they had been meeting. The engine coughed and spluttered.

'To Samaka Church,' said Kawala again, as the engine continued to rev without movement. The little car jumped forward, whining and complaining. City road was quiet and deserted as they reached Musasa. The little Morris made its way up the South End round-about. Cumba, the driver, pressed the accelerator.

'Still to Samaka Church, Bwana President?' he asked.

'Yes. It's late, I know, but leave me there. I'll simply walk across the road to my house afterwards,' replied Kawala.

Cumba was a kind of general-purpose retainer for Kawala. He had never been to school, but he was well informed. He fed his children off the occasional gifts of food that supporters made to Kawala.

Kawala was tense as he got out of the car. Fr Lafayette, although he always slept late, was not used to being interrupted. Looking through the uncurtained window, he could see the priest's spare form silhouetted against the fulsome flame of the candle on the small table. Kawala hesitated. Should he knock or just walk back home? But he had to see the priest in there. Throughout that day and especially that night he had been greatly worried about the things that he saw as inevitable and coming. Years of patient work, years of reasoning by the party with the Colonial Government for his country to be given independence, had come to naught. The masses had become fed up with promises of threats without action.

But now a new plan had been worked out. No more general threats. Just action. His blood raced as he stood looking at the bent form of Fr Lafayette through the window. Suddenly he envied that man praying over his breviary in that small room. At least he was not lonely. At least he had a breviary to keep him company and maybe he felt God's presence. He, Kawala, was lonely. No matter how mildly Chimuko may have put it, ultimate responsibility from now on would be his. And so all the blood would be on his shoulders, including the blood of even the men who would carry out the plan.

Then there was Katenga, the new man, who was the embodiment of all that was violent against anyone who would dare oppose PALP. For him PALP was already a religion not permitting of contradiction. As he had sat in that meeting of only an hour ago, Kawala had felt the rebuke of that man's eyes if he should fail the central committee. Behind those red eyes, the unkempt hair and the fuzzy beard, there was a steely and almost fanatical dedication to the party. Could the plan be carried out without spilling blood? Just burning down bridges and schools? Blasting empty rail coaches and no more? Kawala's heart trembled. 'You are our only saviour. We give you total emergency powers. Do anything with anyone. Even we here.'

Kawala raised his hand to knock at the door. He had come there to seek solace from the only man he knew could give it to him. He was not a 'yes' man, that man in there. Not a 'yes' man to the colonialists or to the nationalists. Many times he had been close to imprisonment for denouncing the Government for social injustice. He'd also fallen out with the party for denouncing it for thuggery. For a moment Kawala's throat choked with anger. Who was he to call the party a bunch of thugs? A white racialist, wasn't he? Should he just go back or should he knock at the door?

He paused, his forefinger set to knock at the door. But he needed to talk to that gaunt man in there, the man with thin white hair, with a long beard. He shook his head, knocked hard at the door. Fr Lafayette jumped up.

'Who is it?' he asked, looking out of the window, his beard breathing up and down with his skinny chest.

Kawala opened the unlocked door gingerly.

'Disturbing me when I am speaking to my God,' mumbled the priest. He was still looking through the window.

'It is I,' said Kawala, walking towards the man. 'I'm sorry I disturb you Father, but really I must see you.'

Lafayette's face expressed surprise, but he relaxed somewhat.

'Is it confession you want my son?' he asked, making for the stole hanging on the bare wall.

'No,' replied Kawala, 'Not yet.'

'Ah. Well, sit down. A glass of water — or can I make some tea?' asked the priest. He looked at his watch. It was after one in the morning.

'Ah. Things of the flesh again,' sighed the priest. 'What's the matter this time? You want to harm your neighbour, my son and absolve yourself by speaking it all out to me. Not so?'

Father Lafayette slid his thin hands into his white cassock. He pulled out a small snuff bottle. Carefully he emptied a little of it into his palm, inhaling it deeply and coughed aloud. He wiped his nose with the back of his hand, and then the beard. All of a sudden he seemed to become vigorous.

'Father, I need your help because only you can help me. We have tried everything possible to avoid violence, as you know. We have threatened, but no one has taken heed. We can't go on like this, always restraining the people, telling them lies about how soon it will all be, how reasonable the British Government is. . . .'

The priest was suddenly listening. Kawala was not now looking at him but talking into the air.

'The rope has snapped. If nothing happens by tomorrow I must put a scheme of violence into effect.'

The priest coughed a little. His grey eyes raised to Kawala, but he did not say anything.

'You can see my problem, can't you?'

Father Lafayette sniffed at his bottle. Slowly he turned the question over in his mind and finally said:

'None. No problem. The problem is always to do wrong. Never to do right.'

'What is right, then?' asked Kawala. 'To do nothing and let the colonialists continue to kill my people? To let my people continue to buy meat through windows as if they are lepers? To continue to see my people treated like dogs? "No dogs and Africans allowed" — are these the signs you want to continue seeing? And all because I must not hurt anybody? If a rat sits on the food, you cannot get at the food without killing it.'

'Kill, my son?' asked the gaunt tall man, alarmed.

'These colonialists are sitting on our birthright, on our right to be human beings. On our right to freedom, independence, liberty, equality. This is our food and so . . .'

The priest sat intently. It was these self same words that drove his ancestors to kill the rich during the French Revolution. 'Liberté, Égalité, Fraternité . . .'

'Tell me Father, if you were a black man and in my position and you felt as completely about my people as I do and you were one of us, one of us; I mean', Kawala looked at the priest, 'you looked at and felt the indignity of your own people, an indignity which even in your own churches reduces us to third-rate Christians, third-rate children of God, how would you look at this whole question of Christianity and colonialism? Wouldn't you . . .'

'There is no discrimination in the church.' The thin figure of the priest had shot up like a stiff poker. His hands were trembling as he held at his snuff bottle. 'You insult me, Kawala. You insult the Church. The Church looks after Christians, black and white. All of them are children of God.' The old man's eyes darted up and down. His face, even in the candlelight, was a lifeless parched white.

'What's the Church in Africa?' challenged Kawala. He too was angry. 'It is the priests, the white priests, their white sisters and the white congregation that fills up St Andrews, because that is the white man's church. It is not Samaka Church. It is not Magwero Church that matters, because these churches serve the black man who has no money to contribute to the Church.' Kawala was now striding up and down the little room. 'I have been to St Andrews. I could not sit on a bench. And that's supposed to be *my* Church. But it's only *my* Church if I am white. That's the trouble and that's why I don't expect you to understand. For so long as the interpretation of moral law will continue to rest with the white man, so long will there be no fair play for the black man.'

Father Lafayette looked into Kawala's face. Then he spoke.

'You have finished?'

He shook his head.

'But you haven't told me what it is you want of me. I have no law to interpret to suit your convenience. I have no law for Africans and another for whites. What's wrong is wrong. Violence cannot be condoned merely because it is directed at one race by another, no matter whether it is in retaliation.'

'It's not directed against the whites, if that's your fear, it's against the Government which happens to be all white,' retorted Kawala.

'You can't kill a person as a member of the Government. You can only kill him as an individual. Your campaign of violence could well result in death, even one death. That would be injustice against the legally constituted Government. But what's more, it would be irreparable injustice against the individual,' replied Father Lafayette.

'There is no legally constituted Government. There are only oppressors.'

'But there are legally constituted beings, human beings, aren't there? With the same right to life as you, Kawala,' said the priest his body once again stiffening into a rod of iron. 'If you want to lead your people, you will have to learn that no way that involves evil is a shortcut to anything. I have stayed long enough in this country to tell you evil has never paid. The existing white Government has an evil basis and that is why it will go. Go!' said the priest, throwing his arms up into the air. 'For God will not permit a Government that treats the black man in this manner. To we human beings, time is money, is everything. But to God, it is the essence of his eternity. Your people expect miracles from you — to deliver violence or independence by tomorrow. You are frightened, frightened lest your better judgement should prevail and you should call off this campaign of violence. Frightened lest you should be kicked out. Is that not really the issue rather than your good people?'

'You're wrong,' shouted Kawala, pounding his fist upon the low rickety table. 'I've never put my self interest before the party's interest.'

'I always thought so. And the party is composed of people. Not so?' Then, without waiting for a reply, the lanky man continued, 'They are the people who will suffer, even be killed, when you start a campaign of violence. Not the security forces. Just close your eyes for a moment, Kawala, and imagine the row of coffins, coffin upon coffin of your own people, some shot in the head, others with chunks of meat riven off their chests, gouged eyes, amputated limbs. Those, my son, are the people who will perish, their children, wives, and relatives — not the colonialists.' Then he looked at him straight in the face and added, 'And not *you*. It is the people who will suffer. Unless your own is touched by this plague, yours will only be a public sorrow, a sorrow which is so small that it has to be cried aloud. And all that, my dear son,' said Lafayette, taking a deep breath and holding it there for a little while, 'will be on *your* head.'

Then Kawala said:

'That's not true! I have to do what the majority wants me to do!' His eyes looked imploringly at Lafayette. 'It's easy for you sitting here, detached, reassuring, moralizing. What do I do? Leave the field to you and your imperialist friends to preach against violence for the protection of the white man? No!' he said. 'I will fight, fight to the bitter end. Even if we have all to become corpses. I will fight. What's life without independence? What's life if it's eternal slavery?'

'If you want to hear only what pleases you my son, why don't you go to the Holy Ones. PALP has been supporting them more than it has supported the Christian Churches. In fact, it has condemned us as puppets of colonialism. Why do you come to me? You talk of eternal slavery as if independence was everything. Some saints only became saints because they knew how to become perfect slaves. The freedom that is real freedom is the freedom of the heart,' said the old man calmly.

'Saints! Saints! Obedient civil servants and the lot. That's how you have brainwashed us. Saints! Saints!' Kawala jumped at the door, slammed it hard behind him and charged up the street, still muttering, 'Saints!'

Lafayette sits a long time after Kawala has left. It's been such a stormy exit and he can still smell the dust kicked up as the old rickety door banged against the ant-eaten door frame. He's trembling with anger at the insolence of the man, and perspiring from the quickened pulse of the weak heart. He looks at the rosary hanging on the wall. He knows he should be praying for that 'poor, misguided and impetuous' Kawala to do the right thing. That right thing means not going ahead with a campaign of violence. It means no rallies of defiance.

But Fr Lafayette, he can't bring himself to hook that rosary off the wall. Kawala's hatred of the white man makes him angry. We are all equal, and that's for sure. But hasn't God given us our colour for a purpose? There may be stacks of purposes, but isn't the preservation of one's species one such purpose? I'm white, says Lafayette. Kawala's black. If anti-white violence erupts, I'll be the first one to go, living so close to this black compound. It happened in the Congo. It's happened in Angola. It's happening in Rhodesia. Why not here? And if it happened here, Kawala would be the cause. He closed his eyes. He will not pray for one possessed, for one who is the cause of evil.

He thinks over Kawala's life. Only he knows the real man beneath that name and that lumber jerkin. There are many things hidden in the deepest recesses of a man's mind which only a priest gets to know and even though he cannot talk about them to other people and not even to the penitent himself outside the confines of the mouldy confession box, a priest is a man and so he cannot exclude them from his judgement of human nature.

Take Kawala's first confession, for example, almost twenty years ago. The little lean boy is panting after the confessional and gasping like a dog. He stumbles over the words, somewhat. He's out of breath as he says:

'Bless me, Father, for I have sinned. Since my last confession — no, this is my first one . . .'

Then he starts all over again.

Bless me Father, for I have sinned.' He pauses, then to get it all over he rattles in a high-pitched voice, 'I have injured my neighbour.'

'Have you finished?'

'Yes,' says the little voice.

'My son. How did you injure your neighbour?'

'I told my young brother he was not a good boy. I know I injured him because he cried. He said, "I will knife you." If he knifes me and kills me, I will die and I will be the cause of his committing a sin against the fifth commandment. I am sorry, Father.'

Lafayette lifts his hand over his mouth in a blessing posture but really it's to hide imminent laughter. At the seminary they had been taught not to underscore or relieve the sense of guilt of the penitent. This one is young, but first impressions are very important. As with the old Christians, he has to be told not to do it again. The encouragement will come in the exhortation to the all-forgiving Almighty. So he gives the little fellow a scolding and when it gets away with only three rosaries, doesn't it romp off with joy! He remembered standing up to get it back into church to say the penance.

Fr Lafayette remembered how the little boy used to come every Saturday, in those days, to practice as a mass server at Lueno mission in northern Kandaha. So keen and radiant. And yet there was a day when one boy hit a smaller boy for no reason. How Kawala jumped at the bigger boy! How he clawed him, kicked him in the stomach, and then when the poor older boy was overpowered, how he spat and blew his nose at him. What a strange boy!

And now this is the man preaching violence, thought Fr Lafayette. What had happened? God has made the priests the instruments of his forgiveness and whatever we bind on earth is bound in heaven. But to dare bind, one must put oneself in the position of the postulant and feel all the forces acting in him. He coughed a little. He was becoming afraid to ask himself the next little question. His lips trembled as he realized that doubt in this field could be heresy. But he had to ask it. Free will. Is there really such a thing as free will? His lips grew bolder as they moved.

'If Kawala orders violence and people die, he will do so under psychological duress. Can he really be held responsible by anyone who knows the full pressures?'

Quickly, Fr Lafayette crossed his chest with the sign of the cross, picked up the rosary and began to recite it. Not praying for anybody and anything in particular, but simply keeping at bay thoughts which it is not right for one who has been so long in holy orders to entertain.

He looked again into that bare white wall before him. Maybe the Church should support the black man's political aspirations. But he checked himself. What was right about Africans being given a vote, he asked. In terms of morality, did a vote secure any moral good as did, for example, giving alms to the poor? Were politics necessary to the moral order and was the just distribution of political power called for by moral law? Was it not possible — nay in fact it has been the case in history, he corrected himself — that the Church thrived most in times of persecution, in times when its followers were denied the most fundamental rights or any recognition by the body politic. The political order is not relevant, he said to himself. What is relevant is that irrespective of the political order, man seeks perfection. Saintliness.

There are saintly people within the white community, his thoughts continued. The Deputy Commissioner of Police, for example, was he not one of his most regular communicants? Take his confessions for example. Every week it's about his lust for his neighbour's wife. But never about the social injustice he commits every day. Fr Lafayette contemplated the lanky form of the Deputy on the other side of the confessional saying, 'Bless me Father, for I have sinned. Since my last confession a week ago, I have committed the following sin. I arrested Africans for demanding immediate constitutional talks.' A smile broke over Fr Lafayette's face, as he contemplated this unlikely confession. So why should the Church get involved in politics, in things of the temporal order? Why should the Church involve itself in politics? Why should evil means ever justify an end?

10

Late that same night, the twenty-fifth of May, Katenga met some miners at the African Mine Club, having gone straight from the meeting with Kawala. That was not very secret. But there was drink. Fortunately, this was Mpengula's night and when the boss of the union was around, drink did really flow. A kind of prince in exile. All the hangers on — a mixture of parched throats and loyalty. Ruffians — if the choice was between protecting the royal personage and, therefore, a free beer or no beer. They were the types who might have been lashers underground. Heavy biceps. Rough language. Not much poetry beyond, 'you-son-of-a-bitch'. Take for example Chimotomoto. Known for his toughness — or is it his tenderness? The story went . . . oh, many stories! But the way how after every drink he contorted his biceps might have made you believe they were true. They called him simply, 'the Conqueror'. Then there was the short man, Kangacepe, a kind of scouter or ferret cat. He always went ahead of the 'presidential' drinking party. A kind of arranger, you would say. It wasn't by accident the president of the Mine Workers Union and the more durable of his supreme council always sat with a bevy of pretties. Someone said of Katenga, 'He is Kawala's man.'

'Shut up!' said the royal voice. It was imperious. There was complete silence in the bar for a moment. What miner would drink his beer in peace knowing the boss is in a temper? The Conqueror stood up:

'Bwana President don't want to hear that name,' he said.

'But he'll hear more and more of it, I'm telling you — and his party.'

'Party!' exclaimed Mpengula. He grunted. 'Kawala's a loafer. He failed here, he left *my* people in the lurch.' And then he said, 'Just over a simple incident. He was too much a villager to talk to the white man. My people, you crocodiles, do you get your meat?'

There was silence in the club as he stood up. They knew they'd all to say, 'Yes', because their jobs depended on him.

'Did you see how I threw Turnbull's stupid tea at his face?'

'Yes, Bwana President!'

'And with what result? Didn't the mine agree to give you boots? Didn't they agree to up your wages? What were you before I came on the scene? Not baboons only?'

'Yes Bwana President.'

'Kawala. What's he got? What did he do for you? Where did he grow up? Here or in the village? What's his wife doing now? Selling insects in the market, isn't she? Why? Why, I ask you? Because lazy louts like him are work shy.'

He paused. Mpengula said:

'Not to mention that reptile here! Drunks from Musasa coming to confuse you. I can tell Bwana Turnbull what I want for my people. Can Kawala do it? He's a villager. He thinks making money means you must drink from the same cup with a white. The whites are his chief, his prince and king. Why doesn't he just tell the Governor all he wants to do is drink from the same cup as I the prince do? Then he'd have a point. Why? Because I won't allow a commoner like him to do it. And for your information, only Turnbull can drink with me. Don't you know that this mine belongs to me? Even Turnbull has to pay a royalty to my uncle!'

Drinks were passed round.

Katenga was not drinking much. He was thoughtful. Mathias Nkolola, the general secretary, said to him:

'You'd better get going. This chap, our boss can rough you up.'

He raised his eyes to the Conqueror as if to emphasize the point. 'He's very sensitive on this issue. No one who carries a PALP card can be allowed to get cocoa underground.'

'He's a sell-out!' exclaimed Katenga. 'You'll never have an African manager here if you carry on like this,' he said.

'No black will become manager. They'll mess it up with politics, politics of loafing. What these curs here want', Mpengula swept his aristocratic hand over the whole club, 'is money. And I get it for them. And it hasn't been necessary to strike for it. I just nod to Turnbull and it comes. Not this stupid politics business. There in town and here on the mine I and the white man must rule. Out there in the village we the chiefs and royal blood must rule. There's no room for jacks.'

It was too late for Katenga to get back to Musasa. So he kept up with Mathias Nkolola. They talked at length into the early hours.

'There's a serious rift in the leadership here, my friend. Mpengula is getting more drunk, more despotic. No one gets a job here these days unless he comes from his area. So they all worship him because out there he's the next chief. But make no mistake, he gets results and its results — money, eh? — which the people want.'

'I see,' said Katenga. 'I've been unemployed for some time now.

Do you think I care for work any longer? Why? Because working for the white man is working for slavery. You fellows here can bring the country to a halt. Everyone's crying for gold in the world. Kandaha is among the large producers of the stuff. Who gets the money? Whites. What do you get? Nothing. Just pennies. That's why Turnbull can afford to give them away to you.' He stood up. He was sober and serious. 'My friend, things are changing. I can see change in the air. A white man's politics my friend, are his stomach. If you could, for example, go on strike, every white man would run away. They did it in Zambia and now they're in control. Why don't you do it?'

'They tell us all is not well there. The Africans there have messed up production. They've messed up the market. No one wants to buy from black men. Even the former white man's guest houses. They tell us they're festering with bedbugs. They say it's not good for giving us more jobs.'

'That's only propaganda.'

'Strike. Strike for what?'

'There's lots of things wrong here, my friend. You blacks are stripped naked, even your anuses searched before you get down into the mine. You are searched again like pigs — as if you've swallowed a human child — when you come up. They don't do this to whites, do they? They don't even search them. If they suspect something, they simply X-ray them. Why not you?'

Mathias nodded slowly. Katenga had a captivating style of his own.

'But there's other things also.'

'What?'

'How can you even ask? As if they're not staring you in the face!' Why do you have to accept even these rations? Does the white donna get them? No. She's given money. They accept she's got a better brain than a baboon. So she can decide what she gets with the money. You? No, brother. You can't. Nor can your wife. So they give you four pints of *Munkoyo* (a local soft drink), sixty pounds of maize meal a week because you got three kids, twenty ounces of cocoa and six pounds of meat. Is that what you want?'

Nkolola said nothing.

'You think you're being done good. Are they doing the same thing by the white man? No way. Why? Because you don't rate. You'll accept everything. Why? Because you've shown the white man that's your worth. Not so? When did you not accept to work long overtime? Just when the Bwana who gets ten times as much is having the fun! When did you refuse to go underground, a death trap? Didn't they say to you, when you'd been underground minding a submersible pump that wouldn't behave itself, just, "Well done nigger"? Just that. And then when you came out, didn't they tell you to go straight out to the Kaffir change room because you "stank" so much? And even after that, didn't they say to their colleague who'd been giving you instructions down there as the swift under river current swept by, "Sorry you've had to spend so much time with blacks mending that pump"! And you say you've got no grievances?

'My friend,' continued Katenga, 'we Africans are exploited. We don't rate. You come from this area and maybe your great great grandfather knew there was this gold here a long time ago. Do they have a Nkolola Shaft here? No. Instead they have Elwyn Shaft, Norris Pump Station. The gold, do you see it? You just crush the ore. If they had their way these whites here, they'd make you crush it with your teeth to save money. We are cheap labour only. Unlike South Africa, their country, we don't see the gold here. The slimes are sent to South Africa so more white exploiters can have jobs and steal the gold. Why don't they put up a plant to finish everything here? When you shit here, do you go forty miles to Musasa to clean yourself? To tire out a fly you shit in two places. That's what they are doing to us. One thing being done in several places so we get tired of trying to find out what these whites are up to. That's why you must fight.'

'How?' asked Nkolola.

'How? Join PALP.'

'Here, I can't. Look at my children. They'll starve. Mpengula will fix any of us if we do, and he's liked and trusted by the Bwanas.'

'Then you must fight Mpengula. I listened to him this evening. He makes me sick. He treats you worse than animals. You must fight him. If I were here I'd have killed him a long time ago. He's the only black I'd be happy to. It would feel so much like digging my claws into white flesh. At least, challenge his leadership. Do anything, man. The party must be born here or we are finished. Norris, his railwaymen in Musasa and these white miners here are the same. That's why he's strong. That's why Baker fears him. Even an elephant, you can only fear it if it's carrying a tusk.'

Nkolola was feeling tired. He would be sitting in that metal chair — winding engine driver — for ten hours, come daylight. Until only a month ago, that job had been one of those reserved jobs which only a white man could do. It was a most responsible job and he knew it. He held the lives of so many people in his hands as he slowly tilted that handle and got the lift moving fast down VVIS (the Vertical Ventrical Incline Shaft). How satisfying it was to feel the men had arrived safely down to the twenty-sixth level. Until now, he'd never thought of those men, their lamps fixed on their helmets, as white and black. They had just been miners. But wasn't Katenga right? Can one forget a leopard is a leopard merely because it shares one's food? Or was he getting confused? He settled Katenga in his room. With two bedrooms, a kitchen and sitting room, the African miners were among the best accommodated in the country.

Later that night Nkolola dreamt a terrible dream. A leopard as large as an elephant was rifling into his intestines. As it did so, it was laughing and slapping him on the back convivially. Then he got frightened, ran and ran and yet seemed never to get away. He tackled the monster, shoved it into the lift at Elwyn Shaft, ran to his driver's seat and sent the lift wildly rocking down underground until the leopard in it was a smashed up mess of blood. Black hands, large black hands with fingers as large as legs, move in on his throat, from everywhere. They are just about to fork off his neck. He screams and the Conqueror's voice cries, 'I kill!' Mpengula's deep voice booms, 'Kill him!' Nkolola jumps up. 'Katenga! Katenga!' he calls out. Katenga has vanished.

A dream? Maybe it is a dream. Nkolola's head tilts. Snores. The large fingers are getting even larger. Together with the head and chest they become one large swollen body. The balloon. It distends. Nkolola grips his stomach. He can feel it swelling up also. He presses it in. A roar of thunder. The crack of lightning. Frothy rivulets of mud are cascading into the balloon. Mpengula's body is swelling, distending. It will split open. Oh, God! How awful. The glassy eyes reddened with drunkenness are bulging. Eyes as large as the head of a new baby. A liquid mechanical laugh rumbles through the balloon. Such a lifeless metallic laugh with no body to it. Then lightning strikes it. The room is on fire. Heavy fumes from the burning pig. Nkolola's hands fly to his head. Such a headache. He pinches himself. Only a dream . . . A cold wind blows. Nkolola breathes it in and with a heavy sigh he falls fast asleep.

I I

It is still the night of the twenty-fifth of May, also the evening of the Chainata Golf Club Dance.

Mrs Eckland was not much of a merry-maker. Even if she had been in her young hot days, she was now a little too old for that. And so was Mr Eckland. But tonight was an exception. They'd not been out to Musasa for many months now. Even if the neighbours at the Southern Estate of the BGS might call them names, and names only because they kept to themselves and lived within their means, Mr and Mrs Eckland, alias 'Mr Smokey Joe' and 'Mrs Nigger Biltong' now and again needed a breath of fresh air. Moreover, Mr and Mrs Turnbull, those ever so socially busy people, had invited some ten or so families from the estate to join them at the club dance. This was, of course, an unusual honour. If you were an employee of the BGS, being invited by its managing director was as good as a royal summons.

Before departing for the dance, Mrs Eckland surveyed the house. She liked everything to be where she wanted it to be. The ornaments in the sitting room were simple. But everyone of them had a story. There was the clock on the mantlepiece, for example. It had stayed so long because it had been so well cared for. It was in fact a simple Zobo clock. Mrs Eckland's mother had given it to her for the kitchen party. So many years ago, but it still worked. There was the ladle with which old mama used to scoop out the soup and pour it into the tiny bowls of her wee tiny children including the present Mrs Eckland. Mrs Eckland as she stood surveying her sitting room remembered her mother's advice when they were young ... 'Look after your things ... Don't break them up because they won't fight back ... A spoon kept well today means you won't buy another one tomorrow ... If only people looked after their things, there would be no profiteering. ...' She sighed with a silent contentment. The cookboy was in the kitchen. He had been with her ten years now, that is, ever since she came to the mine. He married only five years ago. She remembered helping his pretty little bride with the wedding dress and other things. Wasn't it fun? And yet other people say niggers are this and that and every month they are dismissing and taking on new servants! She would not part with her Jeke for anything. His wife regarded her as her mother.

She tiptoed to the kitchen.

'Jeke, Bwana and I are now going.'

'Yes, Donna.'

'You'll look after the house.'

'Yes, Donna.'

'How's the little one?'

'Very well, Donna.'

'Did she like that coat which I knitted for her?'

'Very much, thank you, Donna.'

'Good.'

Jeke looked at the Donna, his white chef's cap striking a rather ridiculous posture against his coal-black face:

'Donna,' he said. 'It's about my wife.'

'Yes, Jeke, anything the matter now?'

'She says she wants to leave me.'

'Why?'

'Someone has told her I'm leaving you.'

'You are not!'

'No, Donna, but someone says you want to dismiss me.'

'I'm not. But you haven't told me why your wife wants to leave you.'

'Well, missus, my wife knows only you. She says you are her mother because only you taught her everything good for a woman to know.'

'Yes.'

'And if I leave this place, she wants to stay and work for you.' He paused then said, 'Donna, I like working here and I love my wife. Maybe if what people are saying is not true you can let me continue here?'

Mrs Eckland laughed aloud. Such a simple and honest African was Jeke. He'd never stolen even a teaspoon of sugar. Where would one go in the whole world to get such a perfect servant?

Mr Eckland called from the sitting room:

'Liz, let's get moving.'

'Coming, darling,' she called back.

'Donna, it's just that what people say I saw also in the dreams.'

Mrs Eckland laughed again.

'What did you dream, Jeke?'

'Well, it's not very clear. But I dreamed I had no job.'

'Because I had sacked you?'

He shook his head in confusion.

'No, I don't remember. It is just that I had no job. I was out there in the bush. With no job. I looked for this cooking stove, it wasn't there. For this house, it wasn't there.'

'Come on now, Jeke. Tell your little wife, mama is not sending you away. You stay. She stays. Now, we must be off. Look after the house.'

'Yes, Donna,' said Jeke, greatly cheered.

They drove off in an old vintage VW. It had come fourth hand from the last owner. Old Mr Eckland had had it gone over himself before buying it. It had cost only £100. But then the mileage clock had gone round twice and no one had expected it to be a buy at £100. And yet it was still running. In fact, beautifully. He'd re-upholstered the inside so that unless you knew the history, you'd think it was a kid. If you were a Turnbull with a Nel and a Jim it might have reminded you of a villager way out in Petauke District of Zambia looking at a VW overtake a hundred-passenger capacity bus and exclaiming, 'Ah! Ah! That young car overtaking a whole big bus! What more when it grows up!'

Mr Eckland looked at Mrs Eckland.

'What a lovely little honey she is! Just like you!'

Mrs Eckland, laughed. She'd never had cause to regret her marriage to him. He always seemed to have that extra something for her. Take this VW business. Wasn't he saying she'd continued warm and strong and delicate in spite of age?

'Yes, darling,' she said, allowing herself a moment of sheer indulgence as she touched his sleeve. 'We've had it so long, haven't we?' Her eyes turned to him, 'And you've had me so long, you old owl.'

They both laughed. 'Owl' was a term of affection they'd each come to live with so that if anyone had come between them and said he or she's an owl they would each have said, 'Oh dear, dear, how charming!'

'Well girlie, you'll have to be on your best behaviour tonight. You'll have to watch young Mrs Turnbull. I gather she can be temperamental.'

'Ah darling, weren't we all temperamental at one time? Remember you couldn't do anything without me being in a flap about something or other, could you?'

Eckland drove on. One thing was sure, he could never be let down anywhere by the girl beside him with silvery hair. For a moment he allowed himself to think about their fate. If only they'd had children! The only one had died in an air crash in the RAF. But maybe this sense of mutual loss is what made them hang so close together. He drove on, enjoying every minute of her joyous prattle. The MD (managing director) had invited them. It's not as if he had invited all the white employees at the estate.

'You remember I read to you what the papers said about the MD. He's a great guy, isn't he? He's got guts too. Just imagine Turnbull telling the Governor where he got off. I thought that was cute and he did us proud.'

'Yes, he really did. But darling, I don't know. I kind of have a feeling that in that speech Turnbull sort of lumped himself and us together with the rest of them, especially Norris. Norris has never had a wife really, come to think of it. Nor has he really come across a good domestic minder like our Jeke. So it's easy for him to lump all blacks in the black group. But I'd have thought, well I don't know really because it's men's business, that Turnbull would have known better. It takes all sorts to make the world you know. And maybe it takes all sorts including these Kaffirs, you know.'

'Liz,' said the man, 'I don't know but I been thinking. I don't understand what the heck everything's about, but give me my plant I know damn well what's bloody wrong with it. I've been on this job donkeys years. But I don't know if we know what's goddam wrong with the Kaffir plant. And what's more I don't know if we know that somethin' could be wrong with us. It's like you say, honey, it's so bloody easy to call all niggers Kaffirs. But are they? So, I been thinkin'.'

'You remember what I told you about my last visit to the butchery before it was burned down. Ever so nice and what a tremendous man is Malherbe. But to do what he did to the black woman . . .'

'Utterly unforgiveable and that's why whenever I see Turnbull in the political headlines I feel like calling it a day.'

'You don't!' said Liz. 'Don't tell me you want us to leave the mine. It's so nice out there. Just peace. No nosy neighbours breaking through the fence, trusting servants and everything you can think of.'

'Liz, I would far sooner trust the African than these people. Turnbull, Norris, Baker, they'll never know what's hit them. You can't go on living off the fat of a decaying carcass. Sooner or later the carcass is bound to fester. And that's exactly what's happening. Justice is festering. There's less justice for the black now than there was six months ago. We'd better watch it because soon enough there won't be no justice even for us.'

They drove on in silence. Then Eckland said:

'Cheer up, sweetie.' Mrs Eckland did not seem so sure. Something seemed to weigh down on her mind. She thought of Jeke. **His** worries about the job. And yet what was he really getting out of it to keep his two kids fed? He had a right to expect this of society, didn't he? She thought about the man's obsession with his dream. No cooking stove. No house. What a ridiculous dream, yet Jeke seemed sold to it right down the middle!

The car laboured to negotiate an incline. Eckland's headlights picked up a figure flitting across the road some fifty yards away. He changed into the first gear. The old VW cried into it as if saying, '*Amama Eee* (My mother, oh)!' Another figure flitted across the road. Then before he knew it there was a heavy bang on the bonnet. A loud smash from the driver's side. The door was forced open. He screeched to a halt. A voice said:

'The keys. Give us the keys or you're fucked.'

Both Mrs and Mr Eckland could see a masked figure at Eckland's window. Then from nowhere a crowd of masked faces surrounded the car. They were horrible, deep tan, black masks with white teeth below the mouth set in a permanent snarl. She screamed and passed out.

'Keys,' said the man at the side window, 'or I shoot.'

Eckland gave him the keys.

'Now you get out. We know you're a good bloke. But you've never fought the system, have you? You're content to bask in its perfidy so long as you've got a job, aren't you? Quick or we'll burn you alive.'

Eckland got out. The man ran his fingers through Eckland. 'He's OK. Gag him. Eckland felt a hard blow. He was on the ground. Something hard was being driven into his mouth. The mouth filled as the jaws opened out.

'My wife!' he cried.

'If she's dead, she dies with the car. You whites keep all the money to yourselves. We'll teach you a lesson. Take all the money and valuables off them boys.'

The boys frisked them. They had £40 between them.

'Is that all?' asked the commander. 'They are a miserable lot. Where's the petrol?'

The man opened the bonnet. Another poured a four-gallon tin of petrol over the engine.

'Drag this woman out.'

Mrs Eckland was limp and heavy.

'She doesn't want to get out.'

'OK, slide her off the seat on to the ground.'

The man's voice felt tense and urgent.

In the crescent-shaped dining room at Government House the same night, Jefferson stretched his legs under the massive and highly polished mopani table. It had been a good evening and everything had gone so well. O'Flaherty was feeling the same. Considering all the stories that had gone on about the Governor and his prejudices against his own people, everything had indeed gone very well. And Lady Elwyn Baker, had she not been an excellent hostess? The sea-food balls had been an excellent hors d'oeuvres. The rich, brown roast duckling and the splash of orange on it had also been fantastic. Then there was the glowing lily-white Alaska pudding. And then the Irish coffee and cognac. The Governor had been charm itself. Jokes about everything.

It's funny, thought the Deputy Commissioner of Police, how the most lasting impressions we form of other people are always at secondhand. Here's this man for example, a full but firm small face, stubborn lines and a set chin. Sharp grey eyes that look as though they were trailing your every movement. A small compact little man, as though the Almighty had meant to get the utmost out of the raw material put into his construction. He gave you the impression of meanness. And people in Musasa talked and before you knew where you were, you believed them; you called him a nigger-lover, even though as Governor he was the Queen's representative. Night-man had come late as usual. He and the Governor had talked briefly. Then the Governor had left the room with him. When they had returned the Governor had appeared slightly ruffled. That had worried Jefferson and O'Flaherty. But since then, it had been charm and smiles.

Jefferson sipped his Irish coffee. He wiped the cream off his moustache. It was a good evening. He looked at his watch. It was 1 a.m. Was it not time to go? Just then the ADC to the Governor stood up and said above the noise of the chatter:

'Your Excellency, Lady Elwyn Baker, Ladies and Gentlemen, the ladies will now take their leave.'

Like one, the table rose, as Lady Elwyn Baker, her silvery curls catching the light, the jewels glinting and her whole person led by the sharp aristocratic nose, slithered through the vast dining hall, hugging her snow-white mink stole to her fulsome shoulders. Even at sixty, four years younger than His Excellency, she was still an elegant sight to behold. The ladies, some with indifferent thick ankles and bent with age, others lithesome and youthful, followed her into the Ladies Parlour. Those were the ladies who were the *de facto* rulers of the country. Some obdurate and uncompromising. Others self-effacing and blushing. But all with a ruthless flintstone determination that Jim, Jack or Tommy, whether limp or ambitious should be catapulted into the highest position in the land.

For Mrs Napier, whose husband was District Commissioner at Chiata, catapulting Mr Napier into the highest office meant tossing him up there into the Provincial Commissioner's chair and holding him down in it in case he should run away from its heavy responsibilities. For Mrs Nightman it meant Nightman becoming Commissioner of Police. She had always felt that he was the best man for the job. Did it matter that as a husband he was not really something hot enough to write home about? As for Mrs Thomson, who else but her man could succeed Baker? For Mrs Jefferson, catapulting her man into the highest office meant keeping him there as Commissioner of Police for ever and ever. She liked him best in his uniforms, looking beefy and brutal. Old though she was, there were times when she felt an orgasm coming whenever her 'lion' summoned his chiefs to his house and she saw him prancing up and down, baton in hand, scolding them. Was there anyone more important than her husband in the whole world?

Mrs Hughes le Bretton, the wife of the Secretary to the Cabinet, had no illusions about her husband. She was not a fool not to know that he required being coaxed out and into every situation. So diffident and almost unmanly, and yet he held easily the most important post in a land where the civil service still ruled. Le Bretton was the kind of man who would be the first to volunteer if the Governor said, 'For the success of the Queen's marriage we require one member of the Executive Council to be beheaded.' Always so devoted to duty, Mrs le Bretton had cause to know better, to know for instance that if the Archbishop of Canterbury banned sex, Le Bretton's manhood would not stir until the ban was lifted. So obliging, so devoted. Mrs O'Flaherty would not have minded her husband becoming Commissioner of Police. But really she had always felt that Chief Secretary would have been better. After all, it was not as if the post had been filled. Ever since Parnell had departed, the colonial office had not named a successor. No, she knew that although he had not been to Oxford, even for a visit, he could make the grade. It was his Irish background in a land of Englishmen which really let him down. Not to worry, she was saying to herself as she followed the other ladies. In God's own time.

With bleary eyes desperately trying to compose his head which he felt was feeling funny and kind of going round, O'Flaherty looked at the procession of long-gowned women making their exit. He looked at the youthful Mrs Jennings, wife of the Private Secretary, her bosom heaving as she held her long neck high and the golden-haired head turning to the rhythm of her hips. He sighed and then reluctantly trailed his eyes back to the head of the table where the Governor sat. Everyone, except the Governor, he discovered, had been trailing that last exit. He pulled together the lapels of his over-size evening suit towards his skinny chest, as if to say to the Governor, 'Mr Governor, sir. Ain't I the only fellow with you right now?'

'Gentlemen,' said His Excellency the Governor, as Mrs Jennings closed the door behind her, 'I have information to the effect that Kawala — or rather PALP — is preparing a massive campaign of retaliation against the Government, if Her Majesty's Government does not indicate quickly whether and when there will be a constitutional conference. In fact a secret meeting of PALP ended only two hours ago.'

O'Flaherty looked up violently. 'What meeting?' he would have interjected. After all, wasn't he supposed to know everything? If it was Nightman who had to inform, shouldn't he have told him first?

'The campaign could involve arson, civil disobedience and even murder.' His eyes stayed somewhat longer on Thomson as he looked round the group of twenty people there — all key men in the Government. 'Of even members of this Cabinet,' he said.

O'Flaherty looked at Nightman. 'Why the hell hadn't he informed me?' he was saying to himself.

'In the past, the African nationalists have issued threats, but they have been nothing more than threats. But there is evidence that they are now desperate and have, in fact, committed themselves fully to a new programme of violent action. Tonight, I am declaring a state of emergency.'

The Governor looked at his watch again and pressed the button on his side of the table. The door opened and the ADC brought in typed copies of an instrument. 'Declaration of a State of Emergency,' read the instrument.

'Government printer is now printing it out,' added the Governor absentmindedly.

The Commissioner of Police rammed on his glasses. States of

emergencies were serious matters. Everyone was reading the statutory instrument quietly. The Deputy Commissioner was also looking at his paper. He grunted, then becoming self-conscious, he looked up at the Governor. The latter was looking at him.

'Is there anything you disapprove of, Decompol?' he asked. Only a few minutes ago as the silver cutlery and copper fruit bowls glinted on the table, it had been 'John'. Now it was 'Decompol', and with that came up the Deputy Commissioner's old dislike of that stuffed little man sitting there as though he owned the whole world and they, little midgets.

'Who's told your Excellency about all these things?' asked O'Flaherty. His hands were trembling as he held the paper. 'I'm supposed to be responsible through Compol for emergencies,' he continued, all restraint gone and his temper rising. 'But I don't get told anythin'. That's the way it's been and I suppose will be.' His eyes flashed at Nightman. 'Who's going to implement this emergency business? S.B. or me? There's no indication here of what should be done. No detentions of people. Nothing. Just a State of Emergency. Meetings will, I s'pose go on as before. In short what are my orders?' Decompol grunted with disgust as his wooden frame slumped back into the chair. He was perspiring.

'Any more contributions?' asked the Governor, looking round the table and his fingers tapping the table impatiently at such a display of boorishness. Then, after a long silence, he said, 'There are to be no arrests of any kind. Everything should go on as before. The state of emergency simply gives the forces of law and order a framework within which to act speedily — if need be — and it had better be with my personal approval, Compol.'

'I'll see to that, sir,' said Jefferson.

'What if these spivs try to murder one of you? We must not act until we have your personal approval?' It was O'Flaherty leaning across the table, irreverently, his eyes narrowed and red.

'That, Decompol, is a straight matter of law maintenance,' replied the Governor sharply, 'and in any case I would then want to know why you have not been guarding the victim concerned.'

'Suppose I don't know of any threats to his life; am I expected to dissipate the small force of white men on guarding every member of the Government?' challenged O'Flaherty again.

'It's your duty to know where the danger lies, Decompol. When that happens, I'll hold you personally responsible.' Once again O'Flaherty's eyes flashed at Nightman. The classic struggle between the secret agent and the regular force was continuing.

'One further point,' said the Governor. 'I think you all ought to know that Her Majesty's Government is committed to granting the country independence in due course. You also ought to know that there may be a constitutional conference in the near future. Therefore,' he said, looking round, 'I don't want anyone rocking the boat.' Saying which, he looked in O'Flaherty's direction. 'Our duty as Her Majesty's Government is to ensure a smooth transition in political power. And that transition, gentlemen, is towards African rule because in accordance with the Balfour Declaration, we the British recognize the paramountcy of the native interest. Are there any questions?' asked the little man leaning over the table, his chin jutting out stubbornly.

'But as yet', he resumed after a while, 'neither Kawala, nor anyone else should be told of Her Majesty's clear intention until I have had categorical instructions to that effect. To do so would be to appear to act under duress in view of the threats already revealed to you. Her Majesty's Government', he said, sitting up and looking round the faces at the table, 'cannot be intimidated into capitulation. Any meetings anyone wishes to hold will be allowed. There will be no arrests in anticipation of disorder, no preventive detentions and above all, officers will go about their duties normally. If disorder breaks out,' he said, lifting his hand and then bringing it down on the table with a crash, 'then Kawala, Katenga or any of them will feel my weight, the weight of Her Majesty's authority.'

'Katenga!' exclaimed O'Flaherty.

'Yes,' said Baker, 'that's a new name to remember.' Then the Governor turned to Nightman, 'You should have informed Compol and Decompol about this.' It was a rebuke.

Abruptly he stood up. Everyone stood up.

'His Excellency will now leave,' announced the ADC after the little man prancing through the hall with a shambling indifferent gait. He stopped at the doors.

'By the way, Mr Jefferson, I want to know by 10.00 hours this morning exactly how many guns have been sold to what and which Europeans in the last forty-eight hours.'

'Europeans, sir?' asked Jefferson, stiffening to attention.

'Yes.'

The double doors swung open. The ladies in the other room stood up and joined their husbands and with Lady Baker standing beside him, Sir Elwyn bid the guests goodbye. He was smiling and radiant as he thanked them for coming. The Deputy Commissioner of Police felt, as he beefed away his dear one to the waiting chauffeur-driven car, like a thin pig bereft of its innards. Jefferson and his wife lingered on a little. Gentleman that he was, he wanted to apologize to the Governor for his subordinate's conduct.

Kawala had reached his home after the confrontation with Lafayette. His wife was still awake. The eldest boy had not returned. He'd gone off in a huff. He'd wanted two shillings from Mummy for a movie show down town. Mummy didn't have it.

'But Johnny's Mummy give him two shillings.'

'His father works. Yours doesn't.'

'Can Johnny pay for me, Mummy?'

'No, your father does not approve of begging.'

'But Mummy, last month Johnny paid.'

'It's too late now in any case.'

The boy had remained standing. Mummy had looked at him then she had gone into the small kitchen and cried. Why did her children have to lack so much? No shoes. Torn shirts. Scraggy bodies. Always picking up what other children left behind. And always the other mothers laughing at her saying, 'Your husband's a loud-mouthed loafer.'

The boy had said:

'Why should we suffer?'

'Dad doesn't work, Mulenga.'

'It's not right children should wear rags, Mummy. Have people point at us: your father good for nothing loafer. It gives me no pride being son of Kawala, Mummy.'

'Shut up!' had rasped Mulenga's mother.

'I have no father. No pride. He's not a good man. If he was a good man he would be home some time. I hear your tears, tears crying for a man . . .'

'Children don't say that!'

'You couldn't have come earlier?' says Kawala's wife.

'No.'

'Politics, was it?'

'Yes, I'm afraid.'

' "Yes, I'm afraid." That's always what you say. And you think I'll go on believing it?' She turned away from him. 'There are stories about your colleagues with whom you go to these strange midnight meetings. Why not you?'

'What are you saying, woman?' Kawala's anger of Father Lafayette returned.

'Exactly what I've said. Katenga for example, you know his background. How does he treat Delia? Does he even remember his child? Is it not a new woman every day? And you expect me to wait and wait and wait for a man who is a stranger to his own house, to his own children. You will find these children murdered. Will independence still be worthwhile with all these children dead?' She turned to look at him in the face. 'My husband, I sometimes ask myself, "Why me?" ' Her voice was no longer a high-pitched scream of anger. She moved towards him. Outside the cocks were crowing and the darkness was lifting. 'I remember the day when I married you. Not the marriage of the village that can last for ever or not last. But the marriage of the church. I wore those beautiful white clothes. And you in your fresh clothes. You touched my finger and you put that ring which the priest lent you on it. You said I was yours, you would keep me and protect me till death parted us. You added, "even after death".'

Her eyes looked into the low flat roof of the little room blackened from the smoke from the wooden kitchen. They were wild distracted eyes. Kawala looked into them. He picked out the heavy lines on her face. He picked up the worry in them, the worry of uncertainty about the children, food to feed them, about himself. He reached out for her hands. They were cold as though she had not slept, waiting for him. They were small and terribly hard hands. They almost felt like coarse sand paper. There were the blisters turned into hard corns.

'Then you took me in your hands, these hands which made me feel so warm. I could have crossed any rough river with you, dared even lions, risked people's gossip. I said to myself, "I will bear him ten, twenty, thirty children. Just like himself".' She lowered her voice, 'And then he will build me a house, a little round hut and all our children will come and live around us. Their wives too, their husbands, their children . . .' Her face had taken on a celestial visage as she lost herself in the make-believe of this idyllic vision. She focused her eyes. The dream had been shattered. Tears rained down her cheeks. 'And now this is what I have. No father to look after me. No father to look after my children. All other women have husbands who stay with them. Not me. Why me?'

She leaned forward on to his breast. He embraced her. She shook with sobs. His heart pained. It was as if someone had bared his chest, not taken the heart out, but passed his bare chest over and over a blazing fire so that not only the heart could feel the pain, but also the nerves and arteries connecting it to the body and the rest of it.

'My wife, I wish you would understand.' He looked into her eyes. She looked up at him. Her eyes were reddened from weeping. 'I love you. You are my gift. You and the children.' His voice became husky. 'I love you,' he repeated.

Her face suddenly glowed and the same proud confidence that had shone in her eyes that wedding day so many years ago, consumed it. Kawala's heart jumped with joy. The pain had melted away and only joy filled his heart. She said:

'Go on. Don't give up.'

'You mean it?'

She nodded her head.

'My wife!' he exclaimed.

'My husband,' she gasped.

The roof was a sooty blackness against the candle flame. But in her mind's eye she could see bright stars whirling around her and floating up into the sky. . . . They lay down. Like one struck by lightning, Kawala fell off into a deep slumber.

His wife jumped up.

'What's the matter?' she asked, shaking him. Kawala was in a dream. . . . His body was strapped to a tree. Coffin after coffin was passing across his face as if on a conveyor belt. Some were expensive black mahogany coffins, polished in a deep tan. Others were simple coffins of light packing wood. Then there were bundles of dismembered bodies wrapped up in blood-soaked, black shrouds. A strong stench wafted to his nostrils. But a loud voice shouting above the din of the trundle of the coffins was saying, 'This is your work, Kawala. This is your carpet to the throne. You cannot close your eyes to this scene now, Kawala, because even the eyes in your mind will still see. See the rows upon rows of coffins and the parcels of your own people's bodies. See the chunks of meat, riven off. See the gouged eyes, the amputated limbs. These, my son, are the people you have killed.' Then the voice rose higher and higher as the coffins trundled across Kawala's face, ever faster. 'Kawala, Kawala,' it cried, 'you reign over a graveyard.'

A blood-stained coffin stopped before him. The liquid mass under the cloth moved, sidled towards him until it was only a few feet away from him.

'Open it!' shouted the voice. 'Open it! Here's a chisel.' 'No, no, no!' cried Kawala. He tried to break away but the straps of wire around his chest and arms cut deep into his flesh. He winced at the pain. 'Open it! Open it!' yelled the voice in a frenzy. Loose now and trembling, Kawala pried off the coffin lid. A blood-bespattered face with a hollow bullet wound through one eye, glared at him with a bare-toothed fixed gaze. It was his late brother's face. He screamed, 'Let me go! Let me go!' 'You cannot go,' commanded the voice in the hollow echo. 'Unless your own is touched by this plague, yours will only be a public sorrow. But now you see it,' said the voice in a suddenly deep vanishing tone.

Kawala wrenched violently at his bonds. But the tree trunk bending over his head held him firm in its wide talons. Frantic with fear he yelled again and again, 'Leave me, leave me!' and with one desperate effort he tore himself away. . . . That is when he found his foot caught in a tear in the old blanket and his body soaked in perspiration.

'Sleep,' said his wife, calming him and wiping the perspiration from his forehead.

But the words, 'Unless your own is touched by this plague, yours will only be a public sorrow. But now you see it,' kept recurring in his mind. These were the self same words Lafayette had uttered. What would be involved? Would there be rows upon rows of coffins? If so, would the blood of all these people be upon his shoulders? He wiped off the perspiration from his sunken chin. Again he felt lonely, so lonely that he said to his wife:

'Come, please I need you.'

Again, like one struck down, he fell off into a deep slumber. It was 3 a.m. now, May the twenty-sixth.

12

It is 3 a.m., May the twenty-sixth. O'Flaherty screamed into the telephone:

'What? Where? No! Good God! When? You nut! Gathering storm indeed! You've informed *your* Compol and the Governor? And what have they done? Nightman, you'll pay for this. I'll get you sacked. At once! You're sacked at once! And I don't care what Baker says. I'm sending your relief at once. Surrender all keys to safes, offices, at once and don't you bloody move. Christ Almighty!'

His wife asked:

'What's happened, Dick?'

'Bloody shit!' said the Decompol. 'That's what it is. Bloody shit! Natives murdering, looting, raping and I can't stop it. Hell!' he cried.

'What are you talking about? asked Nightman.

'Burnt to ashes, do you hear? Turnbull's mad — and so he should be. Norris is mad an' I'm mad I tell you!'

A moment later, O'Flaherty picked up the telephone again. He dialled a number and when the other man picked up his receiver, O'Flaherty said:

'Decompol here. Decompol here, I say. Listen Fitzwilliams and stop yawning. Is all this stuff about a Mr and Mrs Eckland being burned to death true? Don't ask me where. Right there under your nose. What d'you mean you haven't heard? Your bright lad Nightman's brim-full of the news. I reckon he's awakened H.E. by now, so he'll be first with the news. . . . Well, you'd better find out what the hell it's all about. Or else I will. In the meantime, get the paras to Two One Four and I want a report in five minutes' time. What? Never mind my sleep. Mind your job because unless you can give me a report you're sacked. D'you understand? Sacked. Sacked, you bloody good-for-nothing jelly brain. Murder under your nose and you don't know it. If you think you can make a fool of me, you're bloody well mistaken. It's me that's got to survive. Not you!' Decompol chewed at his cigarette, spat it out into the receiver grunting, 'You're sacked. You're just hiding the native murderers. That's all you're doing. Not so, mister? I'll fix you. You're fired. . . fired! Do you hear me, jelly brain?' O'Flaherty sighed, replaced the receiver noisily and stamped away in the lifting dawn, mumbling, 'Whites've been burned by blacks. Nightman twenty miles away here in Musasa can get the news and not I, Decompol. And all because my top aide in the area is asleep. Christ Almighty!'

The telephone by the Commissioner's bedside rang. He turned the other side and drew the blankets over his head. The shrill metallic ring persisted. Every fresh ring sounded like the burst of cannon.

'Pick up that thing, darling,' said his wife, turning in her sleep. Jefferson threw his blankets off. He wore no pyjamas and his well-rounded stomach which always made him look as though he was about to give birth to a large football, jutted out in the general direction of the 'phone, which was on the other side of the bed. He leap-frogged his wife to the other end of the bed. His stomach scraped her mouth. She exclaimed:

'What's that?' and hit hard into it.

He located the instrument and said:

'What the hell's all this in aid of? Who's speaking? Decompol? What's happened? What? What . . .' Jefferson rubbed his eyes. He was now fully awake. He remembered that he had been to a dinner only a few hours ago.

The Commissioner paced up and down the bedroom. The Governor was not given to being interrupted. Should he ring the Governor? Why should he bother about it at all? It was because of Elwyn's attitude that all these things were happening. He felt angry, angry at this bungling amateur sent out from nowhere to preside over Kandaha. He picked up the receiver and dialled Government House. The telephone rang on and on but there was no reply. Then there was a giant croak at the other end and a voice said:

'Elwyn here.'

'I want to speak to His Excellency. It's urgent,' said the Commissioner.

'H.E. here. Is that Dave?' asked the voice. The voice was calm and collected, almost as if it was 10 a.m. Jefferson hesitated.

'Yes Dave. Can I help you? I'm sorry you're up so early. Is there anything the matter?'

Compol, feeling the calm in the Governor's voice felt awkward. But in that moment he remembered what Decompol had just said to him . . . 'Everything's the matter. Whites've been burned by blacks, PALP spies, the very people who you say are going to run this country. And I can't act against them 'cause you say they're holy. Holy savages. And I'm supposed to be responsible for law and order. I tell you Compol, it's all your fault. Just tell me what the hell do I do now? Stand my fellows down and go to church to thank the Lord for this great favour? And wait for all whites to be got rid of until there's only yourself, the Governor and Nightman? You're mistaken. I have got to move in right now. Nightman's gone. I've sacked him. Your sweet boy at BGS is gone too. I've sacked him. From now on you can tell the Governor I keep law *my* way and not his way until *he* learns to keep it the Queen's way. An' I don't care about the consequences. Law breakers are law breakers even though they may be native. . . .'

The Governor hung on, waiting for him to reply. Then he repeated the question:

'Can I help you Dave? Is there anything the matter?'

Compol at the other end of the telephone, tugged at his stomach and then replied:

'PALP have murdered a white couple, Mr and Mrs Eckland.'

There was a momentary silence on the other end. Then:

'You mean the Africans have killed Europeans?'

If he had been O'Flaherty, Compol would have cut in and said, 'Do I speak Hebrew?' That's just what O'Flaherty had said to him. But he restrained himself and merely said:

'Yes.'

The man on the other end of the line bit at his lip with impatience. Then he said:

'Compol come up here at once.'

It was three-thirty in the morning.

Jefferson had hardly walked into the Governor's office and sat down when the telephone exploded into life.

'This is the limit, Your Excellency.'

It was Norris. The little Governor had taken the trouble to dress since saying to Jefferson, 'You must come up at once.'

Her Majesty's evening business could not be transacted otherwise than in, at least, a pin-striped black suit.

'A white couple's been murdered. Do you know about it?'

Sir Elwyn Baker stood up slowly. His grey eyes flashed fire.

'Yes,' he said, 'And do you mind?'

'I'm not putting the phone down. I want an answer. What are you doing about it?'

Sir Elwyn looked in the direction of Jefferson. Jefferson stood up.

'Where's our protection?' asked Norris.

'Sir Ray, you're just a trouble shooter, a damn despicable racialist!'

Ray Norris glared into the receiver. His bulldog forehead wrinkled and he said:

'I've warned you already. We've got the money and now it's gotta be a showdown. If you've ammunition, don't spend it protecting us whites. Spend it on shooting us to protect your niggers.' Norris replaced the receiver noisily. He picked up the 'phone again, dialled a number and said, 'Like I was briefing you earlier, all systems are go.'

Simon Malherbe, unemployed since the Bristol Gold Syndicate butchery débâcle, felt his gun. Nudging Joan in the ribs he whispered into her sleeping form.

'Now, it's us or your niggers, sweetie.'

Kawala was still dreaming. . . . Now he was in an icy-cold lake. An eel trembling with electric fire was creeping towards him. He flapped his arms helplessly against the cold water. He was sinking. Nothing could save him now. Then the water suddenly heated up. The cold eel turned warm. Someone was saving him. Was it hands? The soft warm fleshy hands turned like a spit. There was a momentary flash of fire. Iron clamps gripped his wrists. A voice with a face capped over in mobile unit police riot kit said, 'I arrest you.' 'For what?' he heard himself ask. 'What's the charge?'

'No charge. But what do you expect if you murder Europeans?' It was a thick black voice. It was a dream . . .

An hour later, O'Flaherty rang the Musasa Central Police Station. They had bagged Kawala. He replaced the receiver and laughed with the gleeful laughter of a hyena. His wife moved in her sleep. With the warmth of a man who had fulfilled himself, he nestled to her.

Eight a.m., Friday morning. A grinding rumble rose in the background. The proud tones of 'God Save the Queen' took the air. The firm voice of Sir Elwyn Baker said, 'Good morning.' Santasa listened. He turned up the volume. The voice on the radio continued:

'Over the past few months, the African political organization known as the People's Army of Liberation Party (PALP) has pursued a policy of increasing terrorism in its attempt to force Her Majesty's Government's hand to grant this colony of Kandaha unqualified and immediate independence.'

Santasa opened the door, and called out to Katenga who was sleeping in the kitchen of his little Hut No. 200 Samaka Compound — a tenant for the night.

'The Governor,' he whispered to Katenga.

'This terrorist activity has taken many forms. But what is the point of my narrating in full the macabre story of violence which clearly shows evidence of a carefully organized murder incorporated association of ruthless and dangerous fanatics who will spare no life, especially that of their own black people, in their quest for illusory power?' The Governor's voice was charged with emotion. 'Last night two Europeans were cold-bloodedly murdered, in the inferno of their car, whose flames consumed them beyond recognition.'

Santasa exclaimed: 'Ah!'

Katenga stubbed into the air with his fist.

'They were white and British. But that is not the point. The point is that once again violence has claimed another victim.'

The voice rose higher. Santasa held his breath. Would the Governor go on to ascribe the murder to PALP? Would the Queen's representative anticipate the decisions of Her Majesty's Courts of Justice?

'The majority of our citizens, black and white, want nothing but peace,' resumed the Governor. 'Peace to live out their lives under the protection of the law. This peace is being denied them now and it is not a self-respecting Government which fails to guarantee them this peace. It is not for me to comment on matters that are *sub judice*. But it is my duty as Governor of this colony of Kandaha to draw the attention of the people of this country and outside, to the tragedy now in hand, to the sustained campaign of intimidation, proven murder, for which some members of this political party have been convicted by due process, and the wanton pillage that has tried to establish the law of the jungle upon this, Her Majesty's domain. This campaign will achieve the black people of this country nothing. Her Majesty's Government refuses to be intimidated. In the face of this hooliganism let me tell the peace-loving people of this country that they have nothing to fear as maximum protection will be accorded them.

'To the perpetrators of lawlessness, I say that the fangs of law and order are drawn and that from now on this will be no land for criminals. It only remains for me to warn the leaders of a certain political party — they are all still at large by the good grace of Her Majesty's Government — to show that they can establish discipline among the rank and file of their followers. Unless they can show strength and can control and restrain the lunatic fringe within their party, Her Majesty's Government will have no alternative but to proscribe this party and bring to justice these power-hungry and misguided men.' He paused. The rustle of paper came through over the radio. 'I have banned all rallies of the People's Army of Liberation Party, PALP. I have also banned all political meetings of that same party until further notice.

'For some time now, I have watched with increasing concern the unwholesome and irreligious activities of a self-styled religious sect called the Holy Ones. This sect's teachings are unacceptable to a community with civilized Christian standards. The sect preaches racialism of the most idiosyncratic nature and represents a source of dark savagery and superstition in a world of bright moral promise. I have banned its assemblies. From now on any member of our society belonging to this sect or attempting to further its cause will be guilty of association with an illegal organization.

'God Save the Queen.'

Elwyn Baker was the product of a Welsh Village School. His father had been a coal miner before the war. During the war in which he enlisted, he rose to the rank of Captain in spite of his background and through sheer ability. He would have risen even higher except for an unfortunate illness which led to his being boarded by the Army Medical Board. Fortunately, for him and as happened with a few of the luckier soldiers, he was given an army scholarship to Oxford where he got a double first in PPE. As a student at Oxford he became interested in socialism. Those were the days of the socialist greats like Aneurin Bevan, Clement Attlee and others. The Labour Party had just formed its first post-war Cabinet.

That was why Elwyn Baker found himself a member of that rare breed of people called the British Foreign Service, an organization which without the reforms of the Labour Party, he would have found difficult to get into. He had been only six months in the Foreign Service when his special administrative ability was recognized and he was posted out as a District Commissioner in the then British Somaliland. That had been an exceptional feat − to rise from nowhere and become a DC without ever having been a cadet and then a District Officer first. From there his rise had simply become unstoppable. A Provincial Commissioner of a province in Somaliland, Chief Secretary in Kenya, Governor of the Leeward Islands and now Governor of Kandaha.

But if there was one posting which had prepared him most for the business of dealing with African independence pressures and the pressures of white settlers, it was his assignment in Kenya. Now, as he read with astonishment a top secret report from Nightman which the Private Secretary brought into his office immediately after returning from the Bristol Gold Syndicate dinner, his mind kept going back to Kenya, to the simple and uncomplicated origins of one of the most serious events of British Colonial history — the Mau Mau uprising. That event had only been possible as a result of the distortions and misinterpretations of officials — especially Special Branch. He wondered, as he sat in the office popularly known as the Oval Office of Government House, and read that report, whether something like the Mau Mau might be in the offing. If it was, then the African nationalists would be making a great mistake because he was ready to deal with them. He raised his eyes and started reading the report again.

Finally, His Excellency the Governor set the report down. He sighed with anger, anger that a report so urgent was only being brought to his attention with only one day to prepare. He picked up the receiver and pressed a red button.

'Tell Nightman I want him at once.'

Sir Elwyn brushed back his neat pile of silvery grey hair. He was still an agile, well-preserved little man with a terrific presence of mind and an indefatigable patience for listening. He neither smoked nor drank much beyond a sherry before dinner and an occasional glass of wine which he would nurse delicately through the dinner. He had strong views on the colonial civil servants in Kandaha. He thought a lot of them 'plain, stupid and unimaginative' and for a man who spoke very little, words of such heat always stuck in the white officials' minds.

He stood up from his high backed chair, bearing the insignia EIIR and a crown embossed in gold. When seated in that chair, the crown rested lightly on his silvery head. Now he was pacing up and down the office lined with pictures of the Royal Family, thinking.

Tomorrow was the day of the funeral of the late Mr and Mrs Eckland. Nightman was briefing the Governor, Thomson, Jefferson and O'Flaherty at Government House. Whites, the country over were in an ugly mood.

'Especially so here in Musasa and at BGS. They're unhappy about the time it's taking the courts to deal with the murderers and . . .'

The Governor, Elwyn Baker, looked up.

'I mean the suspects,' Nightman corrected himself. 'Norris' Front has laid on a large symbolic funeral. Almost certainly the fox will find an occasion for a public speech. What's he likely to say? He'll almost certainly chide us for laxity in law enforcement.'

The Governor once again looked up. He was fretting with his fingers. Lines of sleeplessness could be seen on his face.

'Does he want the law of the jungle? He's got it then,' he hissed and let Nightman continue.

'In the last few days Norris has been under pressure to show his teeth.' Said one critic, "We're tired of the snarl." His opponents want him to launch the Home Guard formally to assure whites of protection. Norris has as good as done that, but, of course, he knows the law of treason and has stopped just short of it. But he might, and it could be awkward to do anything at such a time.' Nightman darted his eyes at O'Flaherty and said, 'Decompol has experience of this.' O'Flaherty could have sworn at him. 'Unfortunately, Your Excellency, the situation is even more alarming than this. There is evidence that a number of officers in our Police Force would go along with Norris.'

'No!' exclaimed O'Flaherty. 'That's a fabrication!'

'It isn't, you know,' Nightman was calm. 'I could show H.E. the list and they are all fairly well-placed men. The miners at BGS would be solid Norris men and the safety of the installations there must be a matter for concern. Turnbull's been appraised of this aspect but, like Norris, he's got a stream of invective for an answer and no action. It may be necessary to move the police in there for the length of the day even though the funeral takes place here.'

Elwyn Baker snatched off his glasses. He looked around the oval office. Then at Nightman and asked:

'The Africans. You haven't told us about them.'

'Them? Not much to tell. They're still cowed down by all that's happened, Your Excellency. Kawala's bunch were not involved, so we released Kawala, but we're keeping Kawala and his merry men under close surveillance. We must not forget that they have no guns and this is not their funeral.'

'Tell me, Nightman, is there any Rhodesian involvement in Norris' party?'

'Plenty, Your Excellency. Our border with Rhodesia is wide open. You only have to get into a canoe and you've got the guns. And even men. Rhodesia is, of course, doing everything possible to strengthen Norris' hand. In the last week, there have been at least four telephone calls between the chairman of the party there and Norris. But we are watching the situation.'

'Are you ready?' The Governor turned sharply on Jefferson.

'Yes, Your Excellency.'

'I don't want any trouble. But if necessary, shoot.'

'Shoot Europeans?' It was O'Flaherty.

Elwyn Baker nodded.

'Or anybody else who makes trouble. You might just leak the word to Norris.'

When they rose, Elwyn Baker retired to his library. In the last two months or so he had become a very disillusioned man. He could see the clouds descending thick upon Kandaha. But what could he do? Advice after advice for a settlement of the political question. But Her Majesty's Government had remained indifferent. They had a name for him out there in Whitehall. 'Little Panic.' They said he panicked so much. Only a month ago a sharp rebuke had come through from Whitehall. 'Demonetization of gold doesn't mean gold is now useless.' He had telexed back angrily, 'If HMG wants the gold, they'd better send soldiers over.' A fairly lowly placed official in the Colonial Office had telexed back, 'Try telling that to an African President out there and we will have the whole OAU on our necks. Stop.' That telex had sent poor Baker raving mad. Impetuous Welsh, he had left immediately for London. With a great deal of difficulty, he had managed to see the Prime Minister. Old Tom Caput had come up the party tree every inch. As solid as stone he had never given anyone cause for accusing him of being too clever by half — or even clever.

'Your Excellency, we can't afford to let go of Kandaha. Not a country with a gold mine turning out one and a half million tonnes of ore per annum and carrying twenty-three grams per tonne. This is big business and our friends in the City would not buy it. Don't forget there's an election next year and fat capitalists though they may be, we depend on their vote. Every vote.'

'Mr Prime Minister, something has to give. We've got a classic UDI situation brewing up in Kandaha now. We haven't got an army. Only a police force. The Europeans can overrun the country any time. And that's exactly what they will do if we don't move or make it clear that the majority will have to govern. That's how we lost Rhodesia.'

'We didn't lose Rhodesia,' says Caput. 'In fact we regained it. Any country in Africa firmly in the hands of British settlers is on our side. We lost too much in Zambia. Just think of it. Three hundred million pounds worth of foreign exchange reserves just passed on to the Africans like that. And do you know what else? They even had the cheek to come back, expropriate the BSA's mineral rights. No,' says the Premier, 'Kandaha's too rich to be independent. If we quit, the commies will be down there in no time. You don't want that, do you?'

'But . . .', Elwyn Baker is confused, 'your party policy.'

Tom Caput laughs. He's got such a genial laugh has the Prime Minister of Great Britain. They call him 'Little Greener,' because every time he laughs he shakes his head so much and lowers it as if he was grazing down a village green.

'You've obviously not thought deeply about us Your Excellency. We British are a strange people. There's only one political party here. But we have more than two labels for it. Whether we are the People's Party or the Middle Party or the Great Party, our castle is our home. Home for us still means raw materials from Africa. We lost political power in all those countries except Kandaha. Aid is proving a useful leverage for raw materials. But aid is expensive and I'm damned if we'll let Kandaha go. Just think Your Excellency, without Kandaha what would happen to us?'

'My firm recommendation is that you should call a constitutional conference and decide the independence issue.'

'We've watched our friends go through all that. Frankly, if we had to give independence, we'd do it without any conference. After all what were the objectives of these constitutional conferences? They were meant to devise arrangements for protecting the white minority in predominantly black countries. Which independent black country still protects the white man's position? None. They've all removed any protection clauses.'

'The future. What's the future?'

'Well,' says the Premier standing up and offering Baker his hand, 'It's been nice meeting you, Your Excellency. Frankly we all know this Kandaha business will be an embarrassment and maybe we should be doing what you recommend. But give us time to think. Rome was not built in a day, was it?' Then, his eyes peering wizedly through the lowered glasses, he says, 'I had a doctor friend once. A very good fellow indeed. Pity he's dead. He used to say, "Tom, politics is like medicine. Don't break the boil until it has a head." What's happening in Kandaha is really nothing. Don't forget our friends in South Africa are shooting it out in Soweto. They're not giving in and maybe they'll win. I hope Lord Ventrical doesn't get round to knowing what we've discussed. The House of Lords would be up in flames. I believe you're lunching with him.'

That had been all. And now, what was happening? Norris was moving in. Turnbull was again publicly warning of economic chaos. Through Ventrical in London, he had a strong lobby in the City.

On more than one occasion influential men there had demanded the withdrawal of the Governor. Baker knew it. It wasn't secret anyway. Thinking back over his socialist origins, Baker wondered whether all the sweat to keep intact Her Majesty's Empire — or what remained of it — was worth all the trouble. What did that empire really mean? It meant tight control by the moneyed people in the City. He had tucked himself heart and soul into all his appointments in his career. Each assignment had had so much meaning for him — the maintenance of law and order, establishment of clinics and schools. These were the things that brought satisfaction and made life worthwhile. But what was worthwhile about the way things were moving in Kandaha? Had he worked so hard all this while just to pave the way for whites? He knew them all — the kings in waiting. The Norrises and the lot. What instinct except that for self-survival did they really have? And to talk of people like that as protectors of civilization? He was damned if he would allow a UDI. He was damned if he would allow the black demagogues to carry the day either. Her Majesty's Government would do the right thing at the right time. But who was that Her Majesty's Government? Then as he thought of Tom Caput sitting there in No. 10 Downing Street, oblivious of the swift current of events in spite of the many colonies Britain had lost, at times even giving the impression he didn't even know where Kandaha was, Baker felt like spitting with disgust. But Her Majesty's Personal Representative could not do that. Instead, he hissed:

'Politicians!'

13

On the morning of the funeral, the Government had put out a warning which was being repeated every thirty minutes on *Radio Kandaha*.

'Members of the public, especially Africans, are warned that the country is still in a state of emergency. No rallies are allowed and police will deal firmly with any gathering of people beyond twelve.'

But PALP head office was also a hive of feverish activity. As with the previous night, the men knew they were buying time.

At the Cathedral of Divine Providence there was no standing room. The two wreath-bedecked coffins were being brought in. Norris and Turnbull were at the head of the procession. The pall bearers followed. They were down-looking men, men on whose faces were still the heavy marks of surprise that what had happened had ever happened. Old Eckland, a fitter on the mine, who had never offended anyone in his life. And such a quiet warm old couple. Was this their reward for such a long, faithful service? Why did it have to happen to them? Lepton at the top of the pall bearers was asking the question. There was no answer. So he trudged on. There wasn't much weight to the coffins. They said the Ecklands had not deserved to die, dying like robbers being burnt on the stake! It was a case of mistaken identity. That was the story that was beginning to get round. A white man owning a Volkswagen exactly the same colour as that of the Ecklands had not paid his servant for four months. The servant, a young man of twenty, was about to get married. He had paid part of the lobola (dowry) — five pounds. The girl's uncle was threatening to call it off. Then he borrowed from a friend. The friend became impatient when he wouldn't pay. He said he had a gang that would bump him off if he didn't pay. And from there things happened. And now the wrong people had died.

Fr Lafayette knew the couple well. He used to visit BGS now and again to say Sunday Mass. Funny how only a week before his death old Eckland had said to him, 'If only one could be sure of a priest like you by his death bed!' He did not normally say Mass in that Cathedral of Divine Providence. Priests who served the blacks generally stuck with the blacks. But today was different. Some white Catholics at BGS had especially asked for him to say the Requiem.

Then the Mass started. At Gospel time, Lafayette paused to look at the two coffins. A solitary tear ran down his cheek. He had known the old couple very personally. Forcing sorrow out of his voice, he said:

'A reading from the Holy Gospel according to St John. Chapter 11, Verses 21–27. I am the resurrection and the life.

'Martha said to Jesus, "If you had been here, my brother would not have died, but I know that, even now, whatever you ask God, He will grant you."

' "Your brother," said Jesus to her, "Will rise again." Martha said, "I know he will rise again at the resurrection on the last day." Jesus said, "I am the resurrection. If anyone believe in Me, even though he dies, he will live and whoever lives and believes in Me will never die. Do you believe this?" "Yes, Lord," she said, "I believe that You are the Christ, the Son of God, the one who was to come into this world."

'This is the Gospel of the Lord.'

Lafayette preached on the immortality of the soul.

'Death is the necessary accident for the soul to be set free for its eternal life. If God had not decreed death for Man, He would not have created him. God created us for eternal life. The gateway to that eternity is death.' Then he said, 'The seeds of death are in our birth. In the African way of life, when a child is born and the umbilical cord is cut, the grandmother goes to bury it under a special tree.

'Man's appointment with death, with the soil out of which he came, is thus confirmed. So let us harbour no malice against those that may cause death. Let us only harbour love, warm love for them, the love that bespeaks forgiveness and not revenge. For let us not forget that He that had no cause to be sinned against was crucified on the cross by Man, Man who forfeited his right to eternal life through the sin of Adam and Eve, Man who continues, as though that condemnation was not enough, to sin again and again, over and over. The real death is not the death of the body, it is sin, the death of the soul. Let us forgive for we ourselves like Magdelan, have much need for forgiveness. Let us love for we ourselves need love.' Fr Lafayette stopped. He was trying to smother a sob. But his voice, broken and feeble, rattled through his body. 'Ecklands, of all the people that I have known, you deserved what has happened to you least. Your slaying, burning, murder, is the product of the sickness that has beset our society and made us prisoners. Forgive us. Forgive us.' The voice faded into a whimper. Women bowed their heads to sob into their headscarves. Sir Ray Norris sat impassively, his chin jutted out like a boxer egging on his victim. His black funeral suit was more crumpled than was normal of his clothes. He was, that day, the embodiment of the white man's sorrow, rage, anger at the dastardly and cowardly act of the Africans.

After the service, the long cortège rode to the graveside. Sir Ray's time had come. He coughed, looked at the congregation and said:

'I wish I could say to you things of morality and not things of truth. I wish that truth could not be that the Ecklands died because they were my colour,' he bared his arm before them all, 'your colour, and the colour of all of us cursed by the Colonial Government, by the black man whom we faithfully look after, never to be given the challenge of bringing peace and comfort to life being lost and peace being enraged. We are, and have always been, the black man's keeper. But now, behold', he raised his hands towards the funeral pyre, 'that which we were ordained by the Almighty to keep has turned its hand against us.

'Turned its hand not to say, "Enough care is enough," but to . . . slay us, to cut our throats in cold-blooded murder, to burn us up.' He raised his hands to heaven. 'Is death, simple death, not sufficient atonement for our sins of kindness, humanity, nay generosity, towards the black man? Before we have died, before we have even cried out, "Spare us, O you prince of iniquity," must we be burnt to the stake as though we were heretics?'

He turned to Lafayette, his voice quavering with emotion, 'For I tell you, Father, on behalf of all these humble and simple people here present, people who would rather see peace and love — yes, even the peace and love that you preach — that we are not heretics, that we are not non-believers. Our very civilization, our very culture, cries not against the obscurantism of disbelief.' He paused, threw out his cupped hand to the audience and said, 'And yet this is what the world of Britain, of America, of the whole until-now free world, would have us believe. To these nations and peoples, nations and peoples seeking only the convenience of political dictates for the sake of economic survival, I say again, "We no longer care for your judgement. You've been measured, weighed, and found wanting. Found wanting in the vital and ultimate things, things that are more spiritual than material, that we, the backwood, vanguard of civilization, really care for. Out with you. Out with your civilization of cowardice. Out with your very Christianity of convenience." Did I say, "Out with you?" Did I say, "Out with the double tongue that bates the black man to slaughter us?" I should have said it. But I didn't. Said it because the Ecklands did not need to die, would not have died, except for the fact that murder of the white man is defended by the Colonial Government.' He threw his arms out, 'How else do I explain this dastardly act? How else do I or can I explain all that has happened up to now? Say to the Colonial Government, "That man is a murderer", and he will be set free. Say to the Colonial Government, "That man is a demagogue and cares nothing for even his people", and the guns of impending execution will be lowered in favour of peace, the peace of cowardice!'

The congregation swayed to and fro in frenzied anger. Lafayette fumbled with his vestments uneasily.

'Why did we have to come so far, not only from this town but from Gunsbury and all the centres where the white man resides, to come to this burial? To render human and deific testimony to the burial of that which has already been cremated? Why?' He exclaimed stabbing his massive hands into the congregation. 'Why!' he cried, the rumble of his voice overspilling the crowd into the cold silence of the graves around. 'Why?' he cried yet again. He raised his handerkerchief to his face. His eyes steeped in an unusual murderous mysticism he said in short stabbing words, 'Lift your arms to the Lord, for my metal is already lifted. Kill the evil in our midst — for that evil is the thirst of the black man for the blood of the white man. For this country, our country because we know no other birthplace, has a rendevous with civilization. That will not be until the black man, the Colonial Government, throws in the towel and says "I give up. I give up because the whites of this country protect civilization better than me." Lift up your hearts. Lift up your courage. Life up your dislike, hate, against the agents of the extinction of the world's civilization.' He lowered his voice. 'And when you have done, tell me to count you among the noble crusaders that redeemed Europe, my country. Great Britain, from the fangs of a savage civilization. Do you not dare arm yourselves? Do you dare walk the streets and say, "The Government will protect us"? Do you dare walk naked, unarmed and defenceless? Heed my call. The fangs of savagery are drawn against culture and civilization. Arm yourselves because you will need the guns. Defend yourselves because no one else will.

'Tackle! Tackle the evil in the black men, the evil that slays white men. Attack the Satan that dwells in these people and twists and warps their minds. For it is our role as Christians and forbearers of civilization to continue to protect the black man against the genetic excesses of his upbringing. So as Fr Lafayette has said, "let us unite in love." But let it be the love that chides against wrong-doing and not the love that does not.

'This is weakness. It is not love. So even as we bury these two, these two who did not deserve to die — and Fr Lafayette has said it — let us stand together shoulder to shoulder. Let us confront the enemy eyeball to eyeball. Let us say, nay spit, into the authorities' face and say, "Enough is enough." We the white race will now take our own lives into our own hands.'

A few hours after the service Ray Norris wrote to his son, George, at the Kamolo Secondary School. He always addressed him as 'my George'. Perhaps it was because the mother had died when George was a baby and he alone had had to look after the infant.

My George

You already know the terrible times that the white man in this country is going through. Therefore you must know by now the even more terrible times which I am going through. Seeing all these things happen to the innocent people like the Ecklands resolves me even more firmly that I have a mission on this earth. I have asked myself many times, many more times today than ever before, why me? But is it necessary to ask this question? Is it not a fact that at every period of challenge in the history of civilization one man has come up from nowhere to save civilization from destruction? Was Jesus Christ not that man? Were Confucious, Muhammad and others, not those men?

And yet, what did they get out of it personally? Nothing. That is the first lesson of life that I wish to bequeath to you my son. I say 'bequeath' because I have a foreboding feeling that this part of the world is about to be consumed in a conflagration of horrifying proportions. Stand by your race because that race is the emblem of civilization.

I take this trouble to explain these things because I would like you, my son, to understand what it is that drives your old man to the height of selflessness that I continue to bear. For the understanding of a son is worth more to a father than that of the whole world. You walked out on my address to Parliament some time ago. I was humbled, but I knew that one of these days you would understand. Now I am sure you understand. But I do not call upon you to join forces with me. That, my son, is a decision for you alone to make. But I question whether it is right for you to continue to nurture the seed of the destruction of civilization by continuing to teach in an African school. I am an old man in dotage. Maybe I do not understand. If that is truly the case, then pray for me to understand. the Lord must surely know that in all that I do I seek nothing but his wisdom.

Ray.

When he read it, George Norris buried his face in his hands and cried. So pathetic to know that his own father really believed what he had thought was merely the stage acting of a politician. He thought of his 'famous' speech in Parliament, of his remarks at the dinner that evening. So his father really believed it! Had he been fair with him? George knew that there would be difficult times ahead. He prayed that he might save the old man much pain. But it was too late to go back now. He would have to confront him and tell him that which he had never thought possible.

14

After Sir Ray Norris had just thanked all the people 'who had shown their maximum and supreme contempt for cowardice by identifying themselves with the sorrow of the whole of civilized Musasa', cars began to drive off. Lepton, the chief mourner as far as the mining community of Bristol Gold Syndicate was concerned, had been completely ignored — even in as far as getting a lift back from the graveyard. He and the pall bearers had been especially picked up from the BGS by the Their Excellencies Funeral Parlour, a company which held the sole monopoly for European burials in the city. True to its tradition, that parlour only 'picked up' and never 'took back'. Thus it was that they were stranded. So Lepton had got a lift back — at least into town from a pair of 'underground men'.

The men said it was a very sad occasion. Then they discussed what Norris had said. One of them said Norris was right. With that he accelerated, overtook the other cars getting back to Musasa while he swore, 'Bloody blacks!' Approaching Musasa African Primary School, Lepton noticed the 'children crossing' sign. He said to the driver:

'Slow down.'

But the driver replied:

'Don't worry, I'll take you right through to BGS.'

Lepton saw a child about to cross the road. He said, seizing the driver's thigh:

'Slow, slow down!' in a husky worried voice.

The driver slapped the brakes on flat out. He exclaimed:

'My God! No brakes!'

He pulled up the handbrake and changed in high gear. The car swerved. It was heading for the ditch. He brought it back on to the road. Just then a child dived across the road in panic. Lepton shrieked:

'Stop! Oh God!'

There was a thud, a cry, a crash against the windscreen. A human body lifted off the unbreakable windshield, high into the sky, bounced back over the roof of the car, then on to the tarmac with a crash. Dead. The driver was dazed. Lepton pushed him off the steering wheel. He looked at the child. If it was still alive it could be fatal to move it. He took off his funeral coat, covered it over the child and zoomed off for the police station.

At PALP headquarters, Kawala was angrier than ever before. He was angry with Norris, with Baker, with everything.

'Now,' he said, 'time is running out on us. Since we started this battle, many Kandahaian children have been born into a land of slavery. Soon we ourselves here will have grandchildren who are slaves because their grandfathers knew not how to fight for their God-given land. Mozambique, Angola, Guinea Bissau, all these countries about whom black Africa had despaired, have now got their independence. Why? Because they have fought for it.'

Then he stood up.

'You have spoken about the colonial régime inciting our people to violence so that it can find an excuse for imprisoning them. But there is the other side of the coin: our people are tired of waiting for the promised day when we will stand up to this evil called colonialism and spit into its face with all the vigour and pride of a noble people. We have let them down after working their feelings up to fever pitch. Soon chaos will break out.' Shakala nodded his head in violent agreement.

Kawala stretched out his hand and picked up a parcel which had been lying on the floor. Unwrapping it carefully, he said:

'From now on this will be my dress. He who is dressed for war mocks the spirits if he does not fight.' He put on the skin lumber jacket. Everyone watched in silence. 'And you also, this will be your dress. From now on peace with the Colonial Government will only be possible if it will not be the peace of permanent war.' He looked at each of them in turn. Then he said, 'Now if what I speak is not right for our people, for our nation, please correct me.' Again there was silence.

A gust of hot air blew through the little hut. Kakonkawadia wiped his forehead. When he had joined the party from the civil service he had expected a hero's welcome. Now it was a hornet's nest. Fight. He had never fought before and did this mean killing? His intestines recoiled at the idea. As one who until only recently had been on the Government side, he knew how ruthlessly Government forces of law and order could act. There would be bloodshed. Was it necessary? Had the men whom he had now joined really run out of all sane options? What would become of his family, and the two children? He must speak up. He had not been brought into the party to be a 'yes' man. He coughed a little, leaned forward and said:

'Mr National President, I believe that there is another way out.'

'What way?' Katenga shot up. Then realizing that Kawala was still holding the floor, he kept quiet. But his face was wild.

Kawala looked at Kakonkawadia mutely. Then at Katenga who repeated:

'What way?'

'Yes, what way?' said Santasa, raising his voice at the last word into a tired rebuke.

Kakonkawadia shifted uneasily.

'The way of further negotiation with the Government,' he replied.

'We don't recognize *your* Government!' Katenga snapped. 'A Government which treats people like animals is not a government. It is a usurper! Government indeed! That's exactly what I was saying.' Katenga swept up the President's face with the shaft of his eyes' sword. 'Puppet only!' He stood up, reached for the window, and spat through it.

'What I mean, sir, is that there may be a need for us to present our case in a different way. The English are moved by ideas rather than by threats of violence.' Kakonkawadia seemed still insensitive to the very sensitive issue which he had broached.

'We are no longer threatening. We shall do it!' exclaimed Katenga. 'Why did they behead Charles I then? Why did they kill the Germans? What about the Hola camp massacres in Kenya? Why are they killing our people if they are not moved by violence? Why didn't they sit down with all those people and present the case in a different way?' asked Chimuko.

Santasa cleared his throat quietly. His face looked puzzled.

'Comrade National President, can Mr Kakonkawadia tell us how to negotiate with these people? He himself has been in the civil service and surely he must know how even the Africans in that service have never listened to us. Always treating us like dogs.' He paused. 'Is he saying that we have been wasting our people's time all along and that only he knows how to negotiate?' There was silence again. Santasa's interventions never ever provoked hostility. They simply made one think. So they were all silent.

Then Kawala said:

'Comrade Kako, maybe you can tell us how?'

'It was just an idea, Mr President,' replied Kakonkawadia.

'Just an idea,' said Kawala. 'You make me sick! Sick!' Kawala's face darkened with anger. 'You think you can solve our problems by negotiation. Negotiation indeed. Did you come to help us or to sabotage the struggle? Why did you say "yes" when I called you? Why didn't you say "no" and keep your negotiating abilities for colonial masters? Do you think we are twits? Do you think we are a blood-thirsty lot who want nothing but to spill blood? Don't you realize that in any war with the colonialists our people's blood will be spilt? Why then don't you ask yourself why, in spite of all this, why are we going to fight? Do you think if we thought there was a way out we would not have taken it a long time ago? Look at what happened at Nampande village. Our people were butchered. Five of them. And you say "negotiation". Just an idea! We have called for a commission of enquiry into these killings. We've got nowhere just because Thomson is busy drinking tea. If any of you don't want to fight, go!'

Kawala was perspiring. He wiped his forehead. He leaned back a little. His eyes swept over the bent heads of the people in the room.

'From now on I don't want to hear that word. I want action and action means war. The war to liberate our motherland.' Then he paused. The silence seemed eternity itself. 'My people are animals in their own country. Africa is still a slave to the gun of the foreigner. Will you, her sons and daughters, not free her? Before I go any further, let any of you who would betray her walk out now!' There was silence. 'We are going to have a day of national mourning. Enough is enough. Katenga, get the miners. We want them in on this.'

Later at PALP headquarters in Samaka Compound, activity was reaching fever pitch. They were working against time. Coded messages were being sent to all the towns in the country. Provincial officials of the party, those who got the messages, stood by waiting for the signal to go ahead. When that signal came through, posters would be plastered all over the African compounds overnight. They would urge something. That something was now being agreed and finalized in the little makeshift conference room in Samaka Compound, Musasa. Katenga's suggestion for a violent eruption had been carefully considered. The time had not come.

'It will never come!' he had just exclaimed, jumping up, wrenching the door open at the point of leaving the room. But they had restrained him.

Now the darkness was tucking them in. Mpengula, the president of the Mine Workers Union and his secretary, Nkolola, were waiting outside to be told. Similar briefings of workers the country over were taking place. But the key was the Bristol Gold Syndicate. Anything that happened there was news.

'The time has come to summon the world's conscience to the perfidy, injustice and oppression of the Colonial Government,' said Kawala as the two miners' union men sat down.

The Bristol Gold Syndicate had moved a long way from the days when PALP was taboo. And yet it wasn't such a long time ago PALP members were persecuted. But events of the last few weeks had accelerated the pace. Mpengula was no longer the man to challenge the party out there. He spoke well of it publicly and kept the snide remarks to himself. That was a step towards a climb down and when Kawala said:

'Boys, we are declaring tomorrow a day of national mourning all over the country. National mourning for the many people who have been killed by the colonialists including the ones who died recently in Boko District,' there was cowed silence. 'Under the emergency powers vested in me, no black man will go to work tomorrow. In every town and village of this country people will meet to mourn our many people who have perished at the gun of the oppressor.' He looked at the roof. 'Many more will die yet.' He turned to Mpengula and Nkolola. 'You are the leaders of the most important union in this country. So you have a heavy responsibility — comrade Katenga has worked with you closely to establish the party at the mine. Tomorrow, I want all miners to stay away from work. They will meet instead to mourn the dead.' He raised his voice, 'All of them!' His eyes looked wildly around. 'All of them!' he exclaimed again. 'The gold mine is there because we are there. You comrades have worked there, enjoyed a salary because we, the people, want you to be there. We, the people, now want you to destroy that mine because it survives on the exploitation of our country. We shall rebuild. But we must first destroy. Go back now quickly to BGS. You tell your people, no work tomorrow.' Then looking at Mpengula he said, 'I don't want any black traitors. If there are any, they'll feel the weight of the party. The party has infiltrated BGS whether you comrades like it or not. Do what the party says and you are all right. Otherwise?' He waved his hand into the air. He stopped. Then he said, 'Comrade Katenga will come with you. We will wait here. He will bring us the news.'

That evening Kawala wrote a note to Dr Lal Naik. Since the accidental meeting at the hospital, Naik had become a friend of the party and Kawala's family. He had consequently been dismissed from Government service and blacklisted by the Kandaha Branch of the British Medical Council. The suspension had been temporary. Then he came down to Musasa and established a private surgery there. Kawala wrote to him, 'The battle for freedom is about to start. We shall need many things and among them, medicines, bandages, etc. I rely on you, comrade to help us.'

Mpengula, driving back in an old battered car Nkolola had just bought, was silent. He had grave doubts as to whether the workers supported PALP to the point of risking their jobs.

An idea came to Mpengula. He would have to summon the supreme council. It had better be in Nkolola's home since it was late and his wife was sick.

The supreme council members were easy to reach. Emergency meetings were not a new thing. They had met in emergency sessions before. When they had all gathered, Mpengula said:

'We have a messenger from the party. *They* want us to go on strike tomorrow.'

Nkolola said:

'We *must* strike tomorrow. It's a day of national mourning for all our comrades who have died at the gun of the colonialists.'

'Yes,' said Mpengula.

Katenga maintained silence.

Mpengula said, 'As your leader, I cannot assure you that if you go on strike you'll not lose your jobs. This is not the way we have dealt with our troubles in the past. But . . .'

'But what?' Katenga looked at him.

'The supreme council only deals with labour matters. Maybe this matter should be explained by the party,' Mpengula's mouth curled somewhat in a faint sneer.

'Yes,' said Katenga standing up. 'The party is commanding you, all of you here, not to go to work tomorrow because we are mourning the deaths of our people. If you don't want to mourn them, you can go to work.' He sat down, his face twisted with anger. 'Sell-outs!' he said loudly.

Mpengula smiled genially. On his home ground, he was his real self. Sardonically, he said:

'Do you want to have no jobs tomorrow and forever after?'

Nkolola replied:

'Yes. If . . .'

'There's no "if" here,' exploded Mpengula. 'If you stay away tomorrow, you stay away forever. That's what it means.' Then he added, 'Maybe other people will give you a job.' Katenga tightened his fists to control himself.

'We must go on strike. Why should we go to work when our people are dying? Will the whites here go to work today? Did they not all go to Musasa? They've already been treating us as if we murdered the Ecklands. Everywhere you go they are saying, "We'll fix you Kaffirs."'

'What fixing is this?' It was the treasurer of the union. After

Mpengula he was the most influential man.

'I tell you, this is not the way to handle the white man,' said Mpengula. 'We can't stay away from work!' cried Mpengula, his self-restraint gone. 'PALP is misleading you. Who's got a job in PALP? What are they? Loafers only, aren't they? What can they give you? Promises upon promises. Not so?'

Katenga kicked the seat before him. He had been instructed to listen.

'And what have you given us?' retorted the treasurer.

'Malherbe!' said a voice.

'Yes, Malherbe,' said the treasurer.

Katenga shot up.

'The butcher?' he asked.

'Yes,' replied the treasurer, 'the very man who set a dog on our woman. Now he's been brought in as personnel manager. Are we resisting this insult? No. If we can't mourn our own people, we can strike to get rid of Malherbe. He stinks!'

'You mean Malherbe is here? You mean that butcher who set Kruger against a woman because she was black? You mean the man who used to keep white corpses in the freezer with meat for the blacks is back here? You mean, you mean you know it but you are not angry? Do you mean . . .'

Katenga had again stood up. His face, incredulity furrowed deep into it, cried:

'Is this true?'

Nkolola nodded his head.

'And you accept this?' Katenga cried.

'No!' cried several voices. 'We'll strike tomorrow.'

Mpengula stood up.

'This is politics. It's not unionism.'

'What's unionism?' It was Nkolola's first challenge.

'Are you opposing me?'

'Yes. Why should we accept that dog?'

'He's a boss.'

'Sell-out,' Katenga was madness itself.

'You are all dismissed. I'll call for new elections. Mpengula, you've betrayed the workers' cause.' Nkolola stood up. He said 'Quiet! We have a crisis. I think we must vote.'

'There's no provision for voting on non trade-union matters in the constitution,' protested Mpengula.

'That doesn't matter,' cried Katenga. 'There's a stinking animal in your midst. There's a colonialist. You *must* vote.' He was trembling with rage.

Mpengula was also beside himself with rage. If a president's motion was defeated, this would be a vote of no confidence, in accordance with the constitution. Would Mpengula resign? Mpengula said:

'You are all idiots, only idiots. Tomorrow you are losing your jobs. PALP will not answer for you. I am not resigning. You don't represent the people. You are only sell-outs!'

Nkolola had again stood up to call for order. After all, it was his house. The treasurer stood up immediately after Nkolola had sat down. He said:

'I propose that the supreme council in accordance with Article 4(i) of the constitution should suspend the president.'

Cheers. Mpengula looked around. Katenga watched him with disgust. Then the treasurer asked for a seconder. Several voices said, 'Seconded'. Suddenly Mpengula said:

'I will go along with you. National mourning, strike, dismissal of Malherbe,' and there was silence. Then quickly he said, 'Yes, I have *other* business. I have *resigned*. Tonight I'm going to Mulule. Tomorrow I'm launching my own political party — CACOP — The Consolidated African Congress Party. I don't want dogs to follow me.'

At the Kandaha Broadcasting Station, Cuthbert Mwalema ripped open an envelope. The note inside simply said, 'Yes'. He smiled.

Ten fifty-eight p.m. In two minutes' time it would be the final news bulletin for the day. He took up his position in the studio. He winked through the sound-proof glass window to the man giving him the cue. Exactly at eleven o'clock he got his cue for the news bulletin. He said:

'This is Kandaha calling!'

Then the music of 'God Save Our Gracious Queen' cut into the broadcast. It stopped abruptly. Mwalema said:

'We apologize to our listeners for that interruption,' and proceeded with the news bulletin.

PALP Officials the country over had had their signal. The national mourning was on.

The day had broken. Tall chimney stacks were belching out smoke over the horizon. Lepton, the underground manager, was just touching up his chin after a shave. The cookboy was late. Maureen was frying him an egg. She enjoyed cooking for him. The night underground shift came off an hour ago. He was due to go down and check on one or two things in an hour's time. Two or three whites due to have gone down with the men an hour ago were still standing around at the Vertical Ventilation Incline Shaft. They were feeling thoroughly bored. They'd been to a party the previous night. . . .

Bwana Malherbe was just waking up. Some say they can't sleep soundly in a strange bed, but this was not so with Malherbe. Last night and shortly before turning in he had telephoned Joan down in Musasa to tell her it was wonderful here in his new home, a BGS house, and he would be sending a chauffeur to pick her up over the weekend. Today he would call up the whites in the personnel department, tell them things will have to change. They would have to change. No black politics. If the English fellows didn't like him, it's just too bad. He's been called in to clean up the stables — and that could mean a few of them.

Lepton settled down to his egg. He was a genial six-footer. He said:

'Dear, dear. How nice Maureen,' to the maid. He took a bite and said:

'Whatever happened to Matthew?' Matthew was the servant. 'He's late. I'll have to do something about this. It's never happened before.'

There was a knock at the door. It was one of the white chaps, Serfontein, who had been standing around at the shaft.

'Dick,' he said. 'There's a fuckin' *muntu* strike. There's not even a soul at work. We've seen posters all over. There's, they call it, a "national mourning". This is a *muntu* business. I'm sure it's PALP.'

'PALP!' Lepton sat thinking.

'In fact I've seen lots of Muntus right now going to the football stadium. Do you know if any Muntu here has died?'

'No. I must find out. The new personnel manager has come, hasn't he?'

'Sure.'

'Have you been to see him?'

'That pig? Jesus, no. I don't know what he's here for between you and I. This fellow brought us trouble when he was here before running a butchery. That's how PALP came here. I bet you there will be trouble again. Maybe if Turnbull stayed here with us instead of in Musasa, all of this could have been avoided. It's not the way to run a mine, men. Down in the Republic you stay where you work and you soil your hands,' said Serfontein. His family had always worked on the gold mines in South Africa and he had been brought up among the primary crushers, ball mills, cyanidation tanks and the crunch of miners' boots.

'The primary crusher underground is in trouble. I must go down and check it,' said Serfontein. He hated his day underground being messed up. Lepton was thinking. He gave Serfontein some coffee and rang Malherbe. It was news to him, but he managed to put in a swear word about giving him time to straighten out the Kaffirs. That's not exactly what Lepton had been looking for. He rang Turnbull in Musasa. Turnbull's anger ran amok.

'We can't afford a strike out there,' he said, 'not with the current price of gold!'

'I know,' said Lepton. 'A strike is bad any time.'

'Do you know why they're striking?'

'I said I didn't,' Lepton was getting a bit angry. Turnbull, thought Lepton, what did he care for the safety of the white miners? It was always profit, profit.

'Last week you only hoisted 35,000 tonnes of ore. The mine was 5,000 tonnes down. And the average grade was only 7 grams per tonne. We can't afford this. I may soon have to lay off labour. And that could be white labour also.'

Lepton kept quiet, trying not to explode.

'You'd better check what this strike is about. Meantime, I'll get Compol to send police. These blacks will have to get back to work.'

He checked. Mpengula was not speaking. Nkolola said:

'We've decided not to work today because it's a national mourning day.'

'Who's died?' asked Lepton.

'Many.'

'Many? Where?'

'All over Kandaha. Mr Lepton, we are very busy. If you want the mines not to flood just get the whites to get on with it.'

'You've registered a dispute with the Government?' inquired Lepton.

'Is mourning the dead a dispute?' replied Nkolola.

A small crowd gathered. Lepton realized it could be dangerous. He left.

'What's happening here?' demanded Malherbe in disgust.

'It's a funeral.'

'Funeral? Christ man, who told you to hold a funeral at the football ground? I must see your leaders. Where are they?'

'I am here.' Nkolola looked at Malherbe.

'So you are not going to work?'

'No.'

'You know you'll all be sacked?'

'No,' said Nkolola. 'We won't be. We are mourning.'

'Why do you even talk to this bastard?' said the treasurer breaking in. 'You, is your name not Malherbe?'

Malherbe looked up startled. 'You remember what you did here? You are a dog!' The man reached for Malherbe's neck. 'We are not working today because it's a day of mourning. But also because we won't have you. It's an insult. Can't you read those posters out there?' He looked up.

The posters read, 'National Mourning Day', 'Out with Dog Malherbe', 'We shall avenge the dead' and so on.

'I would advise you to leave Bwana. We will soon be telling the people why.'

Nkolola moved over into the football ground where people were singing funeral songs. They cheered.

'Are all the families here? Are all your children here also because this is a funeral?'

The football ground had already filled up and more people were arriving. Already more than five thousand people had gathered.

'Today is a day of national mourning. Our respected leader, President Kawala wants us to observe it peacefully and sorrowfully. People who are mourning don't go to work because their work is to bury and mourn the dead ones. Many people have died at the hands of colonialists. There are many about whom we have not heard who have died. If you go to work you are a traitor. Remember that if you do we shall never mourn you when you die. Norris can bury you himself.

'As for the mine authorities, we have no quarrel with them. They treat us well. So we want them to leave us alone today. The mine can flood if they want it to. If they don't, they will man the main pumping stations. But if they cause you trouble, then tell us. We shall cause them trouble too.

'After I have spoken, let us sing hymns of God and songs of our ancestors to remember the dead. Then you should all go quietly to your homes because mourning is a thing of sorrow.

'In the meantime, I want to tell you that the day after tomorrow we are calling a strike to protest the employment of a dog as personnel manager. Tomorrow we will give Turnbull an ultimatum to dismiss Malherbe. If he hasn't gone after tomorrow, then we will go on strike. This strike is going to be a long one. Just because we have never gone on strike, they think they can continue to insult us. Malherbe set a dog on a woman. He was a racialist when he was here. This man will never be fair to us.' The crowd roared in anger.

'Away with the dog!' it cried. 'Down with Malherbe! He's a sell-out!'

Nkolola calmed the people down. The crowd had swollen further. They started singing hymns and after an hour they began to disperse back to their homes.

Meanwhile, in Musasa, the stay-away from work was a fantastic success, considering the secrecy and prevented publicity. Government House was a hive of activity. So was Police Force Headquarters. It had become public knowledge that Kawala might address a rally.

15

At the Bristol Gold Syndicate, the national mourning activities were coming to an end and everyone dispersing quietly to their homes. A few men gathered at the tribal games corner of the welfare area. As part of the after-work relaxation, they played *Imbeta*, *Mulambilwa*, *Nsolo* and other African games. In one shelter, a four-man team ranging on one side cheered. They drew chalk rings around two fruit seeds. They were long rectangular seeds, the sort you find in pears. One chap smacked the ground affectionately and said:

'Here, here, *Kapala wa mupamba namwishetela mwe ba senshi*.'

The losing team yelled:

'Well, get him off!' They buzzed their fruit seeds over to the enemy. One seed led, leaned backwards and then forwards as if it was saying, *'Heya!'* and then struck one of the chalk circle *'akapala'*. The underprivileged team exclaimed:

'Eya!'

The spokesman of the four-man team line-up said:

'You've lost. You're not supposed to speak when the *Kapala* is being aimed for. He's the victor of our last round.'

The others grumbled, but accepted the fact. Their leader said:

'No more loud mouths. We'll assault the enemy.' He whispered, 'Here!' Then loudly, 'We go!' The pear seeds zipped, zoomed and sidled across. The other team tried their best to engage the vanquished in hilarity. But they were not playing ball. They wanted to win and every noise that they might have made counted against them because when you fell down the king or the *Kapala* you had to do it in ominous silence — maybe as a mark of respect. It was all so exciting. The occasion of the lively event — the national mourning — had been completely forgotten.

Then a huge truck, roaring, whining in third gear came into sight from nowhere. Then another. Another. Another. Another and another. Until there were ten trucks of fully armed fellows. All wearing masks. But also, all carrying automatic fire.

The children who had gathered round their fathers playing *Imbeta, Nsolo, Mulambilwa* and other games were wild with excitement. They'd never before seen such a toy-like display of sheer hard armoury. A diversion of military display was fantastic they thought. So they rushed towards the black marias. Their elders looked on grinning. A minute's interruption of their keen game was worth everything to look at the display of sheer sophistication of the white man's gadgetry. They too followed the kids, rushing towards the gleaming black marias, with the brilliant sunshine reflecting against their bodies and the black police holding their guns looked incredible. They all rushed towards the black marias. Black was a sign of sorrow — at least they had learned that much about the white man. And if someone sympathized with you in sorrow, did you not have a duty to cheer him up? So the shelters of people regaling themselves in the relaxation of the unmolested holiday of defiance rushed towards the trucks.

The man at the head of the trucks looked at the onrushing mob nervously. He had been told that the blacks at the BGS were in a truculent mood. He grasped his walkie-talkie.

'All stations, stand by,' he said, his voice quavering with pained uncertainty. He glanced at his wrist watch. Noted the time mechanically. If any explanation would be needed, he would have to mention the time.

Another officer, also white, next to him said:

'They're rushing on us. Soon there will be a pile of corpses.' Shaking up his commandant, a nineteen-year-old, two weeks' recruit, he said, 'For Christ's sake, let's fire!'

The first black maria carried only white policemen and, therefore, white officers. That first truck hesitated. But the young police officer's cry, 'Fire!' had been heard in the second, third and maybe even fourth truck, all of which carried black policemen. Fire rang out from the second to the tenth trucks. Men leapt out of their trucks as the accumulating bodies of miners and children who had gathered to watch the native games fell. The whites in the front-line 'scaring truck' also leapt out. Some among the blacks falling were still exclaiming, "*Ehede!*' which means 'Ha ha ha!' thinking the ring of fire and their falling colleagues were a joke. Was this after all not a peaceful holiday of mourning?

Simon Malherbe appeared from nowhere. The white officer in charge of the operation was just about to order a retreat when he exclaimed:

'Christ man, finish the job! These *muntus* have been attacking us since this morning. Why the hell do you think you came all this way? Just to aim a pelt gun at one native?'

The blacks in the shelters saw their colleagues stop, fall back and then explode into blood. For a moment they couldn't understand. Then they understood. Out of nowhere a crowd of yelping frenzied black faces surged forward towards the mouths of the guns chanting blood-thirsty incantations. The white officer in command perspired as the seething mob ran towards him. He cried:

'Fire Muntu!'

There was a whelp, a scream and roaring echo of gun-fire. In a moment all had become silent. Silent apart from one or two bodies squirming their way into death. The young officer, realizing what had happened, ordered his truck to turn back. Ploughing like a rogue elephant through the mine, it galloped, barked, cried, howled through the compound. It was unbelievable. So much death in a matter of minutes. What was it for? The Africans looked at each other with a charcoal blackness.

Then the whole compound rushed towards the trucks speeding away like rhinos gone amok. Stones, sticks, knobkerries rained into the trucks. The police inside, their guns pointed through the peep-holes waited nervously for orders to fire. Then, it all happened so suddenly. Someone threw a grenade in front of the last truck. The driver swerved to avoid it. It was too late. The wheels were upon it. The front wheels lifted like an elephant doing exercises. There was a loud deafening explosion. Into the air, the truck disintegrated. The driver and one other were torn to pieces. It was a reserve truck carrying provisions and further ammunition. The ammunition caught fire. The crowd drew back. Then the crowd recovered itself. As if by design, the masses ran to the offices of the company, pulled out and beat up all the whites who could be found and set the building ablaze. From there the crowd rushed to the supermarket, burning and looting. The police trucks reformed, five miles away after hearing the explosion. In a moment they might have to recharge.

In the compound itself, women were yelling and crying as bodies were being covered with blankets. The mob turned to Malherbe's house. But he had vanished. The crowd set his house ablaze. Terror had come.

At the national mourning in Musasa, a crowd had swollen to an unbelievable size. Kawala, who had started to address it five minutes ago was saying to the crowd:

'If the colonial police come, don't run away. He that has to bury the dead does not desert them. We are mourning our people, the people who have died at the hands of colonialism and imperialism. The graves of these courageous people are all over Kandaha. We are meeting to tell them that their lives will not be lost in vain. Their blood has fertilized our courage. But this is also a protest rally. Unless we get independence, we will cripple the economy — the white colonialist's and racist's stomach.

'For Zimbabwe (Rhodesia) it has run out already. For this country it is running out. Let Baker not forget that behind every discontent there can be steel. There is steel. We will pursue freedom beyond passive resistance, if necessary, to the clamour of arms itself. For freedom is the real self of ourselves which we have lost to slavery. This shadow,' he said clenching his fists, 'this shadow which you call me will search for the real and free Kawala even among the pounding of cannon, the prisons of torture, the graves themselves. Africa! You are not free until all your peoples are free. We summon you free Africa to come to the aid of Africa yet unfreed. But in doing so we do not ask you to fight our battles. They are ours. They are our right. They are our duty. For no freedom that is won by some for others can ever be real freedom. We only ask you for your moral support.'

He turned to his people.

'For so long I have prayed that I will deliver you all to the God of freedom, intact and living to enjoy that freedom. But as I look into the future, fate tells me that it will not be so. For even as Jesus Christ died, so that we may have life and have it abundantly, the cause of freedom will demand yet more sacrifice than we have had cause to make so far. Shall I be plain and say that the defence of our liberty, our very right to life now requires us to fight the forces of destruction. These forces are in every colonialist. They are in every racialist that denies us freedom. For how can we be men worthy of our great God-given destiny if we are not free?

'So I say to you that if you have an axe, sharpen it. If you have a spear, sharpen it. If you have a gun, prime it. For the hour to win that which we cherish, even by force, has come.' He threw up his arms. 'Yes, I am proposing violence. Violence for the cause of peace. For even as I speak, innocent people and children are dying at the behest of the colonial and racist God of destruction.'

The crowd was swaying with sheer raw anger. Kawala stood looking at it.

'Will you fight for freedom?' he cried.

'Yes,' cried the crowd. The echo of its 'Yes' reverberated through the buildings of Colonial Avenue. Someone came rushing from behind Kawala. He whispered something to Katenga. Katenga jumped up to Kawala. He was trembling.

'Twenty-three people killed at the mine. A child killed at the school and the school burnt down!'

'Oh God!' whispered Kawala. Then unable to control himself he yelled into the crowd, 'Oh God!'

There was sudden movement among the people. Someone had heard what Katenga had said. Women began to wail. Then the men surged forward. Kawala cried:

'Twenty-four!'

A burst of fire. It was tear gas. Kawala stood, his shoulders held up erect. He looked in the direction where most of the shots had come from. There was a sudden stir in the crowd. He cried:

'Lie down! Down!'

But it was too late. Two shots rang through the crowd. This time real shots. A child fell under Kawala's feet. Dead. The crowd held back. He looked at the child, its skull shattered. He picked it up, hugged it to his chest and walking glassy-eyed in the direction of the shooting, he cried:

'An eye for an eye!' A tooth for a tooth!'

A shock ran through the crowd. Women cried. Then the shock became an electric one. Like a huge elephant run mad, the crowd seethed forward, then crying, 'Kill! Kill!' it rushed for the police everywhere.

'An eye for an eye!' cried Kawala. A burst of cannon fire. Bodies fell. But the mob rushed on. 'Retreat!' cried a white voice. Trucks rumbled. 'Retreat!' cried the same voice again. But for some it was too late. The mob turned to the offices and shops along Colonial Avenue. In a moment the whole avenue was a smouldering mess. Musasa had gone amok.

An hour later the armed forces re-established order. Kawala was captured, the dead child still stuck to his bosom. The whole central committee including Mama PALP and other party officials had been captured. But Katenga and Chimuko were nowhere to be seen. Had they been shot and their bodies carried away by the police? Had they really escaped? Only Kawala knew. For in the midst of the stampede he had said to the two, 'Escape. Carry the revolution outside. Avenge our blood.'

At Kawala's house that evening a small crowd gathered to console his wife. He would be back. . . . How could she be certain? Now and again she broke into a sob. An elderly woman would say, 'Shut up! You cry as though he is dead. That is only to wish him bad luck.' Her children were all there. Would they be orphans, or were they already orphans?

Later in the night, armed police came to the house. The people did not run away as they would have done if it had been a light matter. But a man taken by the police could be dead by now. Even if you were a coward and cared only for your life, can you run away leaving a corpse? The police, it turned out, were accompanying the white lawyer who defended the party members in trouble with the law. He was visiting the wives of all the people who had been picked up. He had protested against police protection. But the police had insisted it was too dangerous for a white man to go into the compound alone. With him was Dr Naik.

The lawyer said to Kawala's wife:

'Your husband is well, but under detention. They'll have to tell me the grounds for his detention and that of the others in two weeks' time. I'm sure we'll get them out. If they don't, then I'll insist on a court trial. I will be contacting you later about visiting him and Dr Naik here will make sure that no injury comes by him. By the way, while he's in detention you are eligible for public support.'

When the lawyer left the atmosphere became somewhat relaxed. So some of the women began to whisper things among themselves.

'This is a good way to earn your wife some money. Loaf all the time and get yourself in trouble and clapped up,' says one.

The two laugh into their breasts. The other says:

'If my husband had a wife who spent all her time at the

market he would also be wanting to get clapped up.'

The laughter is joined by a third woman. They call her 'The Rabbit's Ears'. Always out listening for titbits of gossip.

'So!' she claps her hands together softly. 'I always thought something was the matter. He must be hen-pecked at home or he would have long put his foot down. What kind of a woman is that one,' she indicates Kawala's wife with a slightly twisted jaw 'who only lives to sell at the market, but can't hold even a cooking stick?'

'Oh!' says a fourth, nestling up to the group like a guinea fowl about to lay eggs, 'if it's that one, don't you know that this woman is very harsh with him? He doesn't say even a word in her presence. Maybe that's why he keeps saying words to crowds. But she will see one of these days. He's quite a handsome man and . . .' She twinkled her eyes upwards. 'Handsome men are like water. They don't stay between the fingers.'

'Maybe you've heard something.' It was the Rabbit's Ears.

'I keep quiet,' said the speaker. 'Some of you don't keep secrets.' The same woman stood up to go and sit near Kawala's wife. She said:

'The father of the boy, how can these white men do this to him, leaving you like a widow.'

Rabbit's Ears had also crept up. She said:

'And yet he is suffering for all of us. This is the trouble with us black people. We are not together. Look around, how many of us are here? And yet when the father of the boy addresses meetings, there are many people. Maybe it is better sometimes to just give it up. These people want to be slaves, slaves eating the white man's crumbs.'

She paused. Kawala's wife was thinking about what the lady had just said. Memories of that episode when she berated him after he had come home so late returned. She remembered the tenderness of the final scene, her promise to him to remain by his side and, as if answering Lady Rabbit's Ears, she shook her head. That was her cross and she would bear it.

Lady Rabbit's Ears sidled back to the other two remaining ladies in the original group.

'As if anyone can want her husband to be released if she gets an allowance! But she'll have to watch out. Even in detention camps there can be women. Well,' she said in a mischievous whisper, 'I think we have mourned the living enough.' She let out a loud yawn. 'I'd better go and look after the grandchildren.' She stood up, adjusted her loin cloth and said aloud, 'These white people, we must simply kill them. That is the only way.'

Later on that night Delia dropped in at the house. She didn't really know Mrs Kawala. But it was her fault. Katenga would not come back. And maybe even dead. All because he followed a fool like Kawala whose wife did not mind him. What right had she to do it? She sat down. Someone was saying:

'It is very bad.'

Delia cut in:

'It is very bad for those women whose men will not return.'

She said it in such an acid voice. The women looked at each other. What man did that harlot have to talk about? A mad one like Katenga?

'Women of these days are strange,' said one. 'I know of one who cried loudest at a funeral as though the man who had died was her husband.'

Delia's heart missed a beat. They were talking about her. Her blood raced. Then she exploded:

'Even if you are married some of you stay like pigs only. Slaves!'

'And you are not a slave being beaten every day by a madman who is not even your husband?'

'I want my man!' cried Delia, standing up and stabbing her finger into Kawala's wife.

Ana sat speechless. The others said as madness was contagious, even she had become as mad as her Katenga. Delia stormed away.

16

The first reaction of the Kandaha situation by the Organization of African Unity (OAU) came from its Secretary General. Monsieur Lantamagne de Masalate Nduoume, a former Archbishop of the Catholic Church, was a suave, polished and highly literate French-speaking man. Nduoume had hoped to become the first prince of the Church in his country. His term of office, however, was reaching its end. His election four years ago had sparked much controversy, especially as he could only speak French and the previous Secretary

General had also come from the French-speaking countries of Africa. Also, he had won because of Arab support. The English-speaking countries had not supported his election until it had become inevitable. They did not trust him. But Nduoume was a consumate politician. He had brought to the OAU job the same single-minded devotion as would surely have made him a cardinal — and maybe even higher — if he had stayed on in the Church. He knew he had to stand for a second and maybe even a third term. So that when the opportunity came for speaking out for Kandaha and thereby winning over to his side English-speaking Africa, he grasped the opportunity with missionary fervour. Nduoume called on the whole of Africa to put an army of liberation into Kandaha. He denounced in a way only he was qualified to do, the forceful imposition of alien religions on Mother Africa. He also warned that the raw materials of Africa would not continue to be available to colonial exploiters, and called upon the British Government in the name of commonplace human decency to release the nationalists, to give independence to Kandaha, to release its rightful leaders from unlawful imprisonment, to pay full compensation to the families of the murdered people, to dismiss Governor Baker and bring him and Norris to trial. He also called for an OAU peace-keeping force to be sent *at once* to Kandaha. As Sir Tom Caput, the Prime Minister of Great Britain, read the details, he knew that the die was cast. He looked at Governor Baker's telex. *Send men. We are besieged*. He had not done so in the case of Rhodesia. Could he do so now? In Parliament that night, the Opposition forced a division. The Opposition castigated Her Majesty's Government for its weak handling of the Kandaha affair. It called for maximum support to be given to the Governor and called for re-affirmation that HMG would not give way to communist-orchestrated pressures to surrender government to people who are 'neither ready nor prepared for self-rule'. The motion was barely defeated and Lord Ventrical, Chairman of the Bristol Gold Syndicate listening to the debate from the Strangers' Gallery felt pleased. It was a timely warning that the people of Great Britain would not be pushed around by Africans, communists, the United Nations, the OAU or anybody. When the results of the UN Security Council debate came through, the following morning, breakfast time though it was, he felt a compulsion to celebrate with champagne. The United States of America, and this in spite of its new role in the politics of Southern Africa had vetoed the motion. Reason — it represented interference in the internal affairs of Great Britain.

Two days later in Kandaha itself all was quiet. The volcano which had erupted had suddenly become extinct. No relatives had been allowed to the mass burial of the people who died at the BGS or at the rally in town. But the warrant for the arrest of Katenga and Chimuko was still out. A reward of £10,000. Dead or alive.

Katenga was striking north. In pitch darkness, he had just crept into a lonely hut. . . . He was starving. The villagers didn't know him. Isolated from the cities, they had not heard of the troubles in Musasa. Nor had they radios. They had not seen a white man for years. But they gave Katenga food.

Katenga informed them of the political situation in Musasa. They listened intently.

'It is the white man who is creating all the problems,' Katenga said.

He heard only the other day that many hundreds were killed by the whites. The people in the huts didn't know. After Katenga's news, the wife of his host said:

'That is why, Sokolo, I will not let you go to town.'

'But our brother, Katenga, must go to spread this news,' stated Sokolo.

Katenga agreed. Sokolo warned him that he was in a game-park area. There were plenty of lions, snakes and elephants around. Katenga nodded his head. Yes, the Lutabo Game Park was the largest after Luangwa in Zambia. But perhaps the richest and most dangerous. Nevertheless, he had to go. He pricked his ears. His fuzzy beard fluttered somewhat. He had developed a kind of seventh sense.

'Here is an axe. You may need it going through this country at night. And some food too. You never know what may happen,' cautioned Sokolo.

This scene repeated itself. Sometimes he fell upon a house where someone knew the driver of the bus that was coming that night and taking off almost immediately. But Katenga always refused the lift. Perhaps it was his seventh sense working, always cautious and sensitive.

It was night. Katenga had finally arrived in the Nampande village, in Boko District. The village had heard about Musasa. Jennings, formerly Private Secretary to the Governor, became District Commissioner at Boko. He sent people to check on Nampande because that's where their troubles first started. Katenga and Chimuko and the search for them almost became legendary through cities and towns. Many claims to have seen visions of

Katenga ever since word went out that he was a hunted man. The village Headman, Nampande, rubbed his eyes.

'Are you, are you my nephew?'

Katenga whispered:

'Yes.'

'How? It must be the Holy One that has brought you here safely. They are looking for you all over the country. It is not even safe to meet in my house. Come.'

Nampande led him off to the edge of the village. Then he went back and in no time a small group of men had gathered.

'We must go back to the assembly, summon all our men and women, tell them the Holy One has sent Katenga in our midst and so we must offer thanks,' said one elder. 'For what man who is hunted by the heirs of the white god can escape without the aid of the Holy One?'

They gathered in the church. They prayed. There was no longer any fear in their hearts. Had the Holy One not told them they were impregnable? Then the elders called upon Katenga, 'the lost son of our religion', to speak. Katenga was tired. But the sons and daughters of Jericho set prayer higher than food or rest. So he stated:

'Sons and daughters of the Holy One, heir to the undying inheritance of Simolonda, I Katenga have come,' he started. 'I have come to answer the call of our founder, the call that I should be the vessel through which the undying Dimintolo will live again and direct the Church through this my sinful hand. For I am a sinner and I confess to you all, even as our leader Dimintolo used to confess publicly to all of you.

But if the sin which I am about to confess is a sin, it is a sin of which we are all, all of us here, all of us black people of the world', he said circling his hand above their heads, 'are guilty of. We have allowed non-believers to trample on our Jericho while we slept or indulged in eating, drinking and sensuality. Thus it is that the body of our leader the Holy One, has been killed even though his undying spirit rises in me now. I am his vessel and now listen what the Holy One says to me to tell you. "Tell my children that he that breaks not open the sore of the land with his hoe will not reap a harvest. He that fights not with the rivers and the lands for his drop of water will die of thirst. But above all, he that sits still and fights not against these who trample on his faith is a sinner unto the Lord." '

He stopped and looked round him.

Then he resumed, his voice raucous with vehemence.

'Arise, O heirs to the city of Jericho! Arise and fight the oppressor.

Arise and fight the white one. For he oppresses you because you are black. He oppresses you and persecutes you for your religion because you are black. Why then, why then', he said raving at them, 'delay you to cast the yoke of slavery that imprisons you? There can be no worship of God in bondage just as God Himself cannot be God in bondage. That is why I was sent hither, spirited out of death to come and unbind the chains of slavery that bind you O sons and daughters of Jericho. Love, that knows no hate is not jealous love. Love that knows no jealousy is not true love. So I say to you, *hate*, *hate* the white one because he imprisons your spirit and keeps it away from worshipping that which it loves. *Hate* the white one because he has raped you of that which you love and treasure so much. Tomorrow or the day after or even the year after, the white one comes to oppress you further. He comes even as it is written in your worship that the devil shall not give up hope, that for as many times as he fails he shall mount a second coming. O sons and daughters of Jericho. O Jericho, city without heirs. O chains of oppression that bind the righteous ones to slavery!'

Then as if anticipating what might come he said:

'Reveal not where your life lies to an infidel. Welcome the infidel as though he were righteous. For the Lord of Jericho welcomes all that repent. But if he that comes to you persists in iniquity even after you have welcomed him, then your duty, O sons and daughters of Jericho is clear. Destroy! Even as the archangel of the gates of Jericho crushed the head of the Archdiablo with the heel of his righteous foot.' Once again he retreated to his seat. Then rising again he said:

'Betray not your teeth to the devil, even as you betrayed not the Holy One. For that is what you do if you sacrifice any of your sons and daughters unto the jaws of the lion that is called the white man's religion and his colonialism!'

The Holy Ones spent the whole night in religious chants. For the first time since the wounding and then death of Dimintolo in Tanzania, it seemed that the promised revel in the joys of the city of Jericho had at last come. Dimintolo had been resurrected. But even more, Jericho itself was in their midst. There was mirth, there was drumming and dancing 'unto the Lord' throughout that night. And Katenga, going from one group to the other would urge, 'Rejoice O you sons and daughters of Jericho! For thine eyes can now see that which thou hast not seen. Thine ears can now hear where no sound existed. Thy lame ones, even if they may still limp, can now walk, nay fly, on the wings of the hope of salvation, the salvation which the white one denied thee.'

The following day around midday, District Commissioner Jennings descended upon the village. A dozen or so policemen preceded him. When they reached the edge of the village they alighted from their vehicles, marched up into the village by their African sub-inspector, their guns proudly slanted on their shoulders. A crowd gathered. The village headman stood grinning. As they passed him, the sub-inspector knew him well from past encounters — they proudly pushed out their chests and saluted him when he said, 'E-eyes-Right!' It was a proud salute, a mocking, sardonic salute which made it clear where real authority lay. The village went wild with cheers of admiration at the click of boots and the smart turn out. Then when they had marched through the crowd the sub-inspector halted the troops. He turned sharply right about and marched arrogantly towards the headman, his sword held high. The villagers shrieked with a mixture of awe and admiration. Would he drive his sword into the headman? He stopped only a few feet from the headman, saluted him and uttered some meaningless phrases. Katenga, of course, had 'vanished'.

Within seconds of finishing this drill the District Commissioner Jennings, rode through the village in a crystal white, plumed uniform. He waved to the ecstatic crowd over and over. His adventurism and his attention to the minutest details were paying off. Before venturing on to the exercise now in hand he had researched the 'behavioural patterns' of religious sects in general and he had, in particular, read Nicolae Branswichnsky's book *Recurring Patterns of Primitive Religious Behaviourism*. The next van carried a gold, white and red throne draped with a high back topped with a black and white plumed hat. It was Jennings' own special invention. The throne was lowered and transported to a place to the left of the village headman. Then Jennings, in all his impish blonde mischief descended and as he strode towards the 'throne' a red carpet rolled off before him and a band of policemen played 'Happy Birthday'. The same dozen policemen and their sub-inspector who had performed for the headman now performed a glorious march past for Jennings. It was a grand, arrogant scene, bristling with pugnacity. Then the same sub-inspector beefed his way to Jennings.

'The troops are ready for inspection, sir!' He stepped down from his makeshift dais. His upright slim form fitted immaculately into the uniform and he walked forward to a dignified and kingly slow march. The troops stood stiffly to attention. They felt proud to be party to it all and there were some among the crowd who wished their sons had been among them. When the formal part had ended, the sub-inspector said:

'Now we want to show the DC something of your hospitality.'

The villagers needed no prompting. They danced for the white one. The white one was happy. Then the head messenger whispered to him:

'We were telling you, sir. The worship of the Holy Ones is no more.'

Jennings nodded agreement and said somewhat loudly:

'It is no more. If they start it up again, they'll be in serious trouble.'

He had meant it for the headman. The headman sat up. Katenga's last words came up to his mind: 'Welcome the infidel as though he were righteous for the Lord of Jericho welcometh all that repent. But if he that cometh to you persisteth in iniquity even after thou hast welcomed him, *then thy duty, O sons and daughters of Jericho, is clear. Destroy!*'

Everyone there remembered those words as what the white one had said spread through the crowd in whispers. Suddenly someone in the back shouted:

'Jericho!' The crowd leapt to its feet, rushed into their huts and in no time a hailstorm of spears and knobkerries rained into the area. Jennings leapt up. He cried:

'Fire!' But his men scuttled into landrovers. 'Fire!' he cried again.

How could they fire when their guns were not loaded! He ran to the landrover stumbling over a policeman who had been speared in the calf. Now his left foot was on board the van. He was just swinging up his right leg when a muzzle loader roared and exploded and shattered the whole of his leg below the knee. Jennings propelled by the force of the impact fell forward into the van. The sub-inspector now at the wheel did not panic. He turned the key in the ignition, the van leapt forward ploughing through the only way available to them, namely the crowd. Later on in the afternoon a fully armed reinforcement arrived. The village had dispersed into the bush. Katenga had vanished and it seemed that at least five of their people had been trampled by the landrover.

Chimuko caught up with Katenga.

They left Nampande a few days later in the evening. They struck towards the Zambian border. The Zambezi lay in between. It poured cats and dogs. About five miles after leaving Nampande they fell into a main road of a sort. The flash of the lightning showed up a white sheet of paper on the tree. Katenga struck a match. It was a 'wanted' poster. £10,000 reward ... Katenga, Chimuko ... Dead or alive!

Dead or alive!

'We don't look very pretty, do we?' joked Chimuko.

But in his heart he realized that they were now wanted men. Men with a price on their heads. Maybe the money was too much for the villagers to understand. But behind every villager who found them there would be a white one to claim the prize. That could be dangerous.

Just then car lights beamed on the dark horizon catching the silvery grey droplets of the rain. They ducked into the bush. It was a police van. It screeched to a halt at the tree. One of the police got out to examine the poster on the tree. It was hanging limp from the rain. He peered into the darkness. He came back to the driver.

'I thought I saw some figures about here.'

'Must have been dreaming. Look it's getting late. My kid's first before this Katenga nuisance.' He turned the ignition. The other man jumped in and the jeep was away.

'We'd better stay clear of the roads,' said Chimuko.

'Don't worry, there's no way you and I will stay clear of death.'

'I wonder what they are doing to comrade Kawala now.'

'Giving him the works. But they are wasting their time,' said Katenga.

They walked on. Another five miles or so. Then a light came up. It was a house. A car was driving up to the house. Its lights played on a tree. It was another £10,000 reward poster. Katenga and Chimuko stood and waited. Then they decided to scout the area. A farm. The labourers' compound was half a mile away.

'Good', said Katenga. 'We need arms and we'll get them. With that kind of money going every white must be armed tonight.'

An hour later the lights went off in the farm house.

'Give them time to make love and sleep,' said Chimuko.

'Now, let's go,' said Katenga after a while.

They crept up to the house. The doors were locked.

'Try the windows.'

One was open. They slid in.

'You look for food. I'll mind the guns.'

Chimuko went to the kitchen.

'Don't get drunk on whisky,' whispered Katenga.

Katenga looked around the study. A gun rack on the wall. He tried the glass door. It was locked. But there were five guns inside. He covered his torch with his shirt. Gently he pressed into the glass. The glass gave way with a clink. He picked the five guns. There was also the ammunition.

'Let's go,' he whispered to Chimuko.

Just then a light turned on. A tall white man stood in the living room, his cheeks ruddy, maybe from pressing them against the pillow. He wore pyjamas and he seemed still half in sleep.

'What the hell are you doing here?'

His back was against the kitchen door. Chimuko crept up to him. His hand darted up to the man's mouth. The man felt a fast cold thing pierce into his back. He collapsed to the floor backwards the kitchen knife driving through his chest. The wife and child heard the faint scream. They rushed to the living room. Angus Morton was lying in a pool of blood. Jane screamed. She slumped to the floor and passed out. The servant heard the cry. He rushed to the house. Two forms leapt out through the window.

The police landrover had second thoughts. It reversed back to the tree after going forward a hundred yards or so. Katenga and Chimuko fell back into the bushes.

'They might be up this tree, these monkeys,' said one policeman lighting up the tree with his torch.

'What's that silvery-grey thing?'

The light rested for a moment on it.

'It looks like a — a snake.'

'Wait,' said another. 'Let's shoot it. And that should frighten the shit out of Katenga if he's around.'

Katenga and Chimuko could hear the loud voice of the one who had said 'shit'.

'Shit your father! I wish we had guns. We would fix this drunken bastard.'

The man aimed for the snake . . .

Four hundred yards away a lion walked stealthily towards its target. It had a high mane and a long slithering body. The duiker slept on. Now the lion was only fifty yards from its target. Its cat's eyes dilated in the darkness and the heavy tail began to flick ominously. The eyes caught the light playing up and into the tree. Now it was near enough to the target. It crouched and began lightly to claw out the earth under its claws to steady its pounce. Katenga picked up the sound. His insides froze.

'A lion!' he whispered to Chimuko.

Had it seen them? He looked towards the road. The policeman was steadying his aim. The snake was coiling itself off the tree slowly. Maybe the light had disturbed it. The duiker shook itself. It cocked its ears and sniffed the air. Something was the matter. It tensed itself ready for a jump into the air. The lion's claws gripped into the earth. The policeman pressed the trigger. A loud explosion. The duiker jumped into the air. The lion knocked its head off with the paw and sunk its claws into the chest with a mighty roar. The cobra, shot in the tail streaked down the tree towards the landrover.

'Lion!' cried the driver.

'Cobra!' cried the marksman.

They banged the doors, drove off in panic fifty yards away from Katenga and Chimuko. The struggles of the duiker had died down. The baritone roar of the lion sent the ants dropping on to the damp, dry leaves of the bush. Then they heard the lion roar again and trot off deeper into the bush with its kill. When the roar faded off into the thickets of the forest, Katenga stood up and shone the light under the tree. There was the cobra lying limp, flattened off by the heavy tyres of the police landrover. He gasped, 'Ugh!'

That night they sneaked into a village. The people had not slept because the police had just been and harrassed them much. It was a friendly village and news of their fleeing had already reached them from Nampande. The village secretary of the party talked with them. The people were fed up with the harassment. Yes, many young men would sneak out to join them, even into Zambia. Others would also follow.

A week passed. Katenga and Chimuko trudged on through the woods. Then they reached the Zambezi and across it they could see the land of freedom that was Zambia. Katenga, tired, turned to Chimuko.

'We shall also make it.'

The two embraced. The bushes were thick. A gentle drizzle was setting in. They looked at a map which Chimuko carried. Five miles south, almost along the river, there was a police station. If the promised reinforcements came, they would need arms, food, medicines. These could be had there. But when?

An hour passed. Then from a distance they heard a rustle. Katenga put his ear to the ground. It trembled with the thud of feet. They could not be police feet. Those would wear boots, in a forest.

'They are coming,' said Katenga excitedly.

Now the feet were getting nearer. Katenga raised the torch and flashed it into the sky twice. That was the sign. They could hear the hurried patter of feet. When they were near their leader challenged:

'PALP?'

Katenga recognized his voice.

'Are you friends?'

'Yes.'

'You know we are armed.'

'Yes.'

'Come.'

The men came on; Chimuko searched them in the full glare of the torchlight. Then Katenga addressed them.

'You have come to fight for your country. If you turn back I will shoot you. You will be here in this area for a week. Training. There's a cave in that mountain which you can just see. We will hide there and other places during the day. The Zambian Government doesn't know. So I don't want any talk. But more people will come. A lot of young men are already crossing into Zambia under the guise of seeking jobs. They will be coming here.'

For a week Katenga trained the rugged troops non-stop, around the area. Climbing trees at lightning speed. Scaling the mountain at night. Eating anything. Carrying heavy stones. So far their luck held and there were no incidents.

Then they crossed into Zambia one night for final exercises. Arrangements had now been finalized for their camp there. News of this camp soon leaked out and there were loud cries of condemnation of the Zambian decision in the Kandaha Legislature and in the House of Commons. A terse Foreign Ministry statement in Zambia denied any knowledge, but said that in accordance with its principles the Zambian Government would give refuge to any political refugees and would not stand in their way if they used these facilities to prepare for fighting colonialism. 'Zambia', the statement continued 'does not manufacture guns and so the allegation of Zambia arming the freedom fighters must be treated with the contempt it deserves.'

The numbers in the camp swelled. Training continued. Then the week of the first expedition came. Katenga gathered the specially trained group together for the last tips.

They moved a mile away into the bush to put the finishing

touches to their land-mining exercises. He placed the mine in the ground, stood up and looked at Chimuko.

'Remove this mine and plant it in another place.'

'This one?' asked Chimuko incredulously.

'Yes, this one,' said Katenga, his voice cool but scornful. 'I've been wasting my time.'

The troops watched. Chimuko dug a hole. Then he bent down to remove the mine from the first hole into the new one. The troops began to back away. Katenga watched them nonchalantly. Chimuko's mouth felt dry. Katenga said:

'Now bury it.'

Chimuko looked at him and shook his head:

'No.' Suddenly Katenga grabbed Chimuko's shoulders, spun the fellow round until he was dizzy and, unsheathing his knife and offering it to Chimuko, he said:

'Now, uncover the mine and remove it from this hole.'

Chimuko got down on his knees. He looked at Katenga. There was no mercy in those eyes. Katenga's face, now hardened, was not giving him any let off. He began to scratch the sand off the mine. Then he uncovered it. He would now have to lift it out with his hands. Then, Katenga's heavy foot stepped on it.

'No!' cried Chimuko.

There was a loud bang. Katenga said:

'I've already told you not to fear fear.'

Chimuko would have struck him out of shame, but he controlled his anger.

That night, it was also the night before the expedition would set out back into Kandaha. The first target would be the police station on the border. Other groups would move swiftly into Kandaha. Musasa especially. There would be a day's difference between the two incidents so that the Government would rush to send troops to the border and leave Musasa and other towns uncovered. The freedom fighters had been put to bed early as they would attack around 4 a.m.

Katenga was uneasy. He was like a sailor with land in sight wondering if the ship would make it in the rough storm. He could not sleep. He wanted to check all round the camp that all was well.

He returned an hour later. All were asleep. Sound asleep. An hour after returning Katenga felt a strange contented peace settling on him. He was just about to slide into deep sleep when a loud shrieking woman's wail pierced the darkness. Chimuko jumped up. The woman was running round the camp like a mad one, screaming. The whole camp sprang to its arms and followed the woman. Katenga took the rear. When the woman reached the place she pointed to a body lying propped up against a tree, blood congealed all over it.

'My husband. They have killed him.'

There was a hushed silence. Anger swept through the crowd at yet another murder by Kandaha colonialists.

Katenga walked forward, took out his blood-crusted knife and said: 'This!'

'You did it!' cried Chimuko pulling out his knife also.

'Yes.'

'You've killed an African.'

'Yes. He was asleep at his sentry post.'

Chimuko's knife flashed towards him. Katenga gripped his wrist and twisted it downwards to the ground. The freedom fighters watched. Any time now someone would plunge a knife into Katenga or shoot him. But they had to await orders. Without even so much as a sign Katenga moved forward. He ripped the heavy coat off the corpse. Underneath it was the uniform of the Rhodesian Selous Scouts — a dreaded murder squad. Katenga had been baptised.

The following morning a party foraging for food went out early in the morning to hunt wild game for meat. They were four, all armed. By the evening the party had not returned. Katenga began to be anxious. Then at midnight he heard a sentry's voice at the gate far off challenging some people. 'Friend or Enemy.' It was three men. After listening to them the sentry went to get Katenga. An accident. Their colleague had gone ahead of them.

'Didn't I tell you you should move in groups of two at least?'

'Yes. He would not agree to wait around for the sick one.'

'Which one of you was the woman to be sick when the fighters need food?' Katenga was furious. There was silence. 'You disobeyed my orders. What's the punishment for disobedience?'

'Death.'

'Death! Yes, death!'

'He's dead. comrade,' said the one who had been explaining.

'Dead? What do you mean "dead"?'

The man looked towards a bundle wrapped up in a blanket.

'A lion.'

'You killed it?'

'No.'

'No?' cried Katenga. 'Didn't I tell you you will kill anything that touches you? Why are we fighting the white man? Is it not because he has touched us, touched our freedom, touched our lives?'

The spokesman could not answer.

'Now you and I, we will follow that lion. Tonight. Now. We will carry no guns. Only spears and axes. We only use guns on strangers. A lion is not a foreigner. We will slay it tonight.' Katenga took one look at the fallen comrade's body. His anger boiled. 'You disobeyed my orders,' he barked at the corpse.

Chimuko, who had woken, said he would come along. They did not have very long to walk. It seemed that the lion, having eaten off only a leg of the corpse had followed the trail of blood down towards the camp. Three miles from the camp they heard a growl from a nearby bush. Katenga whispered:

'Shh. It is he.' Chimuko felt afraid and uncertain. He could fight anything with a gun. He could kill a human being with his blow, knife, axe or any weapon. But kill a lion with an axe ... a spear . . .? Beads of sweat formed on his forehead in spite of it being a cool evening. Katenga marched forward, not for a moment even lowering his frame. He stopped and sniffed the air. His red eyes narrowed in the darkness as he tried to see. His beard fluttered in the wind. A raw animal scent wafted across his nose from the east. That scent reminded him of the hunting expedition with the whole village many years back.

'Down,' he whispered.

The lion could be near.

They heard the violent flick of something twenty yards away. It was the monster's tail. That meant it had seen them and was crouching for a spring. Katenga shone his torch in that direction. It picked up the fiery, cat-like eyes. The lion steadied. Katenga raised his spear. Would he throw it at it? Would he wait until it sprung forward? A gun. There was no gun. Chimuko felt his legs tremble. He could only just stand. Then, a roar. The beast leapt sky high at Katenga. There was a metallic clash against its skin. Chimuko had passed out ...

When he came round, Chimuko found Katenga standing on the dead beast, holding the one and only spear that had pierced deep through its skull, down the throat into the stomach and out on the side.

'You sleep too long, comrade, in a bush full of snakes,' said Katenga.

'If I were in the village now would be the time for a new bride.'

17

It was Sunday. Lafayette woke up unusually early. He had not needed to rise until Complines at 5 a.m. But he had been up at 3.30 a.m. On the eight o'clock evening news broadcast the previous day, the Government had broadcast its appeal to all churches to dedicate that Sunday to prayers for peace. His service would be due in six hours time. That morning he felt a more than usual urge to pray for the success of his sermon. So, while a priest from another parish said the 6.30 Mass, he crept into the church and after listening to the confessions remained there praying. Shortly after eight, the young black priest who had said the earlier Mass came back to the Church.

'Father,' he whispered into the ears of the praying superior, 'Father, there is very bad news on the radio. There is trouble all over the country.' But Fr Lafayette had not really understood what the young priest was saying. One trouble was already enough trouble for his frail body. Besides, his mind was still on the sermon that he would be giving shortly.

'What trouble, Father?' he said absentmindedly.

The other said:

'PALP is stirring up the country. Norris' men are armed.'

Climbing those stairs up to the altar of his Samaka Church on that hot Sunday morning, Lafayette felt as if he was emerging from a cauldron of steamy water into the open fresh air. He knew that Mother Church had to speak out against violence. So he welcomed the opportunity of doing so. He also knew that the subject had its pitfalls. When, for example, did violence cease to be violence and become law enforcement? He had seen many political activists detained on very slight evidence, sometimes mere suspicion. Some of these men had been tortured. Had he not heard of political detainees having matches pushed into their organs and then lit at the head? Assuming those men had been guilty of violence, when did the punishment for violence cease to be justice and become violence itself?

What was violence, he had kept asking himself over and over. Was violence violence only when it left a physical mark such as a scar or swollen limb or the debris of a burnt-down house? Or was violence possible in an abstract sense? Take, for example, the white man who calls an African a 'baboon'. If this insult annoys the African intensely, is it not possible that the humiliation of that remark can be more painful to him than the infliction of a wound upon his body? What of the man who starved his servant, letting him live on £4 a month with his eight children while he spends £30 a month on choice steaks for his dog? Is this man not committing violence to the servant?

When he had started writing his sermon, Lafayette had thought that the job would be fairly straightforward; a condemnation of the thuggery that was gathering momentum around the country and nothing more. He would round it off with an exhortation to his flock to disown the demagogue. He would ask them to remember the teachings of Our Lord Jesus Christ. If someone smacked them on the cheek, they were to give him the other cheek. But now the whole subject was becoming much more complicated. What, for example, caused the first man to smack the other on the cheek? Was it simply a sadistic perversion or could it be his way of reacting against violence physical or mental, perpetrated against him by the other man? That Jesus died at the hands of violent men was not in doubt. But, and here Lafayette would close his eyes in an effort to close his mind against the temptation of unbelief, is it possible that Our Lord through his teachings did violence to the institutions represented by his crucifiers? If so, was their sin as mortal as it is? What would he say to the congregation? What did Mother Church teach? You cannot pay wrong with wrong. . . . The means does not justify the end. In any case, what was this end? Was political freedom an end in itself? What does any freedom mean unless it is freedom from *sin*? And yet freedom from *sin* cannot be had by sinful means, which is what violence really is. Can violence be a subjective matter? Thou shalt not steal. . . . Thou shalt not kill thy neighbour. . . . Thou shalt not commit adultery. . . . Thou shalt not . . . All these are categorical acts of violence against a neighbour which are categorically prohibited by the Church. The Church must speak out against anything that hinders the goal of loving one's neighbour as much as oneself.

The small church was packed. As he concluded the first part of Mass, Lafayette surveyed the congregation. He coughed a little. The little cough gave birth to a bouncing one until his white cassock convulsed into a spatter of coughs. His eyes watered a little. He wiped them off on his sleeve. Still looking at the faithful, he blew his nose into his handkerchief, fumbled with his Sunday missal and the papers under it and then said:

'*Sequentia sancti evangelii secundum Lucam.*'
'*Gloria tibi Domine,*' replied the congregation.

Ever since Vatican II had decreed the use of the vernacular as a language of Mass, Lafayette had never really felt that the Mass was still the same act of prayer that it used to be. He had learnt the Latin Mass as a child, long before he had ever known *mensa, mensa, mensam, mensae, mensae, mensa*. . . . He had not needed to know Latin to feel that *'Sequentia sancti evangelii secundum Lucam'* (Following the Holy Gospel in the footsteps of Luke) was much more expressive than 'The Holy Gospel according to Luke'.

That is why now, as he ascended the steps to the pulpit to read the Gospel in the vernacular he still withheld his last little concession to Vatican II and said:

'Sequentia sancti evangelii secundum Lucam.'

He adjusted his reading glasses on his bony nose bridge, sneezed a little and then began to read the Sunday's Gospel.

When he finished, he said:

'You have heard me read the Gospel of peace. You know that this Gospel is read only at Christmas and yet I read it now, on this Sunday. "Glory be to God in the highest and peace to men who enjoy his favour," I say unto you.'

He took a deep breath and surveyed the congregation. After that Mass, he would mingle among the congregation and hear what they would have to say about the sermon he was just about to preach. Many of the people in the congregation were loyal Christians who had expressed disgust with any form of violence. Perhaps the time had come for the Church to take a stand. Indeed God had so willed or how else could a heretic like Thomson have found the wisdom to ask him to preach a sermon on peace? He took in the air into his lungs and for a while held his breath. Then he let out his breath and he could hear the strange wheezing noise within his chest.

'Today is a day of prayer for peace, a day of prayer against the violence that is sweeping this Christian country. It is also a day of prayer for the men and women who have fallen victims to the rapacities of certain arrogant political groups.' The people sat up. Lafayette could see that he had dropped a bomb among their unsuspecting lot.

'There are people in our community whose respect for life is the respect of a snake for a frog. These men have only one ambition: to kill people for the sake of an independence of their own fashion. Political independence is a good thing. But of its own, without the independence of the heart that comes from freeing oneself of sin, it is nothing. We are fools if we pretend to independence when our hearts are shackled and strapped over to the devil.

'Any man who seeks to attain independence by killing is seeking a shadow which is the devil himself. You cannot kill and still be independent. For even though the people, the powers which you imagine to stand in your way to independence, were to be frightened into giving in to you, the devil, Beelzebub, and all his evil choir take possession of the sinister house of murder which is your soul.'

Fr Lafayette stopped at this point. Then, as if summoning all his powers of exorcism, he thumped the pulpit and cried:

'Murder cannot be justified as a political necessity. You, the Africans, will still be people even if you may not be free politically. If you kill, whether it is the white man or your fellow black people who oppose your political ends, do not deceive yourselves by the sophistry that the end justifies the means. That end is neither noble nor holy. The means is bloody.' Then he lowered his voice, 'I have served you for these many years. Please God, I will do so with a full appreciation of the dignity and right of a people to political freedom. My own country fought to be free even from its own kings and queens.

'The goal you seek is a good one. But it will only be a noble one if the means which you use are those of God. Mother Church supports the quest for freedom. His Holiness Pope Paul VI has said so on many occasions. But the Church will not support murder, murder of the innocent merely because their mind is of a different colour from your own.'

Lafayette straightened himself up, his eyes still dark narrow slits of anger.

'As the Church's ordained priest, I enjoin you my congregation to condemn violence of all kinds. But I do more.' Then he raised his voice again and excitedly waving his thin arms before the congregation he said, 'From today I bind all the sins of those that shall commit or be accessory to the committing of an offence of political violence. If the only way to avoid violence is to leave the political party of violence, then I your priest command your conscience to leave that political party. For not to command you so is to assist you in committing your soul to the devil's house of sin.'

There was a murmur in the congregation. One man stood up but the others pulled him down. Then another man stood up and before anyone could stop him he said:

'If God will only welcome the black man as a slave, then let God know that we black people do not want His Heaven.'

All eyes turned in the man's direction. The man swore aloud and then turned to go. Then when he reached the door, he turned and exclaimed:

'God Bless Africa! God Bless Kandaha!'

There was commotion in the church. Fr Lafayette looking haggard cried:

'Stop making noise in the House of God!'

Someone let out a loud mocking laugh.

'Stop it!' cried Lafayette again.

The same man who had let out a loud laugh exclaimed:

'Take your God to Europe!' The Catechists rushed through the congregation and in a moment there was calm. Fr Lafayette, still in possession of the pulpit, swallowed hard. He would have to continue as though nothing had happened. Then, just when he was about to part his trembling lips, a small figure hobbled towards the pulpit from one corner of the church. The figure walked with the aid of crutches and one trouser leg was carefully rolled over the thigh where it was tied up with a belt.

Lafayette stopped. Bending down on his crutches, the man unfastened the belt and pushed back the trouser leg and when the stump that was once his leg peeped out, he said:

'For being a man of peace this is what the colonialists did to me. For feeding my own son they did this to me a year ago because he was a member of PALP.'

The church was hushed.

'They bound my hands and my legs in my own house. My own children and grandchildren saw their own father and grandfather carried away like a dog. Circulation stopped in this leg,' he said pointing to his stump. 'They kept me in detention. They refused to take me to hospital. When it was too late, they took me there and the doctors cut my leg off. The colonial police,' said the man speaking slowly but in a low, deep voice which commanded attention, 'refused the hospital permission to dispose of the leg that had been cut away. They said it would be required as an exhibit in court. So it was put back in the mortuary. Sometimes it was taken out of there and left on the floor to make room for whole corpses. Then on the day that I was discharged the police took me to the mortuary. They ordered me to wash my festered limb. With these hands', said the man, 'I was forced to dig a grave for my leg while sitting down. All the time they jeered at me.' Then the man stopped. For the first time he turned to the congregation. His eyes were brimming with tears. 'For how long shall we continue to keep peace for the sake of non-violence? Is it really Africans and not white people who killed these two Europeans?'

'Kawala, Kawala, Jericho, Jericho!' roared the congregation.

If Lafayette had had a choice, he would have torn off his vestments there and then and walked out. But holy Mass, once commenced has to be finished, consummated. *'Ite Messa est'* ('Go, the Mass *is*') was that prayer of consummation. So he resumed the Mass and mechanically went through the prayers. As against the scores of people who went to Communion, only two stood up to receive the Holy Eucharist. One of these was the little man hobbling on his crutches. Would he give him the Host?

Lafayette stood transfixed before the bowed, kneeling figure of the little man. He had raised the Host but the words would not come out of his mouth. He closed his eyes. In that closing of eyes, he remembered his visit of many years ago to St Peter's in Rome. There were the bold words running along the belly of the great renaissance dome. Here he was, a small insect in that immense expanse, revolving on his feet as his upturned face followed the letters of the dome . . . *'Tu es Petrus et hanc petram aedificabo ecclesiammeam et tibi dabo claves regni caelorum. . . . Ego rogavi pro te O petre ut non deficiat fides tua . . .'*

'Thou art Peter,' his silent lips uttered, 'and upon this rock I will build my church and to you I will give the keys of the kingdom of heaven.' Then his lips quivered. 'Whomsoever you shall bind on earth he shall be bound in heaven; whomsoever you shall absolve on earth he shall be absolved in heaven. I have prayed for you, O Peter, that your faith may not fail.' He opened his eyes, raised the Host yet higher and lowering it into the cripple's mouth he said,

'The Body of Christ.'

18

'Ha ha ha! Ha ha ha!' The laughter echoed through the high red brick fence of the Selope Maximum Detention Camp. The camp was not really a camp. In fact it was a prison converted into a detention camp for the sake of keeping on the right side of the law. Broken bottles were embedded on top of the wall and masses of coiled barbed wire ran up it, extending four feet above it. St Claus, the Officer Commanding, laughed again and this time he held the sides of his stomach as his body convulsed with laughter.

'So, you've come back home at last,' he said, kicking the man. 'At last I've got you, you ——!' said St Claus.

Kawala did not move. He was sitting on the edge of his concrete bunker.

'You've caused us too much trouble. You knew a nigger couldn't win didn't you?'

Kawala's eyes were still cast down.

'You know, I've shot a Kaffir before? I could do it to you. And do you know what the verdict would be? In the course of duty, my nigger friend. Maybe I'd receive an honour. You know that they've not sent you here for nothing? It's because they know I'm tough. What have you been causing riots for? What did you kill the Ecklands for? Here, my nigger friend, you'll die a slow death. It's a far cry from dreaming about being President of Kandaha, isn't it?'

St Claus' taunting voice was low and chatty. But Kawala did not look up. Then he said:

'Blacks are monkeys my nigger friend. Remember that. You'll never rule this country.'

Kawala jumped up. His deep set eyes fixed on Claus' face. They were fiery eyes, reddened by lack of sleep. St Claus blinked. He had never looked at a black man so close. But Kawala held his eyes. The sunken cheeks depressed further with utter scorn. St Claus felt awkward. He had not looked into such a face ever. Never. Those eyes cowed him, intimidated him. They frightened him. They were the eyes of an angry lion. And yet ... didn't they look the eyes of fearlessness, of deep compassion? He could not remember what it was or where he had seen those eyes. He was sure it was not from a photograph. Some white man he had known years back had had those very eyes, in fact that very kind of face. A white man to have the features of a black? Kawala's eyes were still on him. They seemed to dilate and seered into his own. Those were the eyes of reproach. But it was a reproach which went beyond a person into one's society, perhaps even one's race. And yet there was a way in which those eyes were reproaching the whole of mankind. Feeling awkward and sheepish, he turned his head to avert that glare, and said as he strutted away:

'Bloody Kaffir!' Then turning to the African Assistant Inspector, he said, 'Put him through the works. I want a full confession by tomorrow.'

When St Claus went home for lunch that day, he was an agitated man. As he sat at the table, he was feeling very restless. The servant ladled out some soup. He picked up his spoon to drink it. The spoon dropped to the floor. His wife looked at him caustically, but she did not comment. He picked it up. As he straightened up his head hit against the plate of soup which was on the edge of the table and the soup spilt all over the table soaking through her most prized Irish linen. Claus was that kind of man who ate or drank more of everything than any other man. She held her peace.

'I'm sorry, darling,' he said.

She held her tongue. But it was really too much. Only yesterday she had quarrelled with him about the business of looking forward to the arrival of Kawala and 'roasting him blacker than he had ever been'.

'I wish you'd stop this childish nonsense!' she exploded.

Unlike his usual self St Claus did not take her up on it. He merely mumbled again:

'I'm sorry, darling,' as he poured himself some more soup.

His wife looked at him like a cat and then she observed:

'At least you could try and mop up this mess.'

It was not his day. That was for sure. As soon as he'd finished lunch he pecked her cheek, settled his cap on his head and left the house.

Back at the cell the questioning continued.

'You've got to tell us everything Kawala. Europeans are squeamish. But we aren't because we know you. A trouble-maker only!' cried a huge black man wearing the Assistant African Inspector badge of rank. 'Constable,' he roared, 'cane him!' The Constable lifted his cane and smashed it several times into Kawala. Kawala did not flinch.

'Now you know what's in store for you. There will be a hundred other things to do with you before we are finished or you are. And my friend, we are only carrying out orders.'

'Whose orders? The orders of the devil? Assistant Inspector, are you bound to obey the devil?' replied Kawala.

The African Assistant Inspector chuckled liquidly.

'Shall I tell you the truth. I need my job. You don't need to continue loafing, making mischief, murdering. It's you who's serving the devil and it's you who has to change. Constable we are behind time. Officer Commanding will soon be returning. Next step please. Or do you want to confess you organized everything that's happened? Right, next step.'

The Constable forced Kawala on his back so that he was lying there looking upwards.

'Stretch your arms over Constable's shoulders. Outwards with your elbows looking up. Now go, Constable.'

The Constable held him by the wrists as he heaved Kawala up. The arms were splitting at the wrists. Kawala tried to bend them. The African Assistant Inspector hit them with an iron bar. When the Constable had heaved the body up and down, he let go and Kawala slithered to the floor, his head hitting the bunk.

'Right. We won't be asking you any questions lest you should tell us lies. We know what you did. You've been keeping us busy. Do you know that some of us have lost our jobs because of you?' The senior looked at his programme. He said, 'Next.'

'We can't do it here, sir,' said the Constable.

'Oh, yes, I forgot.'

The senior led the way to another building. He followed a flight of stairs downwards. Kawala followed, handcuffed to the Constable. When they were down below the heavy door behind them called a valve, closed. It was pitch dark in there.

'You want to see the place?' mocked the officer switching on the light. 'We'll treat you kindly so you can confess when the Officer Commanding comes.'

The wall was painted black. On one side of the wall ran a concrete bunker. There were several plugs in it. Above were several gadgets for lifting and lowering things. On the wall there was a cupboard which it seemed contained implements.

'Next,' said the officer, ticking off that number in his notebook.

The Constable lowered a bar with two iron boots stuck to it. He shoved Kawala's feet into it and secured them down with metal straps. He lowered another bar from the high roof. The African Assistant Inspector barked:

'Hold on to that bar! That's your lifeline.'

Kawala held it. Then a button was switched on. The bars with

184

Kawala's feet in the lower one and his hands gripping the upper one rose into the roof.

'Ha ha ha!' laughed the man. 'That's very nice indeed. You wouldn't say we were torturing you, would you?'

Just then, the officer switched on the current to the upper bar to which Kawala's arms were hanging. He shrieked as he let go of it. His body swooped downwards to the floor. Then it swung beyond it and backwards to the other end of the wall. Several times he swung in this manner, his feet firmly secured to the bar.

'Stop! I see our friend is not all courage!'

Kawala's head was pitched downwards.

'Raise the bar,' he ordered. 'Next please.'

The Constable switched on a heater. He put it right under Kawala's upturned head.

'You'll enjoy the warmth, my friend.'

It was getting hot. The Constable was lowering the bar. Kawala tried to swing off the heater. But the man lowered it further.

'I burn!' cried Kawala. There was a smell of burning hair.

'OK, take it off. He's not a strong one, is he?'

The Inspector looked at the next item. He said:

'He'll need something to do in the evening. Get him down. Ready, my friend? Ready, you're landing on your hands or head.'

Kawala dived the hands forward in time to support his weight as the iron feet above unclamped. He collapsed to the floor and passed out. In the evening, St Claus looked at him and said:

'He's coming on nicely, eh?'

St Claus did not return to the camp for three days. Nor did the African Assistant Inspector. But the Constable kept guard on Kawala. His relief was another fellow. This fellow's drinking exercises always coincided with his duty hours. He wasn't much use and indeed many convicts had managed to escape during his duty hours. But St Claus had a soft spot for him. Perhaps it was because with every such escape he was able to make a case for more ruthless treatment of the internees to O'Flaherty. So the drunken Constable was on duty. He said to Kawala:

'You aren't much use, are you?'

'Why?'

'Well, I understand you don't drink. What good is life without it?' He smiled stupidly as he tilted his hand upwards to his mouth. 'I used to be like you once. Never drank.' He furrowed his forehead to appear serious. 'Only water. Then I got into woman problems. Couldn't sleep. The wife, always yapping at me. You did this. You did that. So over a period I says to myself, "Kapini, you are a fool. If you do what she accuses you of, you'll be pals." '

Kawala listened. It was strange how little Kapini worried him.

'If you don't patch it up, well at least she would be on the right scent. You love her so much that it pains you to see her be so wrong about you. So one night, I got real boozed. I came back late. She's not talking. I creep on to my side of the reed mat. She's not talking. Then I says to her — loud and right into her ears — "I'm drunk!" What a hornet's nest that one was! She really beat me up. Said she knew it all along. I go to drink for women. But you know, secretly, I was very glad with myself that I did it to her. So her blows didn't really hurt. I just sort of lay there in seventh heaven or whatever you people call it. So the following evening I did it.'

The little fellow did a caper as if threatening to do it again right there and then.

'And do you know what? I discovered some women like their husbands drunk — especially gentle ones like you, my friend, who can't command and domineer a woman unless you are drunk. So now, she's the gentlest of creatures and I'm the most drunken of the whole lot. Sometimes she even brings me beer home. Buys it for me. Believe you me. But I says, "This is a stupid European way. How can an African he-man drink alone at home? Do you want me to get drunk?" ' Kawala could have laughed in spite of the pain.

'So you want some beer now old man?'

'Did I say no?' asked Kapini. His eyes lit up.

'Not now,' said Kawala. 'You are on duty. I might escape if you got drunk. You could lose your job.'

Kapini laughed silently. His shoulders shook with the effort to suppress the laughter.

'It's not my job I'm worried about losing. It's my drunkeness. I haven't got money now. And when I can't drink, I feel awful. I feel like killing a man.'

'What about the Officer Commanding, Mr St Claus, he wouldn't be happy to see you drink, would he?'

'Ha ha ha, he? Any day. Don't you know he likes Kaffir beer very much? Why do you think he doesn't dismiss me, even though you fellows may escape when I'm on duty? Because I get him the stuff. And so you know where we drink it? Not at his house. Where else can a white man meet Kaffir beer except in a kaffir house?'

Kawala arched his eyes.

'Yes, me, me here,' exclaimed little Kapini and by way of emphasis stabbed his little chubby hand into his stomach.

'If you told people I was around and they know you see me, they might give you lots of beer for yourself.'

'You? Who do you think knows you here? You murdered twenty-four people and many more. Everyone here has been waiting for you. You are lucky we guard you. They would have murdered you a long time ago.'

'Who?'

'The people here in Selope. They are angry with you for murdering those people at the mine and Musasa. It's a good thing one of the demagogue's children died also.'

Kawala kept quiet. In that sudden silence the words of Fr Lafayette came back to his mind, 'Unless your own is ... Yours will be only a public sorrow, my friend. ...' What had happened since then? Many people had died at the Bristol Gold Syndicate. Almost as many at the rally in town. And to make it worse, that child, the skull crushed open, crushed by a European driver. The child he had carried in his arms blind to the dangers that surrounded him. That child too had died. Another innocent infant. Would there be no end to it? Had not the soil enough blood to open out and let the seed of freedom sprout out?

Here he was, far away from anywhere. What would happen to his wife? Would the security forces not torture her and even imprison her? He closed his eyes. Bloodshed was inevitable. But PALP's survival was a must. He bit his teeth tightly and mumbled,

'Time.'

'Time? What have you got to bother about time for?'

'Nothing,' Kawala sighed. 'But time is very important, my friend. Time.' He had stood up and gripped the man's hand. His deep-set eyes had sunk further into his forehead. 'Look, I haven't got much time. The revolution has just started and unless it's completed quickly many people will die.'

'Yes,' Kawala put on a bright face. A plan was unfolding. 'Yes, there are lots of people who would give you beer if they knew you looked after me so well.' He looked into Kapini's face. 'You are a very good man and don't you worry about me. I won't make you lose your job by escaping. You've got a family, haven't you?'

'Yes, nine children.'

'And you are still drinking?'

'Well, wouldn't you if you had my wife?'

'Maybe I would and maybe I wouldn't.' Kawala stopped a moment. 'You want beer? Well, if you got me something to write on and a pencil I could give you a note.'

'No writing here. They search us now and again.'

'You know Kanshi?'

'Yes. Why, he's not a politician?'

'Well, just tell him I say you are a very good man.'

'Yes. Is that all?'

'Well, what else can I say if you won't allow me to write?'

Kapini searched his pockets hastily and thrusting pencil and paper before Kawala, he said:

'There. Quick!'

He loosened one hand. Kawala wrote, *Kapini good man. Help him. Tell me what's happening. I need to know. Time is running out.*

Kapini looked at the note — upside down. He always travelled with sellotape — constant repasting back of notices being torn off by detainees. He pushed his pants down and bending down, he taped the note on to himself just below the 'opening' and quickly dressed up.

'You do this often?'

'No.' Kapini looked surprised with himself. 'I don't know why I'm doing it for you. You know, you don't look a murderer to me. I've met some of your chaps down in Selope. They're thugs, arrogant thugs. But you — it's different. And maybe that's why. Maybe you have as many children as me?'

Kawala nodded.

'My children can see me — at least when I'm going to work. And yet I'm a drunk. They can't see you and yet you are sober.' Kapini shook his head.

There were footsteps from a distance. Two sets of footsteps. 'That must be Bwana St Claus and the African Assistant Superintendent. Don't worry, St Claus might possibly feel out my pockets. But he won't be touching a native's shit place.'

The door opened and St Claus said:

'How's the kaffir doing?'

'All right, sir!' saluted Kapini.

'You bastard! You aren't drunk for a change, eh? Now Kawala, are you in a position to confess? Or would you like to sample our other delicacies?'

'I am hungry.'

'Hungry?' It's only four o'clock and you're unlikely to eat for the next twenty-four hours.'

'I haven't eaten for the last two days.'

'Don't argue with me,' snapped St Claus.

The African Inspector smashed Kawala's knuckles with his

baton.

'Good. Maybe you want to confess and eat later? No? Maybe you want to know what's happening. I can tell you that. Six more of these chaps who were wounded at your rally have died.'

'No!' cried Kawala, standing up and trying to move towards St Claus, his feet and hands chained up. He fell, his head narrowly missing St Claus' leg.

'Ha ha ha! Assaulting me, eh? Ha ha ha!'

Then St Claus turned to the African Assistant Inspector.

'Take that down. We'll have a string of charges soon to justify the fellow's imprisonment.' The officer did. Then St Claus cried, 'Haven't you heard Kawala has assaulted me? What are you waiting for? Justice first, the courts later. Where's the police Constable? Kapini here is a drunk. He can hardly wipe his mouth.'

'He's just coming on duty, sir,' said the African Assistant Inspector. Then to Kapini he said, 'Dis — miss!' Kapini saluted, scuttled up the steps and out of the cellar, glad of the release. The other Constable came down. St Claus said:

'Right, carry on officer,' saluted casually and climbed out.

'I think, Constable, we now move to point five. Strap up his nose . . . That's right. Let's see. Push that electrode right in. Right. Now we are ready. Switch!'

Kawala's body contorted. The expectation of pain was more terrible than the pain itself. The current shot through him. He threw up.

Later the man said, 'Good. Next time, and I suppose that you can now be told in advance, we'll stick a match into your manhood, pour petrol over it and light it up. I'm sure that even a so-called freedom fighter will not want to be freed from the slavery of enjoying sex.' He laughed, very much like his superior St Claus. As he did so, his shoulders shook. 'You,' he said pointing a gleeful mischievous finger at Kawala, 'I know you, you political fellows. You spend half the time playing monkey-punky with other people's wives because they go to work and you are loafers. If any of you ever touch one of my three wives or my two girlfriends, I'll kill you there and then.'

A week passed. No communication with the outside. Even his tortures were some communication. Kapini had not been seen and he wondered what might have happened. Then St Claus came on his own. Kawala had by then been moved back to his first cell. St Claus did not waste much time.

'You!' he exclaimed, pointing his finger into Kawala's eyes. 'What's all this business of all the so-called Holy Ones crossing into

Zambia and planning an invasion? You smuggled Katenga and Chimuko to Zambia, didn't you? I'm telling you, if Zambia tries it, we will set that Muntu country on fire. Chinese arms are getting to these people through Zambia. Chimuko has got an army right on our borders on the Zambian side. He too escaped with a lot of people. Katenga nearly killed the District Commissioner in Boko. And that fellow the Muntu President of Zambia, tell him Kandaha, like Rhodesia, can hammer his brains out. He's been a thorn in Smith's side and South Africa, we and Rhodesia can finish him off. Tell me, you did it all, didn't you?'

Kawala did not reply. He pretended no interest. Then St Claus realized that in his anger he had told too much. Turning away he said:

'Fool! We'll hang you alive.'

That evening Kapini was back on duty. He had been ill. Almost certainly too much to drink. His face was really lit up. He had had an excellent time with Kausha. Drank so much. What's more, he'd been there more than twice since then. As soon as he closed the door Kapini uncorked his gun, drew out a piece of paper and said to Kawala:

'Quick, read it. What does it say?'

Kawala read, *Pot boiling. Send message to all in prisons and front. Friends helping Nga and Ko.* He said:

'Kanshi says you are a very good man and he wants you to go back so you can both have a good time.'

Kapini smiled.

'Good fellow that. Your relative?'

Kawala thought quickly.

'Yes, my nephew.'

'You want to send another message when I go?'

'Yes.'

'This time not in that place. I nearly forgot about it when I was pressed. Look here.' He displayed his blood-bespattered bandage in his hand. 'They've all seen this bandage. Bwana St Claus saw it when I took him beer this time to his office last night. So write now and I can tuck it away here. Here's a pencil. Write on the back.'

Kawala got down quickly. *To all in prisons — I am well but tortured. Keep firm. Say nothing.*

19

Mark Bolton surveyed the area for some shade. His landrover had broken down and he was right at the edge of Kandaha near Zambia. In the far distance he could see the shimmering clearness of one arm of the Zambezi River. With binoculars you could almost see the fish in it. He said to his friend Peter Strong:

'Well, this is it.'

Peter asked:

'What's the matter now? We've had so much trouble with this vehicle.'

'Well, this time I think its a lot more serious. The engine seems to have seized. Well, here we are. Two hundred miles from civilization. Little food, little water. I suppose we can eat a freedom fighter if we can find one.'

Mark grinned.

'Ah, there's a good tree there,' he said looking through his binoculars. 'Let's go get ourselves some shade. We'll have to leave this monster here!' He patted the landrover. They walked on. 'Maybe we can sleep in the tree.'

The sun was just setting. Mark and Peter were geologists for the BGS. They had come out here to gather samples. So far the BGS prospecting project was showing promise. No one outside the inner sanctum really knew what the prospecting was for. That was a secret. Certainly no Africans were allowed to know.

They returned to the landrover to pick up the tent. The best place to pitch it up would be somewhere where it was sheltered, like under the large tree which they had located. Snakes? There weren't many and in any case, from his knowledge of nature there he knew that they were all non-poisonous. When they had set the tent they made a fire. Some coffee and they sat down to eat their sandwiches. They amused themselves with the usual yarns about geology and other things. Around ten they snuffed out the lamp and tucked in. So far everything was going well.

The night was dark and overcast as though it would rain. As they canoed to the shore, Katenga checked his automatic. It was dry. Then he peered into the darkness. A lonely hyena howled in the distance. He waited for the last man to come out of the canoes. Now they were all there. Twenty-two of them. Their newly acquired boots crunched into the sand of the river bank. They nestled their

Kalashnikov to their chests. They were novices, all of them. But their eyes, if they could have been seen, shone with courage. A month of drilling in discipline and the use of arms had had its results.

This was by no means their first assignment. But it would be the most important. It was the first time since the fateful rally Katenga was crossing from Zambia back into his own country. His boots crunched into the sand, up, up to the land itself. Cicadas were singing. Another lonely voice of a lonely hyena let out its baleful laughter. The laughter echoed on on on into the surrounding hills. Then as if rebuffed it echoed back into the valley and died away into the bubbling waters of the river. He lay down his gun, prostrated himself before the soil of Kandaha and kissed it. The others, guns at the ready, watched. When he had finished, each of them did the same. Then Katenga, looking around them, his face charged with breathless emotion, said:

'Comrade National President is in contact. He wishes us our spirit's blessings in this mission. His orders are . . .,' he hesitated. Yes, he thought about Kawala's secret orders issued from jail. He would have said, 'To kill, kill any white skin', but Kawala had not said so.

'Our orders', Katenga closed his eyes, 'are to, to demoralize the enemy!'

Then he added under his breath, 'Shoot!' Katenga whispered, 'We could be here for days, even for weeks. You know what to live off. This whole area is PALP area. The villages have been waiting for us. The food — don't worry about it. The ammunition — keep it carefully. Don't fire unless you have to. Every shot should home into the white colonialist head. Maximum impact for maximum effect. If they get at you, that's the way it was ordained even by our spirits.

'Now, break off, lads. Nearest white farm is twenty miles from here. That's your target.'

The area was called Chimbamba. Next to BGS it was the most important area economically. White farmers. Settlers. They grew beans — hence the name of the area because Chimbamba is the name for beans. Where beans grew, citrus grew in plenty. Some of the farmers had even as many as fifty thousand citrus trees. That was not a few — by any standards.

'We must get there before daybreak,' said Katenga.

'But the enemy could be around us. Remember you are fighting Norris with the colonialists. The vigilantes are here!'

They walked on, Katenga leading half the number while another headed off west. The moon was just beginning to break through the darkness. Its light fell over a strange object. It looked like a van. He said, 'Down!' to the others. Then, crawling on his belly, he scaled towards the object. He drew nearer it. The team trained their Kalashnikov AK47s on the landrover. He was now within twenty yards of it. He no longer had any bush cover because the van was in an open space.

He hesitated. He knew that the guns were pointed at it. Crawled further. He did. Nearer and nearer. There was no motion from it. Then he reached it. He crawled under the chassis and listened, there was no sound of human breathing. He crawled out, raised his head to peep into the driver's cabby. No sign of life. He flashed the all clear to his colleagues. The torch flash picked up a pyramid under the large tree.

He flashed at the others urgently to indicate 'wait'.

The others waited. Down the thick grass and back towards the river bank was a tent. He listened. Snoring inside. Two or more people.

He lifted the tent, flashed his torch.

There were two human beings curled up in their sleeping bags. There were no guns. The two were white. He pulled off their blanket and said:

'Your life!'

Mark Bolton jumped at Katenga, a revolver pulled from underneath his pillow, in his hands.

Katenga looked at him. He grinned into his face. From behind Katenga one of his men came forward, pressed the trigger and Mark, with arms raised high in despair fell back.

Katenga turned to Peter and said:

'Now you!'

Peter raised his hands.

Katenga, eyes glinting in the torch light, said:

'I don't trust you, you white bastards.'

Peter Strong jumped sky-high and crashed back to the ground. Jumping up Katenga cried:

'We are baptized!' Crying 'Capitalist rat!' he stabbed into the two bodies with his boot. One of the troop rolled off Bolton's body with his boot and spitting into his face said:

'Even as you killed my people at Nampande.' Then they moved further on deep into Kandaha to a secret camp some five miles in.

Two days passed. Mark Bolton and his friend had not returned.

Search parties consisting of police and Norris' white vigilantes were mounted. White farmers around the Chimbambu area where it was thought they might have reached, also formed their own search parties. Turnbull threw in helicopters.

The search spread to other parts of the country, also. But nothing was to be found.

Then on the third day a tracker dog picked up the scent. It ran and ran on ahead of a jeep. Then it disappeared. After an hour it ran back to meet the vehicle. The dog was restless and it whined a great deal, howling running ahead and back like one mourning desperately. The sun was setting. Ray Norris leading the farmers on that particular search party raised his binoculars to his eyes as he stood atop the jeep. A tent zoomed into vision. He tilted the binoculars nearer. There was the landrover.

'Boys,' he said, 'we got it. They must have got stuck.'

The party hurried forward, alighted at the tent, went in and — there were cries.

Ray Norris stood transfixed. It couldn't be.

'No!' he cried.

He had not slept ever since the search had started. He had even gone on radio to exhort volunteers to join the search. And now, this was the end of the journey.

Two festering bodies shot up by bandits.

He stared at them. The others also entered the tent. They stood silently, heads bared and bowed. Anger welled up in Norris's heart. As far as he was concerned, only one people could have committed that dastardly act — Africans — PALP. He clenched his fist, raised his arm and said:

'We'll fight!'

They covered up the bodies, loaded them on to Norris's jeep. He and another man silently departed, their hearts bitter with sorrow. They had hardly gone a mile when a huge explosion rocked the silence of the evening. The echo of the explosion was still rumbling through the valleys and hills of Chimbamba when Norris looked back. Then he realized what had happened. The rear truck carrying eight farmers had been blown up by a landmine. Norris turned back. As he approached the scene he could hear cries of despair, anguish. Unmindful of his own safety he plunged into the carnage. With his friend's assistance they lifted the two badly injured into the small van. One man had been killed outright. What would they do?

Norris tore off his shirt to bind the broken limbs and bleeding bodies. They took off the van Mark's and Peter's bodies. Norris would leave his colleague at the junction to the main road to secure transport for the dead. Norris would go on to Musasa European Hospital, two hundred miles away.

At the maximum detention camp at Selope, Kawala sat on the edge of his concrete bunker. A lonely cockroach ran across the floor lazily and then right under the bunker, perhaps to nibble away at the two-day old remains of Kawala's supper. Suddenly, the steel door swung open and St Claus stood in the doorway. He shifted his two-hundred pound weight uneasily as his head scraped the top of the six-foot door. As usual, his khaki uniform was all starch and his reddened bulbous nose was pinker than ever. Kawala looked at him. It was no use fearing the worst when it was already there upon you.

'Last time we didn't get off to a good start,' said St Claus. 'This time I'll tell you everything about me because the situation is very grave. I am Mr Anthony David St Claus, Officer Commanding, Selope. When I enter you will stand to attention at all times.'

Kawala looked at him. That seemed to annoy St Claus. He walked over to the bunker, pulled Kawala off it and pushed him to the floor.

'Now you can stay there and I will chain you to the bunker.'

Kawala struggled to his feet and looked him fully in the face.

'Now, that's better. You've remembered to stand to attention at all times in my presence. They sent you here because they know I am tough. I am the best of them and I'll show you. There have been massacres in Musasa. White men were shot dead on the border. You masterminded all this from here. You plotted the murder of the Ecklands. Katenga must be found and you have to tell me where. If you don't, I know where you are and . . .'

Kawala looked him in the face again.

'I thought you have done your worst already.'

'Are you afraid then?'

'No. I'm not afraid of anything. Even of you. You are worse than death.' St Claus' hand rose and it homed into Kawala with a slap. Kawala staggered. He brushed off the blood in the corner of his mouth. He said to St Claus:

'You cannot knock ideas out of a man's soul Mr St Claus.'

St Claus stared at Kawala and this time, waving his baton in the air, it crashed into Kawala's ribs. Kawala slumped to the floor and for a time he seemed lifeless.

'When you have time to think, we will talk again my friend,' said St Claus closing the steel door roughly behind him.

That afternoon St Claus received more instructions from Musasa. Kawala had to be made to confess or else. So he called for Kawala to be brought over to his office.

'Your friend Katenga has been killed. Good for him. So I won't trouble you about his whereabouts any longer. Next will be Chimuko. Santasa we can take care of any time. So you may as well confess.'

'If you have Katenga bring his head to me. That is the only way you could have had him.'

'You will talk my friend!' cried St Claus jumping up and banging his table. 'Today you will talk!' He sighed then continued, 'And your wife . . .'

'What about my wife?'

'She, too, is in trouble and she won't stand it very much longer.' Kawala looked at St Claus. He said:

'My wife has always had problems. But we have learned to cope and we don't need your sympathy, Mr St Claus.'

St Claus struck Kawala in the face. He had not liked the way he had said, 'We have learned to cope.' Had he not in fact implied that the whites were selfish, always wanting more and more things and never satisfied?

'You'll pay for this, Kaffir. Next time your mfazi (woman) comes here looking for you with her silly white lawyer I'll have her imprisoned.'

'She has been here then?'

'Yes.'

'And you didn't allow her to see me?'

'That's right.'

'It doesn't matter. I don't have to see her to meet her. The cause will even make orphans, widows, of our people. But we shall always meet.'

In Musasa at the market, things had never been easy for her since the upheaval. Women, baited on by the police and some who were jealous of her industry, refused to give her any peace. The day after St Claus in Selope had told Kawala that she was having problems was like any other day for Ana Kawala at her stall. An attractive youngish woman called on her. As usual Ana smiled at her. She always smiled respectfully at her callers.

'Have you had any news of him?'

Ana thought for a moment. Many people had asked her that question before only to end up berating her for everything that went wrong with them.

'I am Delia. I am Katenga's woman.'

Ana remembered their first and only meeting had not been very pleasant. As if reading her thoughts Delia said:

'I did not understand you then. You forgive?'

Ana nodded.

'Your son, any news?'

'No. Since the riots he has vanished. I tell the police and they shrug it off and say, "Ask Katenga". Could he have gone to fight for his father?'

'He will return, have no fear. In this land they grow up into manhood fast or they won't survive. Men are always the same, always wanting to go!'

Ana turned away. She was crying. Delia put her arms around her. Then a group of women approached them. The leader, standing arms akimbo said:

'She must go. She has been nothing but trouble.'

'And how will she live?'

'That is her own business,' replied the fat woman.

'Do you have powers to stop her working in the market?' asked Delia.

'It makes no difference,' said the women in chorus. 'She must go!' Delia reached behind the counter, pulled out a broomstick and cried:

'Get away you crows. You are man haters. That's all you are.'

The women hesitated. They had not met such a mad one before. Finally they left, brandishing warnings that they would still get her. Ana Kawala knew that was no idle threat.

Suddenly Ana kept quiet. In the small rickety counter where she stowed away her merchandise there was a knotted handkerchief. She touched that knot ever so many times a day. It was Kawala's handkerchief. To remind herself of his sufferings. To remind herself never to despair. But was there anything to hope for? With all that was happening, would they not kill him? She crouched behind the little counter, the little dirty handkerchief now in her hands. She put it to her bosom. Delia noticed and put her arms round her shoulders. Now she was shaking with emotion. She could not hold it down any longer. She cried into her hands. Jena her little faithful companion came romping up from playing with the other kids on the road. Folding herself into Ana's lap she said:

'Mummy, where is daddy?'

20

Sir Ray Norris had just delivered the two badly injured people to the Musasa European Hospital casualty ward. Although he had spent five hours driving, he was still feeling as numb as when he had discovered the massacre. He looked it too. The minutes of waiting for a doctor felt like days. He had already made up his mind that that very night he would demand to see the Governor.

He would go even if the Governor refused. In fact he did not even ring for an appointment. He just stormed in, his trousers still spattered with blood, his chin unshaven. He swept past the Private Secretary, his borrowed shirt hanging out. The Private Secretary said:

'Please!'

He pushed the door to the Governor's library open. Lady Elwyn Baker was with him. The Private Secretary burst into the room. He said:

'Sir Ray, please!'

'I'm not getting out of here. Lady Baker, you may not find what I have to say pleasant.' He raised his voice, 'I'm going to tell your husband about people, Europeans, who have been murdered in cold blood.' His enraged face challenged Baker. The eyebrows furrowed, the grey streaks twisting into a thick matt. Lady Baker left.

'Your Excellency. For how much longer must our people continue to die? You can see the blood all over me, can't you? This is what to be white has come to. To be haunted by your Government and haunted by the blacks. Bolton and Strong were murdered, each two bullets into their heads. And now, two more people have died before my eyes. Land mine. And maybe the others will die tonight. Their blood, do you see this blood?'

He advanced towards the Governor.

'Your Excellency, you are the Queen's representative, I shouldn't be speaking to you in this manner. But, but,' he shook his head. 'you are Her Majesty's representative for blacks, Muntus, Kaffirs only!' He lowered his voice, 'But not for me, not for a white man. Yes, I am white. Do I have to be a Kaffir to be protected by Her Majesty? Do I have to be a murderer to be protected by you?'

Sir Elwyn Baker stood up.

'Sir Ray, I know about the killings. Her Majesty's Government is not free to react irresponsibly. The issue is being investigated, culprits will be brought to justice.'

'Justice! Justice! What have you done about the murderers who killed the Ecklands? They were found guilty of murder, weren't they? They are still alive and kicking. Why? Because no doubt there are political aspects to the case. Justice, the law, the police, all these are now paralysed by your prevarications.'

'I'm not used to being told my duty.'

The little Governor strutted up and down the library in a rage.

'I haven't come to teach you your job,' roared Sir Ray.

'I've just come to tell you that this time I'm taking the law into my own hands. We know that the guerillas are being given refuge in Zambia. Katenga is in Zambia. He is the one organizing these killings and maybe even as I speak he is here in Kandaha, here even in Musasa.' Sir Ray paused. He was perspiring.

'We will strike deep into Zambia. We will teach these blacks, Kaffirs . . .'

'They are not Kaffirs,' cried Baker.

Sir Ray Norris grunted.

'We'll teach these niggers a lesson. You may wish to know that a number of my supporters have enlisted to fight for Rhodesia against Zambia.'

'For pay?'

'Yes. And do you know what kind of pay? Not money. Freedom. If we can't fight these terrorists from our own land we will have to fight from another land. And, Your Excellency, lest you should forget, let me remind you that a Britisher can enlist in any army and for any cause.'

The telephone buzzed. Elwyn Baker moved to pick it up. It was from Jefferson, the Commissioner of Police. He had an urgent message.

'What is it? Is it about . . .'

'No.'

'What?'
Baker listened.
'What?' he exclaimed again.
'The armoury at Gunsbury? Who by?'
The Governor turned to Norris.
'There's an emergency on. You'll have to excuse me.'

21

That evening, Mr Norman Mpengula, the leader of the CACOP, paced up and down his little office, puffing at his cigar stub nervously. Every so often he parted the torn curtain of the smudged glass window to peer through it. But all seemed to be quiet as the setting sun gave way to an unusually dense creeping darkness which seemed to strangle the little office, the office whose door plaque proclaimed limply in a limbless scrawl, that it was the nerve centre of the Consolidated African Congress Party, and the official seat of its National President. Plastered all over the wall were portraits of world-famous leaders such as Nehru, Gandhi, Kaunda, Mao-tse-Tung, Churchill, Hitler, Stalin, Kruschev, Banda, Nasser and many others, testifying more to the party's faithfulness to the incongruities of history than inferring any ideological pattern. The National President puffed a mouthful of smoke into Churchill's face which remained stubborn and defiant with a kingsize cigar firmly gripped between its teeth. That stubborn look reminded him again of the way the forces of law and order had been closing in on Kawala, and he allowed a light smile to cross his lips as he whispered:

'That settles him for a long time if not for ever. They'll get him again. All this is just a trap.'

But his mind that evening was not really on matters of state, even though he could not completely wipe out of memory the headline news that his repeated denunciation of lawlessness and savagery were making.

No. He was not really concerned with these matters. Had he heard footsteps? His heart jumped in his mouth with the violence of a foetus kicking at its mother's womb. There was a gentle knock at the door, almost a ratlike scraping. 'That must be it,' he said to himself, his heart pounding. He had been in this situation before and conquered many many times over. But he had never experienced that body-rending expectation. He, an experienced man, why was he gasping for breath?

Had his bodyguard really carried the message to . . . He couldn't bring himself to mention the name, as his mind tenderly caressed it. Here he was, a man who was already conquering many foes in his political life, now hoping and waiting for that soft scratching knock which would give him what no man or woman had ever given him before. He thought of Madyauka, his vice-president, of how he must be that very moment holding house to house meetings in the Cidolo area, at least two hundred miles away. But this was not the time for thinking. He must open the door. There was another faint scratch and suddenly he felt the overwhelming loneliness of all his many encounters with women, women who had walked in through a door like this one, women for whom he had had only one use. It had to be done quickly and forgotten. But this soft scrape at the door was different. The thin rickety wooden door was shutting off an eternity of happiness. He took one step towards the door. Should he open it? Then the voice of Madyauka, two hundred miles away, came through his mind's ear. 'Norman is the only man for you. His party is the only one.' He couldn't bear that voice. With one violent pull he wrenched the door open. But instead of the soft gracefulness of Mrs Madyauka being swept in, Mr Nandabhai Patel bounced in like a rabbit out of a hat. His large, thin-rimmed glasses reflecting the playing candle-light gave him the aspect of benign cunningness.

'Mr Mpengula,' said the man. 'You hearing in dis lunchtime news how Katenga he attacking members of us Injuan community? Ve not Sowists (Sophists) and ve not double tongue. Ve got same one tongue like himself.'

'Yes, yes,' said Mpengula. Then it clicked. It was Mr Nandabhai Patel of Tayetaye Patel & Co. Limited. Yes, that morning's paper had singled him out for Katenga's special contemptuous mention.

'Ve got money,' continued Mr Patel, 'and ve not standing on side seeing dis fellow and his party push us around.' He listened on. 'Vhy Kawala he don't denounce dis man? Vhy? Cha! I telling my friends of cummunity, Mr Mpengula only man for us ve black people in dis country. You and us ve same difference. You peaceful man same like de Mahatma. Kawala no good. He spoiling dis

be excellent, if you don't mind my saying so.'

Mpengula remained quiet. He did not know how to react to the last suggestion even though he liked it. Turnbull, wishing to get to the point of the drink, asked:

'You heard what Katenga has said about nationalization. That sort of talk never did a country any good. Look at Zambia, Tanzania, Uganda and Zaïre. What good has it done them? Mr Mpengula, would you nationalize BGS or indeed Mr Patel's Kandaha Rice Wholesale Corporation or even this hotel?'

Just then there was a knock at the door. Mr Nandabhai Patel, the proprietor of the Porcupine Head was doing his rounds among his clients, asking them how they liked the hotel, did they have any complaints about catering and so on. Some guests did not like this business of interfering with their peace and they would make a point of telling him so. Others welcomed him and even asked him to have a drink. In these cases, he would ask to be excused and move on. But tonight he was not asking to be excused.

He hesitated in the doorway. Mr Turnbull said:

'Ah, Mr Host. Glad to see you. Come and meet a friend of mine, Mr Mpengula. He used to work for us at the gold mine. Now, of course he is as you know, your leading politician out here in Mulule. We have our share too in Musasa. Norris and Kawala, I mean. You chaps are very lucky to have him here. Curiously enough,' said Turnbull still standing in the doorway, 'Mr Mpengula had just asked me about our attitude towards our sister, your organization, if, in fact when, CACOP becomes the Government. He wants to know if we would continue with our holding in it and if we ourselves would continue out here.'

Mr Patel swiftly slid through the door and shook Mpengula's hand. In the clear light of the room Mpengula could see that the man had a hare lip.

'Well, Mr Mpengula, de Rice Wholesale Corporation vill continue because ve have confidence in your coming African Gowernment. I telling all Injian in my company dey applying for Kandaha citizenship now or no chob. Ve knoving our new gowernment it vanting money to dewelop country and ve giving it dat money,' opened Mr Patel, diving his hands upwards, almost into Mpengula's mouth as he pronounced his last words. 'But ve not liking Kawala to vin. Katenga ve not trust. He danger. He communist same like Lenin. He not like Nehru.' Then he looked towards Turnbull who was nodding agreement. 'He great danger. So ve not trusting Kawala. Ve not trusting Chimuko. Ve not trusting nobody except yourself, Mr Mpengula, as I saying. Ve got big interest here, ve and my friend Turnbull here,' concluded Mr Patel, just as his lungs began to itch — an unfailing notice of an impending series of coughs.

'Well Norman,' said Turnbull seizing the opportunity to continue Mr Patel's lapsed thoughts, 'I'm glad you've raised this subject even though frankly, I hadn't intended talking shop. Our interests in this country are, as you know, very extensive indeed. The future Government and ourselves are frankly going to be so interdependent that I couldn't see either of us surviving without the other. That's an arrogant thing for a foreigner like me to say, but I think it's a fact. You will have your voters to look after and we have our share-holders and I genuinely think that our interests are not different.

'You will appreciate, however, that while we welcome an African Government — and you know best how we have supported you materially and morally — every change creates a new set of circum-stances and that very early in the day investors need to be reassured that they can continue to invest. It's not just for the good of BGS or my friend here but for the good of your own people. In fact when you fellows become independent there will be many other avenues of investment opportunities which we would explore and I do mean explore, actively.'

'Such as a fishing industry?' asked Mpengula. His village back home survived on fishing.

'As a matter of fact that's already on the cards. My chairman is very keen on this. And also on rural electrification. We could lend you the money for this. Naturally the terms would depend on whether we were awarded the contract for electrification or not. We believe for example that your rural population needs milk. In fact every child should have a pint of milk a day. These are things the Colonial Government does not bother about. So long as every white child has a pint of fresh milk it is all right. But an independent African Government, a Westminster-style type of government that depends on the voters, cannot ignore this. One of our engineering divisions in Britain has constructed two long-life milk plants, one in Zambia and the other in Kenya. Long-life milk does not require refrigeration and can stay good up to three weeks. Ideal for your rural areas.' Turnbull gulped at his cognac.

'Here again, the money would be no problem. We could either supply it or Export Credit Guarantee Department could finance the whole project. But we would need assurances that private invest-ment is welcomed. In fact I have been specifically asked by my boss to assure you of our readiness to invest.'

'And the milk? Would you be prepared to invest in the dairy industry?' asked Mpengula.

Turnbull thought for a split second.

'Most certainly, if you would want us to. But our experience is that it is nearly always better to leave this to local initiative. We have sometimes been called upon to act as consultants or been given a contract to manage the scheme.'

The conversation went on into the late hours of the night. Mpengula, contrary to expectations, continued alert and enthusiastic. In his mind he could see Kandaha suddenly bloom into prosperity. But that depended upon the British Government agreeing independence and keeping Kawala safely locked away in detention. If Kawala's PALP won, then that would be a vote to turn Kandaha into a desert. As if re-echoing his thoughts, Patel asked:

'Vhat chances you got to vin if independence come? I knowing dey pretty good.'

'Almost ninety per cent,' replied Mpengula.

But Turnbull was not going to have the matter dismissed so lightly. Strictly speaking, it did not matter who won. But it mattered what they did thereafter and it was the *dead* which he had been briefed to try and anticipate. As he listened to Mpengula he became more and more convinced that that man's chances were slim. But the man had his heart in the right place in regard to private investment. It was perhaps more important that he should be at the decision-making table than that he should win. Turnbull had stayed long enough in Africa to know that opposition parties never got anywhere. So he thought about the question that was forming in his mind. He had to ask it even though he might feel offended. After all, it was not as if it would be a new question. Kawala himself had called on 'the erring sons and daughters of CACOP' to repent and join PALP. Of late Turnbull had become very disappointed with Norris. The man seemed to have lost all punch and did not seem to appreciate that his time was running out. Ideally he should be supporting Norris. But others before him had supported Wellensky in Zambia. With what result?

'There's no doubt in my mind whatsoever that you will, Norman. But you know, there's just the rare mishap such as spoilt papers and so on. It happened recently with an important name in Britain. It's happening all the time. And yet such a result would be absolutely suicide for Kandaha. Of course Lafayette would be very happy. But what stake has Lafayette in this country? Nothing. Not even in heaven.' Then he stopped and helped himself to the bottle of cognac on the table. 'Have you ever thought about the possibility of a coalition with PALP?'

'What?' exclaimed Mpengula. 'Never! Never!' he cried, jumping up and stamping his foot into the ground.

Mr Patel sat up. If two could safeguard his interests, that was better than one. Mpengula could influence PALP's thinking.

'I telling you Turnbull is got a point,' said Patel. 'Ewerywhere in Africa, in Injia, ewerywhere opposition party is waste of man-power. Is newer strong to stop a mad gowernment. If you in one party both you and Kawala you win. No loser!' He clapped his hands together with enthusiasm. 'You saying he good man and together you form best man, best gowernment. If he become President and you become Wice President and wice wersa. He old, you young. If you not boss now you boss sooner and later. You giwing him most people, he giwing you more people. Same ways good,' concluded Mr Patel, not soon enough to elude the oncoming cough which transformed the last sentence of his speech into a squeak.

Mpengula who had now sat down, thought. There was something in what Patel had said. But the followers . . .

'If, say,' said Turnbull, speaking confidentially and leaning towards Mpengula, 'If say you made overtures to Kawala to form one party and he rejected them, it would be he opting for violence and surely he must know that that won't help the investment climate. In fact, I would almost say, without committing my chairman in any way, that if your move failed and you were not part of the Government we could certainly offer you an important interest in our twenty per cent stake in the Rice Wholesale Corporation and I know that Mr Patel here would go even further. Bonus shares and all that, you know.'

Mpengula looked at his watch. It was an hour after midnight. He stood up.

'Well gentlemen, thanks a lot. It's been a very useful evening.' Then he pumped Turnbull's hand, 'We want you to stay in this country.' Then to Patel, 'Well Mr Patel, thanks a lot.'

'You won't do anything as stupid as PALP of course,' said Turn-bull. 'I gather they've turned down going to the constitutional talks. You and Norris could well find yourselves in a coalition Government.

That night Turnbull wrote a brief for his chairman in London, Lord Ventrical.

Mpengula is a pleasant and charming character. Perhaps the only respectable black leader. But we should not expect any miracles from him. Like many of his kind, he has formed a party so that he can be called 'President'. He has no policy and it will be a miracle if he finds one. He does not even know whether to go it alone or with Norris or with Kawala. Imagine being indifferent to being either in hell or heaven and you have your Mpengula.

This is a tight-rope affair. But I am sure we can survive. I recommend that we play our support for him in low gear — someone he can always turn to, you know. But let's not dramatize it. After all, he performs the useful function of dividing the Africans — that is if he will ever get any black support worth mentioning. Our best bet is still Norris — he's at least got a policy even though sometimes it looks as though Hitler should have lingered on to learn from this new apostle of racial hatred. I sometimes wonder whether we will not be caught with our pants down if we overdo our support here. But he's a good bait — certainly so from the point of view of the morale of our European labour force. . . .

It is because of this slight shade of doubt that I'm suggesting the ridiculous, that is, that we should not completely write off Kawala. If the transition to independence is going to be peaceful, then Kawala is more likely to emerge than Norris. On the other hand, and if it's going to be rough, then the whites will fight. We could well have a UDI like in Rhodesia. In that case, we'd have to throw in our everything to back Norris. After all, our investments in Rhodesia have remained intact since UDI, unlike elsewhere in Africa where we have sometimes had to sell at prices that amount to expropriation. If it came to an open fight, we might well have to consider unorthodox ways of helping Norris to eliminate his opponents. But let's not forget that our black labour force is mainly PALP, that we are not in politics to make kings but for business, that in the final analysis only our candidate should win. Our candidate is *profit!*'

22

Katenga looked at his Cuban wrist watch. He had changed plans about storming the police station on the border. Any time within the next thirty minutes the Musasa-bound train would be passing through the pass cut deep into the mountain. It would be laden with merchandise from Rhodesia. That is what kept the white man's wheels of commerce moving in Kandaha. They had practised train blow-ups many times and this was as good as any target to start with. Perhaps the best. After burrowing through the mountain the rail road came on to an open valley and a tributory of the Zambezi flowed below it. That bridge was the best target.

Chimuko and Katenga watched as some ten freedom fighters planted the dynamite on the beams of the bridge. Katenga stood with a rifle and two rows of bullets across his chest. Then he waved the other people off the bridge. He had seen the sky light up further down. That could only have been the train. Ten minutes later the train appeared on the horizon. They all scampered away to hide in the bushes. Katenga grinned broadly as the train came on, seeming as though it was picking up more and more energy. He signalled to one fellow to light the fuse. In that moment he could see a passenger leaning out of the window and perhaps savouring the crisp morning air. The man lit it and ran to safety. Then there was a sudden tremble and like a fire cracker the dynamite exploded. The train jumped up sky-high like a long horizontal snake rocket reaching for the sky. Katenga watched with calm as the train and bridge came down with a screech, explosion and great metallic noise, plunged down, some of it into the cold waters of the river. Whole beams hurtled into the bush showering it with splinters of metal rock. Ten minutes later all was quiet except for trapped bodies wailing and crying. The day after they learned that help came too late and that there had been no survivors.

'And now,' said Katenga, 'for the bastard's soft belly — the city.'

Saying which both Katenga and Chimuko looked at their watches and smiled with a grimace. If Santasa had not let down his side of the plan there would be action in the city soon.

It was 2.15 p.m. of the same day. At Bristol House, Musasa a black worker in denim overalls slid into the air vent. He picked up a mop and pail and scaled up to the exit on the eighth floor . . . .

In the warehouse of the Musasa supermarket an industrious workman tidied around the place. The warehouse manager had just left the large room to go upstairs to chat up the general manager about the latest event — the blowing up of the train on the border. Of course such events were terrible. But they could not happen here in Musasa. The black man valued his job and he knew that that meant the white man being around. The worker in the warehouse looked around. It was 2.15 p.m. There was no one watching. No one except a mischievously nude white doll whose eyes always seemed to trail him from whatever point he looked at it. But it was only a doll. He had in any case spent the morning dusting it up for moving into the supermarket the following morning. He smiled at it briefly and said:

'You and I will be great pals.' The man looked around again. No one there. He slid a brown paper bag behind a stack of boxes, took off his dust coat and walked out on to the crowded street and disappeared. . . .

It was still the same afternoon. A middle-aged African stood polishing up the steel grey Mercedes Benz. The official car of the general manager of Barclays Bank, Kandaha. If anyone had watched him, he would have noticed that the man was uneasy and kept glancing around furtively. The man slid a brown bag under the driver's seat. He gave the car another brush up and melted into the street crowds. . . .

A hundred patrons were just winding up their lunch obsequies in the dining room of the Musasa Safari Club, a prestigious joint mainly for rich tourists from Europe and the United States. A tall, grey-haired waiter carried a tray to the back of the room. He looked around. The other waiters were busy with final orders. He set the tray down slowly then again looked around. He uncovered it and removed a package from it and, bending to pick up a pencil, he set the package on the floor. Gently with his foot he helped it on to a position under the counter. He looked around, pretended that he had forgotten something and walked away.

A client called 'Hey you.' The waiter stopped. His mouth dry. He turned. The man beckoned him. He came. His heart beating hard. 'Get us a bit of butter,' said the client. The waiter walked over to the counter where he had planted the bomb. The butter was there. He brought it to the Bwana and walked away to the kitchen. The kitchen was empty with everyone still in the dining room madly serving out as the kitchen had to close by 2.30 p.m. The waiter walked into an alley in the back of the Safari Club. The alley was empty. He looked around, slipped off his waiter's jacket and stuffed it into a garbage tin, rolled up the sleeves of his shirt, walked into the street and melted away with the crowds. . . .

Barclays Bank Kandaha was crowded and busy. It opened for the afternoon service once a week. It was busy because of the panic caused by the various acts of violence that had happened. Already an Angola-type of white exodus was being freely discussed. The door to the general manager's office opened. He was a tall thin man with a razor-cut moustache, grey suit and greying hair. A bit of a dandy you might have called Sir Basil, especially with the brown alligator attaché case dangling off his well-manicured hand. He looked at his gold Omega Sea Master watch. It read 2.30 p.m. He cursed under his breath. He had worked over the lunch hour and his wife was still waiting for him at home. If there was one thing she always insisted on it was that Sir Basil should never pass up his lunch. And if he was lunching out she checked that this was indeed so. And when he returned she would ask who was at the lunch, just so she could be certain he had eaten.

He stopped briefly at his secretary's desk — a young girl of around twenty, pretty with jet black long hair hanging down to her waist. That was the kind of woman that turned Sir Basil on and maybe in a platonic kind of way, that is why he got on so well with her.

'Please call my wife and tell her I'm on my way.'

'Yes, Sir Basil,' replied Janet. Janet picked up the phone as Sir Basil walked away. Then she stopped and called, 'Sir Basil!' Sir Basil turned around. She said, 'Good luck!'

Sir Basil smiled,

'Thanks Janet.' He left.

A faint clock-like sound ticked away in the brown bag under the driver's seat in the Mercedes Benz in the parking lot. Sir Basil headed for the Benz. At that moment Janet ran towards him. He heard her heels and turned round. Janet whispered something into his ears, something perhaps about the call to his wife. It was 2.39 p.m.

Sir Basil looked at his watch again. He had to hurry. The minute hand was just touching 2.39 $^{1}/_{2}$. He opened the door slid the key in, waved to Janet, turned the ignition and — bang! The car lifted up in a huge explosion which sent glass and splinters flying right into the bank itself. Sir Basil, Janet and three white customers in the bank were dead. . . .

It was 2.40 p.m. Something ticked away in the brown parcel in the air vent up on the eighth floor of Bristol House. John Turnbull had just left a minute before for a crisis meeting with the Governor. Lepton who had come in for the day to finalize all the flow sheets in respect of the company's application for financing from Eximbank was sitting at his desk. For the black staff, all of whom were only labourers, that afternoon was their time off. Once a week they got an afternoon off. Lepton had just stood up, having heard something like an explosion downtown and was looking through the window when the whole building trembled, something lifted and there was a deafening explosion which showered debris for a quarter of a mile around. When Lepton ran down to the ground floor and then outside, he found that the eighth floor was hanging together by a string and people were lying all over, dead. . . .

At the Musasa supermarket dead bodies and dummies were lying higgledy-piggledy among the debris of bricks and mortar. A fire engine was rushing towards the smouldering building. . . .

The Musasa Safari Club had been reduced to a shell of smouldering charred bodies. It had taken the worst. . . .

At 2.40 p.m. also a worker from the Musasa supermarket warehouse sat at a table with two boys about his age at the Sanga African Bar. They were having a beer and laughing away.

At that same time the worker who had polished up the Mercedes Benz in the parking lot at the bank stood at his stall hawking fresh fish. The man's stall was next to Mrs Kawala's. He looked at her and smiled broadly. Normally his wife attended to the stall, but to-day he had come to help her out. He only did this on Saturday mornings now and again.

That day there was hell to pay for Jefferson and O'Flaherty. The little Governor was angry, really angry for the first time ever in his life. In the Legislative Council a hasty marathon debate on the situation opened that day at 4.30 p.m. The debate continued into the early hours of the morning. The chamber was stiffly guarded. Norris had defied the Governor's orders and brought his own armed volunteers to stand guard. At all other times that would have been treason. It would have been equivalent to a coup. But vexed, tormented and harassed from all corners and including Mpengula who called for the public hanging of Kawala and his men, that was no time for legalities.

'We will arm ourselves. We have armed ourselves!' cried Norris, raising his arm and thumping the air. 'Katenga and his murder incorporated are still at large, at large to stalk our homes with the plague of a most chilling murder. When Rome gave up its duty to defend the empire, life itself, that is when Rome decayed and died. How can a Kaffir . . .'

There was an interruption. Someone on the official benches said: 'On a point of order.'

The Speaker stood up.

'A point of order has been raised,' he said.

'Is it in order for the Hon. Member for Musasa West to refer to Africans as Kaffirs?'

The Speaker looked furtively at the Government member who had raised the question. He too was angry with the blacks and could you blame him for it? He paused uncertainly and then said:

'The Hon. Member for Musasa West may continue. The point of order was not a point of substance. People will be people by whatever you call them. Hon. Member for Musasa West.'

Sir Ray looked at the member who had queried him. He could have gobbled him up.

'Playing on, at, with words, that's all these people,' his massive hands spread at the Government members, 'are doing when Musasa burns, people die the most horrible mangled deaths. We, Mr Speaker . . .'

There was a commotion outside. A home guard was scuffling with someone. The Sergeant-at-arms brought the Speaker a note. There was a massive black demonstration outside. Santasa and Mama PALP were leading it. The long column of men, women and children was spewing into Parliament Square. The home guard stood at the ready, their guns pointed towards it.

'We want to see Thomson, now!' cried Santasa.

'We want Thomson! We want Thomson!' chanted the crowd.

Posters read 'NORRIS A MURDERER', 'BGS MAFIA CAPITALIST CLIQUE', 'AWAY WITH IDIOT BAKER', 'BAKER COLONIAL BUTCHER WORSE THAN SMITH'. But raised above them all and emblazoned in large deep letters were at least a hundred posters calling for immediate release of Kawala from illegal imprisonment and vowing the war would go on. One or two denounced Mpengula but it was obvious he and his party did not rate much.

An armed black policeman came forward.

'You murderers, what do you want?'

'We want to see your chief dog, Thomson. Aliko Kawala should be released, now!' Mama PALP, the fat leader of the Women's Brigade, and member of the central committee came forward. She had a round moon face, clear brown eyes and for all her troubles appeared to carry her fifty years very well.

'Yes, you are a puppy. Thomson is the dog, the hyena. It is he who has murdered our people with his stupid Governor and Norris. Let them all come out here if they are men!' cried Mama PALP.

'We are under orders to shoot you if you persist!' cried the policeman.

'Shoot us!' said Mama PALP jumping back to the front again. 'Shoot all those wombs here that brought a disease like you into the world. Shoot!'

The policeman looked behind him. He looked at the thousands of men, women and children. All their eyes converged on him. Just then reinforcements arrived. Inside Parliament Norris interrupted his speech to ask the Speaker if, on a point of order, it was right for the debate to continue under conditions of 'savage siege'. He also asked why the forces of law and order were not there to protect the freedom of Parliament.

Thomson stood up. Outside, the deafening cry, 'Release Kawala! We want Thomson! Castrate Thomson! Kill Baker! Skin Norris alive!' could be heard.

When he had sat down in his parliamentary office, Norris rang the Governor and then said to O'Flaherty:

'Tell them, I can speak only to their leaders.'

When the message was broadcast there was a pandemonium:

'No! To all of us or to none! PALP, PALP, PALP! Kawala! Kawala! Kawala!'

The crowd surged forward towards the police. O'Flaherty could see it coming. It would be another massacre. Even he was getting disgusted. He was feeling like vomiting. If they didn't stop he would have to give the order. O God! O God!

Just then Thomson came out on to the porch. He stood urbanely before the menacing crowd. There was silence. Then Santasa cried:

'We will storm and burn this building if you don't release Kawala, if you don't stop killing our people!'

'You are proposing violence!' cried O'Flaherty.

'Yes! We propose and you do it.'

'Kawala! Kawala! No more white dogs in Africa! Africa! Africa!' the crowd shouted. It surged towards Thomson. Thomson retreated backwards to behind the police lines.

'We have not come with guns. We have not come for war!' cried Santasa.

'If you don't want your black brothers to catch the bullet

between their teeth, move!'

'We will not move!'

More trucks ploughed into the crowd. The crowd moved forward. O'Flaherty cried, 'Charge!'

When it was all over at least a hundred people had been injured badly. Ten had been shot in the legs and one fatally. O'Flaherty felt happy with the success of the riot-control drills which he had introduced into the force recently. For him, the casualty figures had not been excessive.

That night a shaken Norris called a press conference. He described the demonstration as 'murderous savagery, performed in full view of the so-called authorities, an attempted coup against parliament by the primitive prince of darkness, aided and abetted by the Colonial Government.' He called upon the Governor to declare a call-up of all able-bodied Europeans, 'arm them with the Government's guns, they too have a right to be protected by the gun of the Government. We cannot trust our security in the hands of black policemen any longer.'

At dawn there was a swoop on the PALP office and houses. Santasa, Kakonkawadia, Mama PALP, all known PALP officials all over the country, were arrested. The Colonial Government declared that PALP had ended. Mpengula wrang his hands with glee. At the Bristol Gold Syndicate workers went down the mine and back to their homes under the shadow of the gun.

That night Mpengula had a dream. There was a vast expanse of carpet-thick green lawn. The lawn's dew glistened in the light of the bright sunlight. Two sets of rabbits, one jet black and the other lily white had lined up on opposite ends of the field. They were drawing to each other, half uncertain as to what the other would do. Then they stopped. The black ones sent one of their number to the white ones. The black rabbit sniffed each of the white ones in turn and then stopped at the most lily white one. It was fat and filled up, the inside of its ears slightly reddened up with health and good living, her face such a beautiful rounded one. The black one said:

'Janita, I love you. I want to marry you.'

The white rabbits cocked their ears. Then there was a horrifying hollow laugh and they scampered away, yelling, crying, shouting 'No, no, no!' until the whole field resounded to a Wagnerian crescendo of 'No, no, no!' But as they reached the end of the field each of the white rabbits became an inferno of burning wood until in the end there were only ashes. The black ones looked on horrified. But when they turned to go and looked at themselves they found that their skins had changed to a luminous white and it was their turn to scamper, frolic, laugh with Wagnerian tumult.

He was still laughing when he awoke to the early morning news about the total swoop on PALP. 'The black rabbit's triumph,' he said. That evening Turnbull called him up to his rambling mansion. Lepton, now more involved in the affairs of head office than ever before, was there. Mr Nandabhai Patel had just been.

'Well Mr Mpengula, now our friends won't be seen this side of life, I thought we might pick the pieces up again and maybe help you. You've always had a hell of responsibility to carry. I wouldn't be in your shoes for anything. But now it's even worse. Like I said to you before, we in BGS have a very high regard for CACOP and its methods. Kawala is a murderer and as far as I'm concerned the sooner he can be brought up for trial and hanged, the better for us all. I suppose you need money.' Turnbull was most tentative and tactical. Since his last report on Mpengula to Lord Ventrical he had cooled off. But now with the vacuum of the wiping off of PALP he had to do something. Moreover, Lord Ventrical had not survived very well from his trenchant reaction to the Prime Minister's statement. He had been summoned by Caput and simply told to toe the line or his investments would go unprotected.

'We are short of money,' said Mpengula.

Turnbull snapped his fingers:

'Let's fix that for starters.'

Lepton handed Mpengula a large, soft envelope of closely packed twenty-pound notes. The money seemed to lubricate Mpengula's tongue and they talked on into the early hours. Mpengula was to try and win over to his party the PALP members now in disarray. He could now be as critical of the Government as he wished. In fact he should do just that, call every one in office and every white politician names. He should stage demonstrations of defiance. Call the police names. Tell the people PALP was a quisling, wasting their time. The Government had agreed not to touch him. Police would be there, but they would not move in against him.

'What we want to do Mr Mpengula is to help the white man understand that only your party holds the future of this country. There's no future in Norris or Kawala. And when you want some more money, please, you know Mr Patel, just say and we'll be there.'

Turnbull advised Mpengula to canvas African support for his party.

'Nothing gives these days without OAU support. You might start with the more vociferous elements. Zambia, Tanzania and Mozambique, for example.'

They discussed the idea.

'It's not such a preposterous idea, come to think of it. We've been approached by these countries to invest there. As for receiving you, these countries are learning to be open minded these days. Aren't the black leaders of the opposing factions in Rhodesia received like emperors in each of' these countries?' Turnbull said. Then, ever so gently and self-effacingly, 'Money would of course not be a problem.'

That settled a lot of things for Mpengula. Within a fortnight his 'courageous' demonstrations had become the talk of the times. Quite clearly, he was gaining a following − even though of a sort. Katenga and Chimuko way out in hiding, followed developments anxiously. Without a following at home, guns were useless. Santasa and the others languished on in detention. Kawala was a caged animal. He could be disposed of any time.

Two weeks later Nkolola staged a daring jail break. He was a godsend to the men in the hide-out near the Zambian border. He brought them the latest situation report.

'He struts around Musasa like he's a Bwana. Giving speeches, giving food to the "poor". He's tearing down everything we've built. Everything we are fighting for.'

'The tool of BGS,' said Chimuko stamping into the ground. 'Mpengula is in our way.'

'You say some members of the party have joined him?' asked Katenga.

'Yes, a few. Not many,' replied Nkolola.

'Traitors!' swore Katenga.

'What's the solution?' asked Chimuko.

'What you said. He's in our way. If a rhino is in your way, you spear it. If it's a tree, uproot it. If it's . . .? Kill him!'

'Kandaha has no room for traitors at this time in history,' said Chimuko nodding his head.

'Even after independence. No room for opposition. That is treachery only,' rasped Katenga. He looked around the faces of the high command − some ten people. 'Any disagreement?' No reply. Then, 'You all agree.' Stumping into the ground again he declared, 'Total! Special Squad.'

In the tourist town of Arusha, Mpengula descended the steps into 'The Cave'. He had his vice president, Modyanka, with him. They had been on a visit to Tanzania for a week. The visit which had been rated 'an official visit', had been downgraded to a private visit. No one in Government would agree to see him. In fact, as he descended the steps to 'The Cave', an official in the immigration department hundreds of miles away in Dar-es-Salaam was preparing to board a plane to serve a deportation order on Mpengula.

CACOP President Mpengula, the Chief's son, settled himself. Spending freely he soon attracted an esoteric crowd of well wishers around him. He had just finished dancing to a Zaïrean tune with a lithesome teenage girl when the waiter brought him a message. He walked up to the counter. No the message wasn't there. Someone had left him a parcel up at reception. Mpengula looked back to cast a longing look at the girl he had just danced with. She walked over to the counter and leaned her head on his shoulder. He said he would be back soon. He was going upstairs to the gents. She walked back giggling with contentment. He was a good generous man. Maybe even the following day he might . . . He looked at her bottom swaying away back to her seat. He smiled.

He changed his mind. He would have just one more dance with her before going up to collect the parcel. Turnbull had said that he had alerted a business friend in Arusha about his visit. That could be a parcel from him. Some present or other. For a moment the thought crossed his mind. Why not leave it at the hotel? But this was not the time to worry about it. He would have just one more dance before getting up there.

'All right for drinks, boys?' ·

'Yes,' said Madyauka. Then he looked at his watch, 'President, we should be going now.' Just then the music came on. Mpengula swept off the girl and led her to the dancing floor. 'The Cave' had soft, bluish lights which sometimes paled off into darkness. Seats were arranged round pillars, giving each party the impression of being in an alcove. The tables were low and the seats were three-legged skin drums topped with small cushions. If you were drunk you might fall off as the legs were too close to each other and did not balance well. The counter was always crowded with 'Safari' drinkers — Tanzania's answer to Zambia's 'Mosi' beer, a stingingly potent variety which makes Simba taste like milk.

The music ended. Mpengula remembered he had a parcel to collect. He went up. The man at the counter had gone down to remind the barman to tell whoever Mr Mpengula was to collect his parcel before someone picked it up. So there was no one at the counter upstairs. Mpengula took the little parcel off the counter. He looked at it closely. Yes, it was from the managing director of a company Turnbull had mentioned to him. Hand delivered and no post mark. Whatever was inside felt valuable. The idea of an expensive, heavy, solid wrist watch came to him. Presents were all part of the game. After all, BGS had already spent a fortune on him. He started to open it. He peeled off the sellotape, unwrapped it slowly, then there was a loud explosion. The counter lifted into the air, the roof down part of the stairway into the club collapsed. Outside, the walls of the toilets adjoining the club crumbled. The steward coming up the stairs from paging Mpengula just managed to duck a brick bullet which crashed into a pillar in the club. The building shook. Voices screamed in sheer terror. Fire had started. Slowly first at the door then, by the time all the people had been evacuated, the flames rose up furiously, gutting the edifice to ashes. When the firemen finally brought the situation under control, the scattered remains of Mpengula's body had burnt to a cinder. The following morning Gilbert Spoon, Turnbull's cook received a telegram from a little post office on the border with Tanzania. The telegram simply said, *Your brother is well*. The sender's name was a fake and Spoon knew that well. Under his breath he muttered, 'That will fix the Bwana. Serving drinks to traitors!' Out in the hide-out when Katenga received the news he stumped a pencil into a makeshift table and muttered 'Good!' The pencil broke into three pieces. As usual there would be anger, enquiries and so on. But if any Government let traitors visit its borders, 'this is the price' said Katenga.

23

The following day Kandaha was in world news and with it activity at the UN and OAU intensified. At the UN the resolution which had been unsuccessful in the Security Council was being hastily rushed up to the General Assembly. Time had already been provided for the Kandaha nationalists to appear as petitioners before the UN Committee for decolonizations.

Further to that resolution, the immediate and unconditional release of all nationalists in prison was being demanded.

In his Washington suite that day the Assistant Secretary of State of the United States sat with the British Ambassador. His manner was abrupt and his expression firm.

'I wish Your Excellency to know that the United States expects you to call a constitutional conference on Kandaha right away.'

Sir Joseph Halifax looked up. He adjusted his monocle, 'Why?'

'Because the United States cannot afford its peace initiatives in Southern Africa to be compromised by the Kandaha situation.' The Assistant Secretary of State leaned back in his brown leather padded chair. He took off his glasses, blinked a little as if to say, 'That's all.' He was a large, tall man with a pointed nose, fat cheeks and a head that, in spite of his size, looked larger than normal.

'With due respect, Mr Assistant Secretary of State, you would not expect me to commit Her Majesty's Government to such a position here.' Then the Ambassador added airily but acidly, 'In other situations such expressions of categorical orders would have constituted interference in internal matters.'

The Assistant Secretary of State stood up. Pacing up and down his office he said:

'Mr Ambassador, the Secretary of State of the United States of America is in Southern Africa. Right now. You don't expect us to embarrass his initiatives by the African heads of Government making the resolution of the Kandaha issue a condition for the Southern African package deal. Do you? In any case, where would you have been in the Rhodesian issue without our "interference"?'

Sir Joseph Halifax, a tall thin man with precise manners wearing a precise suit said:

'Her Majesty's Government will take into account the views of the Government of the United States of America in determining its position.'

'The United States is not giving evidence, Mr Ambassador. It is instructing you to convey the instructions of this Government to your Government. From now we will proceed on the assumption that you will release the nationalists now in jail, summon a constitutional conference and grant independence.'

The Assistant Secretary paused. By way of an afterthought he added:

'The Secretary of State has been authorized by the President of the United States to reply affirmatively to the Presidents of the Frontline States if they should raise this issue.'

Halifax jumped up.

'On behalf of Her Majesty's Government, I must protest this high-handed manner Mr Assistant Secretary.'

'Mr Ambassador, just remember that the United States does not spend billions to save a dime. We are playing for high stakes in Southern Africa.

'First, there's the all-important question of peace. Then there is the question of preventing that part of the world from becoming a military sphere of influence for the Soviet Union. The United States cannot afford its peace being threatened so close to its border.

'Third, there's South Africa itself. Our investments there run into billions of dollars. Pressure in South Africa will let off if the political problems of the satellite countries can be resolved. You will inform Her Majesty's Government accordingly.'

At the United Nations two days before the debate, the Soviet Union put out a statement. The statement condemned colonialism and imperialism. It called for serious measures to be taken against Britain if she did not heed the United Nation's call, the call of the OAU, for immediate independence for Kandaha. The Soviet statement provoked a press conference from comrade Chi Ho Ling, the Ambassador Extraordinary and Plenipotentiary for the People's Republic of China. His Excellency, speaking fast to a packed house in one of the large committee rooms of the UN building said through the interpreter:

'Today our eyesight has been outraged by looking at a Soviet document purporting to be a statement of socialist thinking in the issue of the Kandaha crisis in Africa. This document', he waved it, 'is a total insult to the peace-loving peoples of Africa and it should be rejected by them. It is the work of colonialism, fascism, imperialism, neocolonialism and super-powerism. The super-powers should be pushed out of Africa by the militant and vigilant forces of Africa.

'To the super-powers, African independence and the independence of the oppressed masses of Africa is like a nail in their eyeball. We must be vigilant against revisionists, imperialists, fascists and super-powers. They appear to denounce each other and yet all the time they are trading with each other.

'This particular super-power is going ahead with many things, including a British factory to assemble cars. This very super-power is working hand in glove with neocolonialist and imperialist America to kill black people in Africa. Britain must get out of Kandaha, Zimbabwe, Namibia. Southern Africa must have a black Government.'

That was not very good for Britain. That was not very good for Tom Caput, Prime Minister of Great Britain for whom the morning after the bombing was a red-letter day. Fighting off savage attacks in the House of Commons. Fighting off charges of weakness in the House of Lords. Fighting. Fighting off the hawks and doves at the United Nations. The President of France had summoned the British Ambassador in France. Personally he read His Excellency a long lecture. *The French Government condemns Britain's non-action in Kandaha. . . .*

'I hope Your Excellency realizes why we had serious reservations about your joining the European Economic Community. Because of you atavistic policies, policies which endanger our relations with free Africa — a vital source of raw materials for our industry. Indeed a vital market. . . .' The French President continued, 'We have just had a press conference to make clear our position to the whole world. We have appraised the OAU of our stand and instructed our Ambassador to the Court of St James to make our position categorically clear.'

When he left the Champs Elysée, Ambassador Harcourt-Johnson was a worried man. The summoning of an Ambassador by the President of France for a personal dressing down was unprecedented. But so was the Prime Minister of Great Britain. Worried about world reaction, worried about student demonstrations all over the British universities. Worried about his party, the left wingers, the Cabinet and Parliament. Never before had a remote colonial issue had so much direct influence on the natural life of Her Majesty's Government. At the final meeting of Cabinet that evening he decided it would not be so for any longer. Going straight from

No. 10 Downing Street, he entered Parliament.

The Speaker had already been alerted for a Prime Ministerial statement. When he stood up, Old St Stephen's Chapel was hushed. The Prime Minister started with the background of Kandaha, how the British got involved with it, its rich resources of gold, the multi-racial composition of the country. Then he paused. He sipped at a glass of water and said, 'And now, Mr Speaker sir, on behalf of Her Majesty's Government, I wish to inform the House...' The House listened.

24

The party was being hosted by the Kandaha Commercial Farmers Bureau. Therefore it was a whites only party. It had to go ahead in spite of everything, because it had been arranged a long time ago and it was to crown the annual general meeting of the commercial farmers who wished and were determined to ensure that Kandaha continued in 'responsible' hands. It would not have been good for the bureau to cancel it. Sir Ray had opened the meeting that morning. In a hall bedecked with portraits of the Queen, Prime Ministers of South Africa, Rhodesia and others, Sir Ray had declared his faith in the farmers and in the country. Unlike his former performances he had shown remarkable restraint toward the Government, saying only 'our lives are in our hands'. On a lighter note, he had invited the colonial civil servants to join, 'the stalwart' farmers in multiplying their numbers so that through sheer population strength they could 'still the cauldron of black dissent'.

The party was being held at the Ngweyeye Farmers' Club on the outskirts of Musasa. The Ngweyeye Club was an exclusive, low, red-brick building with a green corrugated roof and a six-inch thick bowling green on the side. It was exclusive because dogs and blacks were not allowed, it was exclusive because that is where the pillar of the nation, that is the white farmers, could go in their greasy pants, take off their shirts and bask in the sun and drink.

Sir Ray was the heart and soul of the party. Already he must have shaken hands with more than a hundred people. He was saying to a cluster of admirers:

'I went to Hyde Park Corner once. I had a row with a twit who was saying all sorts of rubbish. But when I cornered him he came back fighting. I'll never forget what he said. He said the white race on earth has very little time. Unless it sticks together the black race will overwhelm it through promiscuous miscegenation. And d'you know what? This chap was no fool. He put it very pithily. He said to me, "Just remember that black on white or white on black can never be white. It will always be black. Only white on white can be white." So,' said Norris rubbing his hands together while he waited for a refill, 'you chaps have to remember we're in this game together. And the British Government knows that we'll fight if they let out these thugs from jail. The Governor knows we aren't going to allow any Kaffir into a party like this.'

There were cheers. Sir Ray raised his well-filled glass and said: 'Here's to us.'

Then the party cheered and whistled and sang, 'For he's a jolly good fellow.' Simon Malherbe had also been invited to the party, as had many other whites. As usual he was chaperoning Joan Chessman who did not appear to enjoy the gathering very much. Throughout the party Malherbe kept trying to get close to Norris. But there was such a thick crowd around their hero. Then his opportunity came just as 'For he's a jolly good fellow' was getting to the end. He nudged Norris in the belly and looked up at him ecstatically.

'I say man, I was right up in there. And didn't we give the niggers the works?'

Norris nodded, 'Well done.'

'This my . . .' Malherbe hesitated. Then he mentioned her name. 'She's British like you. I am South African. You arranged my job at BGS. And you know, I'm always ready. Jesus! Sir Ray, that was a piece of cake. Bomb at night and back to work tomorrow. I know your son. Great guy and thinks and talks like you, you know. I believe he's teaching in a big school and is very bright.'

Malherbe ran out of drink, out of steam. He broke away from Norris to refill. Norris turned to the girl.

'Mrs Chessman, I believe,' he said.

The girl corrected him.

'Miss,' she said firmly.

'What do you do?' he asked.

'Teaching,' she replied.

'Oh, that's interesting. My son is also a teacher. But he's teaching in a Kaffir school, way out in the country. He's making up for daddy's sins, you know.' Norris chuckled as he raised his other hand to pick out a *samusa* from the tray that the black waiter had placed before him. 'Well then, you must meet. Although he teaches blacks he's got his head well screwed on. Will stand no nonsense from Kaffirs.'

'Sir Ray,' began the girl.

'What?' replied Norris bending down a little to catch her voice and gobbling the samusa at the same time.

'I don't agree with . . .'

The chairman of the Commercial Farmers' Bureau rushed towards Norris holding a radio high. He'd been tipped that the one thing Norris would not miss was the eight o'clock BBC news. There was an immediate silence as the signal came on. Sir Ray was wrapped in attention.

'This is London calling,' said the news reader. 'The news read by Michael Ashton. First the headlines.'

Norris listened. The chairman would have loved a refill, but he had to stand around.

'The small British colony of Kandaha is to become independent and a date for constitutional talks has been set.'

Norris' jaw fell. Then he cried,

'Shut up!' thinking it was someone speaking. The crackly voice returned:

'In the House of Commons today the Prime Minister, Sir Thomas Caput, announced that the Government had decided to grant independence to the tiny colony of Kandaha in central Africa and a date for constitutional talks, to be held here in London, has been set.'

There was silence.

'Speaking to a packed House, Sir Thomas recounted the history of the colony from the days when Britain acquired it in response to native appeals for protection. He said that although the colony had experienced minor incidents of restlessness in the last few months, Her Majesty's Government was satisfied that the majority race there had been sufficiently prepared to govern the country. Asked outside the Commons as to whether the Government had not acted under pressure, the Prime Minister replied emphatically "No" and then added that the decision had in fact been taken more than a year ago. He also said, in response to another question, that there would be no pre-conditions to the talks. Asked specifically in respect of the necessity to guarantee the security of British personnel and investment, the Prime Minister simply said, "No comment now and none after".

'Earlier the Prime Minister had told the House that constitutional talks would open in London in Lancaster House in four weeks' time under the chairmanship of the Commonwealth Secretary. The statement which was listened to in hushed silence in the Commons, received a mixed reaction in the nation. The president of the Movement for the Liberation of Colonial Peoples, Sir George Andrews, welcomed it, whilst the executive chairman of the world-wide multinational Bristol Gold Syndicate, Lord Ventrical, described it as "a mortal blow to civilization and commerce, a mischievous idea invented by a coward and executed by a fool." It is also understood that all members of the only viable African political party — the People's Army of Liberation Party, who are now under detention, will be released in time to enable them to participate in the talks. It is not known what white reaction in Kandaha will be.'

At ten o'clock that evening His Excellency the Governor of Kandaha spoke to the colony. He announced formally the decision of Her Majesty's Government to release the prisoners and hold constitutional talks without any pre-conditions. He reminded the country that it was still in a state of emergency.

PALP's Caretaker Committee issued a statement.

The war continues until all PALP members under detention are released in accordance with the British Government's announcement. We will not talk to the colonialists. UNDER NO CIRCUMSTANCES SHALL WE ACCEPT TO TALK AT THE SAME TABLE WITH NORRIS.

Katenga issued a warning from Zambia.

We have heard Norris tell the whites to kill us by the hundreds; we shall do that which he may do to us in the same manner as we wipe out thousands of mosquitoes by fumigating our houses with the burning roots of an African tree. Under no circumstances will we accept peace imposed by the defeated. It is the peace of cunning.

'You must not make any more statements,' said Chimuko.
'Because my words stink to the white man's nose? If my voice stinks it is the voice of all black men that stinks. You want to disown us because we stink. Don't you?'

'You haven't heard from the President. We have to consult first with the party.'

'Which party? The party that wants to pander to the whites or PALP? Who founded PALP? Did you? Was it not Santasa? I am sure that Santasa does not like this,' Katenga, who had sat down, now stood up again.

'I am PALP,' he said, pointing at himself. 'PALP is not Baker's creation. It is not Lafayette's creation. It is not Norris' faeces. People will be hanged wantonly because a black man must always die like a frog! You already smell the cakes, the stupid tea parties, the luxury cars, the mansion of a ministerial house, the black servants whom you will continue to keep in slavery, everything that the white man enjoys, too quickly even before you have got there. Smell out the present stench of poverty of your own people. Then you will act. Then you will do. You will pull the trigger instead of consorting with capitalists. This independence talk is a fraud, a trick, just when we are hitting back at the colonial reptile.' He stopped. He heaved a sigh of disgust.

As soon as the news went over Radio Kandalia, Norris issued a statement calling upon the British Government to observe the seeds of an Angolan situation in the disunity of PALP . . .

'To whom shall the British give independence?' he asked. To nobody obviously. Norris disparaged the 'hasty and indecent retreat' of the British and said:

'The bloodshed which I have so often warned about is now a reality.'

PALP's post-office box that day was choked with telegrams. The telegrams by and large demanded the calling of a National Council. Many pledged support for PALP. But others supported Katenga because Katenga had said more than PALP had said. One read, *Palp and Holy Ones pledge full support Katenga statement stop Imperialist rats must be routed before we can talk stop We demand immediate meeting of National Council to deal with traitors. Ends.*

After the 'shocking' news, Sir Ray Norris went over to London. The trip had been planned a long time ago — the annual meeting of the Commonwealth Parliamentary Association. Now it had of course become urgent for him to go and use it to protest the decision and lobby for a change. On the evening of the opening of the conference, the Commonwealth Secretary gave a cocktail party. Many dignitaries attended. There were members of the House of Commons, High Commissioners and Ambassadors.

The Permanent Under-Secretary in the Commonwealth Office

winked to Sir Ray Norris. The two withdrew into a corner. The conversation appeared intense. Both men were doing more talking than drinking.

'Ray,' said Sir Andrew Mortimer. Sir Andrew was an octogenarian-looking fifty-year-old man. He was pale, slightly built and ruled the Colonial Office with an iron rod. Some of his colleagues called him a moving grave, implying that he should have been dead long ago. Others simply hated his guts. No consultations. Always commands. But it had worked. There was no country which had become independent in Africa which did not remember his acerbic temper and trenchant remarks at the constitutional conference table.

'Ray,' he said again, 'you'll be a bloody fool to press us too far over the independence issue. We've made up our mind on that one.'

'But you did not consult us,' said Norris. 'You've got to understand Andy that we just can't go on being pushed around like this. When I was last here you didn't give me so much as a clue as to what you might do.'

'I know Ray. But that's the problem. We can't always tell even our closest friends what's going to happen. Kandaha independence is part of a global strategy by the PM. It's the only way of ensuring the security of our interests in that country.'

'What about our security?' asked Norris. 'The personal security of we, the British, and other Europeans there? You only care for your interests. You don't care a damn what happens to your own kith and kin, do you?'

'Of course we do, Ray,' said Mortimer. 'Make no mistake that'll be an unspoken condition for independence. But it can be prejudiced if you don't co-operate. The British Empire has to live on. This time it can't be a political empire. It must be a subtle economic empire. After all, this is what we had the great scramble for Africa for. Political imperialism was by default because we suddenly found that the natives couldn't rule themselves. That's why we had to impose *Pax Britannica*. Now that they can do so . . .'

Norris shook his head.

'Yes, now that they can,' repeated Mortimer, 'we must appear to step down. But make no mistake. We'll be running their economies and therefore the white man will continue to be indispensable.'

The Commonwealth Secretary moved towards them. 'Andy's not pumping you Sir Ray, I hope,' he said smiling. 'Relax, we've a long agenda tomorrow.' Then he looked at his watch and said, 'Andy, we've a late sitting tonight. I must go back to the Commons. Take charge of Sir Ray, we'll see you tomorrow'.

'Her Majesty's Government will,' said Andy Mortimer as if resuming his discussion from where the Commonwealth Secretary had interrupted them, 'insist on a clear and unequivocal undertaking that all British investment in Kandaha — public and private — shall be fully guaranteed against (a) arbitrary and unilateral confiscation; (b) capricious changes in the tax law of that country, such changes for example, as might discriminate against our investment; (c) the free and unimpeded remission to Britain of all earnings of British nationals and corporations; and finally (d) an undertaking that the new colony, sorry dominion, will honour all agreements entered into by Her Majesty's Government in connection with the continued payments for patents and royalties of whatsoever description to British holders of these rights. Her Majesty's Government is not disposed to accept anything less. Unless these conditions are fulfilled, not only will there be no independence but, in the event of a rash act on the part of the blacks, all aid both financial and personnel-wise, will be cut off at once. And that means . . .' Andy Mortimer looked up. 'You'll see Ray that we've covered you pretty well.'

Maybe Her Majesty's Government had, but Norris wasn't sure. So later that night he kept a late appointment with Lord Ventrical, the chairman of the Bristol Gold Syndicate, the man who had made 3 Southsquare, London the legendary work place of a business colossus. Norris had taken note of his acid comment on the independence announcement. He was going to use it.

'What do you propose doing now, Ray?' asked Ventrical, looking up from his desk. Norris had hardly sat down when the question was posed. 'Please sit down,' said Ventrical indicating a seat further down the office, abstractedly. 'I'll join you in a moment.' He continued writing. 'This whole Kandaha affair is a shambles,' he mumbled. 'I've sunk a lot of money into the country and', he looked up at Norris, 'into your party, Ray, and into the pockets of your black friends. How do you propose repaying me, Sir Ray?' Ventrical stood up. He walked over to Norris and sank into a sofa.

'What can I do for you?' Norris replied. 'I've been thinking. We've got to fight back. We need money and only *you* can help us.'

'I've given you money before. What have you done with it? You and Turnbull have squandered it on useless causes, useless people, haven't you?'

'That's not entirely correct, unless you're thinking of Mpengula.'

'How much money have you invested in *the only respectable black leader*?' asked Ventrical sarcastically. 'I hope you know by now that neither you nor your Mpengula will ever rule that country.'

Norris thought for a moment. The conversation was not exactly constructive. Ventrical was still fretting and chafing from the events of a few days ago.

'What do you need the money for, Norris? You're finished aren't you?'

'We'll have to fight back if Kawala starts violence.'

'Fight back against who?'

'The blacks and maybe even against the Government itself. Rhodesia has done it. We can do it.'

'I'm not here to finance rebellion,' snapped Ventrical.

'Fine,' said Norris. 'If you want to lose everything you've built up in Kandaha, stay clean and loyal!'

Norris was fighting back. Ventrical thought again. His interests in Rhodesia were intact and this only because the whites there fought back against Africans taking over.

'There are two ways of fighting a war, Norris. One is to fight and win the war. The other is to win your enemy. Why don't you try winning Kawala over?'

'Me?' asked Norris incredulously.

'Yes, Norris,' said Ventrical. 'I've been thinking things over. If you were to undercut our Government and come out in support of no guarantees, you could win Kawala over.'

'Win over a barbarian!' snapped Norris.

'You haven't heard me out.'

'Lord Ventrical,' asked Norris, 'are there no principles?'

Ventrical shook his head slowly.

'None,' he said, 'and you know it. If you want money you'll have to bend your principles. You can't expect me to bend my interests and finance a lunatic scheme.'

'Communists, barbarians,' hissed Norris again.

'Never mind their being barbarians. They are not communists yet. If that's the only way to swing the position and get things moving, it will have to be that way.'

'Incidentally Ray, have you heard the latest?'

'What?'

'The whole damn lot of them has been released.'

'What?'

'Yes, including your best friend Kawala. Katenga is back in Zambia, with his hands still covered in white blood. There was something about giving the murderers full immunity and they say that in a week's time PALP is meeting to debate whether they will join the talks or not. Incredible! They say too that Katenga may be difficult. After all, it's a public secret he's been mixing up with Cubans and commies up there in Zambia. Zambia had better watch it. Incredible,' said Lord Ventrical again.

25

There were eight provinces in the country. Each province constituted a 'region' and sent sixty members to the National Council. The theoretical maximum number of delegates to a National Council was thus four hundred and eighty plus the members of the Central Committee who numbered twelve. The President had to get at least two-thirds of the total votes cast by the regional representatives to be elected, while for the rest of the Central Committee members it was a straight simple majority. An extraordinary meeting of the Council required the written or telegraphic request of seven of the eight regions and already all the eight were calling for an extraordinary session. Notice of an extraordinary session had to be issued within two days of receiving the 'effective' petitions for that session. The meeting itself had to take place within fourteen days of the issue of that notice.

The meeting started on the fourteenth day of the notice. It took place fifty miles to the north of Gunsbury Town on a flat plateau covered by hard aged granite rock which stretched over half a square mile. The Mulungu Rock was an important part and parcel of PALP's history. That was where, years ago, Santasa declared the birth of PALP. That was where when the party was torn by strife and it seemed as though it would collapse, the party elders — the councillors — repaired to argue and fight it out. The fact that the Council was not meeting in Musasa but at this rock in the bush underlined the crisis nature of the meeting. The Rock was a kind of island formed by the Mulungu stream splitting itself and the two rivulets flowing round each side of the rock until they met at the end of it. Just like the way Kandaha came to be. The stream itself was called Mulungu, which comes from 'God', because long ago the ancients who lived in this part of the country believed that that rock was the seat of the ancestral God. How else could one have explained the smooth flat and continuous surface of the rock, the teaming brim in the rivulets below it and the fact that every so often, the rock rose into flat-topped slabs of rock which looked like tables off which the ancestral gods ate the sacrifices offered by the living to appease their restless ire. Since taking over, the party had built grass huts on both sides of the rock. These huts were rarely maintained throughout the period from one such conference to another. This therefore meant that the first day of each conference was taken up in hut construction and the session proper did not start until well into the afternoon.

The whole crowd stood up and began cheering him. Then the clapping started.

'Everywhere! Kawala, Kawala! On earth Kawala, Kawala. In heaven Kawala, Kawala!'

Kawala looked at the crowd. He started the African National Anthem and as the crowd sang 'Nkosi Sikeleli Africa . . .' Kawala steeled his nerves and determined that he would fight unto victory.

'Fellow comrades and countrymen, we have come here in the darkest hour of our nation,' he began. 'Darkest hour indeed. Throughout this never-ending twilight of our struggle, we have fought unceasingly to liberate man from the yoke of slavery. We have suffered for our principles. Our people's blood has been shed. We have been spat at by the little arrogant men who would have us believe that only they are human beings. But throughout this period of bitter struggle we have refrained from paying the colonialists and neocolonialists back in their own coin. Just as we have condemned racialism before now, I ask you now to continue to condemn it. Racialism is a stinking animal and whether rotten meat changes hands or not, it will still stink. But there is another form of racialism which is more insidious, more pungent, than racialism itself. It is tribalism. This, comrades, is more serious because it is a putrid vapour within our midst!' Katenga looked at him but Kawala continued. 'I warn you comrades, of the dangers that can divide man from man — racialism, and brother from brother — tribalism — when our fight is not at an end or victory in sight. And so you may wonder why I talk of this when this conference should be about whether we will continue to fight or lay down our arms. In my opinion, the decision whether to continue fighting the colonial régime or to stop, is an easy one. Very easy indeed. But if we regard colonialism as the only enemy, racialism and tribalism will slip out through the back door to persecute and plague us in a vast deluge of brotherly carnage!'

Everyone was listening. Kawala spoke on about wars in the world. He spoke about the Angolan situation and then said:

'It is not for me to pre-empt any one of the things which you wish to say at this conference. It is not for me to force any particular line. The position is that your Central Committee has not committed you to any line of response to the Colonial Government's offer to talks and independence. You, the councillors, must make that decision now. Shall PALP accept the overture or not? That is the question to be decided. But in making that decision, bear in mind also that whether in continued battle or not, the other equally important question to be answered is, 'What kind of society does PALP wish to see? A society bedevilled by racialism and tribalism or religious intolerance and sectionalism or a society of free men?' When he finished he said, 'It is now my pleasure to declare this special extraordinary meeting open.'

The chairman of the North-Western Region rose to propose the vote of thanks to the President. It had been suggested by Chimuko that he should move the vote. He thanked the President for his 'highly stimulating speech', underlining the dangers of regionalism. Then he continued:

'But comrade National President, in the strains and stresses through which we live, there is a danger of imagination running ahead of us, a real danger of imagining ourselves crossing the bridges even before we have come to them. Let me be more specific, since eyes looking everywhere never caught the maiden's eye. I can understand the President's warning about tribalism and regionalism. It is indeed a timely warning about racialism. How many of us have practised it? How many of us have even had an opportunity of practising it?' Katenga stubbed his foot into the ground. 'If the white man hears that we will not reverse racialism he will become even bolder than now in his insults. The white man must be told now that we will pay him in his own coin when we take over. Pound for pound, as Shylock demanded.'

'Comrade National President,' said Katenga, 'as we debate the present issues we will bear your words in mind. They are very wise words and speaking personally, I am very pleased that you, comrade, have left it to the people to decide what kind of future we want to build for this country. Comrade National President, having said what I have said, let me also say that the greatest threat to the success of this conference is not what decision we take on the independence issue: it is ourselves. Ourselves and the divisions within us.' He received an ovation. Kawala would have cheered him except for the last sentence. The Council then split into committees and remained to discuss Kawala's opening address and the business of the conference for two days.

On the third day of the conference the Council again met in plenary to hear the reports of the committees and to consider their draft resolutions for adoption. Katenga had been elected chairman of one committee, while Kakonkawadia and Santasa had been among the five elected chairmen to the other committees. Chimuko was the chairman of the plenary session. When they had all sat down on the rock he said through an improvised public-address system:

'I call the National Council to order. I will now call on comrade Generalissimo Katenga to present the report of committee 1.'

Katenga jumped up to the deafening cheers of the crowd. His fuzzy beard fluttered somewhat in the wind. He drew near to the only trumpet-shaped loudspeaker. Grasping it by his left hand he brought it to his mouth and cried:

'The God of the white ones said to his Moses when he gave him the commandments: "If any kind of hurt is done to you, you must pay back a life for a life, an eye for an eye, a tooth for a tooth, a hand for a hand, a burn for a burn and a wound for a wound." That God of the white ones further said, "Do not let yourself be led into doing something you know to be wrong because the majority of people favour it."

'Maybe the majority of people here favour laying down their arms even if it is wrong and negotiate with the colonialists and Norris, their lackey. For these people, this is an easy decision. Haven't we heard on this very rock that the decision is an easy one?' Kawala listened impassively. Several necks craned up to take a look at Kawala. 'It is easy,' continued Katenga, 'for people who have never taken up arms to lay them down. These people may even have been in jail. But they didn't get there because they were fighting.' Everybody sat up. Could what they were hearing really mean what it seemed to mean? Those of them who had been in Katenga's committee could not remember having discussed what Katenga had said so far. Their committee had come down in favour of participation in the talks. It had even urged Kawala, in a resolution to be debated in the plenary, to ensure that there was no more delay. Who could Katenga be referring to? His remarks only pointed to one person. But could it be possible? No. It wasn't the President; were the two not too close together for this kind of thing?

A host of wild ducks which had been drinking water in the rivulet below cackled noisily. Then they beat up their wings and soared above the rock and flew away in a splendid marchpast. The people looked up to their glistening bodies. As soon as they had fled Katenga resumed.

'I have fought the colonial reptile. I have taken up arms against the crocodile. I am not going to lay them down just when its gangrenous jaws are opening up even wider than ever in search of a kill. Only flies, dirty flies laden with the pus of the rotting hyenas and jackals fly straight into the mouth of the crocodile. Are there any flies here?' he cried. 'Are there any jackals? Any hyenas?' The sound of 'No' echoed through the crowd, on the edge of the rock into the rivulets and then into the thick bush after him. Katenga smiled faintly for the first time since the opening of the conference. 'I am not going to lay down my arms even if all of you here say we should. I am not going to lay down my arms because I know it is not right to lay them down, even as the God of the whites, the God with whom some of you now flirt as if you were not Africans and you did not have your own God agrees.' He paused for breath, then drawing the loudspeaker back to his mouth he said, 'To lay down your arms before you have avenged the death of all our brothers and sisters who have been killed by the white man, is to offend even the law which his own God handed down to his Moses. Have we paid back a life for a life?' he asked, jumping from one end of the rostrum to the other. Then he sighed and in a low voice he said, 'No. If some of you have, I certainly haven't yet. So obey your God — those of you whose God is that of a white man. How can you stop before you make him pay back your eye with his eye, your tooth with his tooth? He has hanged you by the dozen. Have you also hanged him by the dozen?' The crowd went wild with cheers.

Chimuko stood to call Katenga to order. Katenga was making a speech and not reporting the proceedings of his committee. Time was running out.

'Yes,' said Katenga. 'Time is running out. Have we already become white men, white men who will not even stay to see their own die because time has run out? If you want me to report on my committee's resolutions I will tell you that they are there for you to read. Some of us have been tortured for not agreeing to talk with the colonialists. So why should I waste time on meaningless resolutions? We have even been told to shut our mouths up. Is shutting free people's mouths up any less serious a crime than racialism?

'As this is my only opportunity to speak, I say to you, reject participation in the planned talks. Reject even if Norris and other jackals are withdrawn. Reject any talks with a Colonial Government the numbers of whose guns you do not know. Don't trust capitalists. Trust only the socialists. Why is Jango in turmoil today? Because the people there left the colonial capitalist carcass before they even skinned it. The carcass resurrected. That is why capitalism, with all its guns, is there today. Only scientific socialism is good for us. You cannot kill a cobra by sending another cobra into its hole. You cannot kill exploitation of capitalism by using capitalism. That is what you do when you speak to colonialism.'

Katenga continued amid wild cheers and wild interventions. There were times when the battle with the chairman seemed to shift on to the delegates with Katenga hurling ridicule and near insults at some of them.

'Because there are people here who want to return to their mother's breasts instead of fighting I will sit down,' he finally concluded.

The drums that had opened the meeting on the first day now rose above the din of the clapping cheers and argument to usher him to his seat. He had not said a word about the proceedings of committee 1. But he had stirred up a hornet's nest. Kawala, the man everyone was eyeing wondering what he would say, sat on impassively. There was just a little impatient kneading of the hands to indicate that he did not approve.

Then Kakonkawadia was called to report on committee 2, someone at the very back of the crowd shouted out:

'What about committee 1?'

'Committee 1 chose to make a speech,' cut in Santasa.

There was loud laughter. Katenga shot a sharp look at him and snorted with disgust. Then Kakonkawadia started. He said the observations and recommendations of his committee were straight-forward. He would not make a speech and besides he was not a gifted speaker anyway — especially when it came to irrelevancies. Kakonkawadia had sized up the situation, from experience he knew that no one who attacked Kawala in the manner Katenga had done ever got anywhere. Kawala had a sixth and seventh sense when it came to political in-fighting and when he homed into an enemy, retribution was swift and ruthless. He and Katenga had, in any case, always been at daggers drawn. Katenga did not like the way

Kakonkawadia had become a close confidant of Kawala, even though he had come late into the party. Moreover, he did not trust educated people and Kako was an educated man by the standards of Kandaha.

'I was saying I will be direct and to the point. But considering the magnificent speech of my colleague who has just spoken, I will be pardoned if I allow myself the indulgence to comment briefly. I am not commenting on the business of laying down arms or taking up arms because the decision is indeed a simple and straight-forward one — certainly in the view of my committee which sees no point in the politics of self-aggrandizement and spilling more human blood than is necessary.'

'You never fought, you Kako!' yelled Katenga. 'Just shut up and go to drink tea with your colonial masters.'

The chairman said:

'Order, order,' and, unruffled by the situation, Kako continued:

'There are too many people who know enough about scientific socialism to pronounce the word correctly.'

'Is this an English class?' said Katenga jumping up again.

'I would ask these people to try and understand these terms before misleading us,' Kakonkawadia said.

He then dealt with his committee's recommendations. On the subject of the conference it wanted Norris out of it but indicated that if this was impossible, negotiations should still proceed. Then he turned to other recommendations. The committee endorsed Kawala's concern over racialism and tribalism, and presented several resolutions aimed at eliminating these evils. The committee also deplored self interest among leaders and called for distributive justice. When he finished, Katenga jumped to his feet and said:

'Mr Chairman, I want to formally move that the party endorse scientific socialism or communism as the policy of the country now and that any capitalists should be thrown out of the party. Capitalists are people who find it easier to negotiate with whites than to shoot out their brains.'

There was laughter. Someone said:

'Seconded.'

Chimuko ignored the proposal and moved on to the third and then through to the last committee report. Most committees had expressed themselves in favour of talks for independence. They asserted that if PALP was confident of itself, it had nothing to fear from the talks. Talks did not mean that PALP would have to unscramble its vigilance. What was there for PALP to be afraid of when it was PALP alone which had forced the Colonial Government's hand? The debate went on for the whole day. As it continued, Katenga's views became more and more the views of a minority even though an unduly vociferous one. Then Chimuko called upon Kawala to wind up the debate before the vote by secret ballot would be taken.

Kawala stood up. He had remained silent for all these three days. His voice carried across the rock in a rich quiet tone. He did not need to scream through the loudspeaker. As if anticipating that he would not use the loudspeaker, the crowd crept closer to him. He began:

'Fellow countrymen and comrades-in-arms. We are about to vote on a most important motion. We are about to make the most far-reaching decision for Kandaha on behalf of those people who have perished in the struggle, those who might still perish and generations to come. I am glad that all those who have spoken have spoken courageously and candidly because this is no time for deceit and double talk. A man should never double talk with his destiny. To all those who have contributed personally, whether I may agree with them or not, I say well done. Kandaha is this day proud of you. I say proud of you because you have all, to the last man, spoken with feeling about the future of this country and explored fully the machinations and perfidy of which certain racial white leaders, black stooges and colonialists are capable. I would ask all of you to bear the sincere and courageous views of our colleagues as you cast your votes. May I also end this part of my brief speech with a personal word of thanks to all those who have spoken pointedly and sometimes critically to my own contribution at the opening of this historic conference. I have learnt a lot from their contribution and I am grateful that democracy, free speech, independence of thought and action, are still the thriving corner stones of the party which is destined to redeem this young nation from the servitude of bondage. The party has not lost the salt of democracy. With this it will salt the whole nation, nay the whole earth with the sweet taste of real democracy. I leave this conference more confident than ever before of the party's ability to withstand internal dissension. Where all men and women can talk freely and openly there can only be unity because democracy itself is unity despite diversity.'

There was deathly silence. So much silence that when the wild ducks flew over the rock in their daily afternoon ritual no one noticed them. Kawala stopped to drink some water. The remarks by Katenga and a few of his followers had been so pointedly aimed at him. And yet he had not mentioned Katenga or even shown that he was angry with him. On the contrary, he seemed to have complimented him on his forthright remarks. But were Katenga's remarks really forthright? This was the question many hearts in that crowd were asking themselves. Had they not been meant to discredit Kawala? There had even been a move tö table a vote of no-confidence in Kawala and to call for new elections to the Central Committee there and then. What else could this have meant other than the unseating and disgrace of Kawala?

Kawala set his glass down and then continued.

'Having spoken about the positive side of this meeting let me now, fellow countrymen, speak of the deep sadness of my heart at the lack of clarity and almost treachery, of the tone of some of the contributions. I am sure that if these people really understood what they were saying they would not have prescribed such medicine for the country which they love so much. So I forgive them.'

The crowd cocked its ears. What would Kawala say now? Who would he talk about? Who had betrayed his country? Kawala took another sip at his glass of water. His face became serious and that stubborn chin jutted out for the first time in the three days. He fumbled at his lumber jacket and drank some more water. Everyone waited. He took out his handkerchief and blew his nose quietly. Katenga shifted in his chair uneasily. Kawala raised his face at the crowd. For well over a minute he looked at it. Then his hand reached for the glass of water again. Finally, setting it down he resumed:

'Kandaha is not in Europe. It is not in the Middle East. It is not in Eastern Europe or the Far East or America. It is a jewel embedded in the stone of Mother Africa. Therefore its solutions to its many problems when it becomes independent must be African solutions. Some of you have spoken of capitalism, scientific socialism, communism, as if the world must be either one or the other of these and as if one of them was a saint and the other evil. Don't you know that all these "isms" about which you speak so eloquently are not natives of Africa but importations from abroad, even as colonialism itself was imported and forced down our throats by the strong powers from outside Africa?

'I invite you to follow the history of all these "isms" in the countries where they were born. They are "isms" of blood. Whole generations of men have been wiped out in the furtherance of these ideologies by a few. No "ism" has spread except by the fire and sword. Do you know the millions of people who have perished, been liquidated, because they would not pay lip service to "isms" of oppression of individual liberty? Do you know how many lives have been secretly liquidated or how much frustration of free expression has taken place? And yet some of you have the cheek to say this or that "ism" is the best for Kandaha. If you want us now to give you the instrument for the suppression of your own people, we say "No" to you. "No" because you are a traitor. "No" because you are a Satan lurking in the dark corners, waiting to unleash a plague of oppression and death upon us as soon as colonialism has been buried.'

Kawala once again reached for his glass of water. His hand was trembling visibly. Katenga, sitting there at the rostrum, was doing everything possible to look nonplussed.

'Angola. Yes, what about Angola? You mention Angola as though it was not Africa's most serious tragedy. After all the "isms" have tired of killing and oppressing their own people, they have now turned to poor black Africa. In the service of foreign ideologies of oppression, black brother is now killing black brother and all the time these "isms" are making money from the blood of my fellow black brothers and sisters. Is this what you want for Kandaha, for Africa?' His voice rose into a roar. 'Do you want a divided Kandaha so that you can personally prosper from the blood money that your employers will be paying you? Do you want to re-enact what your ancestors did to your own brothers and sisters, selling them into slavery for the sake of a few sweets or beads? Brothers and sisters, it saddens me greatly. So long as I remain President of this party I must and will insist on an African, a Kandahaian solution, to our problems. That solution must first and foremost put man at the centre of all institutions, all ideologies. Institutions and ideologies must not be created for the oppression and elimination of man by a few selfish people. And by "man" I mean Man and not just black man. I want this to be clearly understood. We will not emulate others. We will do whatever is best for us to achieve the objectives of consolidating our liberties and improving the quality of life for everybody and not just a few. But we will not exchange one form of colonialism with another more terrible type.'

The silence deepened. 'There have been moves at this conference, yes, I know about them, to precipitate a premature election by forcing a vote of no-confidence in me and my colleagues in the Central Committee. If you are bent on this course of action, go ahead. I say "go ahead" to you Satan. Go ahead and be about your father's business of betrayal. If we have lost you a life, let us pay back with a life. I don't fear the death of the body. But I dread the death of the spirit, death that comes out of corruption, the bartering of the lives of one's own people for a mess of potage.' He paused and then cast his eyes above their heads. 'So to help you be about your father's dirty business I am asking you now to express your lack of confidence in me and my colleagues by voting positively the motion that comrade Katenga put to us early today. Namely that this party should endorse scientific socialism or communism or any other "ism" as its ideological policy. Upon a positive outcome of that vote I and my colleagues will resign and leave the field free for you to elect a new Central Committee which can then conduct the vote for the business which this conference is all about.'

He sat down. Had the people heard him correctly? Did Kawala say that he had resigned? Then pandemonium broke loose.

'No! No! No!' yelled the crowd, stampeding towards Kawala. 'Katenga should resign! He is the traitor!'

Women began to cry. Even men could not hold their tears. Then when Chimuko finally calmed the crowd, he said:

'Comrade President. The people refuse. They don't want any vote of no-confidence in you.' He turned to the crowd and said, 'The ballot will now take place. The procedure has already been explained. You will mark an X against either "Negotiations" or "No Negotiations".'

When he read out the results the atmosphere was electric. Four thousand, eight hundred and seven of the four thousand eight hundred and twelve delegates had cast their vote in favour of participation in the talks to be held at Lancaster House, in London. The cheering continued.

'The war of peace is now on!' cried Kawala above the din. 'It will be more difficult, more difficult because the enemy of peace is invisible.'

Just then Katenga, his beard fluttering in the breeze, ran to Kawala and embraced him.

'I am with you,' he said at last.

'My General!' cried Kawala. 'Where is my warrior Chimuko?' he cried again, his voice choked with emotion. 'Come! Come all of you the freedom fighters!'

The cheers were thundering. Kawala's handkerchief went up to his eyes. Katenga's grey-streaked beard hung limp upon his chin from tears raining down. Then Kawala, his face a rapture of shining joy cried:

'One Kandaha.'

'One Nation!' replied the crowd.

The rocks carried the echo 'One Kandaha! One Nation!' into the valley and then lifted it up into the hills and back to the rock until it became a cacophonous babel of 'One Kandaha. One One One Nation Kandaha.'

26

In Musasa, John Turnbull had been feeling rather happy with himself. Since the announcement of the constitutional talks a month ago, the situation at the Bristol Gold Syndicate had become very healthy indeed.

More than five years ago the Bristol Gold Syndicate had made a secret arrangement with the Governor to prospect. A geologist had been very impressed by several samples that he had tested. So he wrote a paper. Turnbull's reaction was hostility itself. No one mining gold had the right to waste the company's time on stupid hobbies like prospecting. He demanded to know from the geologist how much of the company's resources had been misdirected into such futile expensive hobbies. He would dismiss the man. The situation had, however, been saved by the personal intervention of Lord Ventrical, the chairman of the multinational company, who happened to be on one of his infrequent visits to Kandaha.

'Let's send it (the report) to our chaps in London,' he said. 'There might be something in it.' Then he had added, 'Cabinet could be influenced to grant large incentives for prospecting in our colonies.'

That was how the gold syndicate came to form a small, high-powered and highly secret prospecting group. Now the very man whom five years ago he had nearly dismissed was sitting opposite him and going over his latest report with him. The man had a thick-set bulldog jaw which seemed to chew up his words as he spoke. His eyes were small and his arms hairy. He always had a habit of spreading his arms over the table.

That little habit of spreading his arms always annoyed Turnbull.

It suggested a lack of respect and nonchalance which he could not tolerate in any subordinate. But this morning he was not noticing the man's hairy arms. That, whatever report it was, was yet another reason for Turnbull feeling very happy that morning. That night Turnbull flew to London. It was such a sudden decision. But then, what airline would not always have a spare first-class seat for the managing director of the Bristol Gold Syndicate (Kandaha)? Turnbull arrived the following day in London and went straight to see Lord Ventrical. That afternoon the Commonwealth Secretary called a press conference. The conference was to brief the press on the arrangements for the Constitutional Conference on Kandaha which was to open that evening. In fact, the delegates, Norris, Kawala and others were waiting in their separate lobbies. Under the massive glittering chandeliers of Lancaster House, he began:

'Ladies and Gentlemen . . .' He had hardly finished the sentence when a messenger laid a note before him. The envelope was underlined *Urgent* and it bore the stamp of the Prime Minister's office. The Commonwealth Secretary ripped it open. *Joe, you must come at once. There's an urgent development that concerns your negotiations. I can't explain it in a note or on the telephone.*

Joseph Schapper, original name, Shapevonsky — Hungarian descent — looked at the note again. Caput was not used to undue excitement. So he knew that something *was* the matter. He looked at his watch. A quarter past three.

'Gentlemen,' he said, 'we'd better take tea now. It could be a long session. Could you please excuse me, I've some business to attend to. That's the trouble with being a Minister in Britain.'

Lord Ventrical was there with the Prime Minister. There was also Turnbull. They were pouring over a large map of Kandaha.

'Joe,' said the Prime Minister, 'this is most exciting news. Postpone or cancel those talks. We can't afford to let go of Kandaha.'

Lord Schapper glared at the Prime Minister.

'What do you mean, sir?'

'There's uranium in Kandaha. Masses of it. And very rich too. We can't let go,' the PM was shaking his head. He, too, shook his head.

'How can we do that with honour?'

'Never mind the honour Joe,' snapped his superior. 'We simply have to tell the blacks nothing doing.' Ventrical nodded agreement. 'If we don't stay,' continued the PM, 'someone else will be in there in no time. The Commies, the Americans, the Arabs, the whole goddam blessed lot.'

'We'd be fools to give away such a country,' mumbled Lord Ventrical.

'Have you considered the possible international reaction, Prime Minister? And our friends in the Common Market.'

'They can all hang, Joe. With such vast uranium resources we can do anything. We wouldn't even require all these goddam overseas contracts. We could then tell the Arabs where they get off,' replied the Prime Minister. 'Do anything, Use any excuse. But the talks must be broken off. We must re-assess our position. If we go on it becomes doubly important now that we get foolproof guarantees of the security of British business.'

Schapper hesitated.

'What do I tell them, the journalists?'

'Anything other than the truth for God's sake.'

'They must already know about this uranium business.'

Schapper was feeling angry and he looked in Ventrical's direction contemptuously.

'They are not fools you know.'

'Even if they were the Magis the talks must never take place,' cut in the Prime Minister. 'Tell them something about a last-minute hitch. Blame it on something vague. Maybe we want to make sure there's no more fighting.'

Joseph Schapper gave it a cool thinking over. He was not a man for evading trouble. He decided he would return to the briefing hall. He would talk in general about HMG's posture in Southern Africa. He did just that.

As his car began to move off from Lancaster House after the abrupt press conference, someone dashed to the front. The chauffeur slammed on the brakes. Another man appeared at the window. He opened the door, a camera flashed.

'Lord Schapper,' said the scruffy looking fellow who had opened the door and who was now sitting beside the Commonwealth Secretary, 'I represent Newsweek of America. Our syndicated columnist in New York has told us that you've either done or are about to do a deal with Lord Ventrical over Kandaha. Is it true?'

He thrust the microphone into his face. Schapper would have pushed the fellow out of the car. But he controlled himself.

'It's a lot of rubbish,' he said. 'Chauffeur, get out of here, for Christ's sake.'

Other journalists rushed towards the car until it was completely surrounded by clicking cameras and shouting, scruffy young men and women.

'So you know Ventrical then,' said the Newsweek man. Then he pulled out a picture. 'Is this you with Ventrical and the PM this afternoon outside No. 10?'

'What business of yours is it if it is?' exploded Schapper.

'Everything's our business, Mr Schapper. What was Ventrical seeing the PM about?'

'None of your business,' replied the vexed Schapper.

'We put it to you that Ventrical has done a deal with you. There's been uranium discovered in Kandaha and you've given him the OK to go ahead and you've agreed to defer or cancel these talks. Isn't it true that the talks may never be held?'

'Get out of here or I'll walk,' snapped Schapper to the chauffeur. The chauffeur raised his hands helplessly. There were people all over his car.

By that time also the other delegates to the talks had come out. The Newsweek man turned to a man.

'Congratulations, Mr PALP. Is it true you don't want to give guarantees to British investment because you want the Communists and Arabs to come in to work your new uranium country?'

The man looked nonplussed.

'What uranium find?' he asked. The man, a student representative of PALP was wearing a PALP badge.

'You mean you haven't been told that the constitutional talks have been cancelled, that there will be no independence for you, because the Bristol Gold Syndicate has struck uranium?'

Mr 'PALP's face turned black.

'That's nonsense,' shouted Schapper. 'I'll call the police.' Schapper went from Lancaster House straight to the Prime Minister. He was very angry. 'You didn't tell me you'd tipped the press.'

'About what?'

'Kandaha and uranium.'

'You don't say!'

'Yes. It's all over the world now. We won't give independence because of the uranium find. Just imagine the reaction! I told you we were playing with fire, playing into Ventrical's hands and the whole conservative lot. What's going to happen now?'

The Prime Minister thought for a moment.

'It's very bad,' he said.

'You must think of something.'

'Like what?'

Schapper almost felt like crushing the PM's head.

'A credible lie.'

'Yes, something with some truth in it.' Then he thought for a moment.

'I've got it. Issue a statement simply saying the talks will open later than planned. Er . . . somewhere in the statement say that there are interesting indications of uranium but that, as yet, it's too early to say.'

'Is that all?'

'Er . . . whatever you do, make sure hot heads like Kawala don't get violent,' added the Premier.

'Does Kawala know? Norris is in the picture.'

'I bet he does by now. He was somewhere in the wings,' said Schapper.

'Ha, ha, ha! There's nothing like a bit of surprise to pep up a drama!'

The following morning the London papers were all full of the uranium fiasco. A day after returning from the 'shameful' journey, as Katenga put it, Katenga and Chimuko disappeared and Kawala was re-arrested.

27

A week rolled on but nothing was heard further about the 'adjourned' talks from Government House. Governor Baker's residence had become a fortification out of which he rarely ventured. He was under instruction to 'lower the political temperature'. From what could be seen that meant strengthening the guard at Government House and making sure that the people did not forget that there was a regular army. As time passed the nationalists became more restless. Within a week, the deadline which they had set themselves would arrive. If nothing would be heard further then there would be no alternative but for Kawala to openly declare war from his cell.

Baker's eyes roved over the document before him. That document had lain there since morning. It was a neat red file with a black border. He had opened it several times that day. But every time he had picked up his pen to sign the death warrant within it, he had hesitated and then put it back. The blotter contained five execution warrants for his signature. The death sentence had been imposed on all the five men who killed the Ecklands.

Now he was reading the covering letter again.

Government of Kandaha, Cabinet Office, Musasa

Your Excellency
I have the honour to enclose herewith the Death Warrants in respect of the persons indicated therein for Your Excellency's approval and signature. The Committee for the Prerogative of Mercy has in accordance with Section 14 (b) (i) of Chapter 6 of the Laws of Kandaha, duly deliberated the sentence imposed by the Supreme Court of Appeal and decided that it (the Committee for the Prerogative of Mercy) has nothing to say ... I have the honour to be, sir, Your Most Obedient Servant ... McGrowther.

When he had received the folder the day before he had left on the week's tour he had called McGrowther as was the practice. McGrowther had remembered the full proceedings because he had known that it would be necessary for him to recount the full story of the deliberations to the Governor. That, too, was the practice. No minutes could be kept of the deliberations of the Committee. Not even a scribble.

Elwyn Baker remembered, as he sat in his high-backed chair — all the chairs in that place seemed so high backed — what each of the three members of the Committee had said both in the debate and singly when they filed one by one into the room where the Secretary and Chairman sat solemnly. 'Let justice take its course,' each one had mumbled and then literally bolted out to get away from it all. Even the Attorney General had not hesitated.

But Elwyn Baker also knew that the debate had been far less unanimous than the conclusion. Thomson had not queried the sentence: he had queried the political wisdom of executing five black men for the murder of two white persons at that point in time. But when the Secretary for Works had said, 'It would be a massacre,' Thomson's face had flushed with anger and he had exclaimed, 'Justice is not massacre. I object to this!' The Attorney General himself had said nothing. He rarely said anything unless something was seriously wrong... 'That would mean that he is satisfied that the five are guilty,' said the Governor to himself.

He thought further about the political consequences. Were any consequences relevant when human blood had been spilt? 'An eye for an eye', he whispered to himself, 'a tooth for a tooth...' He raised his silverclad pen. He dipped it into the ink.

I have read over this warrant and signify my personal consent by affixing my name and signature to this Document of Warrant of Execution....

Baker dipped his pen into the ink for the umpteenth time. He looked once again at the paper before him. Was 'an eye for an eye' justice? He corrected himself. That question had· already been answered by the courts. His job was not to question justice but to decide whether there were any mitigating circumstances outside justice in the matter before him. The paper before him required his signature. No one else except himself could sign that paper. And when he did the five Africans would be as good as dead. There were no mitigating circumstances whatsoever, or so had felt the Committee. Not even in the psychological reports. All the five men were *compos mentis*. The youngest of them — eighteen — had been to a secondary school. He had passed his O-levels. But there had been no job for him. There were plenty of jobs for white boys with even less qualifications. So he had taken a job at Mrs Martin's fries joint. It was his job to pack the potato chips and the fish into the paper containers. That month when he and the others had killed Mrs Eckland had been a crucial month for the young man. He had been betrothed four months now. It was to be his month of marriage. But neither his uncle nor father could find the money for the *lobola*. Without it he could not marry his loved one. If he had received his pay he would have raised the sum asked for — £20. He had already borrowed £10. But Mrs Martin was going through a difficult time. Her debtors were putting the pressure on. She did her best to fend them off but it was no use. She was due to appear in court a few days before she was murdered.... Was it right for the five to slay in such cold blood a woman who was innocent? Baker dipped his pen into the silver inkstand. He would sign the death warrant. The pen touched the point where his signature would start.

He closed his eyes firmly. In that moment, a fat romping child burst into his mind. Here he was laughing away at his daddy's efforts to crawl with him. Always so happy and beside himself with laughter when daddy returned from the office. That picture of his son belonged to the past. He had been left in Britain to finish his schooling when they had left for the colonies. The boy had done well and gone to University. But at University he had fallen in love with a girl from a noble family. When everything seemed to be going well the girl's father had announced in *The Times* his daughter's engagement to a wealthy millionaire twice her age. Baker's son had asked the girl, 'Is this a joke?' But she had simply replied, 'People don't spend money to advertise jokes in *The Times*!' The boy had tried to win the girl back but to no avail. So one night he had taken an overdose of barbiturates. The following day his body was found coiled in pain.

Governor Baker wiped his forehead. He was perspiring. He opened his eyes and looked again at the name of the boy who killed because of love. A voice within said, 'Don't!' He dipped the pen into the red ink. The pen rushed to the red dot which it had made on the paper. A sharp pain shot through his head. He closed his eyes again. When he opened them there was the signature, his own, in lurid burning red. He closed the folder, bolted out of the room and for the first time in his dignified life, ran, ran to nowhere, ran in circles around the rambling mansion that was Government House.

Two days later at dawn a young man was walked up a gangway. He looked heavily sedated. They stopped at the door. The white man inside opened the door. He smiled into the young man's face. The young man looked at him blankly.

'You have come?' said the European, the executioner.

'Yes, I have brought him sir. When you have finished with him I will bring the next. No problem.'

'The governor of the prison is here. We shall have to wait for the priest. You said he was a Roman Catholic this fellow, didn't you?'

'Yes. Ah, here is Fr Lafayette!'

'Good. A cold morning Father, isn't it?' asked the European.

Lafayette did not reply. He looked at the eighteen-year-old boy who had killed for money to marry with. Earlier that morning he had heard his confession, administered Holy Communion to him. Two Africans came to join them. They were the public witnesses required by the law.

The door closed upon the group when they were in. It was a heavy steel door with three heavy-duty locks. The governor of prisons yawned and said to the hangman:

'Time's running out.'

The hangman smiled at the eighteen-year-old boy. He led him towards the centre of the room.

'Now, let's see,' he said, bringing the noose of the rope down on his neck. 'This is just part of your routine exercise,' he said to the boy. 'The Governor has forgiven you. I hear you talk a lot about your girl.'

The boy looked up. His eyes and face livened up.

'Yes, I know about her. Nice girl and you are a lucky man, my boy. In fact she will be coming just now.' The boy looked at him. 'Now, there we are. Get up on to the platform,' said the white man. He had already worked out the length of rope that would be required for the boy's weight and height.

'There, I can see your girl coming,' he said, turning to the door.

The boy turned also and at that point the hangman pressed a button. The floor boards parted. Just like a flash. A crack in the neck. The boy was dead. The hangman said:

'Next!'

And as he said this he bent down to write 'not guilty' on the charge sheet alleging that he had murdered the eighteen-year-old whom he had just hanged. He knew that it was a mere formality. He had to be accused of the murder. He had to deny it. They had to reprieve him there and then — the judge who had accused him of murder. And that would be the end of it all.

'Next,' said the hangman again.

28

In the Louise Hotel a week later, George Norris looked at his watch. It was time for him to go and get it over with. He was not sure where his father would be that evening. So he decided he would try the town flat first before going on to the farm. He drove to the flat in Mortiz Road. Sir Ray Norris was standing in the doorway saying goodbye to Simon Malherbe and five other people. George nodded to them and walked through into the flat.

'Make yourself comfortable,' called out his father after him.

George poured himself a drink. His nerves were somewhat rattled. How would he start?

'You're very brave to come all this way alone,' said Sir Ray. 'You no doubt know the news.'

George nodded.

'It's not very good,' he said. 'I think HMG should finalize the talks so people know where they stand. A drink, father?'

Ray Norris slumped back into his chair with a sigh.

'What's the news at Kamolo? How are the black piccaninny school kids behaving? Right?'

'They're fine,' said George.

'George,' said Sir Ray after taking a deep swig at his glass, 'I've been thinking about your future.'

George looked up.

'About what, father?' asked George quizically.

'About this business of teaching in a nigger school. It's not good headlines for me, you know. So I've arranged for you to join the European Education Department.' He leaned towards him and said, 'I thought you'd like it. I've arranged for you to teach science at the Musasa European Secondary School. How about that for a good father?' He smacked his lips with exquisite pleasure and then proceeded to recharge them by draining off his glass. 'Some more, my boy,' he said, holding up the glass. 'It's been a hectic day with all these blacks doing their thing. But I've told Baker in no uncertain terms we'll no longer put up with all this goddam nonsense. The chaps you met going out are on night duty. We're patrolling all white homes tonight and make no mistake, those chaps are armed too.'

'But where will all this get you father?' asked his son. 'For years now you've been fighting.'

'Fighting for what?' asked Ray Norris. 'For civilization, isn't it? You think I've paid too high a price fighting for our culture, for our civilization? George when you marry and have to bring up a family, tell your kids you had a father who fought for their future, for the future of civilization, for the future of the white man all down the line. Tell them he was a courageous man. Then they too will take up arms and rise against the barbarians, against men whose only law is that of the jungle, against men who think they can come to terms with blacks.' Sir Ray looked at his issue. He raised his glass for some more. As George poured him the third double, Ray said, 'You know what, your mother was a darling girl. If she had lived to this day, I'm sure she'd have been here, by my side, fighting alongside me. Perhaps this is what keeps me going — the thought that she'd like me to do everything possible to keep off the all-consuming lava of black savagery. You don't remember her much, do you?'

'Not much, beyond the photographs, Dad. But I remember vaguely how comforting and warm she always was,' replied George.

'Ah, she was a wonderful woman. I miss her so much,' replied Sir Ray. For a moment he was silent. Then he said, 'George, you've got something on your mind. What is it?' He looked squarely at his son. 'What's on your mind, sonny?'

'What's on your mind, sonny?' repeated Sir Ray Norris. 'Here,' he said, 'a refill, please. It's not every night I get an opportunity to drown myself like this.' He chuckled to himself.

His son took the glass and filled it up with the 'usual'. George, who was still nursing his first drink, felt sorry for him. Ray's face had become redder than usual and there were ominous bags collecting under his eyes. When he held a glass his hand trembled. The son knew how much he loved him. Although they were rarely together, it would pain him to know that they might be even less together. The father had asked a question. Was this the opportunity he was waiting for? George closed his eyes. He would have to go through with it. He could not do without that for which he had come to ask his father's blessing.

'Dad,' he said quickly. 'I'm getting married.'

His father looked up. There was a momentary flash of pain across his face. Then his mouth parted into a smile, then loud laughter, of sheer joy.

'Congratulations!' he exclaimed. 'Jenny should have been here. This is fantastic my boy. It calls for champagne.' Ray Norris strode over to the drinks cabinet. In no time he had skilfully popped a bottle and now said, 'Cheers!' to his son.

'Cheers!' replied George. His heart was suddenly joyful. 'It's done, it's done,' he kept repeating to himself excitedly.

'Jenny should have been here,' repeated the old man. Then he fell into a brooding mood.

'Dad,' said George going over to him and clasping his hands, 'I understand.'

Ray Norris embraced his son.

'It's such good news for both of us. We'll have a girl in the family at last. How does she look? Will she accept Old Bones, or *Mbatatisi* as the Kaffirs call me, as her father?' Norris Senior chuckled gleefully. 'Maybe she can join my campaigns, eh? Cheers my boy!' He raised his glass and clinked against the boy's.

George closed his eyes. In that closing of the eyes he could see his lover. There she was. Eyes lowered listening intently to him. Then she would raise them, look at him full in the face and she would break into a sunny smile. That was his girl, all of her. 'I love you Anna,' he whispered.

A mile or so away Anna was dozing, a feeling of delicious contentment overwhelming her heart. And as she fell into a slumber, she dreamed of a white Christmas. The snow was falling softly on the tree branches outside and large, lily-white birds were swooping over the trees in a glorious fly past. Her lover was hugging her to his bosom and she was rubbing her face against his white suit over and over. Could any happiness be greater than this, she was asking him. They were laughing aloud. George was now bending down to switch on a cassette record player. It was a waltz. Then they danced until it seemed their dancing would never stop. She looked up at him. The white suit had become jet black and he was standing still and erect with his chin jutting into the air. She looked outside, the white birds and the softly falling snow had disappeared. Instead, vultures were shrieking swooping over the house and flapping their wings against the glass windows in clangorous tumult. She let out a shrill cry. Then she awoke perspiring. She pinched herself. It was only a dream. She slumped back and in no time she was fast asleep.

Now they were up in the Alps. George had so often told her about a skiing holiday and she would wear a red, fur-lined coat . . . George had said, 'Come on darling, I'll teach you to ski.' She had said, 'No, I'm so frightened. George, don't go please.' George had smiled at her. That smile made her feel so warm. He had waved goodbye to her and he had begun to slide down the slope looking back at her and waving. Then it seemed that he had lost his balance. He gathered speed. Her heart jumped. 'George! George!' she cried, 'Stop it!' but, as George flashed down another slope of the mountain, he slipped from his ski. He flew into the air, somersaulted twice. 'George! George!' she cried. He landed on the other side of the slope with a loud thud and suddenly the whole mountain was silent darkness ... She got up crying, 'George! George!' She pinched herself. Only a dream, thank God. But what a dream!

George opened his eyes. A broad smile broke over his face.

'This is real great, daddy. I'm so happy.'

'Another champagne my boy?'

George took the bottle up. He popped it. His father said:

'Save the good stuff my boy.'

But George did not move. The champagne just cascaded out of the bottle on to the floor.

'What's the matter, my boy?' asked Norris.

'Father,' said George 'maybe you don't know yet. She's black. Her name is Anna Alinesi.'

Ray Norris stood transfixed. His face lost its colour. The glass which he had held slid and shattered to pieces on the floor. His lips moved, but there was no voice. The son looked at him. The worst had come and he might as well face it.

In that moment he had become a man, a man, a man to mind only what happened to Anna Alinesi. There was a defiant arrogance about his face. Then a tremour shot through Ray's body. His lips parted and an explosion of anger bolted through them.

'No!' he yelled.

The son simply replied:

'Yes!'

He felt sorry for his father. That yell was meant to be a yell of paternal anger. But it sounded so pathetic, such a pitiable exposure of the real helplessness of a man who found that all he had lived for was being shattered there, by his own son and before his own eyes.

'You can't!' cried Norris again.

'Dad, I will.'

Then Norris' face contorted into fury itself. Summoning all the powers of his strong voice, he cried:

'She's a nigger! A Kaffir!'

'Then I'm also a nigger,' said the boy.

Norris' head went round. He felt like vomiting. He steadied himself against the wall. Was he running mad? Without warning Norris crouched like a lion. Rushing at the boy with hands ready to tackle him, he roared:

'You. . . .'

The boy ducked. Norris crashed into the wall. He stood up, darted into the bedroom. His son heard the ominous click of a gun being loaded. He ran for the door and jumped into the car. The car lurched to a start. A loud bang crashed into the back seat. Norris Senior fell back exhausted. Then despair embraced his heart. He had spent his last cartridge.

The following morning Thomson rang Norris.

'I'm sorry to do it to you, Ray.'

He heard Norris ask:

'What?'

'Your boy,' he said.

Then Norris' voice said in a slur:

'He's dead?'

'What dead? No, no, no, Ray. Awfully sorry Ray for getting you so worried. No. He's all right. At least I haven't heard any bad news. It's about the call-up, the general mobilization. You remember you've been harping on this one for some time now. Well, Government has now decided the situation is grave. So at midnight last night His Excellency signed a general mobilization decree. All able-bodied young men between eighteen and thirty have to report to Police Headquarters by today noon. It doesn't matter how far away from here they are. Your son is among them and I thought I should tell you it will be perfectly all right. The boys will be fully covered and we've now got the latest and most modern weapons. But it won't take them long to learn. We couldn't do it until we'd got these weapons. What's more we now know where Katenga is.'

When he put the phone down Thomson wondered at the flatness of Norris' response. Could it be that it was a blow for the old fellow?

In the Louise Hotel, George Norris read the Government notice with grave concern. He was being commanded along with three hundred others, to go and kill. Kill. Kill Africans. Why? Because they wanted freedom. Because they were black. Because anger had driven them into murdering. The Courts. What was their duty? Then his thoughts moved to Anna. He had driven to her home straight from the quarrel with his father. He had told her he wanted her to marry him. Oh how happy she had looked! How she had wanted to wake up her father and tell him the news. The father had asked if his father approved, he the big white man. George had not told a lie. He had said, 'I don't think so. But in our society when a man reaches twenty-one he can do what he wishes.' Anna's father had shaken his head, 'Even though, when he dies he has to return to his father the limbs that he gave him. It is well for him to be on your side my daughter, this father of your husband. For me, if a white one desires you, can I say "No"?'

Anna had told George everything which her father had said. George had left on wings. Could anyone be happier? Anna's father had also said something about George knowing all her people. If he did not know them he might not give them water, 'or stop you my daughter from giving them water.' And now George felt numb. These very relatives of Anna might be among the freedom fighters. Would he give them water? Would he not give them bullets instead? He looked at the notice which took up two full pages in the *Musasa Times*. *Recruits and their families are warned that refusal to enlist or defection are punishable by death. A military tribunal has been set up for the purpose of summary trial of all offences connected with the proper execution of the war effort.*

It was a week later. George Norris was beginning to get used to the new routine of intensive military training under two colonels flown in from London. But the high command was still Jefferson — and that meant O'Flaherty. He missed his pupils at Kamolo very much. The fact that more than half of his colleagues at the school were also in camp did not improve matters because he did not approve of them and they hated his nigger arse-licking guts. But they were allowed to write home. Home for him now meant writing to Anna. But as the letters were censored he did not post any of them. He just wrote and hid them away. Deep in his heart he knew that she was doing the same. That is what they had agreed. To write each other a letter every day and keep it. 'It will be such fun seeing your replies to my invisible letters when it's all over,' had joked Anna.

Everything seemed to go on well. There might be no war to fight after all. Maybe the mere fact of the guerillas knowing that there was a mobilization would deter them. Since the mobilization, peace had suddenly settled in trouble-torn Kandaha.

One evening the high command of Jefferson, O'Flaherty and the two colonels came to the camp. The troops were to be moved that night to a spot near the Zambian border. The terrorists' hide-out had at last been located. In the 'Main Ops' room the high command went over the maps carefully with the troops. George was put into a platoon which was to approach the hide-out from the rear to create a diversion. Black policemen would be in the front and the whites would give them support. If any of the black police ran away he was to be shot on the spot. The attack would be at 5.30 a.m. Emplacements, trenches and the lot had to be dug by 3 a.m. It would take a good part of three hours to get there. Then the recruits were briefed on the terrain of the area. There were already natural emplacements and trenches, so there wouldn't be much digging to be done.

By 5 a.m. all preparations had been completed. The black policemen had taken up their positions and the various platoons deployed. They waited. George waited breathlessly with despair. He had thrown up several times, on the truck ride. They had laughed at him and some had cursed at his father for bringing this on them.

The first colonel said:

'Now, it's beginning to lift. We'll hit them when the sun is in their faces. That way they will still be half asleep and will think the bullet a hot burning sun.' He smiled.

'Something about the early bird, eh?' said the second colonel.

'These troops aren't much. But they'll do. I gather that's as much push as old Caput could take. He's flatly refused to send an army here and we aren't supposed to be fighting. We are only supposed to be training this army. Boy, what a ragtag of an army this one is.'

'Officially, this is a training session. That's why these guys are here. Jesus, they couldn't even lead a battalion to slay a mole. These fuckin' whites here make me sick. Have you thought for a moment what this great show is all about, Ted? It's all about making sure the whites here have their cookboys and nannies while we in Britain sweat it out.'

'It's also the law, John. These blacks are rebels and we can't sit back just like that,' Ted said.

'We did so in Rhodesia. Look as soon as all this mess is cleared up I'm going to Rhodesia for a fuckin' long holiday.'

They chatted on. O'Flaherty swaggered over.

'Not a stir so far, eh? They sleep soundly these chaps.'

The two machine guns waited. The two men on them waited.

The camp was stirring to life. Men, women, children were getting out of their houses. O'Flaherty looked round. All the men were in position. He raised his hand. Counted three and all hell let loose. A rain of bullets hit the camp. People fell like clay pigeons in a shooting gallery. Some freedom fighters jumped for their guns only to be felled to the ground in an ever-rattling pounding of the guns. It was like a Chinese New Year 'crackers' festival. One freedom fighter crawled up unseen to a machine gun. He raised the gun, groped for the trigger. A hail of bullets hit him and the gun dropped to his side. In every direction in which the freedom fighters ran they were greeted with gun fire. Children exploded in mid-air as they tried to run.

At exactly fifteen minutes after 5.30 the shooting ceased. The army swaggered into the camp. Not a single shot had needed to be fired by the white recruits. Brother had killed brother. O'Flaherty swaggered through the camp. The police were to look for Katenga's and Chimuko's bodies. The few surviving women sat on the ground with the remaining children. They were weeping, weeping for their men, for the breast that fed flesh for the cannon, for the village that had opened out its arms to welcome the freedom fighters and make them part of it. But victory had eluded O'Flaherty. For Katenga and Chimuko were not among the dead or alive captured. Immediately after conferring with the colonels, a scorched-earth campaign started. The police and the white recruits were scattered over the area, to prod into villages, if necessary to cross into Zambia to find the two most wanted men.

The sun set. For George it had been a shocking experience. It had also been so for many of these young men — even the most heartless of them. So much blood. So much suffering. Where did it lead to? There was no answer. So as they trudged the villages, bushes, in search of the 'final solution', morale was very low among them. As he thought, George trailed behind his group more and more. What was there to live for? To carry a badge saying 'On Day X of the month of Y in the year of Our Lord 19QD I helped kill many people'? Lost in thought he lagged far behind the others. They got worried and two of them retraced their footsteps to find him standing, thinking. He had been thinking about Anna. How he would have to tell her the rivulets of human blood that he helped to spill. Some of that blood could well have been her own blood, a relative's blood.

'Hey, do you want to be shot up? Let's go.'

They trudged on. The others ahead also marched on. They

followed a little path which dipped into a thick growth of tall trees watered by a rivulet. It was so dark and dense there. They had been chatting and so did not hear even the singing of the cicada. A voice, at once flashing a strong searchlight at them said:

'Stop or we fire!'

George stood still. Fear did not make sense any more. The other two snatched their weapons up to fire at the torch. Before they could pull the triggers long pangas split open their chests. There was not even time to cry. George passed out.

Later that night and the whole of the following day massive hunts yielded no result. Then, on the third day, a search party saw vultures circling and dipping into a thicket. They followed them and found there the mangled bodies of the two men, one a white man and the other a black policeman. George was missing. Presumed dead maybe.

On that day also the lonely band of freedom fighters that had captured George made contact with Katenga. He had not tried to fire. He had passed out. A woman only,

'That is why we did not finish him off. But, but,' stammered one of them, 'he is also Norris' son.'

'Norris' son!' exclaimed Katenga.

'Yes.'

His eyes reddened with fury.

'And you could not kill him! Hasn't he killed your own people?'

'We, we thought you might like to know comrade before we dispose of him.'

Katenga kept quiet for a long time. Chimuko waited. The others waited.

At that moment Katenga's little baby romped into his mind's eye. That little boy, what would he become in life? Would he grow into a victim of society, to be pushed into murder and then to be butchered? Was that not the worry of every father, every mother? Norris was a father.

'Reptile only,' he said aloud. The fighters looked at him. But he was deep in thought. What would Kawala have done? Kawala would not have touched the son of a father, no matter what that father was, said a voice from within.

'Do we have any alternative?' asked Katenga.

He had not expected any reply. It was a question that meant there was none except to kill. He raised his hand. He looked at the men and at Chimuko. From past experience, when the thumb dipped down the word, 'total' would be uttered. That would mean total agreement, George must die. George said:

'Before you kill me, please do me a favour.'

He was composed. Katenga looked at the boy.

'Please give these letters to my wife, I mean the girl who would have become my wife. Please, please do me that favour.' Tears rolled down George's cheeks.

'You didn't search him then?'

'We did. But we gave him back his letters.'

'Then, take them away,' said Katenga. 'A dying man must have his wish.'

Kawala's visage loomed in his mind. What would Kawala have done about a murderer of his own people? Katenga grew uncertain. He closed his eyes. In that moment he remembered how village Headman Nampande was presumed dead many years ago. But just when the people were about to lower his coffin into the grave there was movement in it and a gasp was heard. Quickly they broke open the coffin and there was Nampande half asleep, half awake but not dead. 'You don't return to death someone whom death has rejected,' someone had said. Had death not rejected the white man who stood before him now? Did he love Norris enough to do him the kindness of inflicting a personal tragedy on him, a tragedy which would become localized and even earn Norris sympathy? Was Ray Norris' crime not a crime against all the black people of Africa and could such a crime be requited by anyone other than Ray Norris himself? Katenga was becoming even more uncertain. He was no philosopher and yet life was philosophy itself.

'We will not kill the son of a reptile. We will kill the reptile itself. Paint him black. Give him a gun. You white reptile, you will be forgiven when you have used this gun to kill your crocodile father.'

'Dog Kawala! Dog Kawala!'

The sharp sound of boots sounded on the concrete floor outside. Kawala's heart jumped. It was St Claus. More torture. Beads of perspiration ran down his forehead. The door to the cell opened roughly. The reddened face of St Claus came in. Anger, real anger clouded his visage.

'We've wiped out the whole of PALP except you.'

Kawala kept quiet.

'Everyone's dead. The whole bloody lot. And', said St Claus

lowering his head and charging into Kawala, 'I'll *get* you, you bloody murderer. But not before you've told me what you've done with George Norris, Ray Norris' son.'

Kawala looked up in surprise. Norris. Did he have a son? Could such a man have a son?

'Yes, you've killed Norris' son and there will be bloody hell to pay. You've killed white men.'

Kawala was lost in thought. Thought about the future of his children. That a father does not know.

'Didn't you hear? We've killed your Katenga!'

'So what else is there then? If you have, you've achieved your earthly purpose. The soul will go on fighting.'

'You bloody cheeky nigger. I must have the whereabouts of George Norris. Musasa is screaming for your head. I'm your saviour, Kawala.'

'I've no need for a saviour of your like.'

St Claus hit Kawala in the cheek. It was a hard blow and Kawala fell back on to the bunk.

'You will sit up!' hissed St Claus. 'Your whole so-called army is wiped out. Maybe your wife can pump some sense into you. But maybe you've no heart to listen to her sufferings, eh?'

'Wife?'

'Yes, the *mufazi* (black woman) is here. This time I'll allow her to speak to you.'

Kawala's heart jumped.

'Follow me, nigger,' said St Claus aloud.

He found Ana sitting in the visitors' room.

Her face was drawn and haggard looking. He stopped in front of the wire mesh which separates prisoners from their visitors. Ana stood up. She leaned to the wire mesh and began to cry. She stopped and looked up at Kawala. Their eyes met. His face brightened up. He reached for her finger through an eye in the mesh. They touched and the two fingers remained together for a while. Then her heart ached. She groped for him, his whole body, behind the mesh. She cried.

'I promised myself I would not cry.'

'How I miss you my little one. How I miss the children.'

'I want you home. The children want you home. They want their father home.'

'My little one, if I could, I would be out of here right away.'

'Then why don't you?'

'Because they want me to sign a piece of paper. To say my people murdered the two Europeans. To say I denounce PALP. I denounce Katenga, Santasa, Chimuko and all of them. To lead them to where Katenga is hiding, if he is hiding. To eat back all that I have said about the justice of our cause. To denounce my very soul.'

'There is no party now. Everyone has been imprisoned. People have been killed.'

'And Katenga?'

St Claus butted in.

'Yes.'

'And Katenga?' repeated Kawala, ignoring the white man.

Ana shook her head. She could not tell her husband a lie:

'I don't know.'

'My dear little one, a party is not an office or desk. It is the people, their hearts and their ideals.'

'I don't understand. I am a plain woman. I want my husband home.'

'Mother of Jena. You don't understand me?'

Kawala looked at her fully in the face searching for the understanding which he thought had always been between them. His face was pained. Her face was shot with pain as she said:

'You could be home if you signed.'

Kawala's head was going round. A throbbing pain seized it. Was this just a horrible dream? He closed his eyes. Opened them and there were Ana's, inflexible and hard, looking into his. 'You could be home.' That is what these eyes were still saying. Then as if what he had heard was not enough she said:

'Other men would have signed. Much stronger men.'

It was a taunt. An insult. But Kawala simply said:

'I do not have their strength.'

Ana looked into his eyes. It was his turn to be hard, granite hard and inflexible. Her eyes filled with tears.

'Explain to me. I don't understand.'

'My little one, I cannot lose myself. If I have your understanding I can withstand anything. If I have your understanding I can redeem my people from this slavery.'

'Others have tried it and failed.'

'I can only try,' said Kawala.

'You don't have my support, my husband.'

'Then there's nothing to live for. I have nothing.'

He turned away from the wire mesh. His drooped back was disappearing back into the corridor where his cell was. The door was closing down on Ana. Ana cried:

'My husband! My husband!'
The heavy door closed.
All was silence. St Claus let out a huge loud hyena laugh.
'Ha ha ha!'
With that laugh Ana understood why Kawala had to go on.
'If he thinks Norris will take it lying down he's a bloody fool.
Ha ha ha! Ha ha ha!'

That evening in Musasa Norris answered a call from Salisbury.
'Very good. And you've got a pretty good idea? Excellent,
Hell, the native presidents and their OAU can howl about that
afterwards . . . The Governor here? He musn't know. After all, their
little effort was bloody ineffectual. They let Katenga slip out and
my son . . . Air support? Excellent. Turnbull will look after all you
chaps . . . Excellent.'
Norris put down the receiver ever so softly. Since the quarrel he
no longer really cared. But . . .
It was 4 a.m. Major Taylor stepped on to the boat. Ten men
stood up and saluted him. He could have been thirty or even forty.
He was tall, well built and with short hair. His black beret was
cocked on one side at an angle. The men he led came from all over
the white man's world. There was an Irishman, a Belgian, an
Italian, a Portuguese, an American, French, Englishman — name
the nation and somehow either through the first, second or third
generation you had it there. They were a crack detachment from the
Rhodesian mercenary force fighting the Patriotic Front up in
Mozambique. Of late and since the breakdown of the Owen-
Young initiatives on the future of Rhodesia, action inside Rhodesia
had intensified. But in the last week fighting had died down in the
confusion of counter recrimination as to who killed the seven
catholic missionaries, including a retired bishop. So Major Taylor,
Irish father, Scottish mother, Spanish grandfather, born in
Yorkshire, wrung his hands with pleasure at the thought of something to occupy his hands. It would be a small mopping-up
operation. Katenga and his crowd were back in Zambia. Zambia
could bark about the incursion, but they could not retaliate. The
money was good. All hard currency paid up in Zurich. US $500,000
between the eleven men and the bomber pilot. He had taken
US $200,000. All paid into a numbered account by the Bristol Gold
Syndicate before the operation could start. That was the law. Law?

Fuckin' bunkum. The law had nothing to do with it. All this hoo ha about an international law against mercenaries just because Nato got jittery. It would die down eventually.

Taylor sat down.

'All ready, Sergeant?'

'Yes, Major.'

Taylor raised his hand to indicate 'Let's go.'

'Air cover.'

'Yes sir, should be setting off about now.'

'Hope he knows what he's doing. These bloody Rhodesian pilots are crusty. Drunks.'

He looked at his watch.

'If we're not back by 6 a.m., we're chopped.'

'I'd give it another hour, sir. Say 7 a.m.' said the sergeant.

'Not more than another fifteen minutes. 6.15.'

'As you say, sir,' the sergeant saluted.

'What time is the bomber action planned to come on?'

'Fifteen minutes after we've started shelling the place, sir.'

'And Katenga is there?'

'Yes, sir.'

'Positive?'

'Positive, sir.'

'Right, let's not have another cock-up.'

Major Taylor shone his torch at a blown-up photograph of Katenga.

'This is our nigger.'

Then he took out a map and spread it on his knees.

'They are staying on a deserted farm about three miles into Zambia. Whites have abandoned a lot of farms out there because of Kaffir politics.'

They crossed the Zambezi quietly. No incident in spite of the normally intensive guard the Zambians kept on the river. When they were out on the Zambian side, Major Taylor spread out the map of the farm. All the buildings on it were marked by letters.

'Frank, take Brian and hit building B on your left. That's where Katenga is likely to be sleeping if ever he is there. I'm beginning to feel the bastard is a bit of a Scarlet Pimpernel. But never mind. We will come in from the right. In that formation hit them with mortars first, then spray with machine-gun fire and then enter.' He turned to the Frenchman. Dupres was short, about thirty-five, a crooked nose. 'Dominique, take out the sentry. There's bound to be some lonely Kaffir soul waiting for the devil to take him to hell.'

'Oui, mon chéri,' said Dominique.

He always made it a point to emphasize that he was French.

They walked on through the bush. Then they came to the farm. Everything was as on the map. Taylor once again said:

'This is the man we are looking for. It's going to be difficult to spot him. All niggers look alike. What's more they stink alike. But don't forget there's a ten thousand quid reward on his head. That should make it easy to recognize him.'

'A mean-looking bastard,' said Dominique looking at the photograph.

They shoved off to the edge of the farm. There was a sentry on duty. Dominique crept behind him, clamped his hand on his mouth and slit his throat. Taylor said to the others:

'Now move off.'

Two mercenaries charged into the camp, their automatic weapons at the ready. One of them, the Canadian called Proudfoot stepped on something cylindrical. It was a landmine and before he could say 'God!' it blew up and his remains scattered into the air in a cloudburst. Suddenly the dark camp was all life. Katenga hurled a flare into the sky. The mercenaries were just in time to recognize him and say, 'There he is', when a bullet caught de Silveira in the neck and he slumped forward, dead. Just then there was a whining sound above the skies. It was the Mirage jet bomber from Rhodesia. The camp, all lit up, made such a fine lame-duck target. Katenga cried:

'Down into the trench!'

He pushed George Norris to the ground in time for the latter to duck a bullet that whizzed above his head. Katenga grabbed his automatic weapon. Taylor rushed towards him, his gun sputtering away. A bullet caught Taylor in the teeth. His head exploded. Five minutes before a Mirage Mark 4 had set off from a field in Rhodesia. It was a bomber carrying eight one thousand-pound bombs. The bombs had been fitted with a five-second, delayed-action fuse. Anticipating fully that the freedom fighters would not be in possession of air-to-air guided missiles with a built-in radar device or heat-seeking missiles, both the pilot and air navigator had fully discussed the matter and settled for the ground-to-air missile and deliberated further over the issue of the installation of the instantaneous or delayed-action fuse. If Major Taylor had been there the matter would have been resolved fairly easily. But Major Taylor was not there.

Pilot Rozensky — Czech — looked at the flaring farm below him. Quickly he set the sights. There was the whole farm and all the buildings within it in sight. He pressed the release button and two thousand-pound bombs cascaded to the earth below. The bombs burst into the camp with a heavy dull thud. Now they were twenty feet into the ground and then a dark spray of dust exploded up into the clouds sputtering limbs and dust. Katenga cried to George Norris 'Down!' But when the clouds cleared, George Norris was dead, sliced into two by a splinter from the ground-to-air missile. Katenga, raising himself from the ashes and dust, looked at George's body. George had not struggled to protect his own life. He had not even turned turncoat. He had just stood there in the firing and rocket range, a glazed contentment on his face, waiting for the inevitable. Katenga remembered it all in the flash of that second. So when the dust had settled down and he said, 'Cover him!' his heart throbbed with a painful doubt. Could it be that a white man so despised death that he did not struggle?

Katenga looked at the skull and cross bow on the beret of a dead mercenary. He shook his head.

'So they hired mercenaries!' he said.

Dominique ran down towards the bank. A youthful voice called from behind him:

'The other boys?'

Dominique turned on the boy. He could have hit him for making so much noise:

'A wipe out you sonnovabitch. They all got chopped. Chopped by bloody Kaffirs!'

The following morning Kandaha made world headlines. In Lusaka, Zambia, the *Zambia Daily Mail* splashed in large letters, *British mercenaries chopped by Kandaha freedom fighters. Zambia outraged by wanton oppression.* The *Evening Standard*, London: *Rhodesian mercenaries attack Zambia. L'Express*, Paris: *France denies selling Rhodesia fighter bombers. New York Times: No American among eight mercenaries killed in Zambia.* The *People's Daily*, Peking: *Son of imperialist running dog killed by fellow mercenary imperialists. Daily News*, New York: *British Government hire mercenaries to attack Kandaha freedom fighters. Daily Telegraph*, London: *Lords demand army of invasion into Kandaha and Zambia. Rhodesia Herald*, Salisbury: *Smith denies mercenaries came from Rhodesia — No bomber aircraft made here.*

29

Ray Norris fell into a stupor.

'Your son is dead,' said Malherbe to him when, after knocking at his door and getting no reply that midnight, he broke it open.

'My son!'

'George Norris is dead. Sir Ray, can you hear me?'

There was no reply. Norris simply looked at Malherbe. Malherbe was puzzled.

'Sir Ray, George has died in an accident. His body is in the mortuary.'

'Mortuary.'

'Can't you understand, man?' Malherbe shook Norris.

'He shouldn't have married a nigger!' cried Norris.

'A nigger? But he's not married.'

'Oh, he's not married, eh?'

Norris fell back into his bed muttering, 'My son married a nigger. Nigger. Mortuary.' Then he let out a loud laugh, 'Ha ha ha!'

'Sir Ray, are you dreaming?'

'I must be.' He jumped up shaking Malherbe by the shoulder and, his eyes popping out, he said, 'Listen, listen, I dreamt a dream. There I was. I saw George, my son George. Arm in arm with a nigger in a black veil. Walking to the altar. To marry. I rubbed my eyes. It could not be true. Ha ha ha! So it was a dream after all. Ha ha ha!'

'Sir Ray, Christ man, you need to see a doctor.'

There was nothing Malherbe could do. He left. He came back the following morning. The door which he had broken had been pushed back by the wind. Everything was as he had left it. Norris was still seated in the chair into which he had dropped after his last laughter. He was not asleep. He was looking at him slowly. Malherbe said:

'You've heard the other news?'

There was no reply. 'They have announced independence will be in three weeks' time. No further talks. No conditions. No nothing. Just like that, man. Christ, man, we should fight.'

Norris merely leered at him.

'Have you been to the mortuary? I have just been. The boy didn't have a chance.'

'Chance,' said Norris slowly. 'What chance did he deserve?'

Malherbe looked perplexed.

'I mean your son'.

'He married a nigger, didn't he?' asked Norris of himself.

'He wanted to marry a nigger. Came here, told me he wanted to, insulted me to my eyes!' cried Norris.

'And so?'

'He left. Now I remember. Did I shoot him?'

'Shoot?'

'But he died in a war accident, Sir Ray.'

'Ah, that's different. So, it's not murder eh? Murdering a nigger's husband. Dirty, dirty stuff.'

'The burial, what arrangements?' asked Malherbe.

'Arrangements to bury a dog? He and the nigger were one flesh. Burn him!'

Just then Joan Chessman came in. News had spread fast and in a few moments people would be calling to pay their condolences. She was dressed in black.

'I am sorry, Sir Ray.' There was no answer. 'He was such a good fellow.'

There was no answer. Joan sat down. Turnbull dropped in. He had really come to talk with Norris about the new move in the political crisis. Norris did not look at him.

'What's happened?' he asked.

'George is dead,' said Malherbe.

'Oh God! Accident?'

'Yes, an accident, two days ago.'

'Yes the nigger-lover is dead,' cried Norris. Then another hollow laugh. Turnbull looked at Malherbe in surprise. 'Have you seen the body?'

'Yes, but not his dad. He's refused.'

'Yes I have refused. Burn the Kaffir, or if you bury him it better be in a Kaffir cemetery.'

'Has the girl been told of this?' Malberbe remembered to ask.

'Which girl? You mean the nigger girl? She can damn well find out for herself when he goes to the Kaffir cemetery. I don't even know her name.'

'And you won't find out?' Malherbe's voice was firm.

'Why don't you go to the pigsty yourself and find out? I've no business with Kaffirs!'

Malherbe said:

'Norris, way out in Chipata in Zambia, I had a girl once. I did not call her my wife because she was a *mfazi*, a Kaffir woman.

But she bore me a child. A lithesome little bouncing imp of a child. Oh, I loved that little baby. I called it Simon. Every evening when no whites were looking the *mfazi* would bring it up to the kitchen and I would spend hours playing with it. Then it was taken ill. Its stupid grandfather took it away to a witchdoctor. By the time they returned with it it was too late. Diarrhoea. I had the *muti* (medicine) there with me, men. But it was too late. I held it in my arms. I embraced it close to my heart. The little creature was limp. Its large eyes looked into mine as if to say, "Dad, where were you? Dad, its too late now". There was a spasm. The little thing clung to me. Dead, Ja, dead, men'.

Malherbe stopped. His eyes were moist. Then he whispered into Norris ears:

'But you, you had a son. He grew up with you. You enjoyed him. I didn't get that chance. And now you can't even bury him because he loved a Kaffir woman, a *mfazi*. Fuck you men, you are a *muntu!* Same as a Kaffir, men.'

George's funeral came and went. Just a few friends all the way from Kamolo African Secondary School and a few white people in Musasa including Malherbe. No sign of Ray Norris himself. The day after the burial, the African girl whom George would have married went out to the cemetery with her father. She asked the attendant for George's grave and when she reached it she wept and wept over it. George had been so good, so loving to her that life without him was unthinkable.

On that day Norris' heart was elsewhere very far away. He was thinking of the long journey he had travelled to get to where he was now. The humble son of a Polish immigrant. The son who had to struggle through life to prove himself. The Pole who was not accepted among the people of his newly acquired nationality. Did a dog have to change to a monkey to be accepted? Was that not what he had done, changing for the sake of a job, social acceptance .... Was his entry into politics the result of a real wish to play a role in serving his community, the human race, or was it a way of compensating for the social isolation which his origins made inevitable? Where were all those people who had cheered him so much in his moment of triumph? Yes, cheered the Pole, the Pole belonging to a nation which had been defeated in the war. He remembered his conversation with Lord Ventrical. 'Are there no principles?' 'None!' had answered Ventrical. None except Ventrical's money, thought Norris.

Then he realized. He was a tool to be used and discarded. But what had he done to those who had not discarded him? His wife, for instance? Had she not died partly because of neglect on his part? Had he brought George up in a home of security? Is that not why he had rebelled, gone to live outside his house, outside his own white community? George. George was no more. He closed his eyes. There was George licking a lollipop, the mouth all smeared with the chocolate stuff. That was the photograph he had loved most, taken almost ten years ago to the day. He stood up. His hands were trembling. He unlocked a small safe, threw out the documents until he found a small khaki envelope. He tore it open and held the small photograph in it close to his bosom.

'George, George George!' he cried.

There was no answer.

Then he remembered Malherbe's question. . . . Has the girl been told . . .? Which girl? I don't even know her name. . . . 'I don't know the name of my daughter,' he hissed to himself. 'My daughter!'

When Malherbe came round that day Norris said, grasping his hand excitedly:

'Come, my daughter, I want to see her!'

'Daughter? Which daughter?'

'Don't you know? Don't you know my son George married a girl. That is my daughter.'

'He did not marry her.'

'No, I suppose. But in spirit, they were as good as married.'

'To see a black girl!'

'Yes.' Where to go? Norris thought a moment. 'I know. We'll go to Fr Lafayette. If he doesn't know he can find out. He knows everybody.'

'Jesus!' It was Malherbe.

They found Lafayette at the African Church. He led them to a little hut in the African compound. People stared at them. Some whispered, 'That is Norris *Mbatatisi*.' But Norris walked on until they stood outside the hut. A mother next door said, 'The wife of the white man who died was taken to hospital.' She said it with such detached contempt that even without saying it, it was clear that she did not approve.

They went to the hospital in Malherbe's car. Lafayette spoke to the sister on duty. Yes, she recognized Norris. He was a VIP visiting an African hospital. She would have to call the doctor. Dr Elliot came.

'You want to see the girl?'

Norris nodded.

'Yes, there was a girl admitted yesterday suffering from delayed shock. Her mother said something about her having lost a boyfriend in a car accident.'

He paused and looked up at Norris, a touch of surprise in his face, 'Was that your son?'

'Yes.'

'I'm sorry sir, we wouldn't have known here. What's the girl's name sir?'

Norris didn't know. Lafayette said:

'Anna something.'

'Yes, I remember,' said Elliot. 'She's in Ward 2. We are very crowded here. All admissions yesterday and today have had to sleep on the floor. No more beds.'

Elliot was a mystical looking young white doctor, eyes blue and a face that looked zealous. Often he volunteered for part of the night shift even when he had done a full day's job. He liked to prowl around the Musasa African Hospital, to talk to the relatives of the patients. Every patient was an individual and he would spend time chatting him or her up. He was six months in the hospital, in fact, in Africa. But already his name was becoming known.

They went to Ward 2.

'How's she?' asked Elliot, of the sister there.

'A strong girl. She's doing well and is even sitting up.'

Elliot whispered something into the white sister's ears. The sister looked surprised. It must have been about Norris.

When they reached the bed, Dr Elliot said to the girl:

'This is Sir Ray, the father of your boyfriend who died.'

The girl got up. She was still feeling dizzy. She knelt on the floor and clapped her hands several times. Lafayette said to Norris:

'You are her father-in-law. That is how they greet fathers-in-law!'

Norris lowered himself. He took her hands in his. He said:

'My daughter, I am George's father.'

The girl burst into tears. Norris pulled out his handkerchief and wiped his eyes. Dr Elliot said, 'Thanks, Sister,' and led the party away. As they walked away Norris could still see the kindly, sincere and loving face of the girl. It was a face searching for some lost love, a face not believing that what had happened had actually come to pass.

'There's fuckin' lots of room in the other hospital. Why can't they give the *muntus* (blacks) one wing?' asked Malherbe.

'The law does not allow,' replied Dr Elliot.

Norris whispered:
'The law.'

Back at his home, Norris remained thinking for days. No food. Could he atone for what he had done to his child, to the human race? What had his life been all about? Creating hate. Hate between blacks and whites. Hate. And yet Kawala had always preached love, justice, Kawala, at least has principles above money. 'I am the poison, not Kawala,' he mumbled. What would be his future? Did a dog have a future? A voice within him said, 'Your future is your goodness.' The voice had seemed so real, so sharp. Now he did not mind what he did provided it was the right thing to do. What did he have to live for? Nothing except goodness. He would try. Maybe people would understand. If they didn't, at least he would understand himself. For the first time he realized that he had never really understood himself. He stood up again, pulled out a piece of paper and wrote his resignation from the Kandaha Front, the party which he had led for so many years.

Interviewed about his action later he said, 'There is no catch. I gave no favours. I accept none. I have full confidence in the leadership of Mr Kawala.' That day also Mr Madyauka announced that he had quit politics. Katenga retorted, 'We didn't know he was in politics. The snake!'

After a bitter debate, the Kandaha Front voted not to accept Norris' resignation. The vote was close. But those loyal to Sir Ray carried the day. Some said that he had a trick up his sleeve. Others said that Sir Ray must know what he was doing.

Father Lafayette sat thinking after hearing the news of impending independence. He had stayed so long in the country that here was his home. What would the future hold? What had it held for him so far? A poor parish priest. A Father Superior now only because there were no other priests available. How many times had he been side-stepped in this or that promotion? As a scholastic he had hoped one of these days to join the Vatican diplomatic service. He might have been at least a monsignor if not a bishop, archbishop or even a papal delegate or ambassador. Soon Kandaha would be independent. A papal representative would be sent. Those men in Rome would never look within the country for their emissaries. Maybe a black bishop or even cardinal would be appointed soon . . .

He checked himself. Was that why he had been so self-righteous to Kawala? What had he done to help Kawala in the new responsibility that he would soon be taking on? Had he even so much as prayed for him in those anguished moments through which the man had passed? He reflected on that midnight conversation about violence with Kawala. Could a man who wanted, thirsted for violence, have come all that way in the dark to consult him? What had he done instead. He had read Kawala a lecture on the Church's position, closed his door and turned in, leaving Kawala vexed and desolate... For I was hungry and you gave me to eat, thirsty and you gave me drink, in prison and you visited me... Did he visit Kawala or any of them when they were in prison? Did he pray that they might be delivered, that salvation might come to Kandaha and justice rain down like manna? He fell to his knees. Striking his chest over and over whispered:

'God, let Thy will be done.'

30

In the east wing of Government House, Mrs Kawala sat in her room waiting for Kawala to come. She had spent most of her married life waiting for him to come. Would he now settle down to eat the little meal of *nsima* and stewed chicken and *mulembwe* with her, the meal which he had loved so much in those early dass of their marriage? Or would he belong to the new nation with not a piece of him left to belong to her? Like the Katengas, they too had moved only that day into Government House. There seemed to be many things even in the room where she was now waiting for Kawala. And the rooms! So large! Any one room was a least twice the size of the whole house they had had in Samaka Compound where she had lived these many years. Somehow she would miss her little hut. She would miss the smell of walls stained by the smoke from the little kitchen. She would miss the rough little floor which she had spent all her life scrubbing. And the children, would their friends come to visit them or would they fear the guards at the gates, or simply shrug their shoulders and say, 'They are now *apamwambas* (snooty people).'?

She and her husband had had lunch with the Governor and Lady Baker that day. Would guests be expecting her to produce so many dishes in so many plates when one plate for the whole family was all that she had ever needed to use? She had noticed at the lunch that Lady Baker was on edge. Was this her natural disposition, or was she feeling bitter about leaving Government House? She was feeling sorry for her because, whatever it was that she had felt, she had been very pleasant with her, pleasant not in a condescending kind of way, but in a manner which was almost as though she had been talking to a long-time friend. She looked down at her dress and then the shoes. They were modest clothes. But they were also her best. Would he like her clothes? How would she put up with the gaze of so many people? From now on she would be in the public eye a lot.

She called to her youngest son:

'Get me the photo album. It's in the brown suitcase.'

When the boy had brought it, she turned to her favourite picture, the picture of Kawala and her standing outside the church. He in a pair of long khaki trousers with a white shirt and tie knotted slightly to one side. She in a long white dress made of the cheapest material and a tattered, but well-washed, mosquito net for a veil. That was their wedding picture. Kawala had always enjoyed laughing at her veil. But that was where life began and here she was. She waited on meekly for the man who had brought her through thick and thin to that night of nights.

But elsewhere in Government House, elsewhere in that portion of the vaulty twin bedroom set aside for her cosmetic exercises, lady Baker's reactions were somewhat different. She was miles away — not in place but in time — and just as a pilot facing imminent death is alleged to see in panoramic and kaleidoscopic fashion the main incidents of his life flash past, Lady Baker was reliving her past. Her thoughts went back thirty years when, as a young District Officer's wife, life had, in comparison, seemed endless and irresponsible. She recalled the flirtations she had with young DOs and, if the truth be known, how on occasions she had in fact been a little naughty. She remembered the parties, the tinkle of crystal, the sparkle of silver cutlery set against the snow-white background of napery, and the floral arrangements.

Then there were occasions when, merely by a stroke of the hand, a red-fezzed regiment of servants would descend on the table, pandering to every whim of the guests. She remembered how the men would retire to their brandies and cigars, while the women-folk would meet in the powder room and chat endlessly about their families and their homes in far off England, what had happened on their last leave and what was planned to happen on the next.

But that was past and done with and now she must look to the future. Sir Elwyn was still a very energetic, and God knows, virile man. What would happen to him? Would he be given a peerage and retire unceremoniously to the Lords to be put on the register of those whose background was calculated to make them experts on colonial affairs, especially in darkest Africa? Would he form part of those interminable commissions which were set up from time to time, a typical Tory device and a Labour necessity for procrastinating action? Or would he be given an undersecretary-ship in the Colonial Office in Westminster? Certainly for Lady Baker as much as for the African, tonight marked a watershed in her career. Life could never again be the same. Her well-bred, aquiline nose twitched and a tear slowly ran down her cheek. When her Lady-in-Waiting said, 'H.E. is ready,' she realized that the watershed had come.

At the stadium Joan Chessman's hand remained tightly gripped in Malherbe's. He had been interrupted when he had said, 'Joan, why don't the two of us . . .', but he was not going to try and finish his sentence. Somehow, she was feeling high, almost blissful. Ray Norris remained quietly in his seat. It seemed that he was miles away in thought. Unlike the past when he would always smile his way into any white crowd and pump their hands vigorously, tonight it was different.

It took twenty minutes of cheering, yelling and crying before the large crowd at the stadium could settle down after Santasa, Kawala, the Governor and their ladies, and Her Royal Highness the Duchess of Halifax, arrived. At exactly five minutes before midnight, Her Royal Highness escorted by the Governor and Kawala walked over to a microphone some fifty yards into the arena. There was dead silence. That microphone would carry the message from the Queen to every part of the stadium and through the radio, to every part of Kandaha. She had been right about making history. History had now offered itself to be made by her.

They waited there, the three of them. The stadium waited breath-lessly. Spotlights which had trailed them towards the microphone also waited with them. Lightning streaked across the dark sky and a mighty labouring rumble of thunder shook the stadium. The second hand of the large clock hoisted up near the microphone chased after the minutes hand. Then it seemed to bolt into a run as it caught up with the hour hand. Her Royal Highness cleared her throat. She raised the declaration of independence to her eyes and then started to read it. Her voice carried well and firmly to the crowd. Then she came to the last part. Her voice rose as she said:

'On behalf of Her Majesty the Queen of the United Kingdom of Great Britain and Northern Ireland, I declare the colony of Kandaha an independent and sovereign republic. God save the Queen!'

The Union Jack wound its way down the flagstaff and from below it the flag of the Republic of Kandaha slithered towards the top. As the two flags met half way they seemed to stop in an ant-like kind of greeting. Then each went on its way and when it was at the top, the Kandaha flag unfurled in a splendour of colour. The police band struck up the national anthem of the new republic.

> O Kandaha our motherland,
> Motherland given to us by God himself,
> How can we tell you O Motherland,
> That we will defend and protect you . . .'

Towards the end of the first stanza, Katenga streaked across to where Kawala was standing at attention with his guests. With tears running down his face he hugged Kawala and then cried:

'Kandaha! Africa! Forgive, but never forget!'

His cry carried over the public-address system and on to the radio sets in every home of the country. The crowd went wild. People hugged each other in a frenzied abandon of joy. Tears rained down their cheeks and some simply ran and ran around the stadium, running nowhere like people possessed. Norris closed his eyes. In that closing of the eyes, he could see his son. Malherbe tightened his grip on Joan's hand and said, 'Christ man.'

On the way to his new ministerial house, the new Minister of Defence, Katenga, stopped at Delia's hut. Delia looked at him and broke into a giggle.

'What a Minister!' she exclaimed. 'Unkempt hair, unshaven beard!' and then broke into laughter again.

'Delia, I've come to take you.'

'Just like that?'

'Yes, now I have a house and you must come.'

'So you need a servant?'

'Yes, is a servant like you not the same thing as a wife?' They both laughed.

'Of course you must bring my child with you.'

'And myself,' declared Delia, laughing.

'You? Yes, why not? Who do you think will look after him if you don't come?'

'But it will have to be a proper marriage. We need to tell the priest about it.'

'These are the white man's ways. Not ours!' exclaimed Katenga. The laughter vanished from his mouth. 'Maybe you can go with the child to tell the priest you want to get married.'

The laughter returned. It was good to see Katenga's frame shake with laughter.

He stopped. He pricked his ears, he could hear the thunderous pounding of the waters of the Zambezi falling over the *Musi-O-Tunya* in the distance. That sound, with all its tempest and fury brought back to his memory the last murderous attack of the mercenaries. The memory of all the men who fell fighting for freedom, of George Norris, standing, waiting there for the cannon that would shred him to pieces. He raised his hand to his eyes. For a moment it remained there, shielding them from the shame of a man's tears. Then he lowered it and said to Delia,

'Let's go!'

At the house, Mr. Nandabhai Patel was on hand to welcome them. Putting a ley of roses around Katenga's neck he exclaimed, 'Aloha! Dat vhat dey saying in Havai'. Then punching his fist into his other half-folded hand he cried, 'Black Gowernment!, Dat vhat ve vanting in Kandaha. Long liwe Kawala!'